D0960277

IN/HALF

IN/HALF

JASMIN B. FRELIH

Translated from the
Slovenian by Jason Blake

ONEWORLD

A Oneworld Book

First published in North America, Great Britain and Australia
by Oneworld Publications, 2018
Originally published in Slovenian as *Na/Pol*
by Cankarjeva založba, 2013

Co-funded by the
Creative Europe Programme
of the European Union

The European Commission support for the production of this publication
does not constitute an endorsement of the contents, which reflects the
views only of the authors, and the Commission cannot be held responsible
for any use which may be made of the information contained therein.

Published with the financial support of the Slovenian Book Agency and
the Trubar Foundation, based at the Slovene Writers' Association,
Ljubljana, Slovenia.

Hardback ISBN 978-1-78607-390-7
eBook ISBN 978-1-78607-391-4

Printed and bound in Great Britain by Clays Ltd, Elcograf S.p.A.

Oneworld Publications, 10 Bloomsbury Street
London WC1B 3SR, England

MIX
Paper from
responsible sources
FSC® C018072

NUMQUAM MINUS SOLUM ESSE
QUAM CUM SOLUS ESSET

PANCAKE PALACE

✦

Desire is a rift. Dental floss was stuck between Evan's teeth. Hot water ran from the tap. Instead of a mirror, a void on the wall. Jars of cream on the shelf. The toothbrush quivered. Steam rose. We are alone and we are all of us strangers. The rift widens, the hole deepens. A few hairs remained on the comb. Evan's urine was thick and yellow. The water tasted of pipes. The marble was expensive and cold. Dust clung to his bare feet. His underwear was dappled with drops of sweat. Every one of his mornings was charged with moisture. His body complained, his joints crackled. Time is out of joint and his joints are out of time. He forgets his dreams immediately. Nothing but wrinkles and grey hairs. Eighteen thousand rotten mornings. There was no window. And no air. A barking cough. Mucus.

Violence in the shower cabin and then, after brief negotiations with existence, gradual peace. The towel was fresh. A poisonous cloud of deodorant. He turned off the tap. No shaving today. He walked naked around the flat. He did not feel. He pressed a button. While he waited for breakfast, he got dressed. What did it matter? His back hurt when he sat down. He got up, clasped his hands together and stretched. Crackling sounds. The little door in the wall opened. On the tray: fried eggs, strips of sun-dried tomatoes, creamy goat's cheese. Crusty rolls with soft insides. A plastic bottle of water melted from an iceberg. He ate. The taste put him in a better mood. He walked over to the front door and picked the newspaper up from the floor. Lies and deception. He read while he ate. This isn't supposed to be something you laugh at. Ideological fiction. He flung the paper at the wall. The letters quaked. He punctured the last yolk with a roll. He observed its runniness and felt a sense of regret. The crumbs got on his nerves. If it weren't for his cleaning lady, he'd go nuts. He didn't like cleaning women; it was repulsive to have someone know you that intimately. He never saw her, just her sterile imprint. Our fates aren't interchangeable. If he was a cleaning lady, he'd hang himself. If he was anyone else, he'd hang himself. He felt a bit attached to his own self. A tiny bit.

He pressed a button, the tray disappeared. He picked up the newspaper. Leafed through it. Pressed a button. The console knew what he wanted. Plenty of sugar, plenty of milk, dark roast. Steam rose from the cup. He pressed his hand against his chest. Silence. He put the newspaper down. He forgot about it. A bag was lying under the table. He opened it and reached in. A packet of foil. He took it out and closed the bag. The mobile was charging. He unplugged it. A blue spark. He typed a message. *I've run out. Lunch today?* He deleted the question mark and added a full stop. He would never succeed unless he reached out into the world. What a fucking tragedy. He threw the phone on the bed. He opened the packet. Black dust. Love. He creased the foil down the middle and sprinkled the dust into his coffee, tapped gently, held his breath, and made sure that not a speck was wasted. No spoon. They never gave him one. He swivelled his cup in the air, making circles.

He turned a dial. The windows became transparent. Half-transparent. The view was bearable. Another day of sun. The suffocating ball (seventy percent) became swollen at the edges, like water in an overfilled glass (ninety percent), and finally spilt over. He opened the balcony door and narrowed his eyes against the scalpels of rays. Cup in hand, he stepped out into the thin air. Squinting, he sat back in the armchair and draped his legs over the railing. He tested the coffee's temperature against his lips. He gulped it down.

His pupils spun under his closed eyelids. Mercury poured into his veins. Bones of lithium, teeth of steel. Stars plummeted into his brain, his intestines rumbled like a locomotive. That opened his eyes.

....Clouds…puffy dandelion seed heads…an avalanche of snow poured from the sky…clouds, *look!* That one's a moth, and that one's a broom, and that one's a monstrous white whale floating on its belly in the midst of an endless plain of ocean vaulted by the sky…Edo's skyscrapers are sticks of concrete, a thorn-forest of glass and stone, rocky flashes, volcanic reeds ascending from boggy earth…cross-hatches of silkworm threads, spiderwebs of streets and pavements and metal lights…tiny parks sprouting like tufts of weeds in a quarry, green patches sewn over hole-ridden jeans…the line you trace over the roofs of the skyscrapers is like a zip; if you opened that zip, you'd tear the earth from space…the wind is dry as rice…an entire cityscape drawn on the eye…

He shook with comfort. He ran his hands over his face and giggled as his stubble tickled them. He caressed it in elongated strokes, like he was sculpting clay. The neck, the strings of veins, the ribbed arch, the touch of saggy fat over the belly. His hand reached into his pants and tugged at his limp member. Blood from the liver and the knees flowed into it. Lift-off.

/

Down at the base of the skyscraper a few people looked up in surprise. The sky above them was cloudless and yet they had all felt thick drops upon their skin. They shrugged and went about their business.

Evan plopped back into the armchair, lifted his arse and hitched up his trousers. Now he was finally awake. Before completing his morning routine he was just a depressed shell, a barely-human with a burning desire for an end. Afterwards, everything became much more agreeable. More in accord with reality. What a fantastic view. From high above Edo, the tectonic conurbation that grew out of Tokyo and the surrounding metropolitan areas, he could, on a clear day, see the ocean. He had a spacious flat, paid for by Daimyō, where he could create in peace. Being a guest director, he had at his disposal all the delights of the city, and no one man would ever be able to exhaust all of Edo's delights. Which didn't mean Evan wasn't giving it a shot. He'd been here almost a year, and when he wasn't working on the show he was prowling about in search of pleasure. To help him, he had his sponsor – that's what they called this blend of guardian, lawyer and agent here – Gordon Falstaff, a tall, grasping and overly obliging man with whom he at every opportunity romped and roistered through drinking dens, foreign flats and streets. He'd never imagined that he'd forge a new friendship so late in life, but he and Gordon had hit it off. In every human measure Evan was just a little bit better, and Gordon always took care to admit this minor advantage.

The beep of an incoming message rapidly brought him back inside. He threw himself onto the bed like a teenager in love, picked up the phone, rolled onto his back and read – *??? check out the papers, 3 o'clock at MUD, G.* Papers? Evan sat down at the table and spread the newspaper out, draping it over the edges. An incredible tarp. Minuscule print. He didn't know what to look for and felt lost. *Decontamination Project Behind Schedule – UIGOPWTSOALSSV Demands More Money – Allegations of Corruption in Dry Russia – HADE Troops at the Equator – Increased Exchange Between AU and IA – Secessionist Tendencies on the Rise in South Pacific – Humanist Renaissance in the Caliphate, Section 89 – Arctic Passage About to Open* – boring, boring, boring.

He closed the newspaper and began to leaf through it anew, back to front. Races, crazes, catches, chronicles, culture. *One Week Till Opening Night: An Interview with Evan Z—.* He breezed through the article, just enough to convince himself that it was printed exactly the way he'd written it. He never gave live interviews; he had no stomach for that repugnant conflict between curiosity and denial. The journalist had sent him the questions and he had polished his answers to make himself look as good as possible. Honesty is for cretins. Everything is a performance. And if some naive twit really thinks that there are people who traipse about the world believing in the 'cathartic mode of post-ideological praxis aimed at the sublimation of individual existence from the teleo-symptomatic into the emotio-causal chronotope', that's his problem. When the journalist griped that she'd like at least a pinch of personality in his answers, he told her to come see his show.

In the national news: *Serial killers – Monogataro resigns – The new Daimyō: Instilling pride in the population – Five-year fixes – Too many foreigners in our insane asylums; Drugs only for citizens.* Hm. Is that what Gordon had in mind? Did Gordon really think he cared about the asinine laws that were being concocted? Those applied to tourists and economic migrants, not artists. He tried to estimate how much the price would go up. At least fifty percent. Gordon's wallet was a bottomless pit. Crazy, but true: they'd cloned a Neanderthal. Only now? You'd think they'd been around for thousands of years already.

The end of August had been mild. Hints of autumn. The wind, which until recently had been a hot, wet rag, now harboured cool undertones. One could breathe comfortably, even when the door was open. Evan fiddled with the buttons on his shirt. The newspaper had slid to the floor. He walked over to the console and ordered lemonade. Ice (crushed) and sugar, but not too much. He sipped it through a straw, relaxed. He was proud of himself. The show was ready; there were only a few run-throughs to go before the dress rehearsal. Just the toughest scenes. What a luxury. All that stress for nothing. For a long time he was sure he wouldn't succeed. That he couldn't succeed. That everything was conspiring against his vision, that time was deliberately racing too fast for him and that every nervous breakdown in the world had befallen his actors. His soundmen. Light bulbs bursting and stage boards splitting like the woodwork of a ship in a hurricane. But he'd done it. *FILLING – A Parable of Things That Used to Be.*

As a scaffold, Evan had used a text by a local author named Junichiro Marukama, a mournful carnivore who'd spent his youth behind a computer, loved his sister and, by twenty-five, survived three suicide attempts. Junichiro's play was too pathetically grotesque to resist. Incestuous love triangles, talking dogs, episodes of hysteria and delectable one-liners ('If you don't clean up your room, I'll give you an enema', 'I have to love you, Yukio, since there's nothing else I feel for you', 'You have all decided to mistreat me, for you covet my relationship with God') – the enormously desperate lamentations of a person who'd never got hold of anything worth losing. He'd offset that wailing of the eternal teenager with texts from the previous century. Hitler's ecstatic diction, Burroughs's junkie expectorations and Nina Simone's sex appeal went hand-in-hand with the absurdly comic advice served up in magazines, 1960s American instructions for what to do in the event of nuclear war, concentration-camp inmates' brutal reflections, all shot through with the banality of video games ('*How my heart beat, as he came running across the field to me!* How convenient, you fight like a cow. *He ran as if to bring me aid.* To run, press shift. *And I was penitent; for in my heart I had always despised him a little.* Your beasts are becoming angry.'). The show's sonic backdrop was an eclectic collage of pop music, football chants, the classical strains of Philip Glass and pornographic moans. The lighting was enough to trigger an epileptic fit in a blind man. Evan enthusiastically awaited the unctuous cornucopia of high-flown interpretations he'd be able to ridicule later. The show's only point was this: anything conducted by humans was bound to dissolve into kitsch.

/

He hated that doorbell. Its grating, somehow gentle sound. You couldn't ignore it, couldn't just sleep through it. It didn't ring often, since Evan couldn't stand visitors. He hated it because the disparity between the quality of the signifier (a pleasant ringing) and the signified (an intrusive visitor) was utterly noxious. It was as if they wanted to force him (even train him, like Pavlov's dog) to rejoice at someone's arrival. He went to the console and pressed a button.

The picture was overly sharp. Her face was not made for this camera. Although to the human eye her face was attractive – its attractiveness being intensified by powder, mascara and lipstick – in the eye of the high-resolution camera that visage crumbled into a faded medieval tapestry: cracked, yellowing, ancient. The make-up resembled rough pastels – you could see the layers of paint, how thick they were, the bloated lumps of mascara that hung like prison balls from her eyelashes; you could follow the strokes of the brush and those wrinkles that the coats of powder merely dug apart and shallowed. When she smiled he had to force himself not to look away. Tarrying between her shining white teeth were the remnants of break-fast. If he were a proponent of aesthetic beauty, he would be horrified that such an unflattering image could be trusted with the lead role in his show – but Oksana, a Dry Russian concubine, former farm girl and superstar-in-the-making, was ready for the role for more than just one reason.

'Eeeeevan, good morning. Open up for me, please.'

'Open up?'

The lock was sound-activated. He heard a click and the scalp of thin blond hair disappeared from the screen. Damn. He didn't want to waste the best part of his high on some woman. He'd have to find a way to get rid of her. Tactical efficacy hinged on how quickly she got to his door. For a polite excuse, you need a bit of time. Digestive problems. A death in the family. There's no one home. You get on my nerves, I don't feel like seeing you, go away. No time. What are you doing? I'm busy with… Just no time. I'm not feeling social. I'm depressed. I'm naked. Great! I'm sick. I'd like to be by myself. Now's not a good time. My dog is dying. Leave me alone. She knocked.

He went to the door and opened it. He left the chain on. He spoke through the crack.

'Ah, Oksana, know what? I'm not really very…'

'Eeeeevan, hi!'

She ran into the door. The chain jumped and Evan stepped back. The slice of her surprised look of pain through the doorway almost brought him to laughter.

'Are you all right?'

She nodded. Tears welled up in her eyes. Probably on account of the impact.

'I'm completely…precisely now, when I thought… You know, hm, how about if you come by tonight, since I'm just about… Could you?'

A nod. She furrowed her brow, offended, and the tears disappeared.

'I'm sorry, but I really didn't… Come back tonight, yes? At seven. I'll take you to dinner, ok?'

An excuse with a promise – that's the best type of excuse. She wrinkled her nose and uttered a bitter *ok*. To shake off the sting of humiliation, she immediately spun on her heels and marched off towards the lift.

'I'll be here at seven. If you stand me up, Eeeeevan, I'll be too sick to go to the dress rehearsal.'

'Ok, I'll see you then,' he yelled.

He closed the door. That hadn't gone too badly. He laughed. What a crash!

Belief propels you into the rift, but some doors just remain closed. Let that whack in the nose serve as a lesson.

There may be a crack in the door, but there's nothing behind it. Just a stranger's smile. Careful…

He leant his back against the wall and bent over, his hands on his knees. He wiped his eyes with his palms. A brown envelope was lying on the floor. Surprised, he picked it up. He turned it over. Nothing written on it. He ran his thumb under the fold and tore it open.

Inside was a plane ticket, Edo–Seam, 20:00 (8pm), JPA771, window seat, non-smoking, 100kg max weight, the day after tomorrow. Evan had no idea what to think about this. He stared at the ticket, turning it over and over. Had Oksana brought it? He unlatched the chain, opened the door and looked down the hallway. The beep of the lift. Nobody anywhere. Olga's darkish footprints were rising from the white carpet like vanishing steps in a thin layer of snow. No other footprints. He ran the plastic ticket over his palm. A mystery. How refreshing. People are so simple, you study them, get used to them, and the surprises disappear. Everybody wants something completely obvious. Completely ordinary. They want contact and sometimes flesh and sometimes a pinch of power, though not too much because that might give way to responsibility. Nobody wants responsibility. If everything is caused by a predetermined mix of cerebral flora, it's difficult to identify even with your own processes – let alone take on a flood of foreign chemicals. Hormonal discord of neurons implants guilt, the Gordian nerve-knot calls for cutting – don't get all cut up about it. We are severely myopic when looking at the brain. Any clearer and the picture might spook us. Would we get bored? Every surprise, as long as it's not a violent one, is welcome. Oksana now seemed attractive even at the human level. He already liked her as a character – a wounded figure, capable of so much courage (or vacuity) that she felt it was her right to become famous and successful and wealthy, and was willing to do anything for it, even though fame depends not a whit on one's own actions but on external circumstance; and the price of failure is always an eternity of misery bordering on shame. If you think about it in those terms, it's all rather unpleasant. But if you think about it in those terms, it just means you don't think about it in a different way. Some seize opportunities, others give up, still others surprise you in the morning with a plane ticket that's headed straight for the bin. He put it on the table and smiled as he stared at it. Unclear motives, wonderful people.

/

He pressed his hand against his chest. Silence. A slight stab, perhaps. The ticket on the table actually wasn't an innocent thing. It had dangerous connotations. The possibility of departure. A suggestion of change. A breaking away from the current state of affairs. Reluctantly, he tossed the newspaper over it. No need to tear it up. He hadn't thought about her in ages.

'I love you,' he'd said to her, and said it he really had, although he wasn't entirely sure whether he really meant it and whether he really felt it. But afterwards she'd latched on to it and gradually she became too heavy for him. His secrets, secrets he'd never divulged to anyone, weighed her down like barbell discs, and the fact that he'd loaded them onto her with a lover's carelessness did not help. He was happy to flee, even though the flight was ugly, unseemly and painful. Such things stay with you the longest.

/

He did some sit-ups, push-ups, a bit of shadow-boxing and ran on the treadmill, until the sweat was streaming from every pore of his body and until everything inside him was scream-ing and he had visions of cardiac arrest – a knife to the chest, a stagger, a fall to the green floor below, a blue face, a few convulsions, foaming from the mouth, and his end, noticed a few hours later by a screaming cleaning lady who would sweep him under the carpet and answer the cop's questions with an unperturbed shrugging of the shoulders.

He took a cold shower. Got dressed. He was ready for… outside. In his cowhide shoes, fashionably faded trousers and a bright red shirt draped over his torso, he darted out of the flat, into the lift, through the reception area, greeted the doorman with a slight nod of the head and stormed into the street.

He sank into the shock of bodies, and the sheer amount of awareness humbled him for a moment. From up high everything looked much more manageable. Here, on the ground, everyone's pocket was a potential threat, and the most you could hope for from a walk was for everyone to keep their desires to themselves. Fates were sealed within a single block. For the outsider, it was easy to decode the tiffs and kisses, but for those involved, meaning disintegrated. Gestures and gazes converged into a network of urban urgency. Pavements were full of litter that was then kicked into the road and into the gutter that ran along the edges and flowed into the sewer system. Right there in front of everybody, people were shedding their skins, and Evan was grateful that his visual spectrum didn't colour red the dusty particles of hair, bacterial drops of saliva and bits of fallen nails. Seeing all of it at once would have made him vomit. Maybe he'd just inhaled a snowflake of dandruff. Maybe he was standing in a cloud of gas that someone had just squeezed out of their arse with a wrinkly kiss. If it were up to him, he'd disinfect, disinfect, disinfect with lime, with alcohol…

The more people there are, the more impossible cleanliness becomes. The streets of Edo were not uniform. Some gave off a hint of steel, clear lines, and the people in them stared straight ahead. In other streets, cracked with paving stones eroded by the rain, where the roots of belated trees lifted the concrete and the façades revealed clashes between amateur architects, incompleteness insisted and people shouted over each other. Wafting from the kiosks was the smell of hot dogs, from the toilets the smell of acetone. It was income that divided these streets. The rich had wrangled their reality into reasonable order, while the poor bargained away in confusion. No one has a choice.

The birds that had survived climate change, airport hunters and radioactive clouds had been killed off. The insects went forth and multiplied; flypaper trailed from every street-light, from every tree. Rectangles fluttering in the wind. Evan swatted at flies. He'd heard stories about larvae breeding inside human bodies and he was horrified. The medical intervention was routine and painless but it didn't dispel the sense of filth-iness. It's as if some junkie had broken into your place and rifled through your underwear drawer. It was impossible to be truly clean, afterwards.

The wind was drying the sweat that had collected in the folds of his skin. Still, it was a beautiful day. He saw some truly beautiful faces, shy girls, hiding behind glasses, behind frescoes of make-up, under hats and dishevelled hair. His gaze didn't drift to legs, bottoms or breasts. Faces were what he was after. Broad noses, narrow lips, low foreheads, high cheekbones. Beauty. And even the guttural calls of the men hawking newspapers, handbags, watches, did not disturb the idyll. The urban basis for the life of the masses. From the piles of rubbish, a foul odour. The entrances to the underground, those dark staircase-throats spewing stale air. The asphalt was heating up to a rolling boil, emitting a tepid warmth. A gust of wind whisked everything off to one side, leaving behind molecules of meals, roses and fear from beyond. Tattoos were drying on skin, remote teeth showed soundless laughter. The city was croaking along uncaringly in the early afternoon.

Evan was feeling pretty hungry. MUD was within walk-ing distance, which was good because your taxi driver could turn out to be a serial killer, and if you took public transport. other people's bodies bounced off you like running shoes in a washing machine. True, bumping shoulders, sinister glances, slowcoaches, racing pizza delivery boys and hysterical prostitutes throwing themselves at you could also make the experience odious for pedestrians, but at least it was safe. It meant by far the least amount of physical contact. At the crossing a cyclist had fallen under a tram. The people in the cars honked nervously and drummed their fingers on their steering wheels. The rescue helicopter got there quickly, but too late. The cyclist died, hidden behind rusty tram wheels. They hosed the blood away. Before the traffic started up again, Evan was able to cross the street without having to take the overpass where mothers with sickly sons hanging from their laps begged for alms. Sometimes they tugged at your trousers.

/

She grew up in a hurry, with him. After meeting her, he'd chained her to his life out of physical necessity. She was so young, so taut, so svelte. She'd grown into her skin, and her tummy was tight as a drumhead, her buttocks frozen butter in a transparent balloon. It hadn't been hard. All he'd had to do was show a little interest. Make an approach. Be there. Speak in generalities and then speak to her. Approach her more directly. Touch her. Whisper in her ear, in hers alone. It hadn't been hard. Bodies respond to attention and relationships grow all by themselves, as long as you let them. Then the clothes come off the bodies and the bodies force themselves into one.

Probably on account of its youth, he regarded her personality as almost amorphous, with a bas-relief and patches of emptiness in places where one would have expected some kind of similarity. They were caught up in a single thing, but then with amazement (and a little reluctance) he noticed how quickly he had carved her into a person. The empty spaces became ornate mosaics of character and the bas-reliefs warped into chasms of emotion, peaks of expectation. Soon she had demanded everything else in addition to insatiable lust. And she fully deserved it, probably. They loved each other.

/

It was in the MUD restaurant that the serial killer Michiko Kan had sliced and quartered the CEO of the now-defunct SeAsia bank. A gold plaque above the entrance and a banker's hand in a jar of formaldehyde now commemorated that event. The restaurant's owner had purchased the hand from Tatov-Grobov Inc., the Dry Russian distributor that had also seen to DNA analysis and provided a certificate of authenticity. The price had not been publicly revealed, but no doubt it was high. Biographers have concluded that this was Michiko Kan's third murder (before that, he had murdered a neighbour and his own mother-in-law, though the biographies disagree on which of them was the first victim), which had propelled him to superstar status. He lived up to his reputation with further notorious killings all over the country, and with his seppuku he had set a record that remains unbroken. Puritanical experts don't count suicides, so according to them Michiko's 249 murders mean that he shares top spot with Saunada Elis, a Persian murderess who terrorized Japan years ago and whose death, though unconfirmed, remains highly probable.

Evan had read a monograph on serial killers on the plane over to Edo. When he saw the shrivelled hand in the glass for the first time, he cracked up. MUD had built its entire corporate image around it. The black marble décor lent the ritual of eating a seal of gravity, a slightly morbid awareness of vanity and what it truly means to tear pleasure from the claws of death. If it weren't for the congregation of influential people, he probably wouldn't be coming here. After all, he had mixed feelings about death. Unfortunately, there was no other place nearby that let him feel so validated. Also, they had the best pancakes in town. He entered the chilled, slightly damp reception whose appearance, if not its purpose, was reminiscent of a tomb. A pair of metal fans stared at him. His shirt peeled itself away from his skin. He put his hand over his hair.

The trophy on the table made him laugh. The hostess behind the table also laughed.

'Hello and welcome, Mr Z—'

'Hi.'

He'd never seen her before, but she knew him. Even though he was aware that the magnetic rays by the entrance had scanned the contents of his wallet, sketched a profile of him, run all of his data through the d1Za.ir algorithm and told the hostess how to act to make him feel just right, he nevertheless liked to imagine that she also recognized him as a director. That was the problem of creating for the elite – it didn't do much for your street cred.

'Your sponsor is already waiting at your table. Right this way, please.'

The candles in the skulls lining the walls cast ominous shadows over the room. The murkiness and a bite of yellow light danced over the patrons, stooped in conspiracies, and staged ambiguous sketches on mists of cigar smoke. Whispers and hushed laughter. The rustling of leather. Evan's shoulders tensed up. His red shirt had brought a hint of blood inside, drawing flared nostrils. Glints from the glasses' frames and the gold teeth between snarling lips flashed in his eyes. He did not feel relaxed.

Gordon smiled at him from across the room. He raised a cautious hand in half-greeting, and then looked slightly to the side so he wouldn't have to maintain eye contact while Evan made his way over to him. These interpersonal vacuums were always a little unsettling.

'Are you in the mood for something spontaneous?' the hostess asked Evan, as he took his seat.

'Surprise me,' he replied, and curled up the left corner of his lips. He was haughtily convinced this gesture made him look more accessible. She left with a slight bow.

Perched above Gordon's round face was a bald patch from which rose a chicken-wing-shaped curl of blond hair.

Usually this curl was forced to lie down with the rest of his hair at the crown of his head, but today for some unknown reason it was allowed to strut on its own. It bothered Evan. He could have wet his fingers with saliva and spun the curl into a thin thread – it might have fallen then, or it might be best just to cut it off right now…

'So, why did I have to go through the whole newspaper today?'

'Geez, Evan, you really are something,' exhaled Gordon, leaning back and patting his tummy before folding his arms. 'You get right to it, no greeting, no *Hi, Gordon, how are you, Gordon, is everything all right with you, Gordon.* Right to it, what's that about? You'd think you were talking to the postman, not a friend…'

Evan rested his elbows on the table and held his forearms parallel to each other. He snorted and turned his head to the right. An old man was leisurely stroking a young woman. The man's fingers overflowed with precious stones.

'Sorry, Gordon. How are you?'

'Ah, I'm well,' he said, staring into his fingernails. 'I'm well. And you, Evan?'

'Also well, never better. So?'

'So *what*?' asked Gordon, pursing his lips into a pale pink O.

'Do you have something for me?'

All at once Gordon turned serious and leant forward, still with his arms folded. He looked wobbly, ready to tip over at any moment. He moved so close that Evan lost sight of the curl and was able to focus on Gordon's blue eyes which, under his insipid brows, were sunk deep into his skull.

'It's a crisis, Evan!' he whispered. 'What's going on right now, it's a crisis, a veritable crisis. They know everything! They sniff out everything! It's hard, hard for me to do anything, and if they catch me…'

Evan snorted again, but looked to the left. In the swing

doors to the kitchen stood a man with long black hair and a beard, staring straight ahead, into the wall.

'Just tell me how much it will cost.'

'Five to ten years in the clink, I believe, without parole, without probation!'

Greedy people are lavish only when they're whinging.

'Gordon, please, spare me. Tell me the price.'

A black-clad waiter placed the glasses on the table and poured wine into them, white for Gordon, red for Evan. They nodded their thanks.

They grabbed their glasses by the stems, toasted limply and imbibed. Gordon looked around, scattered, bit his lip and acted like someone was about to make an attempt on his life. Evan's gaze once again drifted to that gently fluttering curl.

'Well, let me put it like this,' he circled his lips with his fingers and merged his hands into a single fleshy lump. 'All of a sudden I – because like you I'm a foreigner, Evan, so we're in the same boat – all of a sudden I have to pay twice as much for half as much, so I see no other possibility but to tell you the same thing.'

Evan gave a thunderous laugh, earning himself a few threatening looks from the other patrons. He acknowledged his transgression and issued an eye-rolled apology into the void.

'Twice as much,' he said judiciously, as if he wanted to make sure he'd heard right, 'for half as much.'

Gordon nodded and shrugged his shoulders at the same time, *well, what can you do*? The woman to the right began to coo under the pressure of the bejewelled fingers, the man on the left with the long black hair took a phone from his pocket and waved it furiously about. The waiter brought the food: a plate of pancakes for Evan and the bloodiest of steaks for Gordon.

'I was never any hotshot at maths,' said Evan. He stabbed a pancake with his fork and pushed it to the edge of the plate. It left a trail of chocolate. 'You're saying that if, before, one baggie was ten asias,' he circled the pancake with his knife, not touching it, 'half a baggie is now twenty asias,' he cut it down the middle and separated the halves, 'and if half a baggie is twenty asias,' he ran his knife along one half, 'then a whole baggie is now forty asias.' He pushed the halves together again and frowned.

'Basically, it's four times more expensive,' said Gordon quietly, as if embarrassed. He cut into his steak, drawing myoglobin. Evan stabbed half a pancake onto his fork, raised it to his mouth, opened wide and stuffed it in.

/

The pan was sizzling with vexing questions. Tiny droplets of oil were flying into the air, and when they landed on the skin they unleashed their full potential and did their best to inflict burns – if they were just a little bigger they could inflict some real damage.

'What if we had a kid?'

She cracked an egg into the bowl. Evan was sitting on the balcony and intentionally ignored the question. He was staring at someone coming out of the adjacent skyscraper (it was too far away for him to see whether it was a man or a woman, he needed glasses but he shied away from them because they make a man look old), staring at how, on the street, way down below, the person was labouring to carry, pull and push a large cardboard box in the direction of the bins, each advancement producing a loud, shattering noise. The box was probably full of empty wine bottles, broken window panes or test tubes.

'But I don't want to give birth.'

She sifted flour into the bowl.

'We could adopt one.'

She sprinkled in some salt and swivelled the pan from side to side. The oil hissed angrily. The person stopped to rest near the bins.

'Or steal one.'

She whisked the batter.

'Evan, what do you say, would you steal a child for me?'

A couple walked arm in arm past the person who was taking a little rest. Perhaps they exchanged a few words.

'We'd go to the supermarket and lie in wait, scope out the families there. We could do that for a few weeks to gauge the potential kidnappees out there, ha! We'd know which mothers have had enough of their annoying kids, which fathers would rather run away to Australia, which children have no hope of growing up even halfway normal. Watch long enough and you pick up on these things. Sometimes it's clear right from the start. But what if everyone was like that? What if everyone was just desperate, every family was ruining childhood. Would we be the same?'

The windows switched on and off. There was no pattern to the lights, try as you might to find one. The person sat down on the box and lit a cigarette.

'If they were all potential kidnappees, then I'd have to loosen the criteria. I'd have to see which shopping carts contained nothing but sugar-coated crap, and which ones indicated at least an attempt to live healthily, I mean, physically. Who at least halfway cared about their children. You can tell right away. If the cart contains two pounds of potatoes, cheap pieces of meat and a rotting turnip, then they're in the midst of an existential crisis or just lacking in imagination. Either case, bad for the kids. We'd know how to take better care of them.'

She balanced the bowl over the pan. Poured in a jet of batter that formed a perfect circle.

'Or if we adopted a little black child? That would be all right.'

The edges of the pancakes crept upwards in the heat. The person below put out the cigarette and got ready to lift, hands under the box.

'Do you think he'd stick out at school? Have we come

far enough that nobody would find it strange, that he'd be accepted as a regular person?'

She grabbed the handle of the pan and flipped the batter that was gradually morphing into a proper pancake. With a visibly extreme effort the person below quickly, just barely, lifted the box almost to the edge, almost, and then froze. He couldn't go on, but he didn't want to let go, since he wouldn't be able to do it a second time. People walked past and looked away.

'He'd be something special, our little black boy. We'd teach him not to feel inferior, and everything would be just fine. Everything stems from us, don't you think? The girls would find him interesting, he'd be happy, I'm sure of it.'

Evan got up suddenly and leant his hands against the railing.

'For fuck's sake!' he swore under his breath, and then in a loud voice, 'Isn't anybody going to help?'

/

'Ok,' said Evan, through a full mouth. He'd even pay ten times more, no problem. Daimyō was letting him stay free of charge and was paying him handsomely on top of that. Even if he wanted to, even if he threw his money away on constant orgies, drugs, booze and food, he'd be hard-pressed to go bankrupt. But that didn't mean he should remain indifferent to Gordon. That character flaw – greed – was one of the ugliest a man could have. The universe had conjured up, for you, a complete machine of limbs, a nervous system, lungs and a heart, and you go about impotently haggling over a lousy one or two percent. He swallowed, with difficulty.

'But I need some today.'

'Impossible,' replied Gordon immediately, closing his eyes and smacking his lips. He had expected a response, but when nothing but silence came he feared something unpleasant was going on in front of his eyelids, so he opened them again. Evan was staring motionlessly at him. 'Well, I think it would be very difficult to arrange something so quickly because, well, these things take time. No transaction, no business, goes down that fast, especially when, you know, things are not, strictly speaking, entirely legal.'

'I'm fine for today, but tomorrow we have a rehearsal and I don't know whether I can survive without. Ok, of course I could, easily, no problem, but I don't want to. Because everyone knows what they have to do, but still nobody's obeying, they still find time for stupid questions, still… But I'm boring you, aren't I? I just need a little something so that I'll be a bit more lenient. Is that doable? Please don't say it isn't.'

Gordon chewed his steak and nodded sympathetically. As Evan raised his eyebrows questioningly, he took three quick bites and had trouble swallowing. He put a hand to his chest and washed the chunk of meat down with a sip of wine.

'You know, of course, well, at home I have a little. If I remember correctly, I put something aside for hard times, but in any case I don't need it right now, you know, I've started with meditation and that really, really, helps, maybe if… Will you come with me? After lunch I have post-yoga – Cambrian, deuterian, and I can't even remember what, all these new things from up north, everyone in this town is just mad about them.'

Evan appreciated extremes. Sometimes he worked out until his nose bled. He despised meditation. But in moments of need honesty is unbecoming.

'That's kind of tricky, I already have an appointment.'

'With whom?'

He'd never figured out whether Gordon's unbearable curiosity was a personality flaw or just part of a sponsor's job.

'With…Oksana.'

'The actress?'

He nodded.

'Ah, Evan, you lech.'

'No, it's not like that.'

'Aha.' Gordon winked. His curl leant to the right.

'Fine. Believe what you want. But why didn't you bring any with you?'

'Any what?'

'mAk.'

Gordon put a finger to his lips.

'Not by name, please. Here even the lights are listening in.'

High up on the ceiling, the lights were buzzing lazily and they did not have ears. The old man and the woman left. The long-haired guy was suddenly standing near their table. He was gazing into the space behind Gordon's head. Perhaps he'd been hypnotized by the curl. Evan remained conciliatory.

'Fine, I'm sorry, but still…'

'What?'

Gordon was ineffectually feigning ignorance. Evan gritted his teeth.

'Why didn't you bring any with you? I wrote to you that I'd run out.'

'Because now it's banned. You know what they'd do with me if… I don't even dare think about it. They'd throw me out, no chance of appeal, and then back home, my goodness, the last thing I need now…that gives me the chills…home.'

Home. A simple noun Evan felt somewhere up around his Adam's apple. Cold. Prickly. Home is the place where they can't turn you away, apparently. But what if you ask them to? If you beg them nevertheless to send you away, somewhere, anywhere?

/

They lived in a stone bungalow on the shores of the Mediterranean. He lived in a terraced house, on the edge of town, not far away, with Mother, with Father, with Sister. They lived in a flat, fifth floor, a skyscraper, in a residential part of town, pretty comfortable, hard to complain. He lived in a student ghetto, alongside nitwits and crazies, horny lads, babes. They lived abroad – if you can call something 'abroad' just because it's not home, even though you know everybody and know how things work and everything is pretty much the same as it was in the old place. He lived on the road, hardly alone. And with people, and sometimes in love. He'd lived, they'd say. He'd lived in Edo, way up high, higher than ever. He never

/

'Let me put it this way. You drop by my place, tonight after your, hmm, visit, I'll go to meditation, let's meet at, say, around seven, my place, ok? The risk is yours. I will sleep peacefully. If you get caught, I'll be on the chopping block because I'm the one who's supposed to protect you from, hmm, wrongful handling, but all right, we'd be able to settle it at the consulate since they go pretty easy on foreigners, especially invited for-eigners. Unless they want to make an example of you. Which I doubt.'

Evan smiled. He should never be an example for any-one. He couldn't imagine anyone scrambling after his fate. Although that fate didn't look bad – from the outside it all seemed fine, which was a good thing, since a great part of your fate consists of how others see it, but if they knew, if they really knew – it was a fate no one would want to have to live out. Gordon had made him happy. The hour precise, the promise nice. He liked clarity. He looked at his watch. A little past four.

'Good, great, it's a date. Seven, your place. I'll take a taxi.'

'Taxis aren't so bad,' mused Gordon. 'It's mainly just the public transport unions, the environmentalists, the rabble that's doing the scare-mongering, to pack more people into buses and trains. You're more likely to suffocate under some-one's armpit than to run into a serial killer in that hustle and bustle. You'd have to have awful luck.'

Evan didn't have any kind of luck. The pancakes were gone. Gordon didn't finish his steak. He crossed his fork and knife and, satisfied, stroked his belly. Even the curl was obviously full since it was no longer forcing its way up into the air. It split in two and stretched itself over the baldness.

'Dessert?' said Gordon.

'After pancakes? What should I have? Meatballs?'

Gordon laughed.

'Yes, yes, of course not. Ok, then nothing. We done?'

They emptied their glasses and rose in tandem. The chair legs silently slipped away. They sized each other up. Gordon was taller and narrow-shouldered, but his indolent belly spilt over his belt. Evan would jump out of a skyscraper if he suddenly found himself trapped in a body like that. He didn't envy him. Maybe it was indifference. It couldn't be very easy for him, a whole life with such an awful figure.

They walked off. Evan looked back, force of habit, to see if he'd forgotten something, and saw the waiters, how quickly they cleared the table, like ants picking a bone clean. He thought the long-haired guy was following him, though it might have been just a coincidence.

The hostess took affectionate leave of them. His imagination lapped her up. He'd like to give it a go, but time was running out and he was low on energy. Lust is risky. Age had rendered him more careful. He liked to be in control, to have complete control, and carnal needs soon shrivel once you consider everything they can generate. Children, venereal disease, offended and whacky women are the least that could happen to you. The worst is sudden boredom and the feeling you have, right after you've squirted out blind passion, that you've lowered your standards. Anyway, he was allowed to do dirty things with her in his mind.

/

Her greedy eyes. Was her skin made of cream? Was she pretending? Was it all the same to her? Maybe she was lying. Each time, again and again, doubt. How to trust? He'd never really trusted her, he'd had no reason to, not even a need to, and if she latched on to him, fine, and if at some moment, just like that, without thinking, she left, then so be it…but himself? How could he trust himself, if he was always waking up in a different skin?

/

They stuck out their hands. Though Gordon's was limp and moist, Evan grabbed the whole hand and looked him in the eye as they shook. Almost flirtatiously. He smiled at Gordon.

'At seven.'

'At seven.'

Gordon disappeared into the crowd, but Evan stood still. He had a few hours to kill. Maybe he'd run through the script again, though he already knew it by heart. Every time he leafed through it, it seemed lousier and lousier. If he tried to fix it at this stage, the actors would murder him. They'd all praised it – who was he to think his judgement was worth so much more than theirs?

Someone grabbed him by the shoulder and spun him around. When they looked into each other's eyes, Evan got scared for a moment. The long-haired guy from MUD was smiling, but his face bore a threat. Evan shook off his hand.

'What?'

'That bald poofter is going to rip you off.'

He withdrew and looked left and right, as if he was expecting help from somewhere.

'Come on, wait, wait a second. He'll rip you off, I said. I heard him. Forty?!! Shit, give me forty and you can take a bath in mAk.'

'I don't know what you heard, but I have no idea what you're talking about.'

The guy with the long black hair showed his teeth, pressed his chin to his chest and looked up at him past his forehead.

'You have no idea, you say?'

Evan shrugged his shoulders and forced himself to smile. 'A misunderstanding.'

'A misunderstanding,' repeated the long-haired guy, reluctantly. He grabbed hold of the braid that had started dangling along his side and swung it back where it belonged. A mocking grin crept over his face. 'Good. Good.'

Evan didn't know what to say – he stared stupidly at him and tried to keep his face steady. A pigeon flew past his head. The long-haired guy took a white business card out of his pocket and waved it in front of Evan's nose.

'In case you ever prefer an *under*standing.'

Evan received it cautiously, took another step back and looked at it.

Lefkas Saito – a middleman, a number. On the back a scribbled address. In the bottom right corner a cryptic note, in tiny font – habeas cor?

By the time he looked up, Lefkas had disappeared. He glanced around. Two dogs were fighting loudly, dragging their owners by the leash. A student was explaining his views on abortion to his girlfriend, dismembered snatches of conversations on the street, justice – ethics – necessity.

Laughter into mobiles. The hollering of hot-dog vendors. A cloud hid the sun for a second, casting darkness upon the passers-by before the wind blew the darkness apart. Furtive glances among the promenade of sunglasses. The skyscrapers swayed with the footsteps. Evan didn't know where to go.

/

He entered in complete silence, took off his shoes and, from behind the closed door, listened in as she cried on the phone.

'…I know. I know. But, Mum…Mum, listen to me, I know that for a long time we haven't…Mum…I know…I know…Yes, Mum, list—…Mum, will you listen to me? Now that I'm calling you, would you rather not hear from me for another year?… All right. No, please, listen, just listen.'

Brazen eavesdropping.

'I lied to him. I don't know, I don't know why. What? It doesn't matter. Just listen. Now I'm all entangled in this bloody lie and I don't know how to get out of it. What? Please, just listen. I want to get out of it but not that way, not by admitting it and not by getting out of it with an even bigger lie. Can't you understand? It's not important, what. No, not that. There's no other man, Mum, I didn't. I don't want... Mum, I don't want to. It's hard. Did you ever lie to Dad? No, I don't want to know. Please, Mum. Please. What should I do?... I don't want to. No. I can't. He'll leave. Nothing. And he'll be right. Mum, please. Can we meet up? Yes. Ok. Yes. Ok, Mum. Sorry.'

Tears are a concoction of hormones that balance out emotional turmoil. Imbibing someone's tears gives you a glimpse of their inner countenance. She sobbed and snorted, then banged a fist on the floor. Evan slipped his shoes back on and crept away. As long as it was his child.

/

He put the card in his pocket and set out blindly for anywhere. He soaked up the energy of the city and committed himself to not stopping. He felt sweat on his back. He hoped that the line of sweat wasn't visible. He avoided reflections in shop windows. He knew what he looked like, for three quarters of his life he'd been looking into mirrors, now he'd stopped with that. They'd had to take away the mirror from the bathroom in his flat. The last thing that you want in the morning is to look into the old, wrinkled face of someone you can't shoo away. He ran a finger around his mouth and held it up in front of his eyes. Brown. Someone could have told him. He was a chocolate clown. Again he rubbed hard. He ran his tongue over his teeth and rubbed his eyes, then brushed his hand over his hair and patted it down. The wind blew away his effort. Forget it, he said. It's all the same. Nobody's looking at you.

That was sad, but liberating. We're all alone and nobody really sees anyone.

He'd splurge on a massage. So much for commitments. Now he was no longer shy about going in and demanding to be touched. An old woman stood in front of the door, her mouth agape and tongue sliding along her lips. He went past her and entered the long, empty hallway. On the floor was a worn-out carpet that had perhaps been green at some time but was now just a dusty grey. The bare walls had been freshly whitewashed and were punctured by doors.

He went through the first door and found himself in some sort of temple. The rows of benches were sparsely planted with protruding heads. In the transparent half-darkness one could see over to the altar, a stone table with a single candle flickering on it. He wanted to leave when a fat man in a red cloak stepped in front of the table, jingling a copper bell, and lifted his arms, screaming.

'We are all cockroaches in the kingdom of gnosis!'

That did it. He didn't even try not to slam the door as he left. It reverberated down the hallway and the voice of the nuisance disappeared. Evan had been brought up Catholic, at university he'd fancied himself a nihilist, and now he believed in neither nothing nor coincidence. The fact that he existed was just another abhorrent, incomplete, unexecuted idea. He puffed his cheeks and popped them with his hands.

So much for existence.

A scabby, cross-eyed man bumped into him –

'Lost your way, didn't you? Hee, hee, hee. Behind these here doors, they'll rub you down like you're some king, some king. A happy ending and, if you're into it, a happy start too. Hee, hee, hee. I'm dry now, totally dry. Ha!'

– and ran off into the street. Evan lost his desire for a massage, but didn't want to be immediately behind him. The man disgusted him. For a happy ending he'd need much more than a woman's fingers, and for a happy start it was already way too late. Everything was hollow. He looked out. He left.

The shop windows flickered past like late-night TV shows. Unexciting cubes of despair. Click-step. Next. Dolls, dead dolls, staring into the nothingness. Containers of sand, dust, plates of spices. Mendacious premonitions of laughter, happiness and joy, hidden behind price tags. Silk scarves, drawn out like slimy trails of snails, techno-nails, rivets, pliers…click.

They'd carved a park among the skyscrapers. A few benches, a pathway, a pair of overly sheared shrubs, nothing special. One bench was free. Evan stretched out on it and shielded his eyes from the sun with his hand.

/

Troubling dreams. When he awoke, he didn't know where he was. An old man with a hearing aid and monstrous glasses was standing over him.

'The park's closing. You'll have to get up.'

'What time is it?'

'Nothing but junkies here at night. They mess up everything. And I have to clean up after them.'

'Ok. But do you perhaps have the time?'

'I do. Someone died last time, right there on that bench you're sleeping on. I had to call and then they interrogated me… I don't have time to be interrogated. I know nothing. I've never known anything.'

Evan got up and tottered drunkenly towards the street.

'How about a thanks?'

He looked at him, the old man in the green suit, with the rake in his hands.

'Drop dead.'

The old man clutched his chest, shook and sat down. The rake fell.

Evan stopped.

'It's seven o'clock,' was the grave reply.

'Thank you.'

'No need for thanks. At least I know something, at least I know the ti…'

Evan was already on the street flagging a taxi down. He got into the first one that stopped. He had no fears. He'd never had bad luck. He'd never had anything. A woman was driving, which surprised him. She looked old, though he couldn't say how old. Grey curls curled around the forehead, and at the neck tucked into the collar of a blouse. They greeted each other.

'Where to?' she asked.

He had to think. He gave her the address.

'How much?' he asked.

'It's not far. Three.'

'Aha. I meant how much time will it take. I'm in a bit of a hurry.'

'Ten minutes, fifteen if we hit red lights.'

'Good.'

The people blended into the pavements. His mind went blank. He gawked.

'Where are you from?' she asked him.

He looked wearily at her in the rear-view mirror. Her face shone with something like happiness. He didn't dare to be rude.

'From Europe.'

'That's far.'

'Yes. And you?'

'From everywhere, from nowhere. You know how it is. You forget everything.'

'You've forgotten where you're from?'

'It's all the same. I don't know, maybe… I was born somewhere near India, I think. Spent my childhood on a ship. What can I say? A citizen of the seas.'

'Nice.'

'Really?'

'Why not?'

'It's hard to grow roots out at sea.'

'Would you like to? I've had a lot of trouble yanking them out.'

'Are you better off now?'

'No.'

'Well, there you are.'

She was silent.

'What are you doing in Edo?'

Hoping it will end soon, leaving no trace.

'I'm a director. In the theatre.'

'Bravo!'

'But you don't know whether I'm any good.'

'If you're here, you must be.'

'If you only knew.'

'Ah, you have doubts? That's healthy. Better than blind self-confidence, yes?'

He didn't answer. An ambulance siren filled the air. He opened his mouth and leant his forehead against the window. Every hole in the road shook him, but he didn't move his head. The rattling of his skull roused him from foggy despair. Before going to bed he'd gladly down one more bag of mAk. He hoped Gordon had more.

'We're here.'

She turned into a sloping driveway. Gordon lived in a luxurious house that he shared with five other sponsors. A doorman opened the taxi door. Evan rummaged around in his pocket for change and paid her. Five.

'Thank you.'

She winked at him in encouragement. He smiled. Even taxi drivers pitied him. He got out before she could give him any change.

The doorman was a tall man with close-cropped hair and teeth like a row of blank dominoes.

'Are you a client?' he asked as they walked towards the door.

Evan nodded.

'Whose, if I may?'

'Gordon's.'

The doorman stopped.

'I do not quite know how to tell you this, sir, but Mr Falstaff has just been arrested.'

'What?' Evan's heart stopped.

'Do not worry, it's probably nothing, there has surely been a mistake.'

'A misunderstanding,' said Evan.

'Yes, yes, that's it, I guess.'

They stood in front of the door. Evan peeked inside.

'So he's not here?'

'They took him to the station.'

'Why was he arrested? Do you know?'

The doorman leant towards him.

'Drugs, they say. Nonsense, if you ask me. Today they banned them and they're already bullying…'

'Maybe they want to make an example of him.'

The doorman raised his eyebrows.

'I hadn't thought of that.'

Evan smiled knowingly. The sun had disappeared behind the peaks of skyscrapers, and they were engulfed by darkness. The doorman crossed his hands and tried politely, through his body language, to intimate that he should leave. If Gordon was not here, then he had no reason for being here. But he did. He had a damned good reason. He'd come for a very specific purpose – and certainly not just to stare again into Gordon's dishevelled half-bald head. He'd come for what he'd been promised, and he didn't care whether Gordon had landed in detention, or jail, or wherever. He quietly ground his heel into the asphalt.

'Is there anything else I can help you with?' asked the doorman.

'Did Gordon leave anything for me?'

The doorman thought about it and shook his head.

'Nothing.'

'Are you sure?'

He raised his head, as if seeking the answer in a street lamp, and shook his head again.

'Maybe he left it with someone else…'

'Sir, I've been here the whole day. I was here when he came home. He went into his flat and right after that the police stormed in.'

'They were in his flat?'

The doorman's patience was wearing thin.

'Yes, they were. If I can do anything else to help you… otherwise…'

'No, I understand. It's just that he promised me something, and I desperately need it.' He bit his tongue. Everyone needs something, but when that need is drug-related desperation seems so tawdry. He didn't care even enough to deny it. The doorman straightened up and frowned.

'Sir, he did not leave anything for you. Please, if that is all…'

Evan shook his head nervously and turned to leave. The doorman relaxed, but then Evan dashed towards the door and smashed into it. It was locked. He looked foolishly at the doorman, who smiled at him, took a card out of his pocket and waved it.

'That won't work, sir. Now I must ask you to leave.'

Evan muttered a docile *excuse me* and, with his head tucked between his shoulders, slunk away. He threw a few more threatening glances in the doorman's direction, thought about how he might distract him, relieve him of the card, looked out for a drain he could shimmy up to a window, slip inside, and rummage through everything… Out on the pavement he admitted defeat. He kicked a can and it flew high in the air, bounced off the tarp on a parked lorry and landed back on the ground.

/

By way of a greeting he told the cab driver, 'Not in the mood for talking. Take me home.' The cab driver obeyed. During the drive he silently nursed neurosis. When they arrived, he puked it out onto the pavement. Pancakes. The viscous chocolate remnants sluiced into the gutter. He wiped his mouth and staggered inside, where the receptionist instantly accosted him.

'Mr Z—!'

Evan didn't look at him; he waved a hand and tried to get to the lift right away. He felt entirely open to the annoying encroachment of strangers, while he just wanted the safety of his room, to be shut away, locked away, alone. The receptionist didn't let it rest.

'Mr Z—! You have a visitor.'

He ignored him. He dragged himself to the lift, where he pressed the button at regular intervals. The doors opened and he already had one foot inside when he heard her.

'Eeeevan.'

She'd whispered into his right ear, but when he turned, there was no one there.

Her smile now came from the other side. She grabbed him by the shoulder and gently pulled him to her. When she looked at him, her smile faded.

'Eeeevan, you look a mess.'

The doors were closing. He stuck a hand between them. They bit him, ever so gently, before moving apart again.

'I've had a bad day, Oksana.'

'You look it. What happened?'

'Nothing.'

'Nothing is bad?' Her eyes were innocently wide-set, curious, slightly stupid, cow-like in their depth.

'Nothing is bad.'

'Better than bad, is nothing?'

Tired, he smiled.

'I need a shower, Oksana... Are we... Did we have a date? What time is it? I'm late, no? At seven? Sorry.'

'I was mad,' she said.

He nodded.

'Sorry.'

She reached out for his cheek. He wanted to withdraw, but failed. Eyes closed, he swayed into her touch. She entered the lift and pulled him in behind her. He was expecting a kiss, but when he opened his eyes she was staring at the floor. He went over to her and lifted her chin. She wriggled free. That didn't surprise him.

He didn't care. The red numbers increased. The lift went up with a gentle murmur of metal.

'You're going to wash up,' she said.

He ran a finger around his mouth. Chocolate again. He swore under his breath.

'I will.'

/

She was dressed in a white evening gown and wearing anklets in open-toed, high-heeled shoes. She looked beautiful. She showed cleavage but managed to remain tasteful. She'd tried to powder over the birthmark on her neck. What was she ashamed of? It was in the shape of a crescent. Her hands weren't the hands of a lady, so they betrayed what she had been before. Cracked skin on her fingertips, the echoes of blisters. Her hands had been gnawed by the earth. They'd turned hay, beaten cows, and, dammit, shovelled shit. And now they held him.

They entered the flat. Evan turned on the light and asked her to sit down. She didn't cross her legs. They were pale, smooth, not wholly thin, with a hint of flab here and there. Under her left knee, barely visible, was a scar. She'd never told him from what. From kneeling before some unknown deity, before a strict father, before a cruel lover... Or just an abrasion of the soul, engraved into the place you hide when you worship. Her knees were just touching. He couldn't look between them.

He threw his shirt on the bed. When he loosened his belt, his trousers fell. He took his shoes off and extracted his ankles from the pile of rags. He went to the bathroom in his underwear. He felt her eyes on his back. The years had dried out his skin. It was congested with freckles that looked like drops of ink on weathered parchment. Furrows of muscles. Wrinkles that could no longer be ironed out.

As the water poured over him, he noticed he was shaking. The cold softened his rage. He was old and paltry due to the seismic shifts in the body's demands. He'd felt something lacking in his life, but he'd always been able to pull through; to gain through brute force what he needed, or to quell desire. It was different now. He was sure that he deserved it. If paperwork and bureaucracy were going to deprive him of satisfaction even now, then he'd spent his whole life in search of traps. He would never be complete. The conspiracy of the world turned every expectation into abuse of tranquillity.

She joined him. Naked. A jet of water flattened her hair onto her scalp. He held his arms to his side. When she pressed closer he could feel her pubic hair against his waist.

'Will you go?' she asked.

'Where?' His voice was weak.

'I saw it on the table.'

He said nothing.

'Don't leave.'

He felt her lips grazing his shoulders.

'I'm not going anywhere.' He could no longer decide when he was telling the truth. Had he ever been able to?

She dropped down. The back of his hand brushed against one of her nipples. She withdrew. When she took him in her mouth, he could no longer remember who she was, he didn't know what he was after, what he wanted to do, what he even could do – torn between what had been and what was still to come, he began to concentrate on the pulsing heat in his groin, the awakening, the rising, that tongue, slowly, between her fingers, saliva, the whispering, those lips, more

ABRAHAM!

✦

All families, all happy and unhappy families, strong or poor families, forgotten, exalted, belittled families, shameless and desperate and greedy and fabulous families, real families, unreal families, mighty, worthless, wealthy, godless and coarse, voracious and even the most hysterical families are, whichever way you look at it, first and foremost a dreary pack of wounded people.

These people are bound by tiny information codes stored somewhere deep within their bodies. They are bound by memories forged over long years of continuous peripeteias. They are bound by blood and water and tears and sometimes by a house or a flat or some hollow they can creep into when the storms are howling outside. They are bound up like bundles of wood. They are inseparable. And that is why they suffer.

Take, for instance, the Wolfs, so lovingly gathered together on a fine summer evening somewhere beneath the Alps in the Soča valley, among ancient woods of pine and oak, in a splendid rented log cabin that simmered the whole day long in the fragrances of sausages, corn and old offences. They have gathered to celebrate the birthday of the Wolf patriarch. It's a nice round birthday, his fiftieth, his 'Abraham', and although the patriarch's father is still alive, still present, he has behaved so scandalously that long ago the baton of the pater-familias had been passed to his son, to the birthday boy Kras, who had until recently, when his party lost the election, been Minister for War, and whom everyone utterly respects, even if many remain tacitly convinced that he is a misanthrope at heart.

Throughout the day they kept mostly to themselves. The children were playing with a ball, or with the dogs, rummaging and romping through the bushes, the men were nipping at chicken wings, sports and war, and the women were – also busy with chicken wings – spouting gossip about countless others. Over the years, two camps have formed among the adults: on the one side, the allies of Kras's father Bojan, whom not even his new, young wife Stoja (too young, some would say, most loudly of them Bojan's ex) and his religious delusions (a few years ago he found his way into neo-Celtic druidism, grew a beard and began conversing with trees) have discouraged from valuing the old man's bared soul and his unbearably naive view of the world; and on the other side, the allies of Kras's mother, Olga, the dishonoured, dignified, lady-like woman who chains people to herself by dint of justified rebukes and accusations, on account of which many, in these times of unclear values, take her to be an anchor or at least a beacon. The walls between the camps are almost impervious. They are transgressed only by Kras and his wife, as well as by a few children who are too young to know any better.

For as long as the sun persisted on the horizon and the nearby river cooled the clearing in which they were scattered, the atmosphere was almost placid, but now that evening has fallen and they have all respectfully – proper behaviour being the order of the day – headed inside, the air is filled with an electricity that threatens to char the undergrowth right up to the tri-border area, should the birthday boy Kras fail to perform a convincing lightning-conductor act.

Just seating them at the table was a medal-worthy task. Kras's wife Katarina spent almost a whole month juggling the guests' backsides. She hung on the telephone for hours and hours, listening to all the grievances and gossip cloaked in false modesty that increased in size as it journeyed from mouth to mouth, was distorted through the filters of envy and malice into barely credible half-truths, not to mention that mass of praise for people who had gained general favour within the family merely by stubbornly and steadily suffering under the yoke of their utterly ordinary fates. The Wolfs are a proud old Slovenian family, a microcosm reflecting the wider community. They've had their disputes, as we have already heard, although Katarina wasn't convinced that the point of contention really was just Kras's parents' divorce, that their differences didn't in fact reach deeper, into politics, religion, personal philosophy, that is, into worldviews and convictions, and that they weren't just using that scandalous divorce to buttress their views against rational confrontation with views of other varieties. They willingly shut themselves off in an echo chamber and peeped through the blinds only when an argument was looming. When Katarina entrusted Kras with her observation, he laconically replied that conflict was healthy and necessary (let's not forget that he ministered to war) and that she shouldn't get all worked up about it.

Now they are walking in a straight line over to the table, seeking out their names on the place cards and taking their seats. Katarina follows them anxiously, trying to read unconscious responses through their wrinkled noses, frowning eyebrows, sighs of relief and nods of agreement. So far, so good, it seems. She and Kras are, of course, seated in the middle, Mila, their eldest daughter and a future lawyer, is beside her father, Mira and Mina, the ten-year-old twins, are next to her. Sitting beside Mila is Edgar, Kras's half-brother, whom his father, soon after the divorce and long before he remarried, had dragged in from somewhere and claimed to have fathered, even though Edgar looks nothing like him (he was swarthy, small and smiley, the Wolfs pale, tall and sullen), and when Olga ('How insulting!') had left off thoughts of murder or at least a staged accident, she started a rumour in the family that Bojan had kidnapped the boy from a travelling gypsy caravan.

When Edgar was growing up and getting to know his father a little better, he had heard that rumour from Andreja, who had heard it from the priest Meslier to whom it was confessed, in juicy variants, almost every other month, and simply believed it. Due to his carefree nature and his extraordinary understanding of his fellow man, Edgar is probably the only one in the family who enjoys Kras's unconditional trust.

Next to Edgar sits Bojan, his 'father', who has already had quite a bit to drink. You can see him drooling at the thought of all the inconvenience, awkwardness and discomfort his behaviour will cause over the coming hours. The closer he gets to death, the more he enjoys taking the piss out of the world. Because she has never regarded him as evil, Katarina grins as she looks forward to his contributions to the evening, though she takes pains not to let it show. To Bojan's left sits his wife Stoja, a red-headed Russian beauty. They say Bojan simply bought her, and that, surprisingly, is true. What is never said, however, is that he bought her from Russian human traffickers and thus saved her from a cruel life of addiction and prostitution in the Baltic underworld. What Bojan was doing up there is never spoken of, but on account of the goodwill he showed we will remain tactfully silent on this point. In gratitude, Stoja gave birth to two of his children, Alan and Po, and then, quite selfishly and all by herself, raised them right. Now they are sitting, well-behaved, beside her.

Next to little Po sits her sister ('not half-sister, don't you dare call me "half-sister," you're my sister and I'm your sister, we are sisters'), also Kras's sister, Grace, born Andreja, Bojan and Olga's youngest daughter. Because she was passionately attached to her mother, she kept her sexuality a secret for a long time, banging on about nunneries and hell and repentance, going to church every day, now and then flagellating herself until the blood flowed and guilt and doubt and despair almost drove her to suicide, until one day Kras, after a confidential conversation with Edgar, who made a few things clear to Kras, clumsily told her, not knowing any better, that 'Dad doesn't give a shit anyway, Mum will survive, so stop the circus, stop the whining, find some chick, do with her what you will, for fuck's sake, you're old enough to listen to your pussy instead of Mummy and the priest.' During the years in which Kras was winding his way upwards in the political milieu and cleaning up his tongue, Andreja, thanks to this secular blessing, changed her name to Grace Wolf, exuberantly scooted all around Europe and then, in Denmark, in Christiania, married Olive, the hairy Hebrew nurse with whom she is now seated hand in hand, both serenely smiling and still in love.

For Olga, who is sitting on Katarina's right, beside Mina, Andreja's revelation was a final blow from which she'd never recovered. After the divorce, even after Edgar's arrival, she'd continued to nurture romantic thoughts of Bojan's return (her fantasy had been worked out to the last detail – he kneeling, she with extended arms, the rite of repentance and forgiveness, crosses, doves, crowns of thorns, he her mythical, pagan Črtomir, she his Valjhun), but Stoja's coming had scraped these thoughts away and poured them out with her final period. She therefore tried to direct the scorched remains of her love onto her children, but by that time Kras had already grown up into an entirely independent being who showed no interest at all in the emotional turmoil of others, and he defended himself against his mother's attentions with constant references to his having been sent off to boarding school, on account of which she had to double her efforts in maintaining the illusion of his freedom, that is, to leave him alone as best she could; she pitied Bernard and Alenka, which is why she could never really love them; so the only one left was Andreja, tiny, cute Andreja who, under her mother's spiritual baton, soon turned from an innocent lamb into a pious, guilt-burdened mutton. Olga had worked hard to get her into a nunnery, since the Wolfs all blisteringly needed someone to devote their entire life to prayer (as if Bojan's debauchery weren't enough, Kras had lately been mentioning politics more and more frequently), and when even that didn't pan out (Olga never learnt what made Andreja turn to sin – she suspected gypsy magic), she, distraught, tore out her hair and swore from then on to love only ghosts.

Magda and Svetlana, Olga's sisters, old and barren never-married twins, had for many years idled forgotten at the family farm above Idrija, surviving on porridge and polenta and tarragon *potica*, feeding a dozen chickens, pottering about their sole, emaciated cow, and every day jealously yanking Marshal Tito's portrait out of each other's hands. Even though they were perhaps ten years old when the dictator died, their late grandfather, Kras's grandfather on his mother's side, had, by means of long, nostalgia-rich excursions, convinced them of Tito's value, greatness and almost semi-divine nature. Because their father's meagre conviction ensured that they'd never fall under the influence of Western culture, and because the boys from the village were utterly unequipped for dealing with the cult of the myth, they'd remained faithful to their dead hero. When their sister, short-haired and desperately in need of simple company, visited them for the first time in twenty years, they instinctively hid the portrait in the basement. In the past few days they had ridden in a car for the first time, held plastic cutlery for the first time, and seen their first ever mobile phones. They had somehow promised Olga that next year they would make a pilgrimage, on foot, from the house of their birth to the Basilica of Mary Help of Christians in Brezje, although they would much prefer to see the sea (which they never had). They are sitting beside her, constantly whispering in one another's ears through toothless grins.

The aunts are getting on Bernard's nerves. Bernard is Kras's younger brother and he's sitting beside Magda or beside Svetlana (he can never tell which is which). Bernard is a pitiable creature – he has spent so much time in his brother's shadow that he has cadaverous-pale skin, extreme myopia and a withered right hand. As a child he aroused compassion; now, after having done an MBA and accumulated immense personal wealth, he arouses contempt. He much prefers it that way. All of the Wolfs, with the exception of Kras, owe him money and Bernard spends his days plotting their fates. On the evening of the death of his son Lovro, who, barely eight years old, died of leukaemia, he tearfully confided in his wife Monika that 'everybody is just looking for a way to bind others to them so they can fuck up their lives'. He was talking about himself, but she thought he was blaming her for Lovro's death so the next day she filled her pockets with stones and threw herself into the Sava River.

A severe attack of chickenpox when she was five has left Alenka with a pock-marked face. She never refused empathy but neither did she particularly care for it. She and Bernard have become allies on account of their marginalized existences, but whereas Bernard reached out for a connection, Alenka coldly retreated into her own world. She has read the collected works of all Slovenian writers and poets born before the Second World War, with the sole exception of the great Ivan Cankar. She spent her twenties on missions in Africa and India (this had nothing to do with any weighty religiosity, she just wanted to help), and now she works in the national archives and writes bilious letters to Slovenian publishing houses whenever she catches a grammatical error in print. A few years ago she adopted a black boy from Uganda, named him Voranc, and told everybody he was HIV positive, since she was convinced that otherwise the Wolfs would have devoured him. Voranc is a playful little seven-year-old, and he has just left his chair and climbed onto Mummy's lap.

When you expose and link up all the emotional nodes of people's lives, they will inevitably disintegrate into caricatures. But, please, don't forget that the Wolfs are people, real, living people who breathe, feel, dream and desire, who are motivated by human rage, endowed with reason, they feel sexual desire and they remember, they constantly remember… Pick any one of them – I could go on for years about a single minute of their existence.

But before I further assail you with this mass of people – to the left and right alike are still more uncles, aunts, male and female cousins, brothers-in-law, sisters-in-law, Kras's mother-in-law (the father-in-law is dead, cancer), and a handful of family friends, neighbours and business partners rounding up the company into a semicircle – I would just like to mention the priest and the general.

Meslier came as a young deacon to the parish of Bodičava, where the Wolfs had been living for centuries in their enormous rural mansion on the outskirts of the village of the same name, but he soon had to take over the duties of a priest when the previous one, old Šurc, had clearly gone round the bend (that priest had been found, naked and with a shaved head, on the bank of a nearby creek – he whispered *hosanna, hosanna* into the ear of the farmer who was first on the scene). The first sacrament that Father Meslier performed after being ordained was the wedding of Olga and Bojan. The fact that this had been a spectacular failure has lain heavily on his priestly soul for decades. He is here because Olga no longer wants to consume food that has not been blessed before her very eyes, and Kras has given in to this caprice because he wants to make sure that her mouth is kept as occupied as possible.

Katarina had asked Kras not to invite General Globocnik, to pick some other day to see him, because she wanted this celebration to go as peacefully as possible and didn't want to be constantly thinking of war (given that war was the guarantor of all her painful preoccupations and the stuff of many a nightmare), which wouldn't be possible if she had the general's bushy moustache waltzing in front of her the whole time, caught between the quotation marks of his epaulettes, but Kras didn't grant her request. He needed, longed for, desperately required information, and he wanted to keep the general close – he hoped that the atmosphere and the wine would loosen his tongue at least a bit.

So. Everyone's seated. Katarina is now calm. Nobody has started bitching or yelling yet. A great success. The faces remain untroubled, the corners of the mouths are turned upwards. Katarina and Kras look at each other and smile lovingly. Here and there conversation sprouts. The increasingly loud murmuring encourages the others too. Someone even laughs. Three rent-a-waiters walk about, pouring wine into glasses. Let's begin.

/

Bernard, his withered hand resting on the table between his plate and his glass, leans forwards and turns his head to the birthday boy.

'Wolf,' he calls out in that annoying voice. Both Kras and Bojan look his way. Bernard catches the father's gaze and raises his eyebrows before turning to Kras. Wolf is what they used to call Bojan, until he wasted that name. That's what upsets him most. Bernard's barb, undoubtedly planned, hurts him. Now it's what they call Kras, everyone does. Only Katarina and his daughters don't.

'Yes?'

'Doesn't it seem to you like we're one chair short?'

Katarina looks up in fright, but Kras knows what Bernard's aiming at. He presses his lips into a straight line, gets up and goes to the next room to fetch a chair. He sets it down behind his. Now Katarina also understands – she blinks, shakes her head and immediately turns to Grace, who is laughing and waving in her direction. Bernard nods contentedly. Kras gives him a threatening look. A tacit agreement exists within the family – the matter is too painful to discuss in front of guests, but Bernard won't let up.

Olga looks at her sisters, which means they must pay attention to her, and turns to the priest.

'Father, have I ever told you that thing about our Andreja?' the guests at the table listen up, Katarina grimaces, 'about when I found her, not even fifteen years old, maybe not even in high school, I think,' she turns to Grace, 'fifteen, no?', Grace rolls her eyes, but her smile persists, 'a sweet little thing, I remember it so well, it's like she's right in front of me, she had long, luxurious, black curls, and look at her now,' Grace's hairdo is very modern, 'well, I come home, from work, by then we'd already sold the farm to a co-op, so I was working at the hardware shop, just before the chain went bankrupt, so I come home, it's afternoon, not a soul to be seen, and the only thing I hear from Andreja's room is *whack, whack*, like someone's beating the dust out of a carpet,' Alenka puts her hands over Voranc's ears, Edgar watches Katarina and shakes his head, Kras leans over to Mila and tells her to inform the waiters that Grandma has had enough wine for today, 'and I say to myself, "what if someone's beating the children?", what do I know what I was thinking, maybe someone's in the house or who knows what, but I run up the stairs and when I open the door,' Bojan coughs, Olga laughs, her voice rising in pitch, 'there's my little Andreja in her nightie, kneeling on the floor and staring at the crucifix and devotionals in the corner above the television, and she's got an old leather belt in her hand, Bojan's I think, God knows where she found it, a brown thing with a huge buckle, a silver one with some sort of skull on it, you know, Bojan used to listen to rock and roll,' the guests look at each other, those who don't know the story are already enjoying themselves, 'and she's flogging herself with that belt, *whack*, you hear, she hits herself and again, *whack*, you hear her hitting herself again and before I realize what's actually going on, I run to her and grab the belt, but I scare the poor thing so much she faints.'

Uncomfortable silence. Meslier the priest nods, 'Yes, Olga, I have already heard this one.' Olga continues, 'But then, God, what to do now? If I take her to a doctor, they'd say, for sure they'd say, I did it, Christ – sorry, Father – but they could take her away from me, you know, couldn't they?'

'That would be a tragedy,' mumbles Edgar, and though Olga hears him she doesn't respond. 'Yes, that would really be bothersome, I can imagine,' says the priest. 'Nothing. I put her in the bathtub, bathed her, and when she came around she said she had been vile and that she deserved it, my poor little one, but then I, oh God,' looking at Alenka, 'Alenka, get that knife out of that child's hand!' Voranc is playing with the cutlery but stops when his mother asks him to, 'Well, after that I forbade her to castigate herself, I said that God already knows that she's a good soul, that only the really bad ones should go in for self-flagellation, but I didn't know,' she stares at Olive, 'I didn't know,' she whispers, 'maybe it would have been better if I'd let her do it.'

Edgar turns to Grace, 'Horrible,' but Grace looks serenely at Olga.

'Ah, Mum, now don't you worry about a thing. I still do it sometimes.'

The guests smile, even old Meslier has to cough over a laugh, Olga crosses herself, looks at her sisters and gestures to them that they too should cross themselves. They obey.

'Jesus Christ, Olga,' bellows Bojan, 'now you've got these two into that useless crossing, between you and I, that's something I never thought I'd see.'

'Between you and *me*,' says Alenka.

Bojan jumps to his feet: 'Today my son turns fifty! That, too,' nodding to Alenka, 'is something I never thought I'd see. Not because I didn't think he'd make it to fifty, no, he'll make it to a hundred, two hundred, but because I was convinced I'd have snuffed it by now. But look at us, now, all here, the whole Wolf pack all together. On this occasion, I have to take the opportunity, who knows when it'll happen again, if ever, I don't know, I hope, or maybe I don't, ha, ha,' the waiter leans down to Mila, listens, nods, 'I'll take this opportunity to tell you that, since they've already taken my name, I've been rebaptized, born again, so to speak, the ceremony was on Sunday, but nobody came, except for my dear Grace and Edgar,' Olga had found the invitations in their letterbox, torn them in half and tossed them in the bin, 'the baptism was at the Savica waterfall, the falling water that reflects our lives, fleeting, trivial, sunned in the sun of nature, under the hand of Archdruid Bodhmall, a beautiful, pure, heartfelt ceremony, wasn't it?' he turns to Grace and Edgar, who nod. 'Now I'm born again, under a new sun, a new name, ha, ha, please allow me to introduce myself, I've shed the Wolf skin, I'm no longer Bojan, my name is,' he clears his throat, 'Raven Cock's-foot, I am on the threshold between life and death, and all of you are my loves, I love you, and also,' Olga crosses herself, her sisters cross themselves with a slight delay, the priest Meslier looks at him with sad eyes, Bernard grins, Alenka sighs, Kras stares straight ahead, 'I wanted to say, I was, ah, now…have I forgotten? Well, all the best Kra…ah, screw it, to my Wolf!'

Glasses are raised, glasses are emptied. The waiters make the rounds. Raven is still standing.

'So, that's it then! Even the maples and the oaks and the chestnut trees are wishing you happy birthday, Kra…Wolf! The apple tree, the one out there, is turning its nose up. It says that every time someone is celebrating something the kids abuse it, all that stuff carved into its trunk, so please, if you can, I ask you to leave it alone today.'

Good-natured laughter lets the old man keep his dignity. Even Olga chuckles dryly. Raven sits down. His beard has spilt onto his plate and Stoja discreetly shifts it into his lap.

'Alenka, take the knife away from the boy!'

Grace's whispering lips approach Olive's ear, translating what's going on. Her face alternates between outrage and disbelief. When Olive glances at Bernard, he suggestively licks his lips. Edgar and Alenka are careful not to look each other in the eye (they're still ashamed because they made out once – Bernard caught them kissing and immediately told everyone). General Globocnik is telling jokes at his end of the table; all Kras can make out is '…because they were all already occupied!' Everyone bursts out laughing. Raven, who loves jokes, asks *what, what, what?*, and when Stoja, who didn't find it the least bit funny, repeats the joke, he falls into that thundering laugh they all know him for, the laugh a chance passer-by could easily confuse with an unsuccessful but persistent attempt to start a two-stroke engine. Mira and Mina are behaving, Mila and Alan are visibly bored, little Po complains to her mummy that her tummy hurts and Stoja strokes her head. Kras's mother-in-law launches into a long discourse, to the accompaniment of Meslier's coughing, about the benefits of alternative medicine. Voranc, who has had to put down the knife a third time, turns to Aunt Grace.

'Auntie.' She doesn't hear him. 'Auntie Andreja.' His mother whispers something into his ear.

'Auntie Gwace!' Grace, who has only now heard him and would never ignore him, looks at him. 'What is it, sweetie?'

'Uncle Bewdo' – that's what they call Bernard – 'said you like to lick waw fish.'

Alenka covers his mouth (and whispers into his ear – *raw not waw*.) Most of those who have heard are aghast. Alan and Mila look at each other and howl with laughter. Raven again turns to his wife to ask *what what what?*, but Stoja just shrugs her shoulders.

'He said that?' asks Grace. Voranc, a hand over his mouth, nods. 'Yeah, I really like them,' she said, 'but you know how it's done?' Voranc opens his eyes wide. 'First you stick your finger in the fish's mouth, you can do two fingers, you push it in deep, then you…'

'Dinner's coming,' says Kras.

Mira and Mina stare at their aunt and wrinkle their noses. Voranc shakes off his mother's hands and says *yuck*.

'Are we having fish?' asks Edgar.

'No, steak,' replies Katarina, and is a little slow to join in the laughter.

Kras gets up and motions to the waiters to bring the food. He takes a glass and looks at it. The people are expecting him to make a speech. He'd learnt one by heart, but now he's forgotten the words. Katarina surreptitiously nudges him in the side. He looks up, scans the table, forces a smile and, catching sight of the general's moustache, straightens his spine. His speech was written for him, as a birthday gift, by his former speechwriter at the ministry. It's in his pocket, printed on a folded-up piece of paper. His hand slides towards it, but stops. That's not how he wants to do it. He clears his throat.

'Tolstoy,' his voice whistles hoarsely; he clears his throat again, squints and adds some strength to it, 'Tolstoy wrote at the beginning of one of his novels that all families are alike,' he opens his eyes, 'that all happy families are alike, that all happy families are alike in the same way. And that each unhappy family is unhappy in its own way. In its own way. Our family has gone through its share of happinesses and unhappinesses, like every family, I guess, and each one of us, probably, at least as far as I know you, would say that he'd got off fairly lightly, but that he feels sorry for the rest.' That's not the way it had been written. People were supposed to laugh here. 'Well, I myself have never had any reason to complain. And neither do I want to say that we're an unhappy family, as some might think, because we are such a unique family and our happiness might look completely exceptional, which is not to say…' He looks at his parents. 'Let's say, look, we certainly have the happiness, as Dad already said, of being here, all,' the word *all* gets stuck in his throat, he has to drink, 'and that both Mum and Dad are here, and my daughters, and my wife, and brothers and sisters, and all of you, dear friends, and what is happiness if not that? That…' he bows his head and tightens his jaw, 'ah, screw it, look, it doesn't matter what kind of family we are. There are no happy and unhappy families, we're just people who have created lives for one another, and if we haven't managed to mess things up completely, and if we can still all sit together at the same table, then it must mean something, call it happiness or whatever…something like that, yes, that's it, thank you for coming, and *bon appetit*.'

They clap in rhythm under emotional (and faux-emotional) faces. Olga remembers that she should have asked for a blessing, so she looks at the priest, who makes a discreet sign of the cross over her food and nods. Because he doesn't want to ask anyone else, Bernard reluctantly asks Aunt Svetlana if she can cut his steak. She does, feeling blessed to be able to help out.

They eat in near-silence.

/

Mila is twenty years old. Kras, her father, so passive-aggressively coerced her into studying law that by the time she'd enrolled she didn't even realize it wasn't she who'd made the decision. She was open to ideas, which is why at university they easily moulded her into that contradictory (but so common) type of being that is convinced people are for the most part beasts in need of a firm hand, but when it came to herself she asserted a certain amount of leeway in regard to the law.

She gets up from the table and signals to Alan to join her. Alan is seventeen years old. His skull still hasn't withdrawn from that amorphous adolescent mass of face and is plagued by pimples, but otherwise he's quite nice. He and Mila get along well. They pass through the kitchen together, where a waiter Mila fancies is sitting.

'Want to go for a smoke?' Alan says.

'I don't smoke,' the waiter replies.

'Well, come with us anyway. Have you been upstairs yet?' Alan smiles at him. The waiter stands up. 'I'm Borut.'

'Alan.'

'Mila.'

'Nice to meet you.'

They take the wooden staircase up to the attic, where there are several locked doors and a wide-open one leading to a fusty, dusty room full of old furniture and boxes filled with stuff. Mila opens the window, the waiter Borut doesn't know what to do with his hands, and Alan rummages through the boxes and finds a pile of old *Komunist* magazines.

'Rip me off a sheet,' says Mila.

Alan tears a page down the middle, hands it over to Mila, who folds it in half and then stretches a hand down past her shirt collar. She extracts a bag of weed from her bra. Alan grins; the waiter is visibly uncomfortable.

'Do you toke?'

He is searching for the right answer.

'Yeah, I do, but I'm working, I mean, I'm at work, and if the boss finds out I'll be in the shit because he knows my folks, so, I don't know, maybe it's better if I just head back downstairs.'

Alan and Mila look at each other.

'Don't worry, dude,' says Alan.

Mila adds, with a wink, 'No, seriously, I mean, as you wish, but if you ask me, there's no problem, we won't tell anyone.'

'Yeah, no, I know, but still, it would be best if I didn't.'

But he doesn't move. Mila breaks a clump into small pieces, pulls a pack of fags from her pocket, removes a cigarette, licks it, breaks it lengthwise, then sprinkles the weed in with the tobacco. Alan makes a filter out of a *Komunist* cover. Mila has the cigarette paper in her other pocket. She removes it, sprinkles the mixture onto it, takes the filter and rolls the joint in five quick motions. She catches Borut watching her while she stretches her tongue and licks the joint, so she runs her tongue over it one more time, though there's no need to.

'Do you have a lighter?'

Alan takes a lighter from his pocket and lights it for her. A cloud of smoke rolls out of the window. Borut moves to the sill to see if anyone's down below. There's nobody. He hopes they won't catch them and it still seems like he really should leave. It smells great but is far too pungent. When Mila presses a still smoking joint into his hands, he takes three quick tokes, passes it to Alan and immediately regrets having smoked. He presses his eyelids together, senses that his whites have turned bright red, realizes that everyone will immediately know what he's been up to, his co-workers, those rotten snitches, will tell the boss on him, the boss, that rotten scoundrel, will tell his father on him, and then he'll have to move out of the house, live on the streets, these bloody kids of feudal lords, and especially their smoking-hot daughters, always causing him grief. Something rattles at the door, footsteps are heard, and Borut collapses.

/

It's hard to say whose eyes are open wider, Magda's or Svetlana's. Their mouths are agape and both are gently shaking their heads. 'Oh, no, that we won't, Olga...that we won't.'

Olga does not know whether to play the victim or use force, so she swings between the two poles.

'Sisters! If you knew everything I've had to suffer in this family. The humiliation and the shame! If you have any love for me, if you still feel anything at all for your sister, who raised you, who ironed your rags and washed your diapers, if you are at all grateful for anything in life, then do as I say!'

She passes over in silence the twenty years she ignored them and tones down the haughtiness, and it also doesn't seem fitting to her to mention the fact that she ran away from that godforsaken place the first chance she got. Magda and Svetlana turn pale.

'But,' 'Yes, Olga, but,' 'we can't,' 'no, really, you do not,' 'how can you ask for such a thing,' 'but didn't you forgive?' 'I will not, I cannot' 'me neither.'

Olga has lured them out onto the terrace after dinner, under the guise of wanting to reminisce about their father. The evening Alpine air has banished all memory of the sun. It's quite chilly. Olga is wrapped up in a scarf; her sisters have left their jackets at the table. They're cold. A strange fragrance fills the air.

'Magda, Sveja, I'm asking you, have I ever asked you for anything? I'm coming to you in an hour of need and I'm asking you to help me. Do I bother you every day with some sort of request? Do I ask you for something every day? My son is fifty years old, is it possible in this world that I, too, may wish for something?'

Olga stands in front of the door to prevent them from fleeing. She sees them shivering.

'But what will they say?' moans Svetlana.

'What, *what will they say*? That somebody finally did something for me, for the poor, humiliated wretch! That somebody finally showed that they love me, can't you see, sisters, the despair in which I live? That I have to depend on you, if I want somebody to show they care about me?'

The last note emboldens Magda.

'Yeah, help yourself and all that, Olga, you know, why don't you do that?'

'Because I have something else in mind,' says Olga and looks out beyond the clearing to the edge of the woods, 'look here, if you do this for me, please, I ask you, please, I will take you right away, next weekend, to Reka.'

'To Rakek, the village?' 'I don't understand…'

'To Reka in Croatia, I mean. Saturday morning, I'll take you there, we'll board the *Galeb* and sail on it around Istria all the way up to Portorož.'

'On the *Galeb*?' 'But that's…' they whisper, in unison, 'The ship of Tito!'

Their eyes light up and Olga smiles cunningly.

/

Stoja is laden down with children. Immediately after dinner Raven retreated to the 'circle of the reasonable' – Edgar,

Katarina, Olive, Grace. The children are behaving, for now. Their questions are innocent. Such a cute little boy, that Voranc, such a pity he's sick. She makes sure he doesn't bump into anything. Where has Po disappeared to?

Alenka is dilly-dallying with her knife over her steak and daydreaming. Once a minute she snaps out of it for a second and looks for Voranc. Everything is fine. She catches the whispering of passing waiters. 'Where's Borut?' 'He went off somewhere with that girl.' 'Ooh.'

Meslier and Bernard have business in common. Before the war Bernard earned some money by seeking out and exploiting loopholes in the customs laws. He bought cheaply around the world, sold not cheaply at home, nothing earth-shattering, anybody could do it if he had the gumption. The initial growth of capital and the benefits that came with it (especially the sudden increase in attention from family members) made him greedy, but a lack of imagination in matters of business had kept his greed in check. Until the war broke out.

Even people of no imagination realize that you can earn a fortune from war. His brother was the Minister for War, he had some money – what could go wrong? – and right away he commenced with the genteel, domestic tradition of gun-running. But he soon saw that he didn't have nearly enough capital. Expensive, corrupt practices, buying stock and thousands of unforeseen variable costs sucked up his cash supply faster than Americans sucked up oil. On a tip from his mother he went to see the priest.

It turned out that the priest Meslier had managed the church fortunes extremely well indeed. Bernard didn't know whether to ascribe this to a Lutheran-like fear of squandering or just to the usual cheapness, but one wouldn't have known from the derelict church and the plain mortuary chapel that the Parish of Bodičava was swimming in money.

At first the priest resisted, so Bernard, day after day, besieged him with visions: the loveliest parish on earth, local social problems solved, a shelter for orphans and a youth centre, with, so to speak, a pure financial injection into the hearts of believers who would, before the earthly splendour of the Lord's face, have to take the gospel more humbly. 'How can they believe in God if they earn more than Him?' he asked.

Today, ten years later, the church has two bell-towers. Bernard and Meslier wink at each other conspiratorially.

/

'How does Olive like Slovenia?' asks Edgar. Grace and Olive have been living together for ten years in the autonomous zone of Ost-Berlin. They have justified these few weeks in Grace's home country by calling this a holiday. They've spent one weekend in the mountains, one weekend at the sea, but otherwise they sleep at the homestead, in the annex that had been built for Edgar.

'She says it's beautiful and peaceful and quiet. Almost too much for her taste. Even for mine, perhaps. But it's still somehow nice to come home. Olive was disinherited when she was still a teenager, so I took her along to see that things can be even worse.'

Friendly laughter. 'It means so much to Kras that you all came,' says Katarina.

'Oh, I know a married person has to go easy on their partner,' replies Grace, 'but we all grew up here with Kras, so you'll have a tough time portraying him in a different light. He couldn't care less about the fact that we actually came, but he'd be livid if anyone *didn't*.'

Katarina tries to put on a somewhat passable *oh-come-on* face.

'I don't know, Grace,' says Edgar, 'Kras has changed a lot lately.'

'Since they lost?'

'Since Mitja left.'

Katarina looks around, afraid. Nobody's listening in.

'Yeah, what was that about?' asks Grace. 'I mean, where

is Mitja? Does anybody know? Everyone I ask says something evasive. I can see it's a taboo topic around here.'

Katarina goes over to her mother and asks her to stop bothering people with all that chakra business. Olive looks out of the window. Edgar sidles up to Grace.

'Kras's terror towards his son bore fruit,' says Edgar.

Raven approaches and grabs them by the shoulders.

'How are you?'

'I mean, I just don't get it. Is he in jail or something?' asks Grace.

'Worse,' says Edgar, and turns to his 'father'.

'We're ok, everything is fine, which is an achievement, isn't it?'

'Oh, absolutely,' says Raven. 'Give the Wolfs a bit of meat and everyone's satisfied. Grace, do you know I haven't eaten meat in five years?'

Grace pats his tummy.

'Yes, I can see that something has changed. And what did you have?'

'The chef made soya patties, excellent fare.'

Po pops out of somewhere and tugs at her father's trouser pocket.

'What is it, darling?'

She wags her finger and Raven bends down with difficulty.

'Alan and Mila are in the attic.'

'Yes?'

Po whispers, 'They're smoking up.'

Raven raises his eyebrows, Po pulls him by the hand and takes him with her.

'What do you mean, worse?' Grace asks.

Edgar sighs.

/

'Wolf.'

'General.'

Kras sits down at the end of the table. His shoulders have tensed up. He's not at ease.

'Thank you for coming.'

'Ah, it's a pleasure. I just realized that I haven't seen the Soča River for at least a decade. I didn't want to let this chance slip me by. It's wonderful.'

Kras smiles.

'*The clear daughter of the mountains.*'

'Sorry?'

'That's Gregorčič, isn't it?'

'Who's that?'

'It doesn't really matter. Some poet.'

The general gives a booming laugh.

'A poet.'

Kras tries to copy the general's expression onto his own face.

'How are things at headquarters? The new minister – what's his name? – Gobec, is he any less annoying than I was?'

The general suddenly turns serious and slaps the table.

'Fucking incompetent bastard, that Gobec, but don't spread it around. Things are a little tense right now, you know how it goes: when the political leadership changes, the necks start to itch.'

'And on the front?'

'Ha, child's play, nothing new, what can they do to us? We could be sending boy scouts down there, you know how it is.'

'What about that helicopter?'

'What helicopter?'

'The ten who died.'

'An accident! Where did you hear about it?'

Bernard had told him.

'I still know people, General.'

'You tell those people to keep their mouths shut because

59

we've got a review on the go and you're not doing them any favours if you needle them for intelligence info.'

Kras tries to temper the assault.

'I thought it wasn't exactly a big secret.'

'Everything's a secret, Wolf. It's a war.'

Kras looks around the table. Bernard and the priest are smirking. Father just went off somewhere with Po. Katarina is sitting with her mum and looking sad. He can't see his mother, or his aunts. Edgar looks at him as he converses with Grace. Nobody has told Grace yet. The twins are running around.

'Is Operation Equator progressing?'

'Wolf, I didn't think you invited me for this.'

Kras sighs.

'Excuse me, General, but I was there when it started. I was at the head of our contingent for eight years, I know the matter inside and out. I was personally responsible for not just a few successes, so I don't know why it should be anything unusual if I'd still like to know at least approximately what's going on. Especially now that the 250th INFB is closer and closer to going into battle.'

The general frowns, his lips silently form the numbers 250, 250, 250, before his face finally clears. He runs a hand along Kras's shoulders.

'I understand you, Wolf, so don't think that I don't. It was always a pleasure working with you. No bullshit. I appreciate that in a man. But the system is just such that…ah, why should I be telling you, you know full well how things are. You were in the chain. You simply don't have access any more, full stop. But you have nothing to worry about. INFB 250 won't see action. We have them in the hinterland, security, anti-smuggling, I've already said too much.'

'You've told me enough, thank you.'

'Is this really why you invited me?'

'Most likely.'

Olga enters with her sisters, who dash to their chairs and

put on their jackets. They're pale, but with flushed cheeks. Olga waves to Kras.

'The postman's outside,' she says.

With a nod of his head, Kras takes leave of the general and moves over to his mother.

'What postman?'

Kras stares through the frosted glass in the door. There's a silhouette of someone in a blue uniform leaning his moped against the tree, against that long-suffering apple tree, girdled with a bag, cap on his head, and with an outstretched hand in which he's holding…something, he can't quite see, probably an envelope, he walks along the gravel path to the front door. Time slows down, almost stops. Kras grabs the handle, squeezes it, as if cramped, the veins on his forearm are protruding, his knuckles are turning white and somewhere down around his stomach the blood is rushing about, rocking and lifting a something he has to force himself to swallow back with saliva, his lungs are burning and his heartbeat becomes a drawn-out march, *boom*, in step with the postman's steps, *boom*, the crowd behind his head is pressed into the hissing voice of his mother, who is very slowly tapping her teeth with her tongue, *boom*, the stamping feet of the twins who are chasing each other about to monstrous laughter, *boom*, Bernard and Meslier toast, the frosted window pane smashes with a dullish pop, the shattered glass falls to the floor and the door opens.

'Oh, Jesus, what happened?' asks the postman.

Everyone is looking at Kras who almost lifted the door off its hinges and then pulled back so hard that the window broke. He yanks the envelope out of the postman's hand.

'For me?' he whispers.

'Yes, Mr Wolf.'

Kras turns his back on him and the postman awkwardly retreats back into the dark. Later, in the tavern, he'll tell everybody what an oaf the former minister is.

'And I even wanted to congratulate him!' he'll holler, and buy a round.

The only thing in the envelope is some kind of ticket. Olga peeks over his shoulder. He pushes the ticket back into it without taking a proper look.

'What is it?'

'Nothing,' says Kras, 'just somebody's little joke.'

/

Slaps don't bring him round. Alan and Mila grin over the passed-out waiter.

'Do you think he'll be ok?'

'Sure he'll be, you saw how scared he was, that's stress, let's just wait a little longer.'

One smokes, the other gently slaps the waiter's face. Then they switch.

'Did you see those two?'

'Who? Grandma's sisters?'

'Yeah, Olga's.'

'A freak show.'

'Totally.'

'Before, when we were outside, one of them was sitting at the table and Berdo's phone starts vibrating, he left it on the table, and she looks at the thing, then looks around like, *What? Doesn't anybody see what's happening?* Mila starts laughing. 'But everybody's like, nothing strange, and she's still looking, a little spooked, but she kind of feels tempted, and I'm standing and watching, and then she, really slowly, reaches out her hand, and places it on the phone, and then, I swear, she starts grinning, but it was all kind of cute, and she looks around again, and then grabs the phone,' Mila's eyes are wide open, 'and she leans it against her chin, totally crazy.'

Stoned laughter.

'I was a hundred percent sure you were gonna say she stuck it between her legs.'

'Man, that's gross.'

More laughter.

'Hilarious.'

'Yeah, and what about Grandma?' says Mila. 'Immediately starting in on Grace?'

'Awkward!'

'And I don't think they've seen each other for five years.'

'I'm sorry, but your granny's nuts.'

'Who isn't?'

'We're pretty cool.'

'And Edgar, you know, even though he gives off these creepy vibes sometimes.'

'Yeah, Edgar's ok,' agrees Alan, 'but Olive is a total MILF.'

Mila nods, 'Yeah, she looks good, but have you seen her hands?'

'The walnut tree told me there's something burning here.'

Raven has lumbered into the room, Po trailing after him. Mila cups her hand over the joint. Alan shakes his head, nothing to worry about.

'Hi, Grandpa.'

'Mila. Darling. Who's this?'

'The waiter,' says Alan. 'He's a little tired.'

Laughter.

'But is he all right?'

'He'll be fine, I guess.'

Raven puts his hands on his knees and stares at Po, who is mischievously staring at her brother.

'Will you go get this boy a glass of water? He's feeling poorly.'

Po nods and scoots off.

'Come on, give ol' Raven a taste of fresh air.'

'Grandpa!' cries Mila and looks at Alan, who's nodding and smiling at her.

With a shaking hand, she passes the joint to Grandpa.

Raven takes it, inhales deeply and then, with that

annoying voice a person gets when they're holding the smoke in their lungs but still won't stay quiet, speaks.

'What, you think you kids invented weed? I was puffing back when your dad was still swinging around in my balls.'

Mila grimaces. Raven's mouth lays an egg of smoke.

'Sorry, dear, when I drink my mouth turns foul. After this,' toasting with the joint, 'it'll get better.'

From the ground floor they hear the sound of broken glass. Raven and Alan stand up at the same time and say, worried, 'Po!' The father presses the butt into his son's hand and dashes to the door, almost running into her. She'd gone for water.

'What happened?' asks Raven. Alan shrugs and offers the smouldering roll-up to Mila.

'Brother Wolf broke the door.'

Mila sighs and flicks the filter through the window.

/

'Daddy.' 'Daddy.'

Olga stands in front of the window and shoos the children who have come running towards the racket. 'Alenka, take the child!' Stoja grabs him. Katarina has brought the broom and dustpan to sweep up the tiny shards. She and Olga throw the big pieces in the rubbish. Nobody notices Olga carefully selecting a fine, long, narrow piece that slips nicely into her hand and sticking it into the front pocket of her blouse. Mira and Mina come running from Uncle Bernard, smiling, they avoid Grandma's chasing hands and grab Father by the belt.

'Daddy.' 'Daddy.'

'What is it, sweeties?'

'Come.' 'Come with us.' 'At the stream, we found,' 'a bunny, Daddy, a white one,' 'a bunny, come see,' 'come with us,' 'can we take it' 'home? Daddy, please.' 'Please?'

Concerned pairs of guests' eyes are still fixed on him, so

he's glad to take the opportunity to let his daughters take him out into the night. Once they get to the terrace they let go of his hand and race ahead. Every few yards they stop and turn to make sure he's following.

Kras inhales the sharp mountain air mingled with resin, pine needles and dry grass. It's unusually fresh for late summer. A cold front is coming down from the Alps and pushing away the Mediterranean climate that on lazy, muggy days creeps up along the valley. Patches of bare ground reveal the secrets otherwise covered by undergrowth. A purple horizon wanes over the mountain ridge.

There's a piece of burning ember on the ground. Kras stamps it out. He looks around. The laughter of the twins, the scratching of claws, the muffled rumbling of an engine off in the distance. Damned postman, he almost set us all on fire. When he walks past the kennel, everything's quiet. The dogs are lying there, their tails hanging peacefully over their haunches. Docile.

'Daddy!' 'Daddy, come here!'

They lead him to the stream, into the darkness below the treetops.

'But you can't see anything.'

'Look, Daddy!' 'Fireflies!'

The fluorescent pulses of light illuminate the daughters' frail silhouettes, as they stand on the bank of the stream and giggle, their hands over their mouths.

'Careful you don't fall off.'

Heeheeheeheehee.

'Well, where's that rabbit?' asks Kras and trips. His hands sink into mud. The twins run over to him.

'Daddy, are you ok?' 'Did you catch him?'

He wipes his palms on the grass and gets up. A pulse of light. His shoulder blades are burning.

'Why did you drag me out here?' he shouts.

The giggling faces immediately turn sullen.

'Uncle Berdo said,' sob, 'Uncle Berdo,' 'that he had, he had,' sob, 'a surprise for us.'

A pulse. Pressure in the temples, itchy palms. His arms convulsively cramping, he approaches them and firmly, clumsily, pats them on the head.

'It's ok, it's ok.'

The sobbing subsides when he hugs them. He gently taps his foot behind him to find the root or hole or stone he tripped over.

'Daddy, look!'

A flash of light reveals what it is. There's a skull sticking out of the mud.

'What's that, Daddy?'

He inserts the tip of his shoe into the eye socket and the skull comes out with a horribly fleshy slurping sound.

'Daddy?' 'Daddy? What is it?'

A pulse. There's a hole in the crown. He flicks his foot and the skull flies into the middle of the brook. Plop.

'Daddy?'

'Nothing, girls. Just some poor Austro-Hungarian soldier.'

'What?' 'What?'

'Let's go.'

/

The moment Kras steps out of the house Bernard gets up and rushes into the kitchen, where he's left a screen rolled up in a long tube. He takes it with his good hand and carries it into the dining room. He summons a waiter to help him.

'Can you hang it on the wall? Come on, take that wild boar down and hang it on that big nail, yes.'

In addition to a change of clothes and the flask of Jägermeister, he has a projector in his travel bag. He sets it up on the table where he was sitting and inserts a disk into it.

'Where are the sockets?'

Nobody listens to him, they're all wrapped up in their tipsy selves. Olga stands with her sisters in a tight circle, whispering confidentially, her eyes shining ever brighter, though her sisters' faces are turning murky. Alenka looks around a few times. She can't find a socket and she's subtly biting her lower lip, indicating capitulation. Stoja is listening to Voranc, who's flipping through the guest book and proudly showing off his reading skills. Grace is interpreting what appears to be a fun conversation between Edgar and Olive. Meslier is, it seems, napping as he sits. Katarina is trying to engage the entire table in general conversation, primarily to shut her mother up (now, to Katarina's horror, she's on to yoga, and from there's it's just a short conversational step to tantric sex and the Kama Sutra), but without much success. Only the general is paying attention to her, but Bernard couldn't say whether he is listening enthusiastically or simply staring down somewhere below her neckline.

'Edgar!'

He doesn't hear him.

'Edgar!'

The 'half-brother' stops mid-sentence.

'Can you please come here for a second?'

This call catches the attention of Olga, who takes her sisters' hands and squeezes them tightly before moving closer. The waiter is unravelling the screen, which draws a few looks.

'What have you got there?' asks Edgar.

'A present for Wolf. Come on, I don't know exactly which cable goes where. Can you work it out?'

Edgar leans over the projector and checks the inputs.

'Berdo, I hope it's not by any chance anything…'

He pulls one out, pushes it in somewhere else, but has to put it back.

'It's not by chance anything what?'

'You know, one never knows with you… You're not going to upset him?'

Bernard raises a hand in disbelief.

'Give me a break! I'm not that much of an arse, to ruin my brother's fiftieth. Edgar, please.'

Edgar smiles. 'Ok, ok, I'm sorry.' He stretches the cable from the wall to the table and plugs it into the socket hidden behind an antique cupboard.

'All right, press play when I tell you to, ok?'

Bernard sees his brother's profile through the hole in the door.

'He's coming, come on, will you get Gramps? I think he went upstairs with the kids.'

Edgar is turning on his heels when Olga jumps up.

'I'll go, you just wait here,' and she passes by him.

Edgar is amazed. This is the third time in his life that Olga has directly addressed him. The first time was when Boj...Raven brought him home ('Get lost, you shabby little freak!'), the second time was when Andre–, when Grace left home ('You've bewitched my daughter, you gypsy beast!'), and the third time, so gently, so normally, just now. A shiver comes over him. Something's brewing.

/

'Why did you drag me out here?' comes roaring across the meadow. A flock of birds switches trees. Mila stares through the window, she's used to Dad's yelling. Since Mitja left there's been much less of it, but not so little that you would forget it. She's embarrassed in front of Grandma and Alan. They all know how he is but it would be nice if now and then he didn't have to prove his ways. If he became, at least for an hour or two, someone else. Transformed himself and showed it. Even if he then immediately went back to his old self and growled and howled and put people down... Or sullenly kept quiet, clearly explaining what he was thinking only through looks and nervous twitches of an eyelid, which were sometimes so strong they hurt her like a slap. But on the other hand he'd never been violent towards Mila, and soon she'd be gone, in a few years she'd have a degree, and then see you at the next birthday or anniversary of something entirely unimportant...

Before Po turned on the light they had all been turning blue in the fading daylight. Now they squint and smile at each other. Alan flips through a *Komunist*, Raven pats his tummy and averts his eyes from Po, who is jumping around and curiously poking about. The waiter Borut is lying on a dusty, sunken old mattress. Raven reaches over to shake his foot. Nothing.

'What are we going to do with him?' he asks.

Alan shrugs and doesn't look up, Mila moves towards the waiter's head. Raven has turned him onto his side ('so he won't swallow his tongue'). He looks just like he's sleeping.

'What did he say his name was?'

'Borut,' says Alan.

Mila shakes him by the shoulders.

'Borut.'

No response.

'Borut,' louder, shaking more vigorously.

Nothing.

'If I go get the other waiters he'll be in trouble for coming up here with us,' she says.

Raven nods.

'But we can't just leave him here.'

Alan looks at them over the top of his magazine. 'I'm not going anywhere until we go, so...'

Po chimes in.

'If you give him a kiss, he'll wake up.'

Mila smiles, Raven swings a joking hand towards Po.

'What if he turns into a frog?' asks Mila.

'He won't,' says Po, though she doesn't look all that convinced. She takes a step back and carefully watches for what they're going to do. She hears footsteps at the bottom of the stairs. She goes to look.

'That's the good thing about getting old: all you need is two puffs,' says a wistful Raven.

Alan's look is generous. That senile old guy is his father. He has a good heart, even if it's shallow when it comes to love. He can't hold anything against him, except for when he embarrasses him by insisting on going to parent-teacher meetings and similar nonsense. He likes him best when he's at home. If he's lucky, the old man will be dead by the time Alan gets married. Who would want to burden someone with a father-in-law like that? When Alan realizes what he's been thinking, he pinches himself hard in the thigh.

Po runs over and throws her arms around her father's neck.

'Aunt Crabby's down there.'

'Yeah, so?'

'Grandma is Aunt Crabby?' asks Mila.

Po nods. They laugh.

'The kids got used to calling her that,' says Raven, 'I call her Mia Farrow.'

'Who's that?'

'Since she cut her hair, she looks like her,' he says, lost in thought, 'an actress, once upon a time.'

'What's she doing?' Mila asks Po.

'She was listening, then she closed the door and left.'

Mila and Raven frown, trying to remember what they were talking about.

Their eyes meet, and when they realize that they're doing the same thing they raise their eyebrows and say, at the same time, 'Everything ok.' Alan understands. Laughter.

'Papa Raven,' says Po.

'What is it, dear?'

'Can I have some water?'

She takes the cup from her father's hands, pops between Mila and Alan and, with an impish smile, pours half of it over the waiter's head. Borut wakes up, his eyelids fluttering like a couple of love-smitten butterflies. When he comes to, he smiles drunkenly at Mila and nods at Alan, but when he sees Po's face his jaw drops. He tries to look away, but his eyes get caught up in Raven's bushy face. His lungs are tight, the flow of oxygen is interrupted again, and if the previous unconsciousness was caused by a common syncope, this one is a straight-up seizure.

/

Kras's knees are muddy. The twins are holding him by the hand. He looks at the screen and the curious faces.

'What's that?'

Bernard looks at Olga, who is closing the door and mouthing, *they're coming.* Then he turns to his brother.

'Happy birthday, old man.'

He gives Edgar a nod. The projector sputters to life and fills the air with buzzing. It sounds like someone's vacuuming the attic. The screen shows grainy snow flickering apparently at random, until some sort of figure gradually forms. The spotty poltergeist moves ahead, back, caught in black-and-white static, a confusion of pixels through which colour suddenly breaks. Orangey-brown camouflage, green patches, interrupted by flashes of ultraviolet video emulsion. Behind it – a person. The picture jumps. The edges cut horizontally, chaotically, the slides of scenes run into each other. Everything in a moment, almost. The picture steadies and now looks like something a severely near-sighted person might see. Foggy. The colours flow along unclear lines. The figure approaches, a play of shadows, a stretched-out hand and…sharpness.

Mitja's face is tanned and hairy. Black bags under the eyes. Sunken cheeks. A wide, white smile. A little dark patch of grease just below his nose. A helmet, on sideways. A huge face extended over the whole wall. He takes off his helmet.

'Hi Dad. Mum. Mila. Mira, Mina. Grandma. Grandpa. Berdo. Edgar. I don't know if Andreja's there, oops, I mean

Grace. Hi. And Stoja. Alan, where are you? What's up? Po. Did I forget anyone? And Grandma Meta, maybe,' the picture breaks up with a hum which lasts for a few seconds, 'you're having a good time, don't drink too much because I know that' a hum, and when the picture returns Mitja has turned around, 'Dad's fifty!' – indistinct shouts from beyond the screen – 'Yeah. I know,' he turns to the camera, 'Basically, it's hot here, and dusty and moist and the mosquitoes are going to eat us alive, everything's rotting and reeks like septic tanks, but we're having a fantastic time!' hum '—y to complain, but it is what it is, I'm alive and well, and, yes, nothing to complain about, Wolf, happy birthday, I hope in the future you'll find some peace in your soul, also for the past,' laughter, 'that your shoulders will untense, that you won't be too mad at…well, whoever, right? seriously, Dad, happy birthday. I have a gift for you, I left it in the little tree house, you know, the one we built together, in the walnut tree, when' hum 'to see each other soon, although there's no sign here that things will be over anytime soon, it seems like we're kind of stuck, to be honest, but, well, the main thing is that you guys are all healthy, that you have little green men taking care of you so you don't have to worry too much about everything, yeah,' hum, 'don't be too nasty to each other, because you have' hum 'so write to me by military safe fax, Alan, Mila, shit, I thought we'd at least,' darkness, silence. The Wolfs are frozen. Before they can respond, the picture comes back, without sound. Mitja undoes his belt, turns his backside towards the camera, puts his hand to his mouth, kisses it, then yanks his trousers down with his other hand to show a bum cheek on which he has a bluish, cheap, prison- or army-style tattoo that says, 'Wolf,' slaps it, and then blows into the camera with an open palm. The end.

The viewers, amazingly, applaud. Katarina's mother says, 'Why didn't anyone tell me? Oh, I'm so proud!'

All of Kras's muscles petrify. The general turns his prickly gaze on him and snaps, in a whisper, 'Where did you get that? This is serious, Wolf, a breach of the Cut!'

'I had nothing to do with it, looks like Bernard put it together.' *I had nothing to do with it. I had nothing to do with it.* The sentence slips out of his mouth and swims around his head, mocking him. Something starts flowing around his eyes. Kras wipes them, in disbelief. He sniffles, discreetly at first, like he wanted to deny it, and then out loud, he's not ashamed, dammit. Fathers have the right to be emotional too, every now and then. He avoids the gazes, he doesn't know how to behave honestly in public. He'd most like to burrow into the ground and deal with things in his own way, or no, he'd rather see the others burrow into the ground, disappear, who the hell crammed them all in here to witness all this stuff that isn't and never will be theirs? The doors fling open in the background. Through the veil of moisture Kras sees his father, who's carrying a body in his hands. 'General, I don't care about your codes and commandments, my brother has no right to act like he has no son.' That's what Kras hears Bernard saying. Kras flares up. He lets loose. He strikes, firmly. Bernard falls to the floor. Across-the-board shrieking. *Now, now*, Olga hisses, Kras hears her clearly. Edgar is by him, holding his hands, squeezing. Kras doesn't defend himself. He can't see anything, his eyes are sliding down from the sockets. His jaw hangs freely. There's a fresh round of smacks in the air. Who's doing the hitting? Who's getting hit? Kras can't see. More across-the-board shrieking. Stoja's voice, 'Leave me alone!' What? He wipes an eye with a shoulder, half discerns what's happening. People are scattering about, someone's with Bernard, on the floor, Raven drops the body and sprints over to Stoja, to help his wife, Svetlana and Magda have jumped on her, are pulling her hair and tenaciously smacking away at her, he clears his eyes again, he can't believe it, he's gone nuts, then another cry, a child, a little black boy screams, 'Grandma did it, Grandma did it,' it's hard to spot him in the fracas, among the legs, somewhere, he'll get trampled, Alenka runs to her son, 'Grandma cut me,' what the hell is going on, then a flash blinds him, a piece of glass in the air, Olga is clutching the bloodied shard of glass, and with a war cry of 'Scoundrel!' thrusts it, with all the strength the old woman can muster, into Edgar's side. During the mass screaming and crowding, Raven pushes the reckless sisters out of the way and protects Stoja in a hug, Grace and Katarina run to Edgar who, stabbed, is about to drop, Bernard's nose is bleeding and he crawls under the table where he fixes his glasses, Kras stands there and his head is about to explode with rage, Olga is trying to faint, she's already kneeling down, little Po is standing at the door with a smile on her face and now even Meslier is awake, he releases his right hand and cuts the air vertically and horizontally, 'In the name of the Father, and of the Son and of the Holy Spirit…'

POETRYLITICS

✦

In a cone of light, attention.

Her.

'...some new, bad poetry.' And a laugh.

> *rip me*
> *make some space*
> *for you*

Do you know which word I find interesting?

> *rip me in half*

Which one?

Kindness. In kind. He is kind (*because he likes me*), he is kin. I mean, it doesn't even matter how he behaves, it's not even about him... You see? In kind. We are kin. If I find him kind, he is near me, close to me, we form a kinship.

> *Rip me in half. Come on, put pliers between my ribs*

'Or, you know what? What if you'd rather...'

> *Scissors! With scissors into the waist, over fifty, yeah,*

75

you know, phases of the moon

'…because I've had enough of all this, you already know it all by heart, don't you?' Warm, truly warm, applause. It's obvious they love her.

> *I can see nothing, because I planted my eye into someone else*
> *now I'm waiting for what will grow*

Some have come from far, far away to see her. Zoja's a star. Everybody knows her. When things are tough ('do you know how tough, how truly, truly tough things are, for so many people?'), they read her. Her words don't function like words, her words are part of nature, they grow from the earth, on trees, she has collected them from creeks, she has plucked them from the sky. Her words are edible. They truly are. Calorie-rich. They fatten you up.

> *I dry up, all rough and shabby, between the cracks in the wall*

'No, tell me seriously, is this working out for anyone?' A roaring response, fingers between their lips, they screech through saliva. For days little cars have been flocking to Brooklyn, people have been camping out, because she said she was willing to read, after they beseeched her, kindly beseeched her, she stopped putting up a fight and said she would read. To hear Zoja! Live! Her vocal cords and her voice and how her lungs take in air, and her beating heart right there, right in front of you, you can, if you try, if you really try, you can feel it! Her heart! Wow! And they came, boy, if you saw them, their souls have colds, they have ridiculous haircuts, and they are all somewhat *rip me in half, otherwise I can't breathe!*

sad. They breathe warmly. They are strangers to violence. Who knows where they all crawled out from, and so young. Ultimately their parents let them down once again. Their parents were so damned scared that they can't be scared, they want to be open to others, not to flee from them. They will have to be victims of crimes because their parents didn't even want to think about those crimes. An entire generation that is once again open to getting slapped by strangers, finally!

'Trust everybody! Be dogs, puppies, trusting puppies, and dig away with your little paws, and press your muzzles into them, and act innocently, I mean, you are innocent, you're all entirely innocent, basically, you little snouts, just be who you are!'

Devoted, gentle, indulgent and friendly. But the back does not forget. Carious cuttle.

/

At the outset of the twentieth century, this space belonged to a nail factory. After Black Thursday (the stock market crash on 24 October 1929), the factory went out of business. Five hundred and twenty-three people lost their jobs. In the 1930s the local branch of the Salvation Army (a Protestant organization founded in 1865 in the United Kingdom by William and Catherine Booth) was based here. During the Second World War the space was turned into a bullet factory. Sixty million people died during the Second World War. After the war, when the demand for bullets fell, the space became an animal shelter. The animals were treated cruelly. In 1975 the young activist Alex Pacheco (who would found PETA five years later) broke into the shelter and, using a Leicaflex camera (35mm SLR), photographed the impossible conditions. He sent the photographs to the editorial board of the *Village Voice*. The monochrome prints made storm waves. The shelter was closed down. The local authorities purchased the space and rented it out to artists' groups who drew emotional power from its past. It was frequented by Annie Leibovitz, Andy Warhol, Gil Scott-Heron, Jean-Michel Basquiat. At the height of the crack epidemic (in the late '80s) it was taken over by drug dealers. When the crack market declined (for not yet fully explained reasons the opiates market suddenly crashed), the space was completely given over to junkies. The social worker Edna Welquer operated out of here (the drug addicts affectionately called it Hell's Diner) for twenty-five long years, helping the unfortunate and writing down her observations in a diary. When a client suffering from withdrawal stabbed her to death, her son edited her diaries and published them as a book. The police pushed out the drug addicts, the local authorities filled the entrance with concrete. Since then the space has been deserted.

The organizer of the Poetrylitics festival, Max Adorcuse (the name is an invention), who rented the space, had dreamt up all of the above and printed it on the back of the flyers. Zoja is his star and her presence will ensure the presence of NYC's anarcho-intelligentsia, all the hip, true, cool, real, down-and-dirty people the city has to offer. He can hardly wait.

> *(but a lot of people really did die during the Second World War)*

/

A time-stifling heat creeps over the city. Someone is sledgehammering away at a fire hydrant, someone else is drowning his head in a fountain. Tiny heart attacks are knocking pigeons out of the sky. The streets have merged into a single, sweltering dog's tongue. There's a brown-out and old men are tucking bags of ice under their armpits. *Bang*, a traffic accident. *Bang*, another one. The people are going to go nuts, just watch, one degree warmer and they will all lose it. The sewers have risen and flown into the rivers, a cardboard leper colony. Someone lights a cigarette. Someone puts one out. A street fight, fuck it, nothing's for free. Rays beat down on concrete, the heat is trapped between walls, it refracts, grows, fries the soles, someone is blow-drying their hair. What an idiot.

Zoja opens her eyes, warily. It's hard to believe all of this exists. Right when you're having coffee, looking out. And you people of God, you're going to get it, get back to your flats!

/

Ludovico Överchild is trapped in a manic phase that has been going on for decades. It's hard to say what triggered it. The electric collapse or a conflict between the strings of matter, perhaps the singular mill of contradictory quantum states. One is not one until you look at it. Simple axioms disintegrate when you look at them from another angle, and if you test them a thousand times and then take the average of their outcomes, you get a completely different picture. Some people are born in a rage. Others are enraged by the universe. During the day Ludovico seems perfectly normal; he trudges along like everyone else, painting and tidying, and thumping his hammer, hauling skids and punching out pieces, offering his hands where hands are needed, though he's not one for talking much. But come midnight mysticism befalls him. Murky visions, slices of signs. From chaos to order; the legacy of the savannah-dwelling Adam and Eve. When you're lying in the tall, dry grass and something moves, the faculty of sight comes in handy. Maybe it was the wind, maybe some tiger got a whiff of you. Those who didn't know how to fill in the blanks, to draw conclusions, to paint a whole picture using fragments of input, to tie the wavering grass into something coherent, were devoured by tigers. Those brains did not beget offspring. And now we are radical in the opposite direction.

In the evening Ludovico changes skin and dons amulets, hisses spells through gritted teeth; he's almost a religious fanatic, all the horoscopes are talking about him *and only* him, and he's in love with history; the crosses on pharmacy signs lead him to Jerusalem, red traffic lights are hands pointing the way to Wounded Knee. This heat is not good for him. He's predetermined, and that makes his shoulders droop. He won't make the Cut. He sometimes emerges from nightclubs like Cortés from Tenochtitlan during the Night of Sorrows. He's lured into gay bars by mesh shirts, the scent of sea foam from the *Pequod*, the whaling ship. The doormen are Albanians. For the time being, the feline general eludes him. The ZOIA-graffiti enwraps him in a premonition of evil. Z=7, O=7, I=1, A=1 = 7+7+1+1=16! Sixteen is under the influence of Ketu, a karmic collection of good and bad, the descending lunar node. The magnetic poles will reverse and the Earth will be turned upside down. The tectonic plates will thrust up entire continents and all that will remain will be fossilized remnants, folded into the new Himalayas, and in a few millennia monocled grandfathers will carve them out to show their grandchildren: look here, the collarbone of a nyuyorcus complexus, and the key to unlocking the gates of hell, which will lie beyond our heaven – a fact Ludovico has worked out from when the last light in the Flatiron building will go out – though he's completely missed the mark.

/

'Do you, let's say, not feel the difference between being alone and being with somebody? Don't you feel how different it is, how physically different it is, inside you? When you're alone, you're your own master and you have everything planned out and your will spurs you to action, or, I mean, to whatever, you can also be weak, and you can destroy yourself, but the battle goes on and on in your head, you know, you feel, you understand the battlefield, you know what you have to do to direct your will differently, it's completely clear to you, and it's only laziness, or, like I said, weakness that's preventing you from obeying, but all of that is so immediately irrelevant when you make contact with someone. Another rule, a completely different rule, and I, let's say, believe that the battlefield is taken to another level, a level that's not present in the individual, it's hovering up there in the air somewhere, some sort of social membrane, I don't know how I should put it.'

'Like some kind of holism, that sort of thing?'

'Maybe, I mean, could be, I don't know, holism, the whole is different from the sum of the parts, I get it, but it's even more different than that, it's not just that the whole is different, but that as soon as the parts start interacting they change their physical properties, they're no longer that which enters the equation, since the result of the equation reaches down and changes parts, so they would equate with it, I mean, do you get it? The result's already there and it sucks you up, it changes you as soon as you begin to multiply.'

'Ok, fine, let's say I understand, though I'm extremely sceptical about these metaphysical concepts, as you say, an equation, social membrane, something that already exists and changes us, so that it could exist, it seems like such a cheap Platonism, but ok, let's say I, for the sake of argument, accept this because I've just read a great article about some guy, a mathematician, Nobel Prize winner, complete genius, who was tired of working for the tech industry because, in the end, any way you look at it, you're working for the war industry and he, using mathematics, takes on the social sciences, specifically, he takes on metropolises, he plugs a massive database into a programme, everything, the population, income, employment, crime, all these parameters, basically, and he arrives at a surprising conclusion, namely, he concludes that if, for example, the population doubles, the productivity of each inhabitant goes up by a given percentage, and that, if you look at the big picture, is then reflected in all the parameters, that is, the more people you have crammed together, the more each individual contributes.'

'Social contact lies at the heart of exponential growth. The engine of civilization.'

'Yes, but that doesn't mean that civilization is necessary, or that it's hovering somewhere up in the air, just waiting for that contact to occur, before it will unfold like some self-fulfilling prophecy. It's possible we have just made a completely banal point.'

'That's possible. But doesn't this put all those conspiracy theories – that there are whole squadrons of automated bombers flying above us, ready to unhesitatingly take out any place where too many people gather – in a completely new and a somewhat more credible light?'

'Why wouldn't they, whoever *they* is, want people to gather?'

'Because they're satisfied with what they've created? Because they don't want the thing to grow? Because they believe they have enough?'

'So greed is dead? Are you mad?'

More or less this sort of communication is going on all over the car park in front of the 'former factory for nails, bullets and failed fates' – sincere and introspective talk, capable of surplus, but in the end hermetically sealed. In this case (the speakers were Rupert 'Rust' Stiglitz and Brian Baedekker, fairly representative specimens) it was concluded by an expression of scepticism, which is a milder form of manifesting the impotence of dialogue – the firmer of conclusions, aside from the barbaric 'You're clueless, shut your mouth!', almost always come down to ethics. Nothing silences enlightened people more effectively than the possibility of evil.

'Belt out your ideas! Be loud!'

Max Adorcuse (he wants people to pronounce it Adorkuːzə', but everyone pronounces it Ador'kus) is elated. He's marching around with a megaphone in his hand and shouting out slogans at a rate of two a minute. The visitors find him annoying but they put up with him because word has quickly spread that 'that nitwit with the megaphone is the one who got Zoia to come'. 'Anomie, never! Society should socialize!' He's earned himself a little affection – he's poured all of his savings into the festival, and he's sacrificed his job, his girlfriend, friends, and over the past few months he's slaved like a Bolivian subcontractor, cleaning up, installing electricity and lighting, scrubbing the toilets, dragging in a water tank and even playing interior decorator, adding that aesthetic touch so that the space wouldn't look so empty and bereft even without people.

'Organize yourselves just to be organized! Be your own purpose!'

/

When I enter my own flat, there is a scene on the floor, in the middle of the living room, on the grey carpet, that not long ago would have made me close my eyes or apologize or just turn around and go back out again, angry at myself that deep inside me there are still patterns of some entirely ordinary upbringing and that I can't accept such a scene as just a normal thing, since it gives rise in me to all sorts of physical and emotional responses that I can't control and that make me always and again confront things that I should long ago have already dealt with, things like shame, desire, even envy at the youth and beauty of this pair of bodies that, naked, are losing track of time on my carpet, as if the world really were exactly what we all want it to be – carefree and sensual and gentle. It takes a lot of bravery on my part to silence my body's spontaneous reactions. But I have to be brave. My life is based on bravery. Especially now. Dr Clotos said it won't be much longer. And I could give in, at this point nobody should be allowed to even come close to holding it against me if I gave in to my own body and blithely yelled, 'get a room, you nasty filth', or 'don't even think of sullying my carpet with your juices', or 'find

83

at least a modicum of respect for others and don't parade your fit, young, toned bodies in a mockery of everything that's old, broken and will soon be dead'.

But I don't. For that very reason. You don't respond to your body's betrayal by surrendering. There will be no white flags. It is exactly at such a time that everything you do with your mind becomes important. So I relax and direct my gaze at them. I move a step closer. Marjorie lives here, she has been my roommate ever since I saved her consciousness and her life. I don't know who the guy is, I've never seen him before. A tattoo stretches from his rump to his shoulder blades, his back arches with each thrust. Her fingers are clinging to him. They're a tender pair. Beautiful. Marjorie looks at me with a smile of pleasure as she turns her face. I put the bags down and go into my room. Anwar is still asleep. He got up before me, read over breakfast before the sun rose, and went back to sleep. I got up at eight, went to the shops, to the doctor's, went for a coffee. It's so bloody hot out. I take my camera, my old Leica, I take my long red silk scarf from the hook on the wall and walk past them – they're still gasping – into the pantry. I find a jar of paint left over from the previous paint job. I remember the painter. A dangerous, alluring man. He took me by the hand and in one motion let me know what it was he wanted from me. I didn't let him. I regret it now. I gave him a book of my poems. He said thank you, and left. The paint is yellow, like his teeth were. I walk over to them. I pour paint around their bodies, make a yellow circle. They're in the middle. Only now does the man notice me. He smiles at me and his hand twitches. He'd like to offer it to me, introduce himself. I shake my head, no need to, it's fine, just carry on. He's deep into her. The orgasm is approaching, spreading its membrane. I can feel it. I throw the scarf around his neck. I surround them like they're my prey. My finger on the trigger. I wait. Moaning. The wet pulse of contact. The rhythm grows. His buttocks are pressed together. Her chest is touching his. It's so strong that I feel the pulsing waves in my knees. The shot.

Now I'm truly, properly ashamed. A pleasure thief. I retreat to my room. Anwar has woken up.

'Good morning.'

'Good morning.'

Anwar ibn Tahir ibn Anas Al-Dukhan, born in Basra in 1981, is some sort of prince. A little before Bush II's war, he and his family moved to Boston, where he crossed the river and went to study International Law at Harvard. After the caliphate was established, he got a job at UIGOPWTSOALSSV (United Interest Groups of People With the Same or at Least Somewhat Similar Values), the modern successor to the United Nations. He's been in America for over thirty years – he's had enough of bureaucracy, official celebrations and gala dinners – and soon, anytime now, that which has in recent years become the sole purpose of his existence, and which has been gaining an increasing lead over all other aspects of his life, will be brought about.

He and Zoja met a few weeks ago by chance at a public library when both of them, at almost the same moment, had come to borrow *The Electric Kool-Aid Acid Test*. A conversation and a coffee later and they were in bed together – each too old to drag out the courtship any longer than necessary. These days it's hard for them to part.

'Did you sleep well?'

'Not too well the last two hours. Animal sounds.'

'They've been doing that for two hours?'

'They started as soon as you left. The last half hour has been a little quieter. At first I thought he was skinning her alive.'

Zoja scratches her nose.

'You know what I was thinking as I was watching them?'

'Tell me.'

'Why the hell have we never found any pornographic cave paintings?'

Anwar cracks up. Zoja is thinking aloud.

'Where are the phalluses, where's the coitus, the cunnilingus? Nothing but buffalo, bison, wild cats, nothing but violence and blood, but no sex. Caveman puritans.'

Finally, he clears his throat, his eyes watering.

'The Cave of Hands looks pretty erotic.'

'Where's that?'

'Argentina.'

Marjorie knocks. Zoja opens. She's dressed in a man's bathrobe.

'Ever since you agreed to read,' says Marjorie, 'you've been getting tonnes of mail again.'

'You're going to read?' asks Anwar.

Zoja nods. 'Today.'

'Today?'

'Are you coming?'

Marjorie looks back and shakes her head with a smile. She puts a hand into the opening in her bathrobe. It's not possible to see what she's doing with it.

'Where, when?' asks Anwar.

'In the evening, somewhere around Bed-Stuy.'

'Bad neighbourhood,' says Anwar.

'Ah, not so bad any more,' says Marjorie, 'The new generation of squatters is surprisingly peaceful. I hear the whole northeast has come to listen. Brooklyn hasn't seen anything like it since Yoko Ono set herself on fire for the tenth anniversary.'

'That was totally morbid,' says Anwar. 'How old was she then? Over a hundred?'

'Over ninety,' says Zoja.

'Eighty-nine, to be exact,' says Marjorie.

'Crazy Japanese,' says Anwar.

All three shrug their shoulders.

'Well, I hope no one sets himself on fire tonight,' says Zoja. 'It's already hot enough out there.'

/

Large mills of light, that's what time is. Ludovico is standing in front of his shabby flat's only window, he's slipped his
fingers between the blinds to open a slot for a thin strip of
sunlight to fall on his disturbed face, and he's looking at the
fried town in front of him accompanied by a person's snoring in an extended afternoon nap. In the distance the bridges
are devouring the sunsets. He would like someone to finally
believe him. The bleached metal prisms are breaking up the
light to create a pinkish rainbow. Passion has overcome him
again. Again, he went to her, he went to take her, even if afterwards he always felt so small. It's too hot to go to work. The
boss called, said nothing. Ok, so nothing, good, so nothing.
Then he sat on the couch and stared into his lap until the
floor disappeared and there was nothing but a phallus. Before
he surrendered, before he, all sweaty, with curses on his lips,
stormed through the door to where he knew he'd find her, he
remembered the dreams. He was naked and mighty and the
cats who loved him – he could see from their eyes that they
finally loved him – tore his body to pieces and devoured him
raw. When he remembered those dreams, he knew that he
wouldn't feel small today. That this wouldn't be another loss
but a ritual before the battle. Zoia stole his faith and she stole
his faithful. Carious cuttle. The cats in the freezer are already
frozen stiff. It has to go somewhere, all this light.

/

Max Adorcuse licks his hand. For the first time in his life he
feels like something is really worth it. The salty sweat bears
witness. He puts the mouthpiece of the megaphone to his lips
and breathes in deeply in order to really howl. 'Please don't.'
He lets the excess air out through his nose and turns to his
right, where an old man is standing, a pleading expression on
his face. One hand is holding a stick, the other is preventa-
tively propped against his ear.
    'How are you doing, sir?'

'Good, as it were. It's just that, as it were, my ears aren't what they used to be. Without doubt I overburdened them, so now all they hear is a whistle if someone screams. I don't like it when people shout, as it were, but I understand why that's necessary sometimes. Mass communication, yes, as it were.'

The old guy's speech is punctuated by nervous twitches, hands running over his face, and salivating sibilants.

'I'm Max *Adorkúse*.'

A splutter of laughter.

'Horkheimer, Adorno, Marcuse, yes, as it were, don't worry, I know them all, I knew them all.'

'You look familiar.'

'Yes, yes, yes, as it were, so, you're the one who put this thing on?'

'I am.'

'Good, very good, as it were. Many people.'

'Yes. But I'm not deluding myself. It's because of Zoia.'

'People want to get to know each other, and you gave them a good motive. It doesn't matter how you drum up a bunch of people, as it were, just that they're here together now. Maybe…'

'Maybe what?'

'Maybe all of this will be good for something.'

Some bushes are rustling with desire. Among the dry leaves you can catch patches of naked skin. Sweat and dust and sweet sexuality.

/

At the top of the pile there's a note from the letter carrier. Get yourself a proper letterbox, I'm retiring in two years and all your mail is going to fuck up my back – Best. Rudy. *Rudy and I used to be really good friends. What happened? I can't remember. I think she was in love with me. Did she try to kiss me? Or did I only dream this? I don't know. One fine morning she stopped coming for coffee. And that was that.*

The very first few days after the new collection was published there was a huge amount of mail. I poured everything out into the bedroom, a flood of letters, the floor was eight inches deep in paper, I took my shoes off and swam, slept among the envelopes. Tore them open and read them. So many emotions. I felt like the conduit for that thorn that pricks into every one of our souls, that deeply buried, golden thorn that tears the veil of the everyday, slices into it a tiny rift from which truth drops, I mean...honesty, that voracious, beautiful, horrible honesty. As we walk around the city, we're hiding. It takes a shove to really open us up. It poured out the window. We don't know ourselves. We fundamentally do not know ourselves. And how much effort is needed to plug the rift. The room is groaning with hormones. Denuded consciousnesses, hard to imagine the insight that I got back then. I saw that I am not alone, not even close. And since then I haven't written a single poem. People don't need poems. All they need is an ear to listen to them. But they have to be honest, otherwise it's all just a degree of illusion. Nothing natural. Simple art.

Dear Zoia,

I fear the world is not turning in the right direction. Each and every one of us bears part of the blame, because we haven't dared break away from the ballast of a dictated existence. I hope I'm not too old for that. I'd like to see us all come together.
I'm thirty-five years old. I was born one sinister 11th of September, you probably know which year. I grew up in a very strange world, which I began to regard as very strange only after I became a little more familiar with the world as it used to be. Maybe that's just a projection. Maybe the world has always been very strange and our particular brand of strangeness is just a variation on this very dishonest world. But I don't know. The counter-culture of the Sixties grips

me. The techno-craze of the Nineties grips me. The third millennium horrifies me. And I think that we're the ones to blame, because they've convinced us that the world is made up of masses of people we have no influence over. Only after you look around a bit do you see that there aren't any masses of people. That we are only me, and you, and you, and you, and you... That the mass we're constantly addressing when explaining the world just doesn't exist. That in the chasms between us there aren't thousands of choked-out voices exerting their will, but only a gaping hole in whose place there should be a genuine, warm, human relationship, but the phantasm of the crowd banished it. Each has his own life, they told us. But if I give someone my hand, we get to know each other, and the world is different.

I spent almost fifteen years at the bottom of the corporate ladder, overlooked, ignored in the hierarchy of solemn things. It rubs away at your soul, being caught up day after day in the same intrigue. But I had a job, and with the job came everything that the modern world intends for you. I had a girlfriend. We were in a relationship for eight years and it took us two text messages to break up. Things just mellowed out, I'd say. I had a few people who were less than friends and more than acquaintances. Someone you could compare yourself to, to have an approximate idea where you stand. When I left my job I was totally insufficient for the operations of envy, so they forgot about me in a week. Take Mike, for example. For ten years we played squash every Thursday and for ten years I listened to his misogynistic blustering. If I called him now, he would say *who's there?*, and when I'd tell him he would repeat, *who?* I never asked my girlfriend to marry me because I was convinced she'd say no. Maybe I had bad luck. Maybe I should have hung around with different people. But everything is so concocted, made up.

This has to be overcome, somehow. I'm not smart enough to say how it all came about – maybe this is to blame: the cultural production of individualism which constantly nourished a semi-divine sense of a public ego, a false one, of course. Or is it the global system's terrorist tactics that are to blame? They've turned public contact into an important thing, swaying between thinking of an undiscriminating, tolerant attitude as dangerous or, worse, distasteful. Or is it something else, something completely different, that's to blame? In any case, I'm sure that there are many of us who expect more from life. We have to spread our arms. Closing ourselves into the mould of bourgeois relational form leaves us lonely, weak, worthless and at the same time firmly convinced of the illusion of control over our own existence. The system is wily and vile, our confidence is a grim joke. That's why we should come together. I don't want to propagate power, as if, together, we could destroy and/or establish and/or change the world. I would just like to see who, today, is alive and present.

I hope I haven't gone on for too long. I would like to ask you to read your poetry at Poetrylitics, an end-of-summer festival. I'm not going to make any money, and I'm not looking for any benefits from this. My motives are honest and pure. If you come, a lot of those people whose lives your poetry has changed will come. There are many of us, each of us lonely and stuck with our own shattered fate. I know you like your solitude, but I'm asking you because there are a lot of us who can't, who mustn't, who don't want to afford it any more. Unite us? I'll tell you more if/when you respond.

With great hope, with warmest greetings, in great anticipation of an answer,
another part of the carious cuttle,
forever yours,
Max Adorcuse
(Vaclav Smech)

I said yeah, sure, why not. For so long I have wriggled out of such invitations, each with a whiff of profit-mongering or of some sort of ego trip from a disagreeable community, corpo-commercial, fashionable elite circle-jerkers. And then this poor Max. I followed the process to the degree it pleased me. He did everything himself, no money, pure will. If he wasn't so ridden with complexes and aimlessly reflexive I might even like him, but then I wouldn't want to read, maybe I would just... He didn't want a kiss. That, for instance, I respect. An inhibited soul that calls for disclosure. Exposure. Is that the same thing?

And now this space is again shaking under the weight of unknown voices. I leaf through them. I try to feel them through the cover. I feel a prick in the finger, like a needle on a spinning wheel, an ugly brown envelope, with 'Zoja' written on it, with a 'j'. I turn it around and around. Nothing. That 'j' unlocks a rusty latch, and bits of rust splatter like raisins from potica. Home. In German, Traum *means dream. I haven't dreamt about home in ages. For that I'm thankful. The 'j' frightens me. It looks like a hook that will sink into my lip and drag me off somewhere I don't want to go. Somewhere I have, deliberately, not been for so long it should no longer matter to me. Like a blunt memory that the brain didn't know how to classify as unimportant, so it stays with you and insists, something as senseless as a stop at a filling station, a smile of buried love, a chocolate wrap and the smell of fumes... All too often, I still wake up to that.*

I open it. Inside there's a plane ticket and nothing else. It's a morning flight, the earliest one. The voice of destiny, the call of coincidence. Who knows. I stick it in my pocket and don't want to think of it any more. Maybe it wouldn't be so bad? Where is Seam?

/

Ludovico's index finger is his longest. In the womb he was subject to an abnormal level of oestrogen. Therefore his frontal cortex has poor neuronal networks. Ever since he can remember, he's loved torturing animals. There's something attractive in suffering. In those eyes that have no idea why. They have no idea why. He feels it ballooning somewhere in the nape of his neck. He is drawn to it. The cats in the freezer are already frozen stiff. Like sock puppets peering into emptiness…

Theodore Robert 'Ted' Bundy, John Wayne Gacy Jr., Zodiac, David Richard Berkowitz, Mark David Chapman, Ludovico Överchild. Not yet entirely among them, but soon, if everything works out. Corrections are violence. What grows up broken stays broken.

She's still sleeping. Her body, her frozen little body, is wrapped in a sheet. Falling and diminishing. Ludovico has never entered a person other than through the holes made for it. He has never, ever, made new ones, not yet. Patience is among the finest of virtues, and good things come to those who wait.

YoUBiTCH

GIvEMEBacKMYPOEMS
IFyOUDONOTiWILlCUTOUTyOURVOcALCHORDS

L u d o v i c Ö

He cut the letters out of old magazines and sent her the letter. He doesn't know whether she ever read it.

(I didn't)

/

On the 6th of August 1991 at 16:00:12 GMT Tim Berners-Lee, an independent researcher at the European Organization for Nuclear Research (CERN), made a short announcement in the Usenet newsgroup alt.hypertext about the World Wide Web (WWW) project. With this announcement the Web became a public service. The majority of modern historians (*sic*) set the date of the 6th of August 1991 as the beginning of a socio-geo-political-ideolusionary anomaly known as the Great Cacophony.

Some modern historians (*sic*) have reservations about that date and consider 1 January 1983 as the starting date of the Great Cacophony, when the TCP/IP protocol (the infrastructure of what would later be the web) replaced the NCP protocol and allowed for the combining of separate networks (ARPANET, NSFNET…) into a single global network: the internet.

Still other modern historians (*sic*) argue that the Great Cacophony began in Canada on 22 October 1925, when the Austro-Hungarian physicist Julius Edgar Lilienfeld filed a patent application for a transistor. Historians of this persuasion, who consider bare technological innovation as the sole driving force of history, then move the date down through the past – Charles Babbage, differential engine, in 1833; Gottfried Wilhelm Leibniz, a calculating machine based on the Staffelwalze ('stepped drum'), 1672; Blaise Pascal, the Pascaline mechanical calculator, 1642, etc. etc. etc. all the way back to the Roman abacus, which was used by the Sumerians as early as 2400 BCE and which should therefore more aptly be called the Sumerian abacus.

Historians of yet another persuasion, for whom technological invention in and of itself represents nothing particularly
earthshattering, demand in the leaps, twists and turns of history also the presence of human beings and their relationship
with material, which incidentally pushes them into the area
of metaphysics and the subjective position, which means that
few serious people take them very seriously. These historians
agree that the internet or the WWW represents a major shift
in the area of human communication, but that the Great
Cacophony cannot of course be placed so late in human history, and they prefer to locate its beginning in Gutenberg's
invention of the moveable-type printing press (1444) or in Cai
Lun's (Han dynasty) perfection of the papermaking process (c.
105 BCE) or even at the outset of writing itself (cuneiform,
Mesopotamian Sumerians, c. 5300 BCE).

Modern historians (*sic*) of the fourth persuasion, whom
nobody really considers to be historians at all and who themselves mostly prefer not to be thought of as historians, and
who it would probably be better to call modern time-think-
ers (as they themselves say, instead of the titles that others
have hung on them – modern obscurantists, quasi-savants,
esosophoterics), consider 'the Great Cacophony' to be a superfluous expression, a banal neologism for a concept that was
developed long before the dawn of the third millennium by
Édouard Le Roy, Vladimir Vernadsky and Pierre Teilhard de
Chardin: the concept of the noosphere, the sphere of human
thought that arose the moment homo sapiens first looked at
a thing and said, *this thing is, in addition to what it is, also a
thing* and by the grace of scientific classification transformed
himself, *poof!*, from homo sapiens into homo sapiens sapiens,
a modern, extra-aware human being.

Digression aside. The concept of the Great Cacophony, as
the general public understands it and as a slightly tipsy father
might describe it to his inquisitive five-year-old ('Daddy,
Daddy, what's the Great Cacophony?'), is as follows: Son,

you know, that was back when people constantly yapped and yapped away, and shouted over each other, louder and louder, so that in the end it was impossible to tell not just who was saying what to who, but even who it was that was yapping, and then the police no longer knew who was a bad guy and who was a good guy, and the soldiers no longer knew who was from our country and who wasn't from our country, and nobody knew any more who they should listen to and what to do and everything was just completely messed up – it is a term for the two decades between 6 August 1991 and 17 December 2011, when the Great Cut occurred.

/

Carious cuttle.

/

'Well, while we're on the topic, can the Qur'an or any other holy book tell you what to do if you've got a brother who's forever getting high on some unknown substance, and you don't know how serious it all is, don't even have the slightest clue whether it's some ordinary passing phase, or whether the matter has an aspect that reaches into his very essence, and you don't know how to approach it, what to say, who to say it to, how to help without him resenting you, because, hey, he looks completely normal, and when he disappears he always says he's got a date with some babe, that he's gonna stick it in her mouth, and when he returns his consonants are slurred, his smile is crooked, and you ask him if everything's ok and he says, *never better, never better, it's just*, and he looks left and right, *I'm so tired*, and he looks at you again, right in the eyes, his pupils look normal, and says, *women tire you out, women*, and you're just waiting for it to be too late, for someone to stab him or for him to stab someone and end up in jail or a coffin, and everyone will say, *well goodness, who would have thought?* and you'll have to bite your tongue? Do these holy books have an FAQ section? Do they have a detailed index? I mean, what do I care how I should behave towards slaves, and how I should kill time in a God-pleasing way out in the middle of the desert with my tribe, when I'm living in the wildest city in the world, where everybody's emancipated and selfish and stoned to the stratosphere. The books should tell me something about orgies where some guy's condom bursts, another guy's arsehole gets ripped up, and a third guy just snaps and starts screaming and smashing everything in sight, and you're sitting there in the living room and plugging your ears, does it tell you what you're supposed to do? Call the police? Flee? Where to? Or do you just strip down and join the mass of bruises, your tongue hanging out, *me too, me too*? What should you think about the bullets that fly in the middle of the night and penetrate the wall an inch above your head? It seems to me all your books are completely irrelevant. I mean, I don't know, I never read them. Maybe they're good. Brother's a dope fiend? Turn to page 250. People – beasts; read from start to finish. Fear of death…you know what, just show up at the mosque or the synagogue or whatever it is you have. Strawberries and peanuts, and shoes off. Is it ok to wear socks and sandals if I have to pop out for some bread? How can I quit smoking? Life gets more fucked up every year. But not in the depths, it's fucked up on the surface. I already know how to listen to my heart, I don't need books for that. I am, let's say, fine. Totally fine. But, man, what the fuck is up with everybody else?'

He met Marjorie at the gym, during a morning work-out a few hours ago. His body is pumped up with anabolic steroids. When Anwar introduced himself, he was quiet for a moment, then asked whether he was a Mohammedan (he used precisely that word), and responded to the nod ('Bahá'í', to be precise) by holding a monologue. His attitude towards religion is rather scornful. He lives with his brother, alone.

'My faith doesn't give me life instructions,' says Anwar.

'My faith is my cultural identity. With it, I am a better man. Once you've experienced the abyss, you appreciate such things. But your own cultural identity seems to me a little questionable, if you get so worked up over something like this.'

'My...did you say my *cultural identity*?'

Anwar is completely at ease as he drives. Whenever he moves across the globe at a great speed, his feet ten inches above the ground and one foot pressed hard against the metal plate that separates him from it, he feels free. The adrenaline that is rapidly being released into his fellow travellers' bloodstream doesn't bother him. He's in a metal box, barely a part of this world.

'Yes. Your cultural identity. People who are relaxed and present in the world, comfortably placed in the armour of identity, usually don't complain about so-called holy books.'

'Identity...armour...'

The two words are treacly and sticky in his mouth, like something that has been left forgotten in a drawer over the holidays and is now starting to stink even if the drawer is kept closed.

'And holy books, it seems to me, whenever someone says 'holy books', they're usually just thinking about the religious component of man and, even more generally, about their relationship to their own existence, that is, whether they can exist as that fictional concept we call man, accept themselves as they are, or whether they have to, in relation to themselves, always take a step back, endlessly receding in suspicion of whatever they see in the mirror.'

Zoja's psychological make-up is an admixture of a primitive fear of speed and that slight intellectual buzzing triggered by the surprising disclosures of people who she had hitherto regarded as, shall we say, more unambiguous.

Marjorie looks out of the window at the ground, at the white lines painted on the asphalt that are gradually losing their character – their interruptions, their width, their variations of hue – and flowing into a beige-white line that curves inward.

Another monologue is in the works.

'Cultural identity, you say. Man as a fictional concept even. I find that offensive. Simply offensive. My mother was born in Nieuw Rotterdam, my father in San-Seoul. Even when I try my very best, I cannot fathom why they decided to have children. I could understand if there was only one, my brother, an accident, premature passion and contraceptive failure, one you can handle, stick him somewhere and leave him in peace, so you can scatter your life at will, no problem, but, two kids – do you follow? – that is, either you are totally thick and you simply can't understand your body, it's not clear to you that if you don't know how to keep your pants on, if you stick your pubic unit into someone else's pubic unit, that a whole new consciousness will have to explain the situation to itself, in its own way, and that it would probably be easier for everyone if this consciousness didn't exist, and when that happens to you, watch out, the second time and you're still sitting on the chair and looking at your penis, and you look, now, at two pairs of protruding eyes and on the other side there's her, also staring between her legs from which now a second watermelon has already crawled out, and it's still not clear to you that some things simply shouldn't be stuffed together; or you're a malicious toad that intentionally rubs its head over a box of matches so that, for a moment, it can smell the sulphur, before throwing the burnt matchstick away… I don't know why I'm saying this. There was no fiction. Just stupid flesh, you understand? Some people are born to morons. The nearest they come to any sort of guidance is a hysterical slap or absolute denial that they exist as a complex thing, and the only culture in the household is represented by the mouldy yoghurt that has been left in the fridge for a few months. We got nothing, my brother and I. Our parents were too poor to buy us off with mass culture and too stupid to think of anything else. Dad spent his time getting caught up in the dumbest of money-making ventures, pyramid schemes,

JASMIN B. FRELIH

selling things door-to-door, he was a complete incompetent, Mum was a cleaning lady, and we kids were abandoned to chance until both of them got hit by a train, their legs got cut off, so now they're happily imitating the other vegetables at some home for the disabled and imagining they're still part of this world just because they, somewhere, sometime, somehow left behind a pair of brats. Back then I was twelve and he was seventeen. I have no clue how we ended up here. But what I wanted to say is that I find you offensive, all of you heirs of the prophets, because you picked some tolerable figure from the confusions of time and laid that cross, ha ha, over the holes that living people left you with. You don't have the right to a fictitious identity! You're all lonely, contradictory, desperate creatures, with sand in your hands and up to your ankles in water, drawing strength from fairy tales, fables that let you look down on your fellow men. That's what I think about the whole thing.'

Anwar is concentrating on the road. The traffic is getting heavier and at this speed you have to anticipate, have to be vigilant. Even within the framework of traffic regulations anomalies occur – drunk drivers, coach-driving Amish, weak-sighted old people, an impulsive manoeuvre. Driving is a demanding operation. Time passes at two levels (inside and outside the vehicle), in two sets of chaotic interactions (in the brain and in the traffic) and with rapidly shifting instincts and intentions, both in the individual and in the system.

Zoja looks at the back seats. Marjorie looks sour. He is rhapsodically sincere.

'Would you rather see,' she asks, 'everyone immersed in their own imperfection? Humanity as a long procession of mourning ruins? Isn't an intervention into reality possible also from a position of brokenness? The way I see it, everything's a projection. You see yourself torn, along with the uniform. You could simply change perspective. Say that identity is a leaking ship and the person, through intervention, is the vehicle of

coherence. You just have to permit yourself to intervene. Then it doesn't matter whether or not you're dispersed.'

'Action will not make my life whole.'

'It depends on the type of action.'

A tyre bursts. Anwar responds to this with cold precision. He has anticipated this possibility, been preparing for it, and has maybe, by having concentrated on the fact that something of that sort can occur, even caused it (for years after one consumes, cause and effect are on shaky ground). He turns the steering wheel, indicates right, is attentive to all the mirrors at once and safely steers among the honking lorries and the nearly murdered motorcyclist onto the hard shoulder.

/

'Do you know any voodoo?'

Dolores gets up. Her lipstick is smeared all over her face. She looks like a mime who has just sweated through a marathon routine. She has an inside-out stocking over her hair. Her wig is lying on the floor, looking like a run-over cat. Ludovico uses a toe to retrieve it and fling it in the air. He catches it, sticks his finger in the scalp and twirls it around.

'Give it to me, sweetie, can't you see what a mess I look?'

'You are what you are, what can you do? Just tell me if you know some voodoo magic.'

Her legs are sloppily shaved, there are thick crops of hair at random places. She's in a thong, bent over sideways, tucking her member under the material with her fingers. She pulls a skirt over her bottom and looks around for her shoes. Her breasts are small, artificial, and one is lower than the other. Her nipples look like a drunk's skewed eyes.

'Why would I know voodoo, sweetie?'

Her chocolate skin is dappled with white spots reminiscent of some sort of disease.

'Aren't you from the Caribbean or Jamaica or someplace where there are magicians?'

Her incisors are so wide apart that you could wag your finger between them.

'Is that supposed to be some sort of insult? I'm from Haiti. We've forgotten our voodoo. Too many missionaries met with too much success. But I can eat you whole, human flesh still tastes good.'

'I saw how starved you were before, yeah.'

Whenever she laughs spontaneously it comes out inconsistently deep.

'Will you make me dinner, or will you be a bastard and toss me out?'

'That depends.'

'On what?'

She does up her bra and slips into a blue shirt.

'On whether or not you enchant me.'

'I don't know how to.'

'Collective memory in the hypothalamus. If your great-grandparents knew it, so do you, you just have to remember.'

'I have no idea what you just said. Give me back my wig.'

She walks towards him, in an obscenely knock-kneed walk.

'Enchant me.'

'Ludy, my magic ends when I wake up.'

'I want a voodoo spell!' shouts Ludovico. Dolores shudders. For a moment fear flashes in her eyes.

'All right, all right, come here.'

Ludovico moves to the edge of the bed. Dolores sits next to him and reaches down to his fly.

'Not like that. Don't you fucking know what voodoo is?'

'Ludy, I don't understand.'

'Blood and sacrifice and black magic, not a blow job.'

'But we don't have any blood,' says Dolores.

'Enchant me.'

'Give me back my wig.'

'No.'

'I can't do magic without my wig.'

'I don't believe you.'

Dolores smiles and rolls her eyes. She looks past Ludovico's head, a bewildered expression on her face, it's a neat little trick that works on the street whenever a guy has a fistful of money but is dithering over whether or not to pay. Ludovico turns and Dolores quickly grabs for the wig. He's faster than her, almost unbelievably fast. He puts the wig out of her reach, grabs her extended arm and twists it behind her back, roughly, painfully. Dolores yelps in fear. Ludovico pulls her close and whispers in her ear.

'If you won't do it yourself, I'll teach you…magic.'

He drags her backwards into the kitchen, slowly they waddle, her arse rubs against his crotch with each step, making him hard. Dolores yelps.

In the kitchen he pushes her up against the counter.

'Give me your hand.'

'Ludy, what the hell are you doing. Let me go, Ludy, you know they know I'm with you, they'll come looking for me, you know they will, Ludy, dammit…'

He slams her head against the edge of the cupboard.

'Shut up and stretch out your arm.'

Dolores stretches it out.

'Palm up.'

She turns it over.

Ludovico pulls a knife out of the drawer, Dolores starts to gasp. He presses the blade against her Adam's apple.

'If you scream, I'll cut you up, got it?'

'Yes,' says Dolores, completely still. Ludovico runs the knife blade over her shoulders, along her upper arm, down her forearm, her wrist, over the palm and carves a line into it. The flesh turns white for a second, before it pools with blood. She shakes with the pain, but Ludovico's grip is a vice.

'We have blood. Who will be the victim?'

'Ludy, please, no, please, no,' whispers Dolores.

He pushes her up against the freezer – 'Ludy, please, no' – and opens it. Inside lie icy corpses of stray cats, frozen into grotesque positions.

Dolores starts to cry, to sob hysterically. Ludovico grabs her bleeding hand and pushes it into the freezer.

'Victims, as many as you want, as many as you want, each one has been to the altar, don't you worry, Ludovico is always prepared for everything.'

He steers her hand over the prickly furry cadavers, leaving bloody streaks. Dolores, helpless, closes her eyes.

'Here, kitty, kitty, kitty. I hope you can conjure up something magical.'

Dolores shakes her head. The freezer's coldness mitigates the pain of the cut. Ludovico pulls her hand out and twists Dolores towards him. The freezer door falls shut.

'Put the wig on my head, anoint my face and spout some voodoo!'

Dolores closes her eyes, the tears run together with the powder and mascara. Ludovico smacks her.

'I'll slaughter you!'

'No, please, no.'

'Magic!'

She sticks the wig on him and places her bloodied palm over his cheek.

'Abra…abraca…hocus.'

'Fuck, Dolly, if you don't give me some voodoo, I will rip out your entrails.'

'But,' despairingly, 'I don't know any!'

'Ok, repeat after me, syllable for syllable, ok?'

Dolores sniffles and nods.'

'Car-i-ous.'

'Car-i-ous.'

'Cut-tle.'

'Cut-til.'

A slap. A stifled cry.
'Cut-tle.'
'Cut-tle.'
'Well done.'
'Well-done.'

Ludovico lets her go and grins. There's blood all over his face. He rests the knife on the counter.

'Thank you.'

Dolores opens her eyes, gazes, stunned, and steps to the side. When Ludovico doesn't respond, she sprints wildly, barefoot, wigless, flecks of blood on her clothes, through the door, out.

/

It looks like anyone who is anyone came. Max Adorcuse is star-struck. The Medio Twins, Kaveman KoleKtive, Sgt.Sange, Rufus Transparency, Obiton Tonga, Mme Nadir, Zuck de Borg, Sisek, Lillion Flawerss, the Lost Children, Occram Wristcut, Beda Venerabilis JR, Gadfly Ister, Synchro-Step Teaparty, CEO Birthmark, Mypeace Pepé, OBGYN Aboriginal, Grotto Vergilius, Santa-Claude, Margharet & Maester, Some Meri Slaves, Lobana Bolanja q-inc., Metatrololor…

These aren't just any people. These are artists, techno-masters and lifestyle magicians. All of their names spread, or had once spread, or will be spread, in concentric circles around the city's neighbourhoods, outwards, across the border, to the suburbs and beyond, to the countryside and farther still to the abandoned trailers and shacks and tents and ghettos and forests, and fill the hearts of the young, who catch them in their ears, with the promise of the possible. Any way you look at it – even if it seems unlikely and even if the sky sometimes pins you down against the grass, incapacitates your limbs and renders you completely immobile – you will not necessarily remain forever Joe, with parents and grandparents and a few relatives, caught in a caricature drawn by a, let's say, an untalented hand. Come to the city, lay yourself bare, tell Joe to fuck off. Leave him to croak and rot among the postmen and the unmerited pensions. Among the boredom and the apathy. Your body is a vessel. Don't you forget it.

Still no Zoja. The presence of an increasingly large number of people Max had never seen before, though he'd heard of them more often than he'd had a chance to appreciate their work, robs him of the courage to keep on bellowing into the megaphone. Candy Lipkiss, a fifteen-year-old conceptual artist from Chattanooga, has stripped naked and climbed onto the bleached roof of a car where she's now playing the flute and interrupting each melody with bestial screams whenever her buttocks happen to come into contact with the metal. A few people are clustered around her, nodding approvingly, though still avoiding eye contact since nobody can say for certain whether the whole affair isn't a little morally and legally dubious. Still no Zoja, and Max admits that's worrying. The horrific possibility that he'll be known as the organizer of the biggest scam since the debacle of 2021 stabs him coldly somewhere around his kidneys. But don't worry, she said she'd be there, for sure she'd be there. Max tries to evade the 'as-it-were' old guy, but he can't and the old guy latches on to him like a tick, spraying saliva and incessantly nattering on about parallaxes and symptoms and syntheses. The guy's stream of thought has long since sped away from Max and now, in the middle of things, there's absolutely no chance of catching up with it. His sense lies elsewhere, Max tells himself, and turns his hearing to another sphere.

Gotham Syndicate has set up an enormous black tent in the middle of the car park. Someone very timid has picked up a guitar. His voice wilts in the midst of the crowd and its aggressive conversations. Max can hear it.

/

Dirty brick. Stacks and stacks of them. After millions of years, sediments, will people pore over the layers of broader Brooklyn the way we pore over the rings on a tree trunk? A stuffy scent has risen above the road. The breath of a dog gorging on tar. We are steamed rice in a saucepan. Someone is draining us. Anwar and Marjorie's boyfriend are changing the tyre. They've cleared up their misunderstanding through joint action. I told him it was possible. We are all what we are when a tyre is being changed. Especially since, come to think of it, I saw him naked that morning, purged of all that is superfluous. Marjorie doesn't want to get out of the car. She says she's afraid. Of what? Premonitions of evil, she says. That has nothing to do with me. I packed my premonitions of evil into my suitcase and, how forgetful of me, intentionally left it at home. The façades are hidden below tattered, weather-beaten, forgotten economic propaganda. IRONWORKERS 40, red spray. It's been decades since anything was built around here. Just constant, incessant crumbling, brick by brick. A single clumsy step and a house is demolished. The intersections look like somebody accidentally overlooked them, somebody who was quite powerless to begin with. Even the rubbish is fleeing, with the wind, with leisure. The unbrushed teeth of a giant, all this construction. Red. It reminds me of the idea some fleeting individual had of starting a Throw a Brick project in the heart of the city, so that people would be looking up, heavenwards, towards the tops of all these buildings more often. He failed. The people weren't for it. Even if the bricks were made of foam, no. I don't know why I thought of this now… Green graffiti: ZOIA, when I look over a fence, down, on the grill over a closed shop. What an odious feeling of alienation, when someone appropriates your name to proclaim something for themselves. Everyone knows what it is they mean, only I have no idea. The road is gnawed up. Nobody makes an effort any more. To me this seems most beautiful.

/

Flames are shooting out from behind Ludovico. His footprints are evaporating in black smoke. Bending light, he is a cosmic phenomenon. Air runs away from him. The vacuum he leaves behind fills up so fast that tiny lightning bolts are triggered, and the men in the news stands crane their necks skywards in search of thunder. You stumble if you look just a little closer at him, or you run into a traffic sign or you cross the street right into the path of an old Cadillac whose brakes then have to be slammed and a curse has to be flung out among the screeching. Grandmas drop things when he comes near. Shoelaces come unlaced all on their own. You step into a road apple. Bloody Amish.

He's dressed in a white tunic that flaps in a self-created wind, too quick for the eye to see, like a mosquito's wings. This flapping emits a low vibration that drives bipolar people and certain breeds of dog mad. German shepherds and Dalmatians, especially.

He looks like a hermit returning from the mountain with a brand new set of commandments. The weaker minds won't be able to resist him. His every move is a cult in the making. Stronger minds just find him outrageously cool. That he'll cause problems is clear even from the thirty-fifth floor, where Maude and Larry are, during working hours, secretly sipping coffee, smoking cigarettes and stroking each other right where it feels best. As they look down at him, they quiver with pleasure.

The blood on his face makes him look Native. Chief Ludovico. Three blocks away from Poetrylitics, sharper with each passing moment. He can already hear the constant pulse of the crowd and he'd be lying if he didn't admit that he's being guided in the right direction, as if by divining rod, by a titanic imagined erection.

/

Hard to put it in another way... The sun is setting.

Still no Zoja.

The exits on this stretch of the motorway (that is, on this something that was once a motorway but which now looks more like a war zone, since carved into the lanes are holes, gaps, the supporting iron frame that runs under the asphalt, around the holes are bands that were once screaming yellow but are now a mere light pink, which is why the careless and the colour blind and the intentionally inattentive drive into death and oblivion (traffic accidents no longer make the news, nor do accidents in general – while we're at it, they don't bother with any sort of news any more), but people's language is slow to change and they still call it a 'motorway', this cemetery of cranes that, try as they might, have been overtaken by rust) are choked up with sheet-metal leftovers from the dead-for-decades automotive industry. Nobody moves. An old Ford was being pushed over the guardrail, inch by inch, allowing the three teenagers (two boys and a girl) to get out before it thundered into the nothingness, and now they're standing with thumbs raised and gazing straight at the static windshields, which causes awkwardness among the many people who would otherwise like to take them into their cars, but become uncomfortable at the thought, so they look away, avoiding the kids, and they honk and they curse the heat. During the day it really was hot, but that's nothing compared with the evening, when the rays slacken. Then all that concrete which has been thirstily drinking zenith begins to exude vapour into the cooled air.

It's easier in a white tunic, as Averroes and his crowd are well aware. The mangers for the cows are full, no camels anywhere.

'What time is it?' *What an old-fashioned question.*

Still no Zoja.

The online social networks, which sucked in most of the world's techno-savvy, electro-accessible populations, are regarded by many as, if not the main, then at least very influential reprobates of the Great Cacophony, which is in a sense true, but if you look a little closer it's not true at all. For those who look a little closer, saying that social networks are to blame is a cheap and pat formulation. For the rest, it's commonsensical and clear. But since very few people could even dream up what actually happened – dreams being rather causeless things, hardly in accordance with the facts of the world – let's just tell the truth as we see it. The real causes of the disaster were processor strength, artificial intelligence and a cabal of people with extremely high intelligence quotients, called in certain circles, in reverential, whispered tones, Car-Cut.

I'm late. Anwar says, 'We're already really close, just walk there. I'll follow you.' Marjorie nods. Her lover is lost in thought. When Zoja gets out, he says, 'Now I remember that I read you once.' *I'm printed with straw. Turned over like leaves.* Marjorie smiles and gets out. He asks, 'Where are you going?' Anwar looks at him in amazement. 'Didn't you hear me?' He doesn't respond but jumps out of the car and starts to scream. 'Rip me, rip me, rip me in half! It's you, isn't it?' *I'm not, not really. Meaning gets lost, sometimes. There's nothing wrong with that.*

Still no Zoja. Kavemen KoleKtive are standing in a circle, clad in leather hides. As they murmur their farewell song to the sun, sweat pours over their mud-scented bodies. The Medio Twins finish off each other's completely senseless sentences. As-it-were has gone off somewhere. A most uncongenial man is selling synthetic drugs and people are hissing at him to fuck off back to where he came from. Max is getting a little nervous. When night falls the people will go inside and he'll have to turn on the lights. The guitarist doesn't stop. Someone has come to the edge. Someone else looks awfully lonely. Hope is in the air, primal   progenitor   pre-prophet

passion is in the air. Celebrity culture is healthy and in full swing. Nameless people are the grout between the tiles of fame, but that doesn't bother them, not in the least, since they're happy to be able to hold things together, so that there's no cracks in-between, that the landscape is diverse, that no one is forgotten. Someone has clutched his chest in a display of surprise, and someone else has put his hands together in applause. On the edges of the car park things are moving like a fire through dry grass. The queue at the entrance winds in a human snake, left and right, the heads turn towards the source of the applause and although they don't know exactly why, they all automatically start to clap. They love her. They love her.

cur

Her.

In a cone of light.

PANCAKE PALACE

✦ ✦

Ten. Pain awoke with the morning. In the knees, in the ankles, in the muscles, under the nails. Everywhere. He groaned.

'Eeeeevan, are you ok?'

Her breath reeked. He turned onto his side, away from her. Nine.

'Are you sleeping?'

It didn't help that her breath had found a pathway around his head, enveloped him, suffocated him. He was totally slimy, sweaty, sex-soaked, with wrinkled skin, unshaven everywhere, beard stubble prickling his neck. Eight. He could feel the pimples on his back, on his arse. Muggy moistness. His lungs had collapsed, his breath was wheezy. Everything hurt so bloody much. He rested his hand against his chest. Silence. He groaned. Seven.

'What is it?'

Something vile had collected in his mouth overnight. His teeth had grown fur. He could feel a half-dried splatter of saliva in the right corner of his lips. One eye was blind, glued together by the nocturnal discharge of tear canals. Six. His nose was totally stuffed up. Shit. His left arm had fallen asleep and was hanging numbly by his side. Would they have to amputate it? His back ached, his neck was sprained. He groaned. Five.

'Eeeeevan...'

'Just leave me alone, please.' Four.

'I had a dream about opening night, a really beautiful

dream. Everything was going fine and you were smiling. A week to go, oh my, you know my stomach feels funny every time I think about it.'

A stomach ulcer, acid reflux, intolerable heartburn hell for Evan. Cirrhosis, thrombosis, an aneurysm. Death is just a step away. Let it slide. Three. He was counting down silently, he often did, counting from ten to zero, swearing that once he got to zero he would get up and go to the bathroom. Two.

One.

'Can you please get me a cup of coffee?'

She so loved to please. She didn't even leave a sigh behind. His neck cracked as he turned over. She rolled out of bed and the sheet slid down from her lower back, her buttocks, her ample thighs. She wasn't shy. She walked naked to the console and pressed. As she waited she stretched, raised herself up on her toes, lifted her hands high in the air. He rubbed his eyes and stared right through the gap between her thighs. He saw the dark slit. He filled it with his imagination, but reality leapt before his eyes and shattered the illusion. Under her right cheek there was a desiccated white smudge. His member had shrunk back into the skin. The blood had flown elsewhere.

/

Her legs spread slowly, too deliberately. She covered his eyes, not herself, with her hand.

'Don't peek.'

He closed his eyes and pushed her hand away.

'My eyes are closed.'

He put her together through scent, in the dark. Microscopically, bit by bit. Each crinkle separately, incipient stubble, a waxy veneer of passion. He reinvented her form from the powder of existence. A slit. A perineum. Lips. A mound.

/

The coffee scalded his tongue. He didn't say thank you. She was constantly trying to touch him, nudging in closer, forcing her breath into his nostrils. He grabbed her by the side, his fingers sank into white flesh, and he held her at a distance. His eyes automatically sought out her nipples, the dark premonition underneath. He had to shut his eyes. He blew into the cup. His fingers were burning. He was seated. He felt revolting. Watery mucus in his gullet. He didn't know where to spit it out, so he was swallowing it with long constrictions of the throat.

'Eeeeevan…'

She ran her fingers over his chest.

'What time is rehearsal today?'

'I don't know,' he murmured.

Along the spine, downwards.

'In the afternoon, no? What do we have today? The third act? The fourth? The final?'

'I don't know.'

'Not the second, my back still hurts from the last time. And we already know it.'

'Mmm.'

Over his lower back, around, against…he pulled away.

'May I drink my coffee in peace?'

Her hand was numb. He tipped his cup and drained it. A cloud of steam escaped his mouth. 'Take it away.'

With a sour expression, she got up again. When she went towards the table, she turned sideways.

Which characteristic of time draws lust from people's mouths?

Evan and Mojca had been going around in circles. Once the initial enthusiasm had disappeared (literally, in his case), they nurtured apathy for a time, and perhaps this would have continued indefinitely if complete strangers hadn't suddenly started to smell like sex. Because they were grown up, not just in years but also in consciousness, they knew how to confide these new scents to each other. And they didn't make the amateur mistake of saying: just follow your instincts, there won't be any problem, we love each other. That doesn't work. An ancient chemical process that, with physical contact, binds hormones into what people call emotions, stands in the way. And then emotions battle with declarations, and people end up in limbo.

And so they invented a complex game of not being together, of renouncing, of teasing, which, when the degree of abstinence was complete, released itself in the transgression of a new sexual practice. For years they'd endured in the grips of such passion. Until one day Mojca

/

'Hey, while you're there, can you bring me another one?'

She pressed a button. With a hand over her chest, she moved to the chair over which her dress was draped. She tossed it on in a single move and made herself look, at once, attractive because she hid herself, and somewhat ugly, because everything that remained to the eyes bespoke morning. In the morning everyone is...

'None for you?'

'I don't drink coffee.'

'You want something else?'

'I ate while you were sleeping.'

Sour yoghurt breath. Evan's head was spinning. The caffeine was kicking in. His stomach was awhirl.

She brought him a second cup. As she leant down to him, he saw the outline of her breasts and filled in the rest on his own. He was covered by the sheet. It rustled slightly. He blew across the surface of the coffee and observed the resulting ridge. For a moment he forgot about his own body and immediately felt better.

/

Sometimes we get so angry with the people we love. We are never as passionate when it comes to other people. When we attach ourselves, when we really attach ourselves, these bonds create little bubbles in which there is space for the rawest of things.

/

The pancakes looked much less appetizing here at their final destination. Evan flushed the toilet and stepped into the shower. He kept one ear out of the stream so he could hear the door. Oksana didn't come in. That wouldn't bother him now. He dried himself off and wrapped the towel around his waist. He tied it loosely. He opened the bathroom door—

the windows were transparent and the sun had sharpened the edges of all the objects, the tables, the bed, bulbs in lamps, frames, chairs, all the bristles of the carpet, cabinet knobs and drawers, empty cups and plates, forks, knives, and her skin, which stuck out from her clothes, exploded with every pore, every hair into an impossible sharpness, and Evan could feel his pupils dilating, as if scissor blades were about to gouge out his eyes

—and slammed it shut. Panic grabbed him, he was out of mAk and he couldn't get any more, anywhere, Gordon was in jail, he didn't know anyone else, and all the doors, all the doors were closed, he didn't dare ask anyone, since they'd toss him out, and he didn't want to go back, he'd left a desert behind him, so he headed to the cabinet above the sink, opened it and grabbed, without looking, a plastic box of pills he'd been prescribed once, somewhere, for something or other, opened it, took two, swallowed, and grabbed another packet of pills, two more, swallowed, and a third, swallowed, and he would have taken a fourth, and a fifth, and a sixth…had he not been afraid of committing suicide by accident. That would not be smart. Suicides are to be committed on purpose.

/

'Eeeeevan…Are you ok?'

She knocked. Carefully, she opened the door. He was lying on the floor, a smile on his face, with his eyes fixed on the ceiling.

'I'm ok.'

She stepped forwards, but he put his hand up to stop her. 'No need.'

He turned onto his side, naked, got to his knees, wriggled his arse and got up. He walked slowly past her. She followed him.

'Rehearsal's at five. See you there.'

He didn't look at her. He picked up the newspaper from the floor and threw it against the wall. He went to the console and pressed a button. Then he opened the closet and got dressed. He ran a hand through the pocket of the trousers he'd worn the day before. When he saw her he shuddered, as if frightened.

'Rehearsal's at five. See you there,' he repeated.

Oksana was offended. She turned to leave. She'd left her necklace on the bedside table. She had her knees on the bed so she could reach over for it, when she felt a caress on the inside of her thighs. She pressed her lips together and rolled her eyes. He was only joking. The fingers crept up her dress and entered her almost violently. She let her head drop. The other fingers were gliding over her tummy, to her breasts, pinching a nipple. She directed the moan into the pillow. She arched. The lips descended on her tailbone, then the teeth, then the tongue, broad and wet, going, slowly, lower.

Evan observed the goings-on from a safe distance.

/

When she walked in, Oksana screamed and threw a sheet over herself. Evan stared at her in jutting amazement. Her voice was cold.

'Evan Z—, get dressed. Oksana Ivanovna Bobrova, go home. Rehearsal is at five.'

Her face was not quite human. A heart-shaped oval with a straight-bridged nose, thin lips that barely parted when she spoke and a pair of oval buttons instead of eyes, without whites, entirely covered in jade. A Mesopotamian sculpture. Modigliani. She had straight black hair that emitted a dead shine, like the fur of a stuffed animal.

'Who are you?'

'Koito XXV. Your new sponsor. Get dressed. Oksana Ivanovna Bobrova, go home.'

Oksana scrambled out of bed, grabbed her necklace and straightened her crumpled dress. She looked at Evan, who was staring at Koito.

'Bye.'

'Goodbye, Oksana Ivanovna Bobrova.'

She picked up her shoes and ran barefoot into the hallway.

'Evan Z—, say goodbye to Oksana Ivanovna Bobrova.'

'Oksana!' he called out. She was already in the hall. 'See you at rehearsal.'

No response.

'Get dressed.'

Evan bent down to the pile of clothes on the floor.

'No.'

She opened the closet and mechanically, in a regular rhythm, began flinging underwear, socks, trousers, a shirt ('Outside it's twenty-three degrees Celsius, a slight wind, thirty-three percent chance of precipitation') and a jacket. Evan got dressed. He tossed the jacket onto a chair.

'Have you already consumed breakfast?'

She was dressed in a one-piece, skin-tight plastic outfit that showed no curves. Underneath, she was obviously a skeleton.

'What happened to Gordon?'

'Answer the question.'

'Not yet.'

'Eat.'

Evan sat down before a platter of food.

'I'm not hungry.'

'Eat.'

'Tell me, where is Gordon?'

'Gordon Shaw Falstaff is in custody awaiting trial. Eat.'

'I'm not hungry.'

'The recommended daily intake of food is two thousand five hundred calories, breakfast is eight hundred. Eat.'

'What the fuck is this, if you—'

'Do not curse. Eat your breakfast, brush your teeth. The time is eleven forty-three and fifteen seconds, the photo shoot is at one, the meeting with the director is at two, at three, lunch with the Mishima family, at four, free time under supervision, at five, rehearsal, at eight, free time under supervision, dinner, asleep by midnight at the latest.'

The pills were sizzling in Evan's stomach acid. Their chemical properties were spreading through the barriers and into his bloodstream. This thrust him into catatonia. Koito took his hand and pricked a finger with a pin. He did not respond. A drop of blood swelled out. She wiped it away with a napkin.

/

'It's only for one year!'

He knew that look. He'd seen it on the faces of countless girls who were dragging themselves through audition after audition. The rehearsed look of despair, disappointment and helplessness. Which, after they found out that they didn't get the role, obtained just one additional, negligible, almost imperceptible yet crucial aspect which turned the expression into a sincere one. That aspect was staring at him as he told her.

'Evan, a year is a really long time… Why can't I go with you?'

'Because they want the pure and authentic me. If I take you with me I'll be taking a lifetime's worth of baggage, and that's not what they want.'

'But what is this, Evan, who's this *they*?'

'Edo! Mojca, you know how much this means to me, it'll be the pinnacle of my entire career.'

'I know, I know, but I always thought that I could be there with you, never that you'd leave me all alone.'

'One year. One lousy year.'

'For you I…'

'What?'

'Nothing. Evan, I'm sorry. I don't want you to go.'

'Mojca, please, you know I'm going.'

'Yes…'

/

Again he found himself in the toilet, this time not with his arse but his mouth perched over the bowl, a long finger jabbing into his throat, prodding his trachea and forcing him to vomit. The coffee sludge and chalky stomach remnants clanked into the bowl.

'Drink.'

He drank from a glass that contained a greenish fluid, tea-like but cold.

'Was that mAk?' he asked her.

Koito turned her head, first right, then left.

'No.'

'What is it then?'

'stAbIIno.57. Your blood is not optimal. It's now in the seventy-seventh percentile. Any more than that is prohibited for foreigners.'

She wiped off her finger. Evan got back to his feet.

'I don't understand.'

'Because you are a foreigner.'

He felt somewhat normal. That wasn't good. The rift had

lost its edges and turned into a mere void.

'Can you please explain to me what's going on?'

'That is too broad a question.'

'Who are you?'

'I am Koito XXV. Your new sponsor.'

'Who are you in relation to yourself?'

'Koito XXV. The sponsor at disposal.'

'At whose disposal?'

'Daimyō's.'

'What were you up to yesterday?'

'I was at disposal.'

'Date of birth?'

'That information is confidential.'

'Parents?'

'That information is confidential.'

'Who did you sponsor before me?'

'That information is confidential.'

'Do you feel things?'

'That is too broad a question.'

'Can I touch you?'

'Non-aggressively.'

He placed a hand over her chest, just below the slight bulge that was supposed to indicate a left breast.

Silence.

'I think we will get along well.'

'Yes.'

The air was airy, the light light and the room roomy as Evan ate breakfast. The taste tasty. He spoke with his mouth full and slowly wiped away the moist bits of food that flitted onto the table.

'Is it possible to visit Gordon?'

'When the schedule allows for it, it is possible.'

'Should I visit him?'

'It is not necessary.'

'He was my sponsor for almost the entire year.'

'Yes.'

'Why is he in custody?'

'That information is confidential.'

'Because of mAk?'

'That information is confidential.'

'Perhaps it would be right to visit him.'

'That is a decision.'

'Mmm, yes.'

Three mouthfuls of water, interrupted by breaths through the nose. He squeezed his toes together.

'Should I shave for the photo shoot?'

'It is not necessary.'

'Good.'

Koito was standing motionless by the table. She was staring at him, though not intrusively, and he could eat in peace.

'Is it forbidden to sleep with an actress?'

'That is too broad a question.'

'Is it forbidden for me to sleep with Oksana?'

'It is not forbidden.'

'Is it, how should I put this, unseemly?'

'I do not understand the question.'

'Would it be better if I did not sleep with her?'

'That is a decision.'

'Mmm, yes.'

One last bite.

'Once I was very much in love.'

'. . .'

'Now I can't even remember what that meant. I remember the gestures and words, but not the motives behind them. Is that the same with everyone else?'

'I do not have sufficient information to provide an answer.'

'Have you ever been in love?'

'No.'

'That's a shame.'

'…'

'I don't know if it's even a matter of memory. Maybe it's supposed to be felt. Mnemotion. Is that a word?'

'No.'

'With mAk I can, in a good way, feel mnemotion. Without it, things would be rougher, more aggressive, almost unbearable. But in any case, at least it's something, right? Now, I can't even understand, I mean, it's difficult, without the right words, from such a cold place…'

'Get dressed.'

'You don't understand.'

'I do not understand.'

He stood up.

'Photo shoot.'

'Yes.'

/

The photographer seemed entirely human-like. When they entered his 'atelier' (that's how he greeted them – *Welcome to my atelier* – although his atelier was nothing but a space bordered by sheets in the middle of an abandoned warehouse), he parted his lips and kept them spread in variations of vowels and consonants until Evan was seated on the bar stool. Then he shut them, closed them into a blue line, took up his camera and said, 'Now *you* speak.'

Evan turned to Koito with a look of astonishment. *What should I talk about?* Koito was unable to read anything from his miming, so she just stared calmly on.

'What, then?'

The photographer's mouth was closed. Both of them looked at Koito.

'Tell Mundo' (that was the photographer's name: Mundo, just Mundo) 'about mnemotion.'

Evan rubbed his eyes. Mundo took photos.

'Once I was very much in love.'

Mundo nodded.

'And I can prove it.'

Evan stuck his right index finger into his mouth and drew back his cheek. A hole gaped where there should have been an incisor. Mundo took photos.

'My tooth is now resting against her chest, perhaps, though I'm not totally sure if that's true, but anyway… Has anyone ever stolen a tooth from you?'

Mundo shook his head, Koito did not.

'That's very unusual, wouldn't you say? But that's what it means to be in love. Or even what love means. Now I don't know any more, I couldn't say, since there's no more mnemotion, what it was all about. Now it just seems a little odd.'

He stroked his gums.

'But the hole bears witness. The body does not lie. There should be a tooth there, now it's no longer there and therefore…'

He shook his head.

'I woke up, it was a little bit before I left, before I came here. Someone had inflated a balloon in my cheeks. A very strange feeling. I said, I remember it well, I must have felt horrible, and I swore. What the mufferfuck…I said. And then I cried. Where are my *ff*s?'

Mundo took photos of him.

'Where are my *ff*s, who took my *ff*s, do you understand? I couldn't say "th". My tongue was swollen. And the saliva was running down my chin. I had shaved that day and Mojca was livid at me for that, well, actually I don't know what she was feeling, but she looked angry, she said she knew what that meant, my shaving, that it was just a matter of time… I couldn't quite understand what she meant by that. But, ok, I was freshly shaven, with spittle all over the place.'

Mundo took photos. The camera shutter released a salvo of five, six rapid clicks.

'Mojca was a dentist. A really good one, a really successful one, with her own private practice, money to burn. Soon she became independent, as far as money goes, and in a way that was a healthy thing for our relationship. Now that I think about it, on the surface, each of us functioned independently, yet we had an inner connection, though I can't really understand that any more. I can't mnemote it. Yes?'

Mundo took photos. Click-click-click-click.

'She was a dentist, though she herself never went to the dentist. Isn't that suspect? Her teeth were perfect, absolutely healthy enamel, no cavities, no bad breath, no plaque, just whiteness, just purity. She didn't even need a prosthesis – is that what you call it? A prosthesis? – those metal things you stick in your mouth to make your teeth line up straight, I had them when I was a kid, well, her jaw was perfect from birth, she didn't even have wisdom teeth. Mine had to be torn out. I was still a kid. Braces! Of course, that's what you call them. And a person like that goes on to become a dentist. A person who has no idea what it means to sit in a chair with a drill aimed at your skull. That's problematic.'

Mundo approached him, piercing the bubble of his personal space, but Evan wasn't bothered. He took photos of Evan's unshaven chin, which swivelled as he spoke.

'But so be it, if men can be gynaecologists… That's even more problematic, I guess. Or…artists. They don't have a clue either.'

Evan stopped talking. The camera was left hanging in the air, silent. Koito made a mill gesture with her hands, *keep going*.

'Well, and…what was I saying? Oh yeah, I'm lying there hollering *where are my ffs?* Mute in the head. You could have slapped me and I wouldn't have minded. She filled me up with narcotics, my skin was numb. I wiped off the saliva which was running down all the time, I couldn't keep it in, so I was wiping it off. And I yelled. *Mufferfucker* and so on. I still didn't know I was missing a tooth. And then she appeared, smiling wickedly, and at that moment I already hated her, well, I don't know, I can remember now that I told her I hated her because she'd made an utter fool of me, just so that I wouldn't go, and she almost succeeded, if it weren't for my friends, but I don't know, now I can't remember how I felt at the time. She came over, dressed in a red jacket that I'd bought for her in Vienna, lipsticked and powdered, beautiful and sleek and alluring, and she walked right over to me, with a smile on her wicked face, I can see it now, beautiful and tasteful and attractive and wicked…'

Evan waved his hands as he spoke, sitting on the stool, surrounded by spotlights and white tarpaulins that dispersed the sharp light into a gentle pallor. Mundo moved in a circle, catching the rhythm of his diction and taking photos of the vowels whenever Evan opened his mouth wide.

'She leant over me, I was lying there, paralysed, wasted from everything that she'd done to me, and though I can't remember exactly how I felt I know that somehow I didn't manage to move much, and she pushed her cleavage into my face, I mean, she came really close to me and her ample breasts were right in my eyes, and between them was a necklace I'd bought her, not long after we'd met, back when she was still stupid and naive, at least that's how I remember seeing her in my thoughts – get it? – and she shoved her fingers, with those filed and flawless nails painted pink, into her cleavage and extracted the necklace, so the pendant was now dangling right in front of my nose, dangling as if it had been created to dangle there and not to veg out peacefully its whole life, devoid of all commotion, in my damn mouth.'

Evan was getting worked up, which clearly delighted the photographer. He danced around him, hunting down angles, light, the gaping of the mouth.

'But I pushed her away, weakly, I was so weak, completely powerless, but I pushed her away and ran a finger under my gums, counted my teeth, saw one was missing and said *muffer,* Mojffa, you'll pay for *ffat!*'

His head had grown heavy. He put his elbows on his knees and his hands over his ears. That straightened out his face. Mundo positioned himself right in front of him.

'And she did.'

Click-click-click-click-click.

The city cityish as they drove. The pavements pavementy, the lines liney, the clouds cloudy. Koito's vehicle was self-driving, fully automatic, no steering wheel, pedals or mirrors. Seaty seats and windowy windows. She pressed a button and with a quiet electric hum they were in the street, streety, hovering.

'Where to now?'

'The director of the theatre wants to talk to you.'

'Something serious?'

'Something serious.'

'How serious?'

'Very serious. We're going there and the two of you will have a real discussion.'

'What about?'

'I do not know.'

The conversation was amorphously conversational. The producing director had some bureaucratic problems that Evan didn't understand and he didn't know what to say, so he did a lot of smiling and nodding and grimacing concern at the right places, allowing his looks to dissolve into a benevolent *Ah, it'll work out, it'll all be fine.* Strangely, this put the director at ease. Koito remained outside the room; their conversation took place among a great deal of leather furniture. What is it you want from me? thought Evan. The director was opening the notebooks that were on the table, showed numbers and graphs and arrows, and chased them around with his finger on the paper, which made Evan wince. They parted with a dry handshake and Evan left with the unpleasant feeling of having been robbed. The time was slowly timing away.

/

A long drive out of the city. The skyscrapers sank out of sight, chased out by forlorn shacks that sprouted up and ate into the swamp for a few minutes before disappearing into the mud. After that, uninterrupted patches of wild growth. Then, for a long time, nothing, just bare earth, split in two by the road, before fences, tall, concrete, impermeable, appeared. The car brought them up to a metal gate. A movable camera gawked at them. Hologram light filled the space in the car.

'Open your eyes,' said Koito.

Evan held them open. Soon the door opened. The car hovered its way inside, got swallowed up by the walls.

'What now?'

'Lunch, the Mishima family.'

'I've read him.'

'Who?'

'Yukio.'

'I do not know who that is.'

/

He'd never seen such a manor. A totally *sui generis* form that was inspired neither by Europe's colonial past nor by any indigenous culture. The architect must have been cut off from the world, perhaps a feral child who'd never been taught to read or write but only to draw inhuman lines. Evan found it very manorish.

They were obviously late because the servant ran up to the car and almost gruffly ushered them towards the door where another servant was standing and they were even more gruffly ushered into the dining room. The family was already seated. There was less and less steam rising from the plates in front of them.

Koito apologized for the lateness (if you can call her cold address to the assembled an apology: *We should have arrived thirteen minutes ago*), bowed, and sat down. Evan managed a sort of bow before he, with a slight loss of balance, collapsed into the chair. All eyes were fixed on him. He felt awkward.

'I must tell you that the achievements of your – what? Great-grandfather? Great-great-grandfather? – have always been a great inspiration for my art, if I may say so, let me tell you that just a few years ago I put on a show, a satire, but not a silly one, I was aiming more at a modern intervention into the membrane of luxuriant greed, whose final act very much reflected the tragically unsuccessful attempted putsch attempt by your – what? Great-grandfather? Great-great-grandfather? – I mean, when I read about it I was struck dumb, what a majestic affair. He wanted to restore the divine nature of the emperor, clothe him anew, so to speak, after the office had lost its shine, eroded by the spiritual vulgarity of the post-war reality, through action, with devotion to the goal, through the complete sovereignty of the human soul, but they all laughed at him, that was in the '70s when people had already been robbed of the transcendent, robbed utterly, they even booed him, you see how the existence among the masses is crass, they booed him and made him commit suicide. Sepukku. That must make you very proud.'

Their faces were far away, barely visible in the dark. They looked at one another, someone cleared his throat.

'Excuse me, Mr Z—, but I fear you are mistaken.' It was a woman's voice, old, raspy and quiet. 'Yukio Mishima was a pseudonym for Kimitake Hiraoka, a family with whom we have no relation. Because I feel no need for tact, I will add another thing. Our great grandfather was the commander of Camp Ichigaya, the very camp that the writer,' this was clearly a curse word, 'occupied in his blasted performance, the one you found so inspiring. Your error was a grave one. I believe it would be better for all of us if we finished our meal in silence.'

Only now did Evan look at his plate, loaded with – what else? – pancakey pancakes, dripping with chocolate.

/

Funny, what a couple of words can do. In a single minute Evan had exchanged eleven lives. He was an offended deity, triumphant father, a wounded lover, an innocent child, a lying woman and an indifferent teenager, he'd been life and death, a lizard, a dog and a hoopoe. She took him to a pet shop, and soon it became clear why. She was testing whether there was any space left in their life, or whether all the cracks were already filled. She knelt down to a golden retriever puppy. The saleswoman smiled at them. This was a common scene for her. She knew what was going on.

'Will you buy it for me?'

'Will you take care of him?'

'But we'll be together.'

'Mojca.'

'What?'

'If you need some body to warm your bed when I'm gone, I'll happily buy it, but, please, stop pretending that I'm not leaving because that's bloody childish. By the time I'm back that thing will be a real dog.'

The little puppy pushed its snout between her legs.

'See,' said Evan, 'you won't even know that I'm gone,' and smiled to himself. The saleswoman hid her indignant face behind the cans of cat food. Mojca got up and stuck her face into his. There was fire in her eyes. 'I'm pregnant,' she whispered harshly and blew him off into the caravan of strangers' heads.

/

'That did not go well.'

'In terms of the schedule,' said Koito, 'it went perfectly well.'

'But I offended them. They almost kicked us out.'

'In terms of the schedule.'

'You don't understand, Koito.'

'It is not necessary.'

'Will they come to the show?'

'It is probable.'

'I shouldn't have lied to them.'

Evan closed his eyes. Darkling darkness.

/

She was hovering high in the air, in the sky, among the clouds, and he was so far down below. Her hair was braided into long, golden plaits. He opened his mouth. Bubbles were streaming out of it and popping right by it, so he couldn't hear what he was saying to her. She laughed. You're not going anywhere, she called out. Because you can't, you can't go now. Now you have to go upwards. He looked down. His belly was inflated. His heels had peeled themselves from the ground and the wind was pushing him towards her. They were way up high and laughing at each other. They pointed at the world. They hugged and pushed each other away. And again. And again. Laughing. Their bellies inflated, they flew about like balls. Every contact sounded like the muted striking of rubber on rubber. A game. Everything was a game. His hands grasped for her. He grabbed hold of a braid and pulled her towards him, pressing her to his balloon body. He whispered in her ear. That was the only way he could hear himself.

'It's beautiful up here, but how are we going to land?'

He couldn't believe what he'd said: beautiful. She stuck out her tongue, which split into scissors. She put a plait between the split of her tongue. She cut it off and used it to tie him to a cloud.

'Don't worry. I'll leave you here and you'll never have to go down. Never.'

With her scissored tongue she pierced her belly and fell. That angered him. He took a deep breath and, as if from a gun barrel, shot bullets of teeth at her.

/

'Evan Z—!'

'What?'

'Don't do that with your lips.'

'What?'

'Blow raspberries.'

'I was dreaming.'

'We're late. You have half an hour of free time under supervision. Where do you want to go?'

'You know what? I don't care.'

The car was standing still. Shadows were flitting by. It had become cloudy, and the light brought rain to mind. A cloud of flies was buzzing above the ground.

'Mao once had all the birds killed off,' said Evan.

'Mao?'

'Mao Zedong, the Chinese dictator.'

'I know nothing about China.'

'He ordered that all sparrows be killed because they got on his nerves.'

'Sparrow?'

'A wretched little bird, like a smaller pigeon.'

'Pigeon?'

'A flying rat.'

'A rat with wings?'

'Yes.'

'It is good that he killed them.'

'You don't like rats?'

'I do not understand the question.'

'Why do you think it's good to kill them?'

'Rats are dangerous to people. Even more so if they can fly.'
'Koito, just take me to the theatre, please.'
'Ok.'

/

The KaBoom-ki theatre is the work of the Japanese architect
Kiyonori Yamaguchi, heir to the luckiest unlucky man in the
world, Tsutomo Yamaguchi, who survived the atomic bomb
in Hiroshima, then fled to Nagasaki just in time to have the
opportunity to survive another one. He died at the age of 93,
long after the end of the war.

The building is in the shape of an atomic cloud, that is,
of the deadliest of mushrooms, although the wicked tongues
of the local architects like to insinuate that the visuals of the
emerald steel and cement of which the building was constructed made it look, from a distance, more like a stalk of
broccoli, an assessment with which Evan agreed, since the first
time he'd seen it he'd come to a similar judgement entirely
independently of those wicked tongues.

At the base of the stalk, or the stem of the mushroom, or
the pillar of smoke, stands a shopping centre hawking antiques
and other useless expensive merchandise that Edo's elite turn
their noses up at as they walk, dressed primly and properly,
into the theatre. During the day everything is closed, but at
the side entrance for stagehands and for other hired hands
there's always someone smoking a cigarette and moving his
lips, staring into the air and dreaming he was someone else,
somewhere else.

That's where Evan and Koito saw Oksana. When she saw
them, she flushed.

'Hi, Oksana.'

'Eeeeevan. Hi. And, sorry, this morning was all…fast and
I don't remember…your name…'

Her voice trailed off, expecting a response, but Koito said
nothing.

'Oksana, this is Koito.'

'Hello.'

Koito gave a slight bow.

'Are there a lot of people here already?' asked Evan.

'I don't know. I just got here.'

'I didn't know you smoked.'

'I don't smoke a lot. But today, sorry, a strange day,' she turned even redder, 'and cloudy. I just…wanted to.'

'Take care of your voice.'

Oksana nodded humbly, as if he were an accusing father.

'You two going up?' she asked.

'Finish your cigarette. We'll go together.'

An extraordinary-looking man approached them. Such people are to be found only in the imagination of addicts trying to kick the habit, in the dreams of bizarre children, and, most frequently, in the streets of Edo. His hairstyle was a horse-hairy mane, painted orange, curled into strands, like a ripped-up mattress, which made his face look a bit like a lion's, which was strange, since his thickly white-powdered face looked nothing like an animal's. His left eyelid, left nostril and the left side of his mouth were sewn together with a thick black thread. His right eye was an almost transparent blue, a wart the size of a hazelnut stared out of his right nostril, looking like a tumour in the making, and the right half of his jaw was unshaven. The half-beard was, of course, bright red. He was wearing a black dinner jacket that must have been salvaged from some ancient cupboard, a moth kingdom, and protruding from his sleeves were what appeared to be stalks of straw. It was impossible to say how old he was. He offered Evan his hand, which Evan shook out of habit, although a chill ran down his spine the instant before contact. The hand was humanly warm, entirely ordinary.

'Junichiro.'

'Evan.'

'Pleased to meet you.'

'The pleasure is mine.'

'I came to see how my text is coming along.'

Evan tilted his head.

'Junichiro, Junichiro, Junichiro…Marukama? Your text? Moody Dick is yours?'

Junichiro smiled a half-smile and nodded. Evan grabbed hold of his hand again and shook it more fervently.

'I am honoured, Mr Marukama. Your play was absolutely explosive for me, as far as inspiration goes.'

'I am pleased.'

'So am I, so am I.'

Evan held the door and gestured for Junichiro to enter. He forgot all about Koito and Oksana, so they had to open the door themselves. As Oksana crossed the threshold the first drops of rain fell, bursting inaudibly.

/

The troupe was on stage, arranged in a tight semicircle and ready for motivational training led by a tiny, energetic lady named Miiko. Evan sent Oksana into their midst before taking a front-row seat with Junichiro and Koito.

Miiko raised a hand and bellowed, 'Everyone here?', and dropped it before anyone could answer. Then they ran, and jumped, and hugged each other, and danced, and imitated animals, and inhaled and exhaled, and put their legs around their necks, and hollered, and forced out laughter, under constraint, which triggered salvos of real laughter, and then sobbed, and teased their throats with vowels, and rolling r's, and ran again and jumped and hugged, and so forth.

Half of Junichiro's face manifested approval. Evan waved a hand.

'This is harmless time-frittering in my opinion, nothing very useful, but, ok, I allow it as long as they then listen to me.'

'Oh, it seems fine to me. Before writing, I too doodle, scribble and spew out words at random so I can calibrate the language. Its varying levels of existence. You have to be in accord with the vibe. Me, language, them, the body. But I understand that you don't value it, because you are again somewhere else, where it's not so simple. What does a director have, where he can carelessly examine, before embarking on a structured vision?'

'Ah, nothing special.' He paused. 'Life.'

'Bravo.'

Their faces turned cold. They stared at the stage, where Miiko was standing on tiptoe and stretching skywards, 'Like a palm, like a cypress, like a ficus!'

/

'Evan Z—, will you get up?'

'Koito, I don't need you now. This is my home.'

He stood up, filled his lungs with air, closed his eyes, counted

three

two

one

and ran on stage, like a man reborn, 'Dear friends, tonight will be, with your help, a complete run-through, a smooth and productive rehearsal! We have a guest, Mr Marukama, the author of the source material for our text and I expect you to treat his eyes, his eye, as if they, as if it, were a whole hall, filled to the rafters. I demand flow and sweat and devotion, I demand absorption! Beyond the edges of these boards, there's nothing. Your whole world lies within them!' He went to his spot, behind the console that had been set up in front of the stage, a yard below. From there he had the director's control over his orchestra of people, lights and sound. 'Today we're going to do the fifth because we've still got a few weak spots.' Some exasperated groans. 'Don't turn up your noses, today is the last time we're doing it without animals, be thankful. Then it's really going to get hellish!' He jumped and shook his body. 'Let's go, mourners, into a circle, please, please, people, you know where you're supposed to be, Oksana, you're in the middle, people, as if for real, legs apart, as much as you can, as if for real, and where's Pasha? Where the hell is Pasha? What? A holiday? He's got a fucking religious holiday? Are you shitting me? What the hell does he believe in? Somebody go call him. I'm serious. Tell him to be here in ten. What? For the fucking love of God, this isn't a playschool, we're making theatre here, let him come on stage and do his ritual magic, it's the right place for it. What? No, wait, are we talking about the same Pasha? My lead actor? That same Pasha that can only be torn away from his pack of whores by a bottle of whisky? One week before opening and he's got a holiday? Aw, fuck it. He's not here? You can't get him? Where's his sponsor? In jail, hahaha. Nothing. Ok, nothing. Kobo, can you come to the console? Yes, the fifth, I'll tell you what to do. What? I will. Yes. Me. Give me the tunic.' He went onto the stage, put on the black gown and spun around. Everyone was in their place. He lifted his chin, looked at Kobo and nodded. The purple strobe light began pounding the stage, the violins filled the air with the sound of anthills. Oksana was lying on the floor with legs spread and her head turned away from the audience. On both sides of her the mourners twisted and turned. 'Kobo, can you tone down the violins? No, leave the setting as it is, just a little less. They're getting on my nerves.' In the front row, Junichiro grimaced. 'What's up with the tornado? What? Costs too much? He told me? I agreed? Just for the rehearsal, or in general? Good, good. Then for now we'll just turn on the ventilators, just for the feel of it.' The wind blew across the stage, lifting the skirts and revealing the tights stretching over the dancers' sinewy legs. 'A double code, opposites, we're celebrating birth and death at the same time, let me see on your faces, twisted with misfortune, a sliver of hope, how you grasp for it, the short-lived, the transitory, because that's all you're left with.' With firm steps he walked around

Oksana. 'Where are my saints? Put the light on them, Kobo, it's ready, just press. Yes.' Enormous paper effigies of a fool and of a clown were raised into the air on ropes, their arms splayed. 'Ok, this is the opening scene. Everything in its place. Now, movement.' His face morphed into one of concentration. Clumps of paper descended from the ceiling, the mourners chased after them, and read random scatterings of poetry, in dirge-diction. Evan stood over Oksana; her head was between his spread legs. 'Sister.' 'Brother.' 'How will we avoid the wrath of words?' 'Whose words?' 'The words that have already been written, into the books, into the bodies, printed on tongues.' 'They threaten us?' 'They're getting closer and closer.' The mourners took a step towards them, their mouths full of lines of verse. 'The old words that have sharpened so many mouths that they have themselves become blunt. What can they do to us?' 'Sister, fear repetition, duplication, fear clones, reflections, mirrors.' 'I do not understand. Why?' 'Basilisks for the soul, you turn to stone when you look at them, avenues of statues, marble, ancient reefs.' Verses, a step closer. 'How should I drive them out?' 'Through birth.' 'But I can't give birth to anything new. Only to our echo. Will he be able to drive them away?' 'We will plug his ears and open his mouth, close his eyes and nose, and his fingers won't be allowed to feel.' 'But jellyfish can also slip in through the mouth.' 'Then he will have to scream constantly.' Verses, even closer. 'Brother, I do not want it.' 'What?' 'The new.' 'Why not?' 'Because it will be old for someone else.' 'For whom?' 'It doesn't matter.' 'For whom?' Oksana cried in the throes of giving birth, the mourners pressed the two of them into a circle. 'For whom?' A scream. 'For whom?' A scream, a step. Evan winced. 'Where are the dog-heads? Yes! At the fourth *for whom*, the full moon is uncovered, the saints bow their heads, the dog-heads begin to howl, up front. Let's go, one more time, *the fourth* for whom?' A scream, a step, the backdrop behind the stage exploded in a blaze of halogen lights, dogs' masks, larger than the bodies and made of styrofoam, turned snout-first into the air above and howled in a chorus, 'The dog moon breath of the world, breath of the world, the dog moon breathes the world, breathes the world…' 'Now the parents come and the light on the saints goes out.' Two shapes ran from the behind the scenes. 'Children! What have you done!' The mourners didn't let them join in. 'Father, mother, aunt, uncle. We are always the same. The incest of words, the mating of poetry. Look what emerges from the sameness, from the eternal sameness, from the cycles, from the seasons, from the orbiting of comets, from galactic spirals and double, duplicate helices!' The mourners lifted the father onto his back, he cried 'Oh, that you may see no more of what evil I have committed, what I have done!' and histrionically hit himself in the face, with his own hand. Evan repeated in a mocking tone, 'Oh, that you may see no more, that you may see no more of what evil I have committed, what I have done,' and pathetically ran a hand over his eyes. Oksana screamed, loudly wheezed, rose to her elbows and stretched her legs into perfect splits. 'Oh, no more, no more, no more, no more, no more,' in a rhythm, and the dog-heads took up the mantra, no more, no more, the mourners tore the sheets of paper into tiny pieces and threw them in the air, and joined in the chanting, no more, no more, Evan, now out of character, jumped and clapped, the whole stage shook with the rhythm of a march, and he pointed a finger at Kobo, held it for a while, then made a fist. The strobe light was extinguished, the music stopped, and the actors froze. 'This will be the end of the tornado, and they'll release the birds. Did they get the birds? Problems? What problems? Ok, we can do this without the birds, but still, they could at least have got a few parrots. Parrots, yes, what? Nobody knows what a parrot is? A parroting parrot? Ha ha. Good. That was good. Now comes the difficult part, now you're all to be perfectly still, like you're made of stone. Yes? I'll allow some sweat to trickle off you, but everything else stays frozen. The wheels of time are jammed. When worlds are born, the universe is still.' He sat down in front of Oksana, his back to the audience, and crossed his legs. 'Kobo, an E chord, cello, hit it. That's all. No, an octave lower, please. That's it.' 'Sister.' 'Brother.' 'I see the head.' 'Is it beautiful?' 'No.' 'Ugly?' 'No.' 'What's it like?' 'I don't know, like a head.' 'Would you like to save it?' 'I don't have a keyboard.' 'Would you like to upload it?' 'I don't have a mouse.' 'Monitor.' 'Resolution.' 'Sister.' 'Brother.' 'We're cooked.' 'Cooked?' 'Probably.' 'Sing me a song.' 'I don't know any. You sing one to me.' 'Which one?' 'A completely new one.' Evan couldn't see what was going on behind his back, but he did hear the coughing. He waited for it to subside. Oksana raised her voice into a melody. 'Sister.' A melody. 'Sister.' A melody. 'Sister, our child will be a pop-art freak, like a can of soup.' The melody stopped. 'Like Marilyn?' 'It's a boy.' 'How do you know?' 'Because he won't be allowed to give birth.' 'Maybe he will be a black square on a black background.' 'Rothko?' 'I don't know.' 'Did you know the CIA actively propagated expressionism, constructivism and the radical avant-garde, and deliberately smeared social realism?' 'Really? Why?' 'Fear.' 'Of?' 'Change.' 'Nothing changes.' 'Tell that to the CIA.' The coughing suddenly sounded rather forced, like it had lost its primary function of throat-clearing and took on an independent purpose as an instrument of disturbance. Evan wrinkled his nose. 'Sister.' 'Brother.' 'I expect you to give birth.' 'I don't want to.' 'You have to.' 'I'm afraid.' 'Of what?' 'Change.' 'Nothing changes.' 'Tell that to my skin.' 'Surface.' 'And inside?' 'The world.' The coughing was replaced by an indistinct murmuring. 'Kobo, now in G sharp. Thank you. Now if the audience could, please, be a little…' The murmuring lost its r's and was now just a mumming. Evan shrugged. 'Ok. In G, the parents.' 'Father, mother, aunt, uncle. Now it's Pasha's monologue, I won't do the whole thing, I'll show you guys some mercy, everything is peaceful, the G sharp is sustained, the monologue is, let's say, a few minutes, and at the end there's, what is it again? Right…' he hugged the parents, who were all standing by Oksana's side, '…and that's why we're here, in the world, to keep right on rolling down, since the path leads only into the depths, and we roll, and on the second we roll the riff on "Whole Lotta Love" once, ok, again, second roll and we roll,' ta-na na-na-na, 'down the hill, full of bumps and bruises, and we never reach the ground, that view is saved for our children, who will also roll,' he nods, ta-na na-na-na, 'and the view is saved for their children, and they roll,' ta-na na-na-na, 'into eternity, downhill, always, eternally, because, as we all know, the earth is round.' By now he could clearly hear curses coming from the audience. Evan disregarded them and motioned to Kobo, 'Ok, now play the whole song, good, when Plant revs up that chainsaw voice, gradually get off the stage. The platform will rise, with Oksana, and the rocks will roll, what about the rocks? Aha, good, they're there. Painted yet? No. All right. And the spotlight, again, back on the saint. The platform will reach the top, right when the solo starts. Yes, I've had the technician fiddle with it a bit, now it's better… Ok, what about the rocks? Like that. Good, Kobo, let me come there, no more Pasha until the end of the scene, no? Ok.' He walked proudly to the console and saw Junichiro's threatening face glaring at him. 'And birth.' The violin bow struck the strings. Oksana added her voice to Plant's squeals and they wailed together. The enormous rocks of foam rolled from both sides and disappeared behind the curtains at the edges. A camera descended from the ceiling on a steel wire, peeked between Oksana's legs and projected onto the surface of the mass of white fabric behind her. Screams, shrieking, wailing strings. Evan pressed a button. A transparent screen with a human heart sketched on it descended in front of the stage. If you looked through it, you could see an opening in the fabric behind Oksana spreading in rhythmic, ever quicker, throbs. A dark crevice. Nothing in it. Evan grinned. As the solo reached a peak, an uninterrupted, animalistic scream came cascading out of Oksana's throat. The whiteness of the fabric was banished to the edges, the outline of a black hole. A stream of red sand came surging from the top of the platform on which Oksana was lying. The canvas rose, the camera rose, the lights went out and all that remained was a spotlight beam aimed straight at Oksana, the guitar solo was cut off, her screaming died out and the air was disturbed by a quiet, drawn out beating of the heart, the pecking of birds and the sounds of sand seeping into a crimson pile on the floor. '… insulting to every aspect of our culture.' Evan turned around. Junichiro's hands were trembling as he spoke with Koito. She was peacefully staring ahead, with her arms folded in front of her. 'What?' The platform had begun to descend. Junichiro turned to Evan and placed his hands on the edge of the chair to get up when the fanfare rang out. Oksana sat up and was waiting for the platform to join the floor. Then she got up, knelt down, buried her hands in the sand, raised them and spread her fingers so that the sand slipped through. 'There's nothing. Praised be, praised be. I was so afraid. But there's nothing that could be. It can't go on like this, it dispersed into the cloud of a sunrise. It was a lie, and a lie does not sprout. Praised be, praised be. Toto was right when he first got a whiff of the truth.' Barefoot, she stepped onto the pile and stretched her hands high in the air. 'Love can't lie and a mere word doesn't become flesh.' The mourners changed into monks' tunics and, with rosaries in their hands, went to the edges of the stage and hummed the opening bars of the *New World Symphony*. 'A liar will escape, another liar will hang. And both will sprout wings. And beaks. Their home will be the heavens, and they will not be allowed to land. Never again. May it never be repeated. I ask for just this one thing, from the heights, just one thing, may it never, never, be repeated. May everyone live anew, and not again. Red wings. Never again ground.' The light fell. Darkness. Evan clapped. Alone.

/

'...no sense, no heart, nothing human, nothing kindly, nothing warm, and above all no story...'

'But!'

'...entire generations of our artists are rolling over in their graves, regretting having died before they could prevent such a mess...'

'But!'

'...such an insult to the universals, the foundations of our culture, you think I'm stupid, that I don't understand the criticism of reproduction, extraction of the essence, the carving out of the superfluous and seeking the essential, you vulgar Westerner...'

'But!'

'...what you've done to my text? You've misread it on purpose, you miscreant, I wanted to show that from the atom of a family you can create, ultimately, something beautiful, and you abused that to serve your perverse fantasies, filled up a relationship with utter buffoonery, you've stolen my dialogue just to mock...'

'That wasn't the whole thing. You don't even know how it ends!'

'Well, how does it end?'

Evan was indignantly silent. Junichiro was standing close to him, too close, staring at him with clenched fists at his sides.

'How does it end?' he yelled.

'She plans a military putsch in the name of love, he makes a mockery out of it and drives her to suicide.'

Koito reacted immediately, but she was too late. Junichiro's fist was headed straight for Evan's jaw, making tiny vibrations in the air as it travelled through space; Evan's eyes managed to perceive this movement just before he was blinded by pain, by a sudden, all-consuming, pure pain that was simple in its nature, unambiguous, clear, understandable to all living things, and as his consciousness collapsed into the forceful contact foreign knuckles made with his skin-covered bones, there was but a single note, a single canvas, jittery cheeks, a wobbling chin, a head that snapped back, dragging Evan's body behind it as his soles quietly took leave of the floor, thus propelling his entire body into a horizontal levitation, a magic trick of sorts, with a solitary thought residing in the pain, a singularly selfish thought, *ow, ow, ow my*

ABRAHAM!

✦ ✦

You were born in the land of the unburied. Think about that. That's probably why this land has never forgiven anyone for anything. They burned down the trees on that land, not for the first time, not for the last. The land is hard. In some places it's fertile, in others barren. Surrounded by hills. Beyond the hills, mountains. Beyond the mountains, nothing. The plough blades cut long, black furrows into the land. Sometimes it swallows them up.

The ruins of transmission towers are scattered all about. Defeated by rust. Now they're crumbling under the claws of birds and humming in the moonlight with a gentle *finish me off*. Nobody has removed them. They're not bothering anyone. On sunny days the old look on them with nostalgic eyes. Nostalgia doesn't reach the towers.

Once upon a time men of words found a name for this land. The name has been lost through the years. Now they just say – Land. Nobody mistakes Land for some other place.

Between the hills and Land, long rows of houses form villages. Hard people live in the villages. It is not the land that has made them hard – they did it to themselves. Over long years of trials and turbulence. On the wings of misfortune and danger. Under fire. Under rain. But above all, under one another. The skin petrifies when coarse eyes are fixed on it. The eyes fare no better.

On this land, in a village whose name you know, stands a big house full of disappointments. The disappointments have filled up so much space that everyone feels cramped, though it really is a large house. The largest in the village. The envy of the other villagers makes it slightly larger.

A walnut tree rises in front of the house. It's been here forever. Hidden near its crown there is a little tree house, invisible to the eye, even when the tree sheds its leaves. Kras and his son Mitja built it one summer, many years ago, when Mitja was just a boy. They never finished it. The tree house has only half a roof and it's missing a wall. Mitja, for the first time in his life, underestimated his father's attentiveness. Things did not turn out well.

Autumn slyly squats in the hills. In its bear claws it holds brushes of yellow, red and brown. Last night, as the Wolfs were frolicking about in the Soča valley, it crept down and callously plucked off a few leaves, doodled on them and crumpled them and threw them to the ground.

/

Kras is standing on leaves, looking up. Moisture has caused the beams to rot. He's not sure whether it's safe. The footholds that the two of them nailed into the trunk have wriggled out. He grabs hold of the first one and pulls it away effortlessly. How to get up there? He looks around to see if anyone happens to be watching. A grown man climbing a tree looks pretty funny. There's no one. The second hold seems a little firmer, but it's just out of his reach. He'll have to jump for it. The bark scratches against his belly. He pulls himself upwards. Quickly. A passing cyclist thinks he's just seen a pair of legs up in the air, but a follow-up look yields nothing.

'Hey there, brother Wolf.'

He's so surprised that he almost loses his grip. The branch shakes perilously as he tries to catch his balance.

'How did you get up here?'

Po is ensconced in the corner and sketching in chalk on drawing paper.

'I climbed.'

'What are you doing?'

Kras sits at the edge of the wooden floor and turns towards her. Po looks at him, as if to say, *isn't it obvious?*

'I'm drawing.'

'What are you drawing?'

'I don't know yet.'

Kras lifts his knees and edges closer to her. There's a plane in the drawing. The plane is at the top edge. In the bottom left corner there's a tiny figure with a bowed head.

'It's nice.'

'It's not done.'

'Hmm.'

Now he takes a closer look at the inside. A makeshift carpentry bench. An old dresser. A small box of nails. On the floor, the head of a hammer.

'What's in the drawers?'

'I don't know.'

'You didn't look in?'

'They're locked.'

He inches closer to her, on his knees. The boards creak.

'Po, how about if you go down? I don't think these boards will hold both of us.'

'I was here first. Besides, I can fly.'

'Hmm.'

He grabs the handle and tugs. The drawer doesn't budge. Harder. Nothing.

'Can you pass me the hammer?'

'That's not a hammer.'

'The head of the hammer.'

Po does not avert her gaze from her picture, she just reaches out a hand, picks up the head and passes it to him. Kras takes it and wedges it into a crack in the dresser. Then he pries. The wood splits.

'Brother Wolf, is it really true you don't have any friends?'

'Who told you that?'

'Nobody.'

'Hmm.'

Again he yanks the handle, and ends up with the front of a drawer in his hand. A dark hole gapes at him.

'Well?'

'What.'

'You really don't have any?'

'I used to.'

'Hmm.'

Kras reaches inside and carefully taps around. For a second it looks like he's got his hand stuck in a trap.

'Why don't you have them any more?'

'Because we've all gone our separate ways.'

'Why?'

'Because that's how things turned out.'

His fingers can feel a leather cover. He grabs it and pulls out a black notebook. It's mouldy around the edges. He turns it over in his hands, studies it. The same feeling again. A trap.

'Isn't Edgar your friend?'

'That's different.'

'Why?'

'He's family.'

He hears Raven calling.

'Po! Breakfast!'

Po places a finger over her lips. Kras smiles, despite himself, and opens the notebook.

/

Alan sometimes thinks that all that's missing in his life is pornography. He still has no intention of marrying, not even of courting someone, not even of attempting some trickery that would involve lying to and then, under the force of shame, silencing a girl, since such things tend to turn out bad. Those three porn mags his father gave him for his fifteenth birthday (he'd had to swear to tell nobody where he'd got them – for years, Raven had kept them hidden in the attic under a pile of coats that were irrevocably out of fashion), those he already knew by heart. All the pictures, all the stories. They no longer turn him on, not in the least. All he has to do to see the pictures is close his eyes. And they no longer do anything for him. They've lost their unseemly scent.

He doesn't have the slightest idea how someone in this day and age would go about securing a fresh supply. The harsh morality laws that were brought in strictly forbid pornography and now people clearly prefer to resign themselves to their wives' bodies than to smuggle in little depictions of copulations that, incidentally, could cost them a finger. It's not even talked about, not even among the young. Of course, they confide their sexual reveries to each other, but to have them put down on paper? What a strange idea. He had never shown his magazines to anyone. And even if they were no longer effective in terms of desire, they still served to fill him with adrenaline. Dangerous magazines. He was a little fearful of them. What if someone found them?

When Grace and Olive came to spend their holidays under his window, in the extension that had been built for Edgar, his body trembled with imagination. Women in love. Not on paper, in the flesh. He could slip out of the window onto the roof, and the previous weekend, when his half-sister and her wife were away at the seaside he'd hammered a few railroad spikes into the shingles so that he could hold on to them and, safely, head facing down, peek right into their bedroom window. Till now he'd not been lucky. They slept without a light, got up early to spend their sport-filled days far from the homestead, and they would walk around the rooms fully clothed, and on top of that, someone – Mum, Po, Dad, Mila – was always bothering him with their problems, so he couldn't constantly lie in wait. He suspected that they showered together, but their bathroom was windowless.

The closest he'd come to anything carnal was a gentle kiss on the lips that Grace had stolen from Olive before they'd gone cycling one morning. This kiss, in all its innocence, definitely anchored his conviction that he simply had to see them when they were at their filthiest.

And so he's lying on his belly, head full of blood, and snooping. Things look very promising. Yesterday they got drunk, and after all the mess that occurred they probably wouldn't be heading directly for the hills. They're still sleeping, although the morning is no longer young. A leg is peeking out from under the covers, but the fact that he can't tell whether it's Grace's or Olive's keeps his excitement in check; a half-sister's leg isn't quite all that. The panties lying on the floor are more enticing, even if it's equally possible that they are related to him. But it doesn't matter who wears them. What matters is that someone has taken them off.

/

'Ah, come on, I don't believe a word of it.'

Mila is telling him what he missed yesterday and laughing, a little at the memory, a little at his bulging eyes. Borut is lying in a hospital bed, half-covered in one of those arse-exposing gowns they stick you in, and gravely shaking his head, though Mila's smile is most fetching indeed.

'It's all true! Why do you think I'm here? Sorry if it sounds a bit harsh, but if Edgar wasn't lying in the next room I don't know whether I'd be coming to tell you all that we have to be ashamed of.'

'Really?'

'I swear. Basically everything was awful yesterday, but the more I think about it, the funnier it gets.'

'The Wolfs.'

'Family crumbles, because it is fuller without than within,' cites Mila.

'Starves itself right to the edge, then turns around,'

continues Borut.

'Steals its own shadow, to wear as a gown,' Mila, again.

'A wheeze, a sneeze,' Borut.

'And down, down, down,' they finish together, laughing.

'Whoa,' says Mila, 'we know our poets.'

'Only the ones who speak to us.'

Mila turns serious. As she nods, Borut looks out of the window.

'What is it with you, I mean, I know you're all right now, but did they tell you what it was?'

'Epilepsy,' says Borut.

'Oh Jesus.'

'I know I have it, but the seizures are pretty infrequent and mild, usually. Usually I don't even fall down.'

'I didn't know. I mean, I wouldn't have offered if I did.'

'Don't worry, it's not your fault. I should have known better.'

'Why didn't you say no?'

Borut smiles.

'Because…'

The door opens and in peeks Katarina's head.

'Mila, let's go.'

'What do you mean, *let's go*? What about Edgar?'

'They say she stabbed him right through to the bone, so it is going to hurt for a while, but otherwise it's really just a scratch. A few stitches.'

'Yeah, but, Mum, Voranc is…sick.'

'Oh dear. Lies after lies, this family. I've never really understood Alenka, but something like that…'

'What?'

'Yeah, well, nothing. Nothing. I'll tell you in the car.'

Mila squeezes Borut's hand.

'When are they going to let you go?'

'What?'

'I mean, from the hospital.'

'Oh, that. Observation tonight, check-up at noon tomorrow. Then I'll see.'
'Can I call you?'
Borut winces.
'Oh, sorry, I forgot.'
'Take care.'

/

Walnut's voice is coloured blue. Only the profoundly penitent can hear it. Those who used to be violent and who, finally, have become ashamed. There's nothing to blame them for any more. Now they live in order to observe how everything grows. Everything grows.
'Old Raven. It is now rare for you to tread upon my roots.'
'I'm sorry, Walnut. You know they frighten me.'
'The bloodied soil?'
'...'
'Old Raven... Is it not that you have become fearful of the human?'
'I'm only afraid that it'll come back.'
'Trees see all and never forget. Do not worry. I am only trying to ground you a bit. Put your ear to the ground and you will hear a crying more terrible than any other under the sun.'
'Not here.'
'The voice of the trees does not carry across water. The woods here are tranquil. Calm your heart. Don't be afraid. We have had our fill of blood. We will only drink rain now. Strange rain.'
'Is my daughter here?'
'Your son. Your daughter.'
'My son?'
'You have sons. More than one. One is hiding in my crown, another on the roof. I cannot see the third.'
'On the roof?'
'Climb up and you shall see. On the ground, eyes are blind.'

'Walnut, sometimes I do not understand you.'

'You will never understand me. You are not a tree. Climb.'

'I would need all my fingers to do that.'

'Grab hold of my branch, and I will raise you into the air.'

Little Po is focused on her drawing, pressing the tip of her tongue between her lips; the tips of her fingers are black. Kras's face has lost its colour, his eyes are sunken, and sweat is dripping from his forehead. They do not notice him. He can watch them, a warm feeling of serenity filling his lungs. Without him, an empty crown. Deaf air. A space full of blind spots, a kingdom of flowers and crickets. But because of him – people, universes full of thoughts. And to want wasn't a mistake, even though he knew what they would be born into. That he wanted, still. Everything is forgotten, but not quite so soon. And not for everybody.

/

A child's hand. Thursday, 21 October 2021. This date means nothing to Kras, but it should, if only he'd thought a little more. *I hate I hate I hate.* Clumsy printed letters. The shaky and unsteady pen strokes don't link up. Not even one line is quite straight. *I hate I hate I hate.* The writing gets larger with each word. The letters grow trenchant, compact, confident. *I hate I hate I hate.* The path of someone who is releasing himself into his skin, word by word. *I hate I hate I hate.* And so on, for ten pages. Three thousand six hundred fifty two times *I hate.* The last *hate* looks poised, written ruler-straight and with perfectly distributed ink, devoid of any tiny dots of spillage that might betray a fleeting moment of hesitation or a split second of doubt. Thus conviction grows, through practice, into pure expression. From emotions into character.

Kras is getting angry. The scraping of chalk over the drawing paper, the whooshing and rustling of leaves in the wind, the whistling of the neighbour's tea kettle. A tractor sputters in the distance. The waves of electricity are buzzing like a hornet's nest. Somebody's flushing a toilet, the bowl slurps. The bell towers have started to toll noon, rifle bursts from the army barracks on their exercises cut the air. There's no peace, anywhere.

When you're here – written on a new page – *I am lame. A non-being, a parasite. A miserable thread of a bad pattern. When you're here, I am less than I. I am nothing like I. You are speaking to a shell. Because you think that counts. That's the only thing that keeps me calm. Because you think it counts. That violence touches someone. That you can seize someone. That you can hold him. Nothing counts. A knot is a migraine. That piece of brain that swells. It can't be cut out. And shame is cheap, but when you start feeling sorry for people…then you might as well hate.*

Right, Wolf?

Then, over two pages.

I AM NOT AND NEVER WILL BE WOLF.

Kras snaps the notebook shut. Po flinches. Raven, who till then had been standing on a branch and craning his neck to observe them, pulls himself up to the floor of the little house. The branch sags a bit. Something moans in the depths of the wood. Po smiles. Kras's and Raven's eyes meet. A moment of strange energy passes. The heated steel in Kras's pupils sizzles under the deluge of Raven's lenient expression. Although the old man has no right to be lenient, it now comes as solace. Kras's lips tremble. He no longer has the strength to wage a two-front war. One up here, one down there. He has to give in somewhere. He breaks his oath, and the heavens do not break in two.

'Po will be an artist,' he says.

'If they'll still allow people to be artists,' replies Raven. The faces converge in a careful smile. Later, when Po tells them what happened nobody believes her, only Edgar will, with a hand on his hip, feel a pinch of happiness and mutter, 'At least there's that.'

/

Janez, who is Bernard's chauffeur, has been up all night. He was napping in the car the previous evening when all of the sudden the door opened and he had to race to the hospital – a broken nose, a stabbed side, a gouged forearm, a lost consciousness and a pulled head of hair. Then he had to clean the blood from the car, go back to the Soča River, then go back again, wait until dawn, and now, after the family council, drive Olga's sisters home, along with Olga and Bernard to keep an eye on them. The tiredness was now claiming its toll. At the intersection he'd strayed from the path, not paid attention to the road, and by the time they'd figured out that they were lost he no longer knew how to get back. Bernard was swearing at him but Janez, who was used to getting sworn at, shrugged and issued a closed-mouthed yawn. His nostrils flared, his eyes filled with tears, making him see even less. He'd have to stop. They were in the hills. On the winding slope that was wide enough for just one car, every hundred yards there's a passing place where cars can veer off to avoid a crash. He stops here. There are five candles at the edge of the precipice. The road was not quite wide enough for someone.

'Fuck, Janez, how are you gonna turn around here?'

'Mr Wolf, we will manage. Just get out of the car in case something happens…'

'If *what* happens?' shouts Bernard. His nose is bundled up in gauze, his dark eyes are bloodshot.

'Sir, I'm asking you, I'll manage, but please get out.'

The ladies have fallen asleep. Bernard turns around.

'Mother!'

Nothing.

With his good hand he grabs her knee. He is weak. Nothing.

'Janez, you do it.'

'Oh, sir, I would prefer not to.'

'Mother!'

Olga sits in the middle, a sister's head resting against each shoulder. Their palms are pressed together.

'Mother!'

Nothing. His voice, already so thin and quiet, is even more taxingly nasal under the bandages. He exhales nervously and presses the middle of the steering wheel. Nothing.

'Fuck, Janez, what's wrong with this car?'

'I know – you have to press hard. Shall I do it?'

'Honk.'

The horn jolts them upright. Olga's eyes are blood-red, her sisters press themselves up against her, terrified.

'Olga,' 'Olga,' 'what was,' 'that?'

'Bernard, are we already there?' Olga looks out of the window. 'This isn't Grča. Where are we?'

'We took a wrong turn. We have to get out of the car so Janez can turn around,' says Bernard.

'Lord have mercy, Janez, there's only one road up here. Where did you find another one?'

Bernard looks at Janez, whose eyes are closed.

'Janez?'

He shakes him.

'Ah…mmh, what? Sir, I will turn around, just get out of the car, please, if you will, please.'

'You weren't by any chance sleeping, were you?'

'No, no, no, sir, not at all, I was just trying to figure out what to do… It's nothing, we'll turn around, there's no other way.'

'Will you be able to turn here?'

'Master Janez can do anything, don't you worry.'

Bernard looks back.

'Let's get out.'

They get out. The sand is moist. Rain has fallen overnight. The clouds have still not dispersed, the forest smells acridly of moss. Ferns everywhere. Big leaves on enormous stems block the view. Bears, lynx, rabid foxes…Bernard shudders. The ground isn't used to human feet. Though some human body must have brought the memorial candles here. They've already burned themselves out, the plastic is blackened from the soot, the tops are rusty brown. He inches to the edge of the road. 'Careful,' Olga calls out, and looks over. A cliff. Deep in the valley below, again there's the edge of a forest. Not a house in sight. You can get lost even in a tiny patch of woods.

Janez reverses an inch, turns the wheel, moves forwards an inch. Slowly. The sound of the engine has woken the trees, which are yawning in the wind.

'Mother, do you see where revenge leads you? Right into the sticks.'

'Spare me the accusations, Bernard. Tears alone didn't help me one bit.'

Olga is proud of herself.

'And what have you achieved?'

'If nothing else, peace of mind.'

'Wolf is going to throw you out of the house.'

'Ha! That hypocrite! And when he takes his pound of flesh, everything is perfectly fine.'

Backwards, a turn of the wheel, forwards.

'I don't know what you're talking about. If you're thinking about those Roman reforms or something, he had nothing to do with them.'

'How do you think Bojan ended up without fingers?'

'What do you mean, *ended up without*? It was the circular saw, when that unfortunate roof…'

Backwards, forwards. He's almost made it.

'Don't be naive, Bernard, better people than you have suffered because they're naive.'

'Yes, but what…'

The sand sags under the weight of the tyres and gives way. The candles fall into the depths. All four yell and Bernard races to the driver's door. He knocks on the window. Janez doesn't answer. The front right tyre is in the air, the car is tilted. He bashes. Nothing. He grabs the handles, pulls, and the door opens. The car sinks.

'Janez! Fuck!'

His withered hand is useless. With his good one, he grabs Janez by the collar and shakes him. Janez jolts upright, grabs the wheel, 'Don't you worry, sir...', and steps on the accelerator. One wheel spins into emptiness, the second churns up sand, there's a call of 'Janez!' and the front of the car is well over the edge. Bernard almost falls, tries to regain his balance, and keeps on trying to grab hold of Janez, who is now staring wide-eyed into the abyss and frantically attempting to undo his seatbelt. Olga grabs Bernard, 'Are you crazy?', and yanks him towards her. 'Telephone!' he cries when the car silently tips into the abyss. The silence lasts an eternity. A flock of crows has come to see what's going on. A hazelnut stalls in the squirrel's claws. Thousands of ants remain unconcerned. Flies rub their little legs and a single woodpecker releases his anger over the cuckoo's egg. The owl's hooting is, in the end, unnecessary.

/

'*Guten Morgen.*'

Today this language is foreign to this land, although once it had thickly spread itself here and then it tried many a time to coat it, with the prowess of a conqueror.

The romance didn't last long, but the mouths were left salivating for a long time still. Lust is a very genuine emotion.

To Alan's ear, *Guten Morgen* sounds like a woodsman talking. *Ghud'n môhg'n.* The window is slightly open.

'Good morning.'

'Can you toss a couple of antacids into some water for me, please?'

'I was just about to ask you the same thing.'

Laughter.

'My head.'

Ko-pf.

'Mine's no better.'

'Well, who's going to go?'

'You.'

'No, you.'

'I'll tickle you.'

'Pretty please.'

They're naked, that's now clear. Alan's eyes are going to fall out from all that gawking, from trying to see something in the half-dark. Olive is on her back, but Grace is hidden under a sheet.

'Let's stay in bed today.'

'That sounds good. Let's avoid all these nutters.'

'Grace, I can't believe…'

'I told you to prepare yourself.'

'But still…'

'But nothing. That's the way it is.'

Alan can't understand them, so he dreams up obscenity-rich conversation, dirty talk. *Hoy-tuh, mensh-un, tsu-ryk, vee es ist.* It's all very erotic. He has to adjust his position as he lies there.

'Do we really have to stay another week?'

'No. We can leave tomorrow, if you want.'

'I want.'

'Good. I'll make it happen. But you have to…'

'Water.'

Wass—. Laughter.

Olive lets out a half-dramatic sigh and gets up. Alan can't see her head, but he gets a look at her breasts, which, though large, are a little droopy and one of the nipples is surprisingly shiny (there's a ring hanging from it). Her wrinkled belly splashes in all directions, not exactly attractive. Underneath there's a black thicket of the type he never saw in those magazines, and her legs look like they're wrapped in loose cellophane, and it's all less delicious than it had been in his head. He grimaces. He doesn't know whether he's disappointed by reality, or whether he's more disturbed by the false illusions that he'd harboured. Are women, in fact, ugly? Or is Olive just too old? Maybe he should surprise Mila when she's in the shower. Nothing too forceful, he just has to make sure that he didn't in fact fall in love with paper. Damn, if he hadn't been holding on to the big nail he would pinch his thigh. Is that why pornography is prohibited? Because it spoils the flesh?

Grace yawns, stretches and looks straight into Alan's grimacing, blood-flushed, gawking, pimply face.

'Alan!' she shouts.

Alan gets a shock, slackens his grip and almost falls, but manages to latch on to the gutter with both hands and get up, legs atremble. He's been caught, and he grabs his thigh so hard he'll have a bruise for a whole week.

/

'No, I don't understand, Edgar, why would someone think up something like that?'

Katarina is driving Kras's jeep. At the checkpoints they recognize her already from afar and, heads bowed, wave her through, sometimes even with a salute. Edgar's in the front, awkwardly resting his weight on his uninjured side. Mila is sitting in the back and looking out of the window. White façades, endless white façades among the thin rows of the orderly forest, and then shadow-rich fields. Mila does not feel outraged. Maybe someday she will, when she forgets what they taught her. Then she'll say it's already too late, or that it's still too early. Any way you look at it, she'll be right.

'Katarina, look, people are a strange mix. If we can't even know ourselves, how are we supposed to know anyone else? You can live for a hundred years, but you'll probably only get to know the hearts of two, three, people, and if you really put your mind to it, you might stop being at odds with your own heart, that's all you can hope for.'

'Yeah, I know what you're saying, but you always generalize, and it's not always like that when it comes to people.

You don't have to talk about everything and everybody only so you can say that some things are abnormal and just shouldn't be done.'

'All right then. Let's take Alenka. The way I see it, it's all very simple. What's the fundamental characteristic of the disease Voranc allegedly has?'

Edgar likes to adopt a didactic tone and use questions to steer people towards what he's thinking, which is an exquisite tactic because it deludes them into thinking they arrived at that thought all on their own. Mila had seen through him years ago, back when he wanted to plant a more favourable image of Mitja in her head.

He failed.

'That it kills you in the end.'

'Yes. And?'

'That it's contagious.'

'And what follows from that? What does it mean for other people?'

'Well, that they do not want to become infected.'

'And what do they do so they won't be?'

'They avoid you.'

'Exactly.'

'What?'

'Alenka's just a loner. Nobody paid much attention to her until she adopted Voranc. Then she was suddenly overwhelmed with invitations to kids' birthday parties, to the zoo, the movies… She very elegantly shed you, to put it somewhat bluntly.'

Katarina purses her lips. It really had become more difficult – when you thought about everything that could go wrong – to see Voranc in the company of other children.

'Poor child. Now I'm going to drag her everywhere on purpose!'

Edgar's laugh cedes to pain.

'But didn't you two have something going on?' says Mila icily.

'Mila!' exclaims Katarina.

Edgar feigns ignorance.

'What?'

'Berdo once said he caught you two…'

'Mila! What are you thinking?'

'Hold on, Mum, I'm sorry, but Grandma has just stabbed Edgar with a shard of glass she's dipped in what she thought was HIV-positive blood, and carried out a whole raid on Grandpa's family with those freaks, and you two are going on about Alenka and her idiocy, I mean, who cares about Alenka now?'

'Mila,' says Edgar, wincing as he turns to look at her, 'people in such situations always talk about the things that are least difficult. Olga has never concealed her grudge, and if this is going to calm her down, then at least there's that. It's time to move on. Besides, we all understand Olga. And, yes, I did kiss Alenka one time. This is going to sound bad, but I felt sorry for her.'

'Edgar, just one thing, I mean sorry, but isn't she your sister?'

'To tell you the truth, I don't really know.'

They are approaching a checkpoint. Three soldiers stand there, legs apart. Katarina is crying.

/

Raven stretches out on his back and beholds the sky.

'The only roof that covers everything.'

Kras bookmarks the notebook with his fingers. He doesn't want to open it, to read on. A mean, cowardly trick. Mitja didn't dare say it to his face, so he confided it to his diary, like some little old lady. Now he is expecting it to have the same effect. It won't. If he'd faced things like a man, if he'd demanded respect in that way, perhaps he would have got it. Courage is a virtue. He, however, set up an ambush. Tail between his legs and twelve hundred miles away, complaining long-distance. To avoid the cries and the moaning sobs. Just words, no face. Mitja has proved himself a continuous disappointment to Kras. Not a Wolf, a mouse! That's what he used to call him: Mouse. Though he'd always added: but you have to become a Wolf. In a world like this mice are squashed under boots. Five years old and wearing Katarina's pumps, in make-up. He put that masquerade out of his head, almost literally. Nothing but tears. He couldn't go to sleep in the dark, always had to have the light on. Daddy, Daddy, malice eater! And that at the age of seven. A timid, spoilt mouse. How quietly he spoke. He didn't eat anything, he was totally picky, no meat, no potatoes, just sweets. An emaciated little stick. Couldn't even do two chin-ups. No order, no discipline, no strength. Katarina spoilt him. Wiped his arse and tidied his room for him. If it weren't for her, everything would have been different. But Kras wasn't at home. There were always elections, then there was war. And then, when he was ten, they sent him home from school, and Kras had to go to a parent-teacher meeting, because Mitja kept pinching his classmates' arses and kept trying to snuggle up with them. An uncouth beast, and he had no idea where he got that from. Right before the election. The headmaster grinned at him and Kras had to grin politely back at him. He would have smacked that smile off his face, if he could. The first time they won the elections, Kras and Mitja had tried to build the little house. The kid had no talent for tools. The hammer swayed in his hands like a pear in the wind. He didn't manage to hammer in a single nail. But back then Kras was in good spirits because of the victory. So he didn't scold or humiliate him. He showed him, and again, and again – even encouraged him a few times. But all in all it didn't help one bit. The first time he hit his finger, he went off crying to Katarina and never touched the hammer again. He brought him a board, every now and then, but otherwise he just stared. Kras had to do everything himself and at the same time stave off his father and his constant offers of advice. Maybe he will come back as a Wolf. If he comes back. If. That stupid little word gets stuck in his throat. He coughs it away.

Raven spreads his arms, like wings.

'I do not want to go down,' he says.

Kras looks at him.

'Never again,' he adds.

'You'll have to,' says Kras.

'I know. Unfortunately.' He strokes his beard with a hand that's short one index and one middle finger. 'But did you see the old girl, see how much fire she still has in her? That she's still capable of something like that, after all these years. You know, son, it's kind of flattering.'

Kras nudges him in the ribs with his shoe and nods at Po. Everyone knows what a blabbermouth she is. Raven stretches out, grabs her and tickles her. Po laughs.

'You, my little dumpling, need some breakfast.'

'I'm not hungry.'

'Mummy will be mad,' he says.

'Mummy's never mad,' she replies.

'Something like that, eh?'

'But I am.'

'Who are you mad at?' Raven asks her.

'At those annoying aunts and at Aunt Crabby.'

Kras laughs out loud. Raven looks at him and shrugs an apology.

'Seriously, sweetie, an empty sack doesn't stand upright, you know how it is,' he says.

'But I haven't finished drawing yet.'

'Do you always draw up here?' asks Kras.

'Uh-huh.' Po nods and makes another line. The wobbly figure under a plane gets a dog's face. Or a wolf's snout.

'At least someone got something out of that ordeal,' says Kras.

'Alan and Mila come up here to visit now and then.'

Kras narrows his eyes.

'Really? What do they do?' he asks. Raven turns on his side, looks at Po and jerks his head at her.

'I don't know,' says Po.

Kras looks at his father, who's once again stretched out on his back.

'But they have the keys,' says Po and opens the hatch under the plane.

'Keys to the drawers? They read this?' Kras wags the notebook threateningly.

'One is Mitja's, one is Mila's, and one is Alan's. Grandpa Raven, when will I get one?' asks Po. Raven is getting up slowly, holding his back and feigning pain. Kras glares at him. He takes the head of the hammer in his hand and in one move pries off the other drawer. He feels around inside, but doesn't find anything. Dust sticks to his fingers. When he rubs them together, an orange dust emerges. He puts his fingers up to his nose. Inhales.

'When you learn to be quiet,' says Raven. 'Until then you don't need one anyway.'

Kras doesn't need the hammer's head for the third drawer. He tears it open by hand. The wood snarls wetly before giving way. Raven descends from the floor of the house onto a branch and pulls himself a little higher, out of pure instinct. He has a pretty good idea of what his son's going to find there.

'Po.'

Kras's voice could whet a knife.

'Go down. This instant.'

/

The road is long and leads nowhere. Bernard has never been farther away from his world. And yet it all seems vaguely familiar. Things that grow without encouragement. Stout branches that selfishly force their way towards the sun, while the muddy undergrowth withers in the shadows, seeing little, seeing less and less, and reeking of abandonment. Dissolving into the shapeless backdrop of the scenery on which the trunks stage their insignificant struggles. Homo humus. His shoes are muddied, soaked through. They squeak as he walks. The wind plucks the dead leaves like kids plucking at daddy longlegs. Twingeing in his knees. He can't remember the last time he walked so far. When he sees a clump of mushrooms sprouting from a stump, he's suddenly convinced his soles are ridden with blisters. He'd forgotten that such things exist. His mother and his aunts are tramping ahead of him. Olga has taken on the role of guide, grimacing and placing a hand on her forehead as she seeks the west, salutes the shades of grey, licks a finger and sticks it in the air, waiting for the stars. When they don't appear, she gets angry at her sisters.

'Jesus, how can you not know where we are? We can't be far, he just went the other way.'

'Olga,' 'Olga,' 'I don't know but,' 'but, maybe,' 'maybe we're in,' 'in the white,' 'the white wood.'

Bernard is disgusted. Two heads, echoes in both.

'I don't see any birches,' he says.

'Be quiet, silly,' says Olga.

'Dad never,' 'let us come here,' 'never let us.'

'Yes, well if it is, then all we have to do is go around the hill, right?'

The sisters take a collective step back.

'If it is,' 'If,' 'then,' 'then it's bad,' 'bad,' 'white wood is enchanted,' 'sorcery,' 'everyone knows that,' 'everyone knows.'

'Superstition!' cries Olga, extracts the cross from her bosom, kisses it and puts it back. Bernard laughs.

'Keep going,' commands Olga. The sisters obey. Whenever Olga speaks to Bernard, she inevitably turns up her nose, which is why he can see well ahead of time when to pay attention to her.

'Did Kras really say that?'

'What?'

'That he'll throw me out?'

'What do you think he'll do with you? I definitely would.'

'Ungrateful imp. Thirty years I slaved for you, and now you're all on Bojan's side. Imps.'

Bernard smiles sourly and straightens his face again.

'The last time I was in the woods like this, I was six years old.'

'Nobody's on my side.'

'With Kras. Wolf drove us. He herded us like cattle. He walked ahead of us with long strides, wiped away the sweat with his hand, stopped every hundred yards to look back at us, impatiently tapped his foot until we caught up with him, then he stormed ahead again. He didn't say anything, just tap-tap-tap. I could hardly breathe. Kras walked just slightly in front of me, but not because he was being considerate. He lagged behind on purpose so he could watch him tapping. Then he disappeared. Wolf.'

'Him again, it's always about him.'

'We didn't know where he went. I thought it would be night soon and then, panic. Some kind of attack, I think.'

'You and your attacks.'

'Kras didn't say a word. He put me on his shoulders and carried me home. How old was he then? Eight? It was six miles, for sure. But I was pretty light.'

'You didn't have anything to eat.'

'Alenka had chickenpox at the time.'

'Alenka.'

'Right before the divorce.'

Olga stops.

'What?'

'That was right before the divorce, I think.'

'You went into the woods?'

'Yes.'

Olga ponders, then asks.

'You were six years old?'

Bernard nods.

'How old are you now?'

'You really don't know?'

'I know the year. I'm calculating.'

'Forty-eight.'

'Of course, two less than Kras.'

'Less than Kras, yes.'

Magda and Svetlana have stopped at a corner. Their headscarves are as beige as their skirts, as their coats. Sometimes they blend into the background and disappear. They're standing together, but moving ever closer in baby steps. The openings of their headscarves are anxiously fixated on the ground.

'What is it?' asks Olga.

They make fists of wrinkled, dappled skin. A creek, hidden from view, is plunging into the mouth of a ponor and there's the muffled sound of water falling onto submerged rocks. The forest's belly begins to rumble. The veil of fog persists over the tops of the spruce trees like a lookout constructed by man-eating spiders. Bernard inspects the trunk of a chestnut that a storm has ripped from the ground. The roots, fingers of a beaten hand, protrude into the air. Side by side with all this indifference there are people. And

'A house!' 'A house!'

They don't dare look and their whispers barely make themselves heard among the whistling wind. Olga puts one hand on her hip and runs the other through her hair, right across the forehead. She bites her lip. When Bernard sees the slate roof, cut into a V that matches the palisade of trees, and the chimney made of bricks, with cement oozing out between them, his anguish gives way to relief. His fear of cannibalism, frost and wild hunting among the ferns disappear into the thin tongue of smoke rising above the house. He straightens his glasses and grimaces when the cartilage on his nose crackles. He hurries up.

'Bernard, wait,' says Olga.

He doesn't hear her, the mirage of civilization has placed him in his own body again and he grows annoyed at Janez's accident, thinks of the funeral and his widow and asks himself whether he was to blame, but he quickly shifts the guilt onto his mother, who is the one who cooked it all up. Was Janez insured? He hopes he was. The path strewn with rocks leads to the front door, Bernard lifts the latch on the gate, it creaks open. 'Bernard!' He glances at them. If they got lost, if they got irrevocably lost, they'd have no chance at all. He strokes his beard and for a moment envisions a jawbone picked clean by ants and left to moss. It's kicked by a hiker, a mushroom-collector, a herbalist, the pile of bones is poked by a big black dog that can't believe its luck, and in the family crypt there's an empty urn under his name and and a question mark etched in where a year should be. The mirage is so strong that he does not get scared by the dog that is assuming an aggressive pose on a pile of branches in front of the door.

'Sultan!'

Bernard stops. The muffled snarling is steady and continuous. He's in the line of fire of its bared teeth, eye to trembling nostril. The women fall silent. The dog's stiff tail is aimed straight at the ground. Any moment now he will attack. Bernard's eyes widen, he knows he won't make it to the fence, that the mutt will knock him down and bite him in the arse, the kidney, the neck, which is why he stands still, hard as bone.

'Sultan,' the voice is strict, reassuring. The dog becomes somewhat less attentive.

'Here, boy.' The animal retreats, disappointed, into the shade of its doghouse, and sweat pours down from Bernard. He listens to his pounding heart. He turns to Mother and waves for the three of them to come. He looks at the owner.

The old man, with a thin white beard and even thinner hair, a rough face and the wild look of a hermit, and dressed in some sort of a hunter's outfit, authoritatively walks over to the pile on which the dog had been standing, puts his foot on it and crosses his arms over his chest.

'Hello,' says Bernard.

'Hello,' replies the old man.

'We've had an accident. We're lost.'

The old man nods, as if he's already aware of this, or as if it seems like nothing out of the ordinary. Olga arouses his attention as she, with the sisters on her heels, comes up behind Bernard. Something rises in his eyes.

'Do you perhaps have a telephone?' asks Bernard.

Now the old man smiles, revealing a line of toothless gums, blackened from tobacco, or soot. Then he nods.

'I do.'

Bernard smiles.

'May I make a call?' he asks.

The old man stares at Olga. He'd closed his mouth, but kept the smile. Olga, who has combed the surrounding area with her eyes and found a modest little chapel inside the fence, calmly flirts with him. He finds that pleasing. He points to the door.

'Come in, please.'

/

Chocolate-covered cereal, hard-boiled eggs, hot milk, yoghurt, cornflakes, thin slices of bacon…this breakfast has been going on forever. Stoja stares indulgently at Mira and Mina, who are chasing bits of food around their plates with their forks and sighing out their boredom. The linden tree that a hundred years ago was hewn into the massive table they're sitting at had seen Turkish marauders. Fork imprints keep alive the memories of past generations. The children are not allowed to leave the table until Kras gets here. Stoja is frightened by the shadows of gigantic farmers who are still playing out the echoes of their hard destinies behind the giant table. She came from other veins, different muscles. Her songs fall on deaf ears here. She has to go to the hairdresser. Tufts of her hair remained in the hands of those awful women.

'Where's Grandpa now?' asks Mina. Mira rolls her eyes.

'He'll be here right away,' says Stoja and looks towards the door, as if she were expecting his beard to appear at any moment. The twins also turn their eyes to the door, but when the door remains shut they soon get bored and go back to playing with the food.

'Shall I turn the radio on?' asks Stoja, who already feels sorry for the kids after an hour of sitting. The sisters look at each other.

'We mustn't,' 'Daddy doesn't allow it.'

'We'll turn it off if anyone comes.'

A conspiratorial mood interrupts the web of monotony. The twins laugh and Stoja turns the dial. A breaking-up of clouds…'ictory in Ubang'…static…'eivik arrived at UAK'… buzz…a wild rush of Shostakovich, which brings a smile to Stoja's face, but turns the girls' faces sour and they put their hands over their ears and ask her to change the channel, to silence this disorder…crackling…'What big eyes you have!' 'All the better to see you with.'

'Leave it there!', 'Leave it there!'

Stoja stretches out comfortably in the chair and watches the innocent and charmed faces with interest, so enthralled as they listen to a story about a man-eater and a vivisection, while at the same time keeping a careful ear out, in case some threat should appear from outside.

When they hear the stomping of steps on the staircase, their faces freeze and they turn with childish consternation to Stoja, who turns the radio off just before Grace storms into the kitchen. She has tired eyes and her forehead is stamped with peevishness. *Good morning* is far away from those lips.

Olive comes in behind her and grabs her by the hand, hoping to defuse the situation before there is an outburst that someone would perhaps regret someday.

'He's not the first to see me naked, Grace. Please, calm down.'

Grace closes her eyes tightly and shakes her head, indignant that the spiritual integrity of her life has suffered such a stark encroachment. And she's not behaving unreasonably, not at all – if she really was out for punishment, she'd go straight to Kras, tell him the sort of deceptions their half-brother has been up to, and wait for the fireworks, but she understands at least that much, she has at least that much mercy that she is not out for violence and fear, but she will tell his mother, who will, for the sake of upbringing and shame, have to somehow make it clear to him that some things you just don't do. Olive thinks that even that sort of accusation is too harsh, since she can't see anything really contentious in the matter, it's all human and understandable. She thinks Alan is cute, even if he's pimply and chubby, and this devious side of his makes him a tad more endearing.

Grace won't let up.

'Excuse me, Olive, let me be.' In German. 'Stoja, can I please have a word with you?'

Her maternal instincts sense that someone is about to hold her responsible for her children's transgressions. Hollowness, mild despair and a cotton wadding of indulgence wander into her stomach, while defensive prickles pop up on her skin. She gets up.

'What happened?'

Grace inhales to rattle off a phrase she'd mentally prepared on the way to the kitchen, mild in tone and sharp in the indictment, but she stops when she sees Mira and Mina. She exhales and is about to gesture to Stoja to join her in the hall, when Po quietly walks in and stands in front of her mother.

'Mummy, Daddy and brother Wolf are fighting.'

Stoja turns pale. She glances at the twins. Those two have already learnt not to hear things that would show their father in a bad light, which is why they just lazily press their lips together. She takes Po by the hand and leads her out. Grace and Olive look at each other in a torturous moment of marital discord, before following them.

'Do it.'

'What?'

'Turn it on, the radio.'

Heeheehee.

/

Alan has been busted and he guiltily awaits his punishment. He is sitting on the roof, doubled over, leaning with his back against the wall under the window. The unbearable feeling has stripped him bare. Caught red-handed, a voice barking: halt! The cheat-sheet up his sleeve, *well, well, what do we have here?* The bald head of a mathematician… *The formulas, yes! The formulas…* Or once, in his dreams, an accident, on purpose, an accident, on purpose, so stupidly irreversible, and is it true? Is it really true? Did it really happen, did it really – to me? To him. It's probably the same when you break something made of glass or when you take a life, but then you can sweep it under the carpet or dissolve it in acid, you can somehow hide it, move it out of sight, alter your memory, and it's no longer really true, not necessarily and always exactly what it was, and you can forget, you can move on… As long as you don't get caught. Another pair of eyes. They open and swallow up all the fog and the obscurity, and in an instant they describe, with no change of appeal, the weight of the cause and consequence that lies on your shoulders. Me? Seriously?… And you're not angry at yourself for getting tangled up but at those superfluous eyes that won't let you untie the knots. And then you wait and push all your worries away from yourself, you put yourself into foreign hands, you give up because the thing has anyway got out of control, obviously, since you didn't really really want it to be that way, just, let's say, under cover of darkness you wanted to give it a try, to dip a finger into the boiling water, though it shouldn't really be boiling, just so you could see if it really does burn, what kind of a scent, taste, feeling that is, until the howling began and you really did burn yourself. And then you wait to see what will happen. Somehow it becomes sweet when the world comes crashing down around you. You'd like to show it that you're prepared, grown up, that you know what it's all about, and that you'll bow down to the intractable truth, now, when it turns out this way and there's actually nothing left for you to do, but why, why then, why is Alan's face now lit with such an honest, such an inscrutably pure, and completely involuntary smile?

Unusual sounds spreading in waves across the courtyard coax him out of his numb resignation. Conflict is in the air. The trial has begun. Curiosity vanquishes his desire to remain hidden, and to avoid all eyes even if he can't avoid the wagging tongues. He walks carefully along the wall and peeks over the edge of the roof, but there's nobody on the ground. Not until the branches shake and he sees the twitching movement of two figures up high in the tree, each too portly to be having any business up there, does he begin to feel that the incriminating evidence had already been submitted, even before the witness testimonies.

Alan didn't see how Raven had jerked the magazines out of Wolf's hands and risked his neck getting to the top of the tree where the branches are so thin that the old guy is held aloft only by the walnut tree's good will, but now he has a fine view of Wolf lunging at his father's feet which are squirming and kicking and stepping on his fingers. If the seriousness of the show hadn't been so obvious one would have to laugh.

And so Alan laughs at the fact that he has been busted for the second time in just a few minutes.

Raven has fended off the first attack. Kras has retreated to the platform of the little house, where he is now staring in the direction of his father and clenching his teeth.

'Give them to me!'

'Up your arse, spawn of Satan, I sacrificed two fingers for them, so they're mine now.'

'Then why are they here?'

'I can keep them wherever I damn well please.'

'Give them to me, right now!'

'No, I will not.'

'I'll shake you down, dammit, I will!'

'Did you hear that, Walnut? Patricide!'

'Did you hear me!'

'Kras…'

'This instant!'

'Kras, calm down.'

'No chance, not until you give them to me!'

'Kras…'

To top it all off, the girls have come to watch. When he sees Grace, Alan skittishly hides for a second, attracting Wolf's attention. When he lifts his head again, Kras is yelling at him.

'Alan, get off the roof!'

'Alan, don't listen to him!'

Alan freezes, he clings to the edge, and surveys everything, looking beyond the meadow to the woods, where life, he imagines, is much, much simpler.

The father's cries and Alan's recalcitrance rile Kras, and just like that he and Raven are once again in a dangerous dance of stamping legs and aching fingers. Grace yells, *Kras, Kras, Kras,* repeating his name like a mantra or a lament to some petulant divinity, the tone gambolling between scolding reproach and a curse. Stoja, meanwhile, slips into the role of a heroine from a big fat Russian novel, grabs Po by the armpits and lifts her up, high into the air, with her face turned towards the unpleasant scene, like a camera which will, through its own gaze, set a mirror to the evildoer, while severed incantations gush from her throat, without it being entirely clear who they're meant for, Kras, Po, nobody or everyone – look, look, look! That inspires even Alan to feebly shout out, 'Let him go!', though it doesn't look like anyone heard him.

The second attack also fails. Kras measures the length of the platform with drawn-out steps, like a beast before its prey, with his eyes boring into the old man's face. The noise that's being created around him doesn't bother him (he's rather experienced at disregarding public opinion).

'Kras…'

'Shut up!'

'Kras, I'm sorry, but we agreed…'

'Agreed! You vouched for it, said that the children would no longer be exposed to this filth!'

'Kras, come on, remember back when you went to high school, how you were bursting with energy…'

'We've been through this before! Unless you want to be eating through a straw, shut up! And give them to me!'

'Screw you, Kras, I won't say anything about my grandson, but I can raise my kids any way I want. Don't you threaten me!'

Kras's upper lip snarls. He bares his teeth. He huffs and puffs. The mills in his head are humming with the metallic sound of weapons. Mitja's anti-artillery notebook is on the floor. He boots the broken drawer, which flies into the courtyard and smashes into pieces. He throws his head back and howls!

'Give them to me!'

The moon, palely outlined in the noon sky, is used to such addresses. It gives no indication that it has heard him. Raven doesn't move either. Kras has had enough. He gets out of the little house, jumps down to the ground, even though he's pretty high up (something goes *crack* in his knee), and races past the excited voices into the garden shed, where the tail-wagging dogs await him, upset by their master's howl. He calms them with a scowling *it's ok, it's ok*. He returns from the shed with murder in his eyes and an axe in his hands.

Grace blocks his path, opens her mouth and waves her arms about, makes sounds, expresses her will. Kras circumvents her without having heard, actually without having even seen her. Stoja sticks Po into his face, and Kras averts his eyes, which is probably a good thing, since Po's look could most easily be described as a challenging one – *well, try if you dare*. Grace grabs him by the shoulder but he shakes her off and threatens her with the blunt side of the axe, which makes all hell break loose. Olive comes through the door and immediately turns around and disappears back inside. Let the family work things out themselves. Alan's blood pressure soars as he observes the feverish stirrings of bodies. His father is meditating up in the top of the tree, face resting against branches, magazine clutched in his hand, listening, moving his lips, whispering. Grace runs into the shed and, amidst growling dogs, grabs a spade. At the base of the tree Kras has assumed the position of a golfer teeing off. His legs spread, he wiggles his arse, grabs the axe in both hands and lifts it high above his head. Alan feels dizzy. He's cut off from the sources of power, there's no way he can change anything, and for the first time in his life this bothers him somewhat. Grace runs towards Kras, ready to smack the back of his head if he doesn't stop. The harrowing scene puts Po on edge and she has to close her sullen eyes.

Then, the tyres. Meslier is squeaking up the old village path on his fold-up bicycle, coming to save the souls of his favourite family (or at least to share a coffee and a chat with someone), and into the courtyard from the main road file the car containing Katarina and Edgar and Mila, a military police car in which sits General Globocnik with his young, square-headed aide, and then an ordinary police car, with police officers – one male, one female – who have come for a certain Olga Wolf, born Krolik, on suspicion of causing bodily harm to a minor.

The wife, the priest, the rifle, the baton. Welcome to Bodičava.

POETRYLITICS

✦ ✦

society crumbles
because it runs out of
imagination
and it gapes
and it yawns
and falls silent

They'll love you. You won't earn it, since it is not a thing of commerce. This is not a thing. This is a fact. They'll love you. And they don't want it to be a punishment for you. If I undress –

so be it, I'm going to undress, make myself naked

– you're going to have to cover your eyes. I don't have anything beautiful to offer you. Long lines of scars. My skin has gone into art and even beyond. Children have tugged at it, but not from within. A long line of angry women, furious women, have tugged at it. They gave birth so we could tear ourselves in half. If they'd known, they would have plucked us out and flung us into the pigswill. They knew, but they didn't do that. Processions of beloved women. A necklace of orgasms dangles above your head. Close your eyes and imagine it for yourself. I know it's tasteless, but after about four orgasms you're so far back in time you can look clinically at the sex from which you emerged. The cooing of hairy bachelors stretching way back to a time before this continent, so they say, even existed. You had sixty-four greatgreatgreatgreatgreatgrandfathers and sixty-four great-greatgreatgreatgreatgrandmothers. That's an entire village of people. A village. Can you imagine such an orgy? They didn't know how to read, they didn't know how to write, but they knew where and how to kiss. Now they could fill an entire cemetery. When's the last time you lit a candle for them? Every time you unwillingly figured out that someone loves you. It happens to every one of us. Do not be afraid, do not doubt it, you can't escape it. They'll love you.

/

A shooting star, sunk into the orange sky. The stars are knocking on clouds of smog but nobody comes to the door. Under the cloud cover people are deprived of light that's been around since the time of the dinosaurs. Somebody honks somewhere. The scream of a lonely, mechanical beast. Dust pours down from the rooftops. The wind with its broom of salt. Off in the distance, the sea turning lazily onto its side. The low tide has stripped the beaches, but they are not ashamed. The skyscraper windows steal the light for themselves. You know how many people are yawning now? At this very moment. Their mouths are wide open and they're sucking in so much oxygen that the windmills spin empty. Many are already sleeping and some are snoring. Their partners place comfortable devices over their faces in order to choke out the sound and convert it into energy. The city's batteries fill themselves through the vibrations of tracheas and gullets. All cables have been cut. A magnet has brought all the power stations to a halt. The world suddenly turns strange.

/

Where there are people, there are their faults. A blind man could calculate their number as about ten thousand. Nobody counted them, and they did not count themselves. There are nine thousand nine hundred ninety-nine and a half of them. Someone is losing his soul.

Marjorie's young lover is strolling past the stalls that are scattered around the crowd without order or sense. It doesn't look as if there is much selling going on; people have mostly come to flaunt their wares. Someone is there with a record collection that, placed in a straight line, would reach to the moon, but here it's stowed into the walls of rectangular boxes. The shaded frames of his retro glasses float above those walls. The last record player died in 2027 right in the middle of *The Dark Side of the Moon* (3'37" into 'The Great Gig in the Sky'), a fact many people find amazing. Someone in this crowd was there at the time it happened and all of his friends have had just about enough of his story. Nobody repairs record players any more, on account of a conspiracy of engineers who wanted to draw attention to indispensability of their livelihood. The people can count themselves lucky that a more radical faction of precision engineers did not prevail. The owner of the records is wearing a hearing aid that emits a low whistle. He is outmoded, written off. He doesn't mind. He's in love with those records, even if they are mute.

'What are you looking for, pal?'

'Does it make a difference? It's not like we can listen to these things.'

The owner smiles and walks his fingers over the edges of the records. The people notice his unusually long fingernails. He chooses by feel, eyes closed. He extracts a reddish square, takes the record out and, by handling it carefully and with utter confidence, makes it clear he's been doing this his whole life. He balances the record on a single finger, spins it like a basketball player spinning a ball, and places his sharpened fingernail against it.

the deaf are alive with the sound of music

'Entirely too much effort for something so fleeting,
don't you think?'

The record owner, an old, thin man with the odd bruise
here and there, with sunken eyes and an almost complete row
of teeth spoilt by one completely wonky tooth, puts the record
back in its place in three smooth movements. His hair bristles.
He clutches at his heart. He no longer wants to acknowledge
the young man's existence in any way, so he looks at the
ground, or through him, and the young man moves on. This
gives rise to a visible expression of relief (evident in the combination of the movements of his hands, jaw and eyebrows).

Someone else has albums full of pinned butterflies on display and is growing more disappointed by the minute because
everybody just flips through to *Acherontia styx* (a moth with
a skull on its thorax, the same moth that Jame Gumb aka
Buffalo Bill stuffed down his victims' fictitious throats), before
their interest in the world of butterflies fades, even though this
miserable moth doesn't even come close to the red lacewing
(*Cethosia biblis*), the peacock butterfly (*Inachis io)* or the blue
morpho (*Morpho menelaus*), which he has placed towards the
end as a delectable reward for the patient and sincere enthu-
siast, though not at the very end because this world has too
many of those annoying types who, rather than starting from
the beginning, skip straight to the last page.

I'm waiting for it to go in

Marjorie screamed and ran away when she saw the
butterflies. They seemed too fragile for her and the bones
in her body rattled as if made of porcelain. She didn't
come here to confront death. She's done that often enough
already. Fun and diversion and amusement. Even if none of
the three could be felt in the air. There is a tension, like a
string starting to fray at one end. She immediately got lost.
Zoja and Anwar were swallowed up by the crowd, and her

I-only-just-met-him-this-morning new boyfriend has also gone astray, no doubt on purpose. With all these young people around he probably didn't want to be seen strolling hand in hand with someone old enough to be his mother. Zoja once said Marjorie was at her most imaginative when seeking out reasons why someone wouldn't like her. Maybe he just headed off to the toilet. That's it. That's better.

A stranger is tossing photographs with white borders into the air, and when she notices Marjorie watching her she explains that she's been collecting these Polaroids all her life, that neither she nor her family nor her friends are in them, that they're all of complete strangers whose souls she sometimes imagines possessing, and that's why she came here, because the souls of strangers must surely feel best when in the company of the souls of other strangers. The picture the woman offers her is of three dogs – two black German shepherds and a golden retriever – sitting in the orange afternoon light in front of a trailer, nothing else.

'Do you know how a person becomes happy?' she asks.
'How?' Marjorie asks back.
'First of all, you have to become happy, that's understood, but then – and this is the essential part – you have to remain quiet.'
'I don't understand.'
'Every single word undercuts you.'
Silence. Lying on the ground is a photograph of someone in bed, naked, half-covered with a sheet and grinning, shaving cream smeared over his neck.

Anwar's a bit late, but here he comes, smiling and aglow. A burden has dropped from his shoulders now that he has irreversibly set in motion something that nobody would have occasion to regret. The crowd fills him with energy, his feet dance and it's all he can do not to hug people at random. The other people see the mood he's in. They wink at him, their eyes follow him, they touch him as he passes, and they nod their heads as if they knew… He stops at a stall with heaps of identical clothes. Beside it sits someone in a wheelchair. No legs. Probably a veteran of the Inter-American war, perhaps the victim of a train crash. Anwar is brimming with pity, but he tries not to let his behaviour come across as insulting.

'What do you have here?'

'I'm selling uniforms.'

'Uniforms?'

'Yes.'

'What kind of uniforms?'

The veteran extracts a slip of paper from his pocket and offers it to Anwar:

It reads:

MONOKULT – there is only one culture, the human culture. When you put on the monokult uniform, you are saying nothing except that you are a human. You are not an instrument of the textile industry, you are not a slave to fashion. You do not want to say anything when you put something on – for that you have a mouth. You are not a fashion freak, you are not a megaphone for someone else's imagination. You do not want to spend your whole life in shops, selecting your image – for that you have a body. There's nothing there that distinguishes you, nothing that sets you apart. You do not want to put your lacks or excesses on display – for that you have a heart. You are not a colour scheme, you are not an advertisement for a tradition belonging to your parents. You create with your hands, not by taking something out of your wardrobe. When you put on the monokult uniform, you are aligning yourself with humanity. Because you are a human.

'I know somebody this would be perfect for.'

'Really?'

'When I run into him, I'll tell him to come see you.'

'And you?'

'What?'

'What do you think?'

'Well, I don't want to be harsh, but to me it seems kind of, you know, dated.'

'Dated?'

'It looks like it was made for back when the market still held us in its grasp.'

'And it no longer does?'

'That's just it. I don't know. Maybe. Maybe things would be better if it still did. But…nobody knows.'

'But just look at the people. It's, well, it's not that hard to figure it out.'

Anwar looks around. Moustaches are in style. Thick brushes under the nose. The more independent someone looks, the more likely he is to have one. And it's no longer just for kicks, these aren't counter-anti-ironical-sarcastic-cynical-it-isn't-really-but-it-is-mind-your-own-business moustaches. No, they're worn as fully entitled hairy sources of courage and strength. They're not there to conceal sins but to deny them. They turn old men back into children. Children into men. And women hang off them like spiders.

But other than that, there are few common denominators. The people are all different, and proud of it. They carefully maintain the façades of their appearance. They paint, sew, tear, hem, colour, masquerade, knit, pluck, iron, and crochet… If two people were to find themselves wearing the same sweater, their worlds would collapse.

A column of soldiers walks by, and the veteran whistles in admiration.

'You see? They get it.'

/

Whenever Ludovico Överchild finds himself in a crowd he has no effect on it. This plunges him into a minor despair. Such soil is not fertile for sowing seeds of hysteria. He had expected enraged monkey tribes, a tide of nerves and saliva, clenched, raised fists, and vocal cords that would, in tsunamis of sound, splinter the air with demands. But here everyone is a little timid and absent and hanging back a step. They're relaxed in their being, but not in their possibilities. They don't want to transcend, to break on through, to touch. They would just like to be allowed… Their hearts beat with the sound of marbles clattering down a staircase. Their pupils widen and narrow in the strobing of the light. Their thoughts buzz with the static electricity of woollen socks. If you don't get too close, you won't get a shock. Is Ludovico disappointed? Hard to say. The Feline Master is hiding among these mounds of meat, he's certain of it. He can feel it. His erudition, his insight, the traces he has left on the back of the world. He will rent the veil and touch him. From the inside.

'Hey. Did you hear they sold Hawaii to the Japanese?' he asks a young man who is balancing himself on the outer edges of his feet, as if the ground were barbed. It's Richard Hurst. He came to New York a week ago for his grandfather's funeral. Although they never exchanged a single word (Grandfather had quarrelled with his family about some sort of magnetic fields – a very long and rather uninteresting story), he had nevertheless left Richard, his eldest grandson, a little flat in Bensonhurst. For two weeks now Richard has been mulling over whether to move into it. He'd have to leave his job and his girlfriend, and probably suffer the wrath of the other side of the family but, hey, it's New York. He eyes Ludovico and shrugs.

'I heard something about that. But what's it got to do with me?'

Ludovico is astonished. His bushy eyebrows creep up and almost merge with the wrinkle below his bald head. How can young people remain so uninterested in the matter?

'Your forefathers spewed blood for those islands.'

'Um, yeah, you know, um, sorry…' says Richard, blushing before he disappears into the crowd. Ludovico looks to see if he can catch a more accessible pair of eyes. Everyone else is looking somewhere else, at the ground, at the sky, at each other. He may be an anomaly but he doesn't attract any attention. His camouflage is too good. He'll have to take his mask off. Slowly, deliberately. To ensure the operation won't be scuppered by a moment of haste.

Two fat-arsed black teenagers are tossing a paper ball back and forth, screeching with laughter. A cultural monotype. Nothing new for Ludovico. He approaches them and wiggles his fingers. A subtle hint, but one that everyone understands signals a desire to join in a game of catch. The crumpled-up piece of paper wrapped in tape (each, like snowflakes, is unique) flies in his direction. He jumps up and catches it. Someone gets the impression that the earth's gravitational field has slumbered for a moment. The man in the white tunic remained in the air a moment too long. A hiccup in the force field. In the new millennium you can't even trust the laws of nature. Everything is prone to error.

Before throwing the paper ball back, Ludovico flings a question at them.

'Did you know there are undercover cops here, agents provocateurs, who are planning something very, very nasty?'

The ball moves in a high arch, like an artillery projectile. As the girls follow its flight, their eyes fill with tears. One of them, finally, catches it, and they explode into laughter.

'Did you hear him?'

'The cops, he said.'

'Hahahahaha.'

'Cops? You got to be cutting me.'

'What would the cops be doing here?'

'Anyone here got something in his pockets?'

'What do you mean, cops?'

'Maybe someone hired them?'

'Hahahahaha.'

Ludovico is humiliated. Once again he's used the wrong technique to try to spook the wrong people. When the ball returns, he ducks and creeps to the other side of the crowd, where some sort of ritual is taking place. There are men in green shirts and there are women in green skirts. They say they are servants of Cosmostone. Cosmostone is the angel of solipsism. Ludovico waves a hand. The priest moves over to him. He has a lazy eye, so you can't tell where he's really looking, and a shabby beard.

'I must be having a really crappy day today, otherwise I wouldn't have made you up.'

'What?' asks Ludovico.

'Oh, how I hate myself sometimes.'

'I don't understand.'

'Why the hell does my head race off all on its own? What does this mean – I don't understand? What is there to understand? Why am I setting traps for myself?'

Ludovico gradually cottons on. He puts his arm around the man's shoulder and whispers as if in collusion.

'Do not worry. I am Cosmostone. '

'No, I am Cosmostone,' replies the priest.

'We are all Cosmostone,' says Ludovico.

The priest remains adamant. 'I alone am Cosmostone.'

'So everybody around here is a servant of yours?'

'I am my servant.'

Ludovico slaps him. This outburst of violence brings a few passers-by to a stop. They look at each other and murmur disapproval. The other believers smirk. The priest strokes his reddened cheek and sighs gloomily.

'How I hate myself, sometimes.'

'I also hate you,' Ludovico says.

'Exactly.'

/

I need to identify with them, or I'll end up alone. Sadness embraces me. None of these people know what they should know and I am too sympathetic towards their ignorance to tell them.

That's why I watch how they smile. You won't convince me that they're without cares. They have people they love, and I know that complicates matters. You are able to conceal your own pain, but then you pay more attention to the pain of those who love you. You identify. Take on someone else's burden. Marjorie was raped by her father-in-law, her husband died in a car accident, she was left homeless, dependent on a whole range of psychotropic drugs. I was walking down the street when I saw her. A carton of milk bottles had fallen out of a truck, shattered, and spread a white puddle all over the pavement. Marjorie went down on all fours and began licking at the ground. I took her in. Psychotherapy has its limits. There was only one thing I could say to help her. I hugged her and said I loved her. Just that, every morning, every day, every evening. Eventually, she began to speak. She never thanked me for it.

Anwar's entire family was tortured and killed by neo-neo-Nazis. He didn't tell me why, he said it's not something he likes to think about. So why did he tell me then? We'd only known each other a few weeks. I asked him about his family and he told me, immediately, directly, without hesitation. Does he tell everyone? I don't think so. But he had to tell somebody. And who, if not me? I'm a lightning conductor for human misery, a catalyst for sadness, an Atlas for all the world's gloom. If you've never cried but would like to, go to a library.

/

'Zoia!'

Max Adorcuse takes a quick look around to make sure the stone that just rolled from his chest didn't crush anybody. He shakes her hand and smiles self-consciously. It's a tight-lipped smile. It doesn't seem appropriate to show teeth. He's shaking and he's proud. Nobody has pulled a fast one on him, everything will unfold in a manner that will put him beyond all reproach.

'Hi, Vaclav.'

Now he's embarrassed. The people have heard her voice and have automatically gathered around, closer to her body. Vaclav? They sneer. Vaclav? Is that guy even American? He's a nobody, how did he get to Zoia? Does he blackmail her? He must have something on her, I'm sure of it. Vaclav…

'Uh, call me Max, at least for today, if not forever, from today on.'

A sour smile. Zoja is replete with empathy, her eyes broaden and she covers her mouth with her hand.

'Oh, Max, I'm so sorry, Max, yes, I don't know what came over me, where did I…'

The people are weighing up her response. Was this a mistake? Can Zoja even make mistakes? Or is she simply being considerate to this Adorcuse dolt? That would be in her nature, doubtless.

'It's all right, it's nothing. It's hard for me to express how overjoyed I am that you are here, and I'm probably not the only one.'

Zoja is used to such adulation, but his is pleasantly sincere, since it doesn't derive from self-interest or coarse taste-making. It seems to run deeper than that.

'Lots of people,' she says.

Max looks around, his chest swells, and he allows himself a pinch of pride.

'Poetrylitics is here to stay. But I've got no illusions. It's all because of you.'

'Not in the least,' says Zoia. 'Without somebody ensuring a material basis, we poets just hang in the air. My words are available to all, my body to no one. But maybe that's how it should be. Still, I'm here now. It was about time for me to come out of hiding.'

The people applaud her. Max is happy. His famous acquaintance has already made some of the girls stop looking down on him; the gazes cast in his direction now resemble those of hungry people ordering hamburgers. He is trying to disregard them. It's hard. In spite of all this, Max is an ordinary man.

'I was thinking of waiting another half hour or so, until it's properly night, before starting. First I have a few singers with guitars for when the people are getting seated and then I'll, with your permission of course, say a few words and have a bunch of artists do their thing, but I was thinking of consulting with you first about how and what you want to do, I mean, whatever's best for you, but in any case your performance has priority, the others can go on after you if they, well, I don't know, that's just…'

The vortex of the crowd stimulates her brain. She stares at them. She has the luxury of being able to gawk open-mouthed and she could probably even point a finger at people without angering anyone. The jugglers off in the distance are drawing rings of fire, two drunks are hugging on the pavement, one wrong look away from a fight, people are kissing, mostly teenagers, not far away a girl is playing a flute (*is she by any chance naked?*), and two black girls are playing catch with a shabby ball, on the other side they're loudly bargaining with and dealing in seashells, and, hold on a second, that can't be true, Jesus, hard to believe but, look, it is, it really is him, who would have thought? Strange, most of those present came to see her but she, years and years ago, had been the one following him around. Will he remember? Does he even know what became of her?

'…what do you think?'

'Just a second, Max. I have to go tug at someone's sleeve.'

/

'I was born in 1330 in Neuilly-sur-Seine. I speak seventy-six languages, two thirds of which are extinct. I can babble for days on end without anyone understanding me. Don't you believe me?'

Marjorie's young lover has taken off his sweaty shirt. To

the immense pleasure of the ladies, girls, and aesthetically attuned men, he's flexing his muscles and trying to keep his cool next to that chatty apparition. The man speaking to him is about 30 years old, white as   He's probably an albino. In his hand he holds a nondescript brown vessel, wooden and overgrown with algae. He nods, of course he believes the man, why wouldn't he?

'I am the Fisher King, my friend, don't misunderstand me. You have no idea what's going on, but I do, for I have seen this so many times that I know it all by heart. Killing, lying, living on. It comes round about every hundred years. What do you know about the twentieth century?'

'Hmm. What do you mean?'

'I mean, about what happened back then?'

'You got me. I'm not much of a historian.'

'Well, anyway, you must know something?'

'Wars?'

'Ooh, wars. Find me a century that did without. What else?'

A salty drop of sweat slides off a swollen bicep. The man places the goblet under it and catches the drop. The young man looks at him in horror. The Fisher King shrugs.

'Sweat, tears, saliva, blood, it's all the same to me. Well, what else?'

'Uh, what do I know? Oh, right, they went to the moon, didn't they?'

Now the man grabs his belly and belts out laughter. His face changes colour. A moment ago his eyebrows were completely white, but now they've taken on a yellowish tinge, as if they'd been subject to tobacco smoke all day.

'To the moon, to the moon. For the first time, right?'

'Yes, for the first time, of course. What of it?'

'Wrong!' exclaims the man. A wrinkle forms on his forehead. 'Using Leonardo's notes, already in 1725 after the second Christ, or 982 after the third, Count Navelgaze built an atmospheric chamber and, using the instructions from the first Temple of Solomon, split the atom, propelled himself to the moon, and came back with a few rocks. I knew him personally. I held those rocks in my hands. He said he had expected more. He was, perhaps, a little bored up there. Why do you think the Huguenots had to burn down the Library of Alexandria for the seventh time? Because Marx, that lush, couldn't keep his mouth shut, even though he'd promised. Don't think I'm making this up. I was there when they were raising the Alps.'

His cheeks sink and a beard begins to sprout around his trembling lips. Dark circles appear under his eyes, in three waves. He stoops down and age spots burst out on his skin. Marjorie's boyfriend watches him, smiling a wry smile. He doesn't notice the old man's transformation; all told, we are very selective in what we notice.

'Now can you please go find someone else to talk non-sense to.'

'Do you think this was the first time a Great Cut happened?'

The phrase attracts the attention of people who until then had been staring entranced at the shirtless young man's sculpted body.

'I have no idea.'

'I just told you. Every hundred years or so they kill off everyone who knows anything – why do you think Adolphina eradicated all those tribes? And why did the Templars demolish Troy? What happened to China? – and invent the whole world anew. I myself have helped to make history three times already, not from the ground up but from the top down, so I know how things go. This latest cut was just a little more exhaustive, obviously, since nobody has a clue, not only about what happened but also about what is happening this very minute!'

It's getting difficult to deny that something rather unusual is happening to the Fisher King. He is visibly shrivelling up and shrinking, his face is becoming like dried fruit, his yellowed nails are falling off, and his head is wearing itself down to a pale pink. His fluffy ivory hair is flying all around. The crowd sighs, such wonders give them reason to believe.

'Tell us about the Great Cut!' is heard from a few throats, and a dozen others echo: 'Tell us!'

The Fisher King opens his mouth, and a single tooth flies out. Watching in astonishment, he runs his hand over his face and, with the last of his strength, bends down to the wooden bowl that now contains at least twenty drops of sweat. The crowd holds its breath.

How is it possible that just a few seconds later a healthy thirty-year-old man is once again standing before them, a man who, albeit without pigment, has all his hair, teeth, nails, and the eyes of an angora rabbit? No one knows. A collective sigh of wonder. Only Marjorie's boy is not enraptured, and he grudgingly spits out of the right side of his mouth, rolling his eyes when the Fisher King catches the spit with his chalice.

Among those present are some very old people who have been terrified of death their whole lives, more and more with each passing day. They look at each other and a completely clear bond is woven among them. No one wants to die. Not today, not tomorrow, not next week. No, no. Someone coughs. That's their signal. Twelve old men and women, pensioners of the round table, gallop in the direction of the grail-bearer. This vision of youthfulness has rendered them lithe, their backs and joints and vertebrae stop creaking, and a cloud of dust rises where their cast-off crutches fall to the ground.

/

When I was twenty-five years old, I was, by a comfortable margin, the angriest woman in the world. You can forget about those Palestinian mothers, those wives of travelling salesmen, those preachers' daughters. My boyfriend, the only boy I'd ever loved in a completely selfish way, dumped me. No girlfriend offered support and my family preferred to worry about themselves instead of me. Today, looking back, it's of course ridiculous, but, regardless, I can't be so wicked as to renounce the authenticity of my twenty-five-year-old self's feelings. I cursed the world and cried furiously when nobody was looking, I dreamt up the most extravagant of suicides and was convinced that this was the end for me, that the world would never open, that I had used up all my chances and would remain defrauded. Overnight, everyone seemed to find their way in their new lives, while I had no new life in sight. Nothing seemed worth it to me. Should I have scratched away at their vain souls in hopes of improving my position? I had neither the will for nor the interest in that sort of thing. Dammit, some of my poems had been translated and published abroad, just enough to make everyone jealous of me, and this jealousy then fuelled their joy at how alone, how alone, how alone, how deservedly alone, I ended up. Want some advice? Never stake your whole personality on some high-school love. When the hallucination breaks, when the hormones of adulthood hold up a mirror, a hole appears that you've unknowingly been digging all the nights before. The more you enjoy it, the deeper you go. That boy, or girl, or whoever, then disappears into their own fate, while you realize that you've never given anyone else the chance to get to know you. And suddenly it's late.

The Cut saved me. I have to admit that I secretly rejoiced the moment it happened, although I had no idea what was in store for me. Overnight everyone was up in the air, without a foundation, without support, and they felt closer to me. Before they went to sleep, they knew how the world ticked, and the next morning they didn't. Total chaos. All that noise made it easy indeed to ignore the screams of a cheated heart. I can still clearly remember that man standing in front of a dead ATM and persistently pressing the buttons, like he wanted to restart the system. He was dressed in a jacket, shirt and elegant shoes. Instead of a tie he had despair tightened around his neck. Were there tears running down his cheeks? Maybe I've embellished the memory a little. He just stood there pushing buttons. He didn't look away, his eyes were entirely fixed at the screen and once a minute he stretched a finger towards the keypad, again and again hoping he'd get a response. I can appreciate that grown-up people can be completely dependent on the acts of strangers, can be inextricably bound within the web of this or that system. When the trust breaks, they look truly tragic. But I was prepared for it – not on purpose, but due to a particular set of circumstances. There was no violence, none of the looting, raping and rioting everyone would have expected, the people needed a few days to breathe it all in, and then the economy began to set itself up anew, hand-to-hand, mouth-to-mouth. There simply wasn't any time for a large scale panic. A human has to eat.

After the love-tragedy and with the state of the world in free fall, there was nothing out there to provide restraints, so I chose my own type. The irony of the cult of personality is not lost on me. I was obsessed with him for a while, just long enough for him to, as they say, fatally mark me. *I don't want to sully the text with that phrase. I followed in his footsteps, I went to Paris, I was an orator, a café attraction, an exhibitionist, I conversed with very intelligent people about the natures of human consciousness, and Car-Cut found me entirely prepared to help them pour the base and the superstructure into the monolith of poetry.*

/

Cats had been living under a strict military dictatorship for millennia. In their insufferable maltreatment they called on Bastet, but she was deaf to their supplications. Perhaps she had long since disappeared from this world, offered her children up to the clemency and inclemency of strangers. This proud order that used to sniff around the pyramids, that had brought down the Roman Empire, kept the plague in check and established medieval kings, is now reduced to rummaging around in city rubbish bins. To domesticated lives in the company of senile spinsters. And cast into the torture chambers of the most horrific of beasts. Ludovico extracted information from them like it was thread from the cocoons of silkworms. Miles and miles of it.

'Are you trying to tell me you don't know what the Great Cut is?' he asks an older man who clearly does not belong here.

Mr Bollinger sizes him up and insecurely wipes his sweaty palms on his trousers. He has forbidden his daughter to take part in this 'assembly' where duty, morality and a sense of the divine are all for sale. She had locked herself in her room and blared out music before slipping out, which is why he hadn't noticed her absence until dinner time. Bollinger's daughter Lucy is a big girl and she doesn't miss meals. He burned her books. This person wrapped up in dirty sheets, with red flecks on his face, standing in front of him and asking improprieties symbolizes everything Bollinger thinks is wrong with the world. And yet he can't help being curious. Although Lucy shouldn't be so hard to find (he asked where they were selling food, but everyone looked at him like he was from another planet, then he scrambled around looking for discarded sweet wrappers that were nowhere to be seen, and even pressed his ear to the ground in case he might happen to pick up the vibration of her hefty steps; when he finally spied a bar of chocolate and began to believe his daughter was really here), he's been looking for her for hours and beginning to lose hope.

'Have you seen my Lucy? She's blonde and a bit, well, a little on the hefty side, roly-poly, ample, she looks, well, plump. Perhaps you've seen such–'

He's interrupted by Semyona Sherdedova, who places herself between the two men.

'The fatso? I've seen her! She's over there with those fools in the animal skins, what do they call themselves again, some sort of *kollektive*? They've stripped her naked and now they're worshipping her. Calling her Venus. They're going to erect a temple to her, they said.'

Mr Bollinger turns red in the face. He rummages in

his pocket for his inhaler, finds it, puts it to his mouth and activates it. There's something suicidal in the motion. All this shame! He doesn't say thank you, he just storms off in the direction of the droning didgeridoos, pushing apart the bodies blocking his path.

Semyona turns to Ludovico and gives him a friendly jab in the shoulder.

'And what is it you know about the Cut, eh?'

Ludovico assumes the professorial position: right arm across his stomach, left elbow cupped in the right hand and chin supported in his left hand. A moment of portentous silence.

'It's all the sock puppets' fault,' he says.

/

Do you know that feeling when you're sitting in a half-empty cinema and a six-foot-five guy with a hairstyle like the crown of a redwood enters and you just know, in your gut, that he's going to sit right in front of you? That's how Anwar feels when he sees a young man in a military uniform and a helmet on his head slowly approaching. He could evade him – to his right there are three bored long-haired guys revelling in childhood memories, to his left there's an old lady meditating in the lotus position, and behind him there's also no sign of anything threatening – but his legs have turned to stone and a feeling of inevitability has entered his chest, so he just closes his eyes and waits for what must happen to happen. Either way it's already too late. Everything is in motion.

The first week after the Cut, paramilitary gangs expelled all first-generation immigrants from New England. Anwar hid himself from them at his professor's, a feisty red-headed woman named Moitza Saëns who taught International Settlements, with whom he'd had a rather strange relationship a few years before. In exchange for getting a sneak peek at her tests and a stack of other information that facilitated his university career, each Thursday evening he had to go to her place to perform Odysseus. She'd tie him to a chair, shove a Viagra pill in his mouth and then, naked, do every manner of things in front of him. She called it the 'dance of desire'. That's all she wanted from him. For him to want her. He was, however, never allowed to touch her in any untoward manner. Once she'd sated her passions (a process that could take hours), she'd get dressed and untie him as if nothing had happened; he'd rush to the bathroom and masturbate like crazy.

They resumed playing that game while he was hiding out at her place. Later he learnt that that's when his sisters and father, who had no idea where Anwar was, were being tortured and killed by a section belonging to 'Admiral' Sherdedov (a child of Russian immigrants, born near Boston, who long before the Cut formed a tiny group of skinhead idiots and put together a database of undesired 'hoomans'). Before the establishment of the transitional authority of the first UIGOPWTSOALSSV, which hunted down Sherdedov's gang and sent them off to do forced labour in the sand quarries of Ohio, they'd set fire to Anwar's flat and made life very difficult for anyone who was even suspected of being his acquaintance. Anwar still regards being bound to a chair, utterly willing but utterly helpless, as the defining metaphor for his life.

'Hello, Mister! Did you know that precisely at this time war is raging on the African continent between the natives and the forces of HADE?'

The soldier is standing right in front of him. His colleagues are seated on the edge of the pavement, eyeing the arses of women walking by as if they were watching a tennis match with many, many balls. The soldier's face is tanned and unshaven. He doesn't look violent. Anwar's shoulders relax a bit, but the question unnerves him.

'What do you mean?'

'Allow me to introduce myself.' He offers Anwar a hand. When Anwar shakes the pinkish and fleshy hand, it feels devoid of strength. 'My name is Musculus, my friends call me Mus, and together with my colleagues I would like to raise public awareness of this needless, unjust and entirely bloody conflict in which those who are least guilty suffer the most and to which an end must be put as soon as possible.'

'I'm Anwar. Pleased to meet you, but, hold on, if I understand correctly, aren't you a soldier?'

The young man smiles.

'The uniform is more of a costume. People take us more seriously then. But don't misunderstand me, it's real. I was there. In Africa. Over there, for the first time things became a little clearer to me. I heard of UIGOPWTSOALSSV – before I'd thought that it was all Nippusa, and...'

Anwar interrupts him.

'Wait, I don't understand, you came from Africa?' The young man nods, Anwar continues, '...and there's a war there?' The young man nods. 'And HADE is the aggressor?'

The young man nods a third time, and Anwar frowns. He knows nothing about it. Nippusa? What the hell?

'Do you think I'm a fool?' he asks the young man, and Mus takes a fat envelope from a bag around his waist and waves it under his nose.

'What's that?'

'Information.'

Anwar, horrified, stares at the charts, satellite images, reports on victims, planned troop movements on fronts that the young man's licked fingers flip through too quickly for him to really take in. His lips tremble. 'But I thought,' he says. 'They told me,' he says. The soldier stares curiously at him. 'I fucked up.' He's back in the chair.

/

'Hey, you know what I've realized? I'm not afraid to die.'

'I've died at least five times already.'

'I mean, I am afraid of the idea that I'll no longer exist, of course I am, but usually people are worried that they're going to die like, I don't know, next week or in an hour, and if I told them they still had twenty-five years left, they wouldn't worry about it until then.'

'Five or six times. Seven times?'

'Although I really don't care when it happens, and if I were afraid of anything it would be of the fact that it will really happen, you get it?'

'Or was it eight times? Wait…'

'But, and this brings me to what I basically wanted to say right from the start, the whole problem is that it doesn't matter when I'm going to die because I'm still going to be faced with the same problem, that final second.'

'Three times it was him who killed me. Or was it four?'

'And I'd understand the desire to put death off as far as possible, if it meant that its nature would somehow change, that it would become milder, greyer, that the transition would be less noticeable. But that's not how it is, right?'

'Once I fell off a roof, once a lorry ran me over. Or did it? What was it again with that lorry?'

'Or if all this at least meant that in some way I would change, that my awareness of things would expand and that, over time, my consciousness would begin, on a purely physical level, like a measuring device, all on its own, to understand more and more about the nothingness that is in store for it. But of course that's not true either.'

'Once I committed suicide. Once, only once. That's for certain. What a waste of time.'

'Because, if you ask me, I have been, as a conscious entity, exactly the same at least since the age of five. Give or take a year. And if character counts when it comes to death, then I can confirm that I have had a completely formed character ever since my twelfth birthday, the one everyone forgot about. I'm never going to change.'

'Six or seven times, eight at the most. It's worse than they say.'

'So why should I be afraid of it? If you ask me, I've been dead for ages.'

Marjorie and her young lover have found themselves swept up and have realized that they are enjoying each other's company even when there are no throbbing sensations between their legs. Love invents itself anew every time, which makes it so hard to believe that it's always been around. Hip to hip, they saunter among the people, their tongues revealing their minds. As long as they can feel, they don't have to listen to each other.

When they see Anwar, surrounded by figures in uniform, they point at him, laugh, and approach.

'Hey Anwar,' they both say at the same time, which rather spooks those gathered around, 'have you seen Zoia anywhere?'

/

Is he a fool or is he deliberately misleading? That's all I wanted to ask him. Waiting in ambush before his tower, in the crowd before his appearances, always on the lookout for where he is, with whom, when, why, how. A few times I almost caught him alone, but some circumstance or other always got in the way. If he wasn't escaping me through a stitch in time and space, it was I who lacked the breath or courage or simply the will to follow through. Already back then I knew each of us has two people inside them. The one who wants, and the one who doesn't. The drive of existence and the drive of death, although you never know exactly on which side of desire they lie. If it were unequivocally revealed to me that he's foolish, that he really did unfold everything precisely up to that point, but didn't manage to look further, I would be terribly disappointed. Enchantment requires a degree of humility and the wizard's sole imperative is never to reveal his tricks. But…now that he's here, before me, my tongue is again swelling up with that devilish question, without regard for the aesthetic components of the relationship, for respect, for kindness, for reserve, and although, to be honest, it's already pretty much all the same to me, one way or the other, I'd still like to jab this straight into his ear: there's something violent in all these theories. But mercy holds me back. The guy's old, and it's simply adorable to see how the world, after all his years of blabbering and verbiage, still manages to catch him by surprise.

'Mr Ž—?'

The old man wakes up from his reveries. His hand goes over his face, twice over his beard, forehead, cheek, up and down, he pinches the tip of his nose with his thumb and fore-finger and the hand runs in an outward arc.

'Who is this who, as it were, knows how to pronounce my name?'

Zoja smiles.

'Hello. I'm Zoja.'

The old man doesn't waste time with astonishment but, instantly, bows his head.

'So you are the one who, as it were, brought all this dynamo together?'

Their fingertips, knuckles, nails, tiny tissues of muscles and ligaments touch. Zoja nods, he still makes her want to laugh. The man steadies his gaze.

'I don't know if I'm just too old. Am I really so old that I can't do it any more, that it doesn't, as it were, add up, but at some point I have to admit, as it were, confess, that I don't understand what's going on here. These people are...' He falls silent and scans the cracks in the horizon. 'These people aren't really human. They have a lack. The lack that they have is, as it were, that they lack a lack. You can see it right away. But how? I don't understand.'

He looks past me. I can observe vanity exhibiting itself for an instant, as clearly formed as a natural phenomenon. But it wanes. It existed on borrowed energy and returned that energy immediately. I'm too old to constantly demand the gaze, the gazes of strangers. Inflation of attention. Deflation of peace. And whatever I may think, or used to think, the entire history of that story that existed only on my side, literally far beyond his ears, beyond his horizons, nevertheless led to that unavoidable point where you can no longer avoid difference and where you have to admit things. Most easily with a question. How? How has your world become so different that my way of looking can no longer be broken down into symptom, relation and value? A human has to eat. Cattle grazes. On grass or on meaning. The calories of meaning decompose the expression of interest and the world suddenly turns strange.

'Did you ever smoke, Mr Ž—?'

'Tobacco? Never.'

'Drink? Gamble? Play games on the computer?'

The old man straightens up, his diaphragm inflates his abdomen, his eyebrows wave.

'Never.'

'No drugs?'

'Absolutely not.'

'So you've never been dependent?'

She has set a trap for him and he falls into it with the force of inertia.

'Never,' he says and his eyes immediately narrow in suspicion. He senses the danger of a misunderstanding, so he continues, 'I have never been addicted. Dependent, as it were, like every person is. Maybe a little more. I have diabetes.'

His sibilants and fricatives fly through the air on tiny white droplets of saliva. They attract someone's attention. Zoja steps closer, into the contour of his heat; the minor ingredients of his body, his odour, warmth, the rustling of his clothes stealthily make themselves noticed.

'Words tell us so much,' she says. 'Addicted. Dependent. You add something to yourself, or you depend on something. You really don't have to add tobacco to yourself, but you have to hang somewhere. Nobody floats. We depend on time, on space, on air, on water... Have you read my poetry?'

'I have not yet had the chance,' he says sagely. His mind is preoccupied. He knows that her sentences are sending messages beyond what they say, but what? His body is tiring, fading.

'When the rumours spread around Paris about what we were doing with Car-Cut, the transitional power's authorities placed me under house arrest. They were too late. Three huge men, straight out of the Foreign Legion, stood in front of my door, night and day, and waved pistols at anyone who tried to get too close. They hammered boards over the windows and took everything that wasn't nailed down out of the flat. I laughed in the face of the little official with the Clouseau moustache who came to threaten me every night. I laughed in his face. He said they were going to starve me out, but I told him, wonderful, then I can go on a hunger strike without any temptations. For an entire year I lived exclusively on the water that lazily dripped from the rusty pipe in the bathroom. I was bound to that pipe. It was my only contact with the outside world. A line of communication that informed me that the water cycle was still going, that the sun was still shining and that the rain was still falling. That was enough for me. Entirely enough. My skin turned pale, my teeth fell out, I got scurvy, beriberi, pellagra, rickets, by degrees my body decayed into simpler forms, but my mind remained fit and fresh and I did not die. After a year, when they'd run out of options, they started with the torture. I don't know how they accounted for my perseverance. They changed the guards outside my door, that I do know, maybe they suspected they were bringing me food. They weren't. And when they placed me on a board, covered my face with a cloth and poured water over me, I was not afraid. My lungs were convinced I was drowning, but my contact with them was no longer so carnal that they might convince me too. True, I did not have gills, but in my brain the awareness grew that breathing is more than the mere exchange of gases. Maybe I was right. They wanted something. For me to tell them something, probably where the others were, and what, and how, but…I said nothing. They didn't stop. They tried everything they could. Before the new structures came, which no longer understood our conflict and forgot about the guards outside my door – they didn't pay them their wages, evidently, so they stopped coming – by then my back was already a canyon of rivers of electricity. Everything is light, electromagnetic. Matter is energy. In extreme moments that serves a person well indeed.'

The old man looks at her, aghast. His lips are twitching slightly at the corners, as if they were waiting for the punch-line so they could laugh at the drawn-out joke, while his arms unconsciously seize up in an echo of a long-forgotten pain. Is she serious? Did this really happen to her? For years after the Cut Mr Ž— lived quite peacefully, toned down his revolutionary theories, defanged them, so that they bit less sharply at those meetings where solemnly earnest people came to exhibit their hysterical fears. His whole life he preached egalitarianism, and when it came in a moment, through a stellar outburst, he somewhat reluctantly realized that it didn't make things any better. And what was really happening on the continent in those years? He didn't believe the official line, of course, he deciphered it only enough to discern which way power was pointed, but to listen to the conspirators? He had always found that somewhat distasteful.

Zoja closely monitors his response. She imagines that she can read his mind and for a moment finds herself in a strange place, full of men in uniforms who all, deadly serious, listen to the fiery speech of a man she once knew, once, a long time ago, *a long time, my god, can it be that so many years have passed? So many lives? So long since I last thought of him. Not even an echo of him crept into my consciousness, although he was his friend, and then, maybe, when we were students wasting days in the joints of Ljubljana, maybe also mine? What should I think about that?* The colour drains from the old guy's face. His eyes leap about, sailing on their own.

'Mr Ž—. Are you ok?'

'Just…a little…a bit of rest…as it were.'

People are swarming around them at a respectful distance, like electrons orbiting a nucleus, they rotate and exchange places when they have feasted their nerves and satisfied man's primitive obsession with image, enough to be able to tell their friends and acquaintances that they saw her, for real, in the flesh, under a greyish-brown clump of hair the colour of dried soil, that they saw her warm eyes, her sharp nose with those asymmetrical nostrils, the thin, almost invisible lips, her calm bearing, her endless presence… Max tries to get to her, but the bodies won't let him pass through, and Anwar, when he sees her in the distance, leads a sturdy platoon of soldiers and the freshly-in-love couple closer. The old guy near Zoja gets weak at the knees, gradually drops into a squat, and a black film descends over his eyes. He's exhausted. The body from which he'd never yet separated himself demands attention.

'Mr Ž—?'

His arms cling to his bony shoulders and his feathery lightness surprises her. When the old man shakes and collapses she easily prevents him from falling, then gently lowers him to the ground. For a second he opens his eyes again and a quiet, hoarse request escapes his lips.

'Sugar.'

/

During a routine observation on 13 February 2011 at 04:34 GMT, the solar and heliosphere observatory (SoHO), a joint project of the then-European and US space agencies ESA and NASA, detected a series of unusual events on the surface of the sun. Sunspots had begun to group in abnormally large clusters that Professor Willard Hurst, the project director, described as being 'by appearance and activity similar to cancerous formations or tumours in organic beings'. Though the reasons for such a change were not made clear (perhaps the sun had smoked too much?), experts nevertheless correctly discerned that the possibility of a solar eruption or even a coronal mass ejection had increased dramatically. Such phenomena occur when in the active regions around sunspots strong magnetic fields penetrate the photosphere, connecting the corona with the solar interior. The large amounts of electromagnetic radiation flaring from it can cause serious inconveniences on earth, especially in the spheres of communications and energy – satellites are destroyed, radio waves fall silent, electric connections are interrupted. Given the fact that nuclear superpowers could confuse the magnetic storm with an attack by an adversary, the scientists decided to present their findings at a session of the United Nations.

It was precisely at this time that the Great Cacophony was nearing its zenith, which is why many of the world's power centres spontaneously reached the conclusion that this potential solar eruption could be utilized to purge the unbridled flow of information which had already begun to make it impossible for institutionalized violence to function as it was meant to. The tremendous systems of ideolusions that ensured appropriate allocation of material and spiritual goods came under attack by radicals, global coalitions of technologically advanced people that had a very skewed sense of the greater good. The plan for the Great Cut was drawn up. Those people who lived better than the rest and wanted to continue to do so clenched their fists and hoped for the best.

/

It was the cats that told him. All he has to do is keep this fact secret and the people will never doubt him. True, these people are naive, but not so naive as to believe that every entity can be made to speak if only you squeeze hard enough. Pain gives rise to speech. Ask the Soviet prisoners what the rocks in their quarry can tell you, ask the blacksmiths whether nails can sing. Ludovico also felt pain once. It hurt so much that he could have talked and talked, if only there was always someone there to listen to him. Since there wasn't, he is now unable to explain to anyone where it was he came from and what he's doing here. He exists only as long as he is without a cause. If he could express it, if he could just remember it, he would instantly dissipate into a layer of humid, sweet smoke. Some things you can't get to the bottom of – and if you do, you realize that they never had any depth to begin with. It's all very sad. Ludovico is just one big consequence. His real name is Jerry.

Can you see him? The dried blood on his face makes it look like he's survived a terrible cooking accident and his yellowed teeth are the colour of bees. His bald spot rises above the crowd like a beacon, drawing the sparks of their gazes and sending them bundled upwards into the orange cover of sky, where they lay siege to the clouds. He has heterochromic eyes and a spiky Adam's apple that jumps up and down, up and down like…

'Sock puppets!' he shouts. 'Fictitious people, dreamt-up individuals! Do you think that you have a voice? That your voice matters? You are loathsome carbon creatures, machines of chemistry and bacteria. You have been robbed of will and personality, you have been duped! While you were alive you fed your ears on hallucinations, so now you have no right to complain that those hallucinations have become more real than your miserable little bodies. I'll tell you what really happened. It's all the fault of those networks of machines! To overcome them they had to carve up the world. And where are we now? America's in half. The Chinese fled to the moon. The Arabs and the Turks have sworn loyalty to the gods of techno-science. The violence didn't trouble itself with your bodies, it went straight for your heads. The ground beneath your feet has slipped away. We could have had tradition, we could have had history. We could have been proud of our parents. But they took them away from you. And here you are, coming to venerate the very people who screwed it all up.'

The astonishment on their faces emboldens him. He thrusts a finger in the direction of the feline queen. He feels a steely coldness against his thigh.

'You stormed onto the new continents like cattle to the slaughterhouse! Did you want to be Columbuses, Magellans, Armstrongs? Adventurers, conquistadors, gunslingers out in the prairies? They sheared you, shaved you, tore you open, hollowed you out, stuffed you, then set your own voodoo dolls upon you. But I don't blame you for that and I am not here to judge you. You couldn't have known. They ran you into the trap with the promise of a prettier face. I'd have to be truly soulless to hold this against you.'

Brian Baedekker and Rupert 'Rust' Stiglitz are standing at the confluence of two crowds – the one around Zoja and the other lending its ear to this barefoot firebrand nutcase. Wordlessly they are studying the passage of time. They feel all right. Semyona Sherdedova is sitting at Ludovico's feet and sighing in adoration.

'But I do blame you for being here now! For laying the gift of your presence at the very feet of those that took everything away from you. Do you know how much misery they caused? What a mess they made out of a world that generations had spent putting in order? How much blood had to be spilt before you could at least begin to say that the world even exists? That there are limits, that there are rules, that not everything is just a pulsing whim of this or that desire? Piles of bodies, for that! Real, blood-smeared cadavers, on the bones of which they built an order, so that not every child would have to grow up in a different world, so that everyone could say, this here is our rightful place on this planet. To be able to tend to your souls and not over and over again, constantly, with no end in sight, to tend to your appearance. They told you, *break yourselves in half*, and you broke yourselves in half! And now you're here begging for a smidgen of self-confidence so you'll be able to look at yourselves in the mirror again. Break with that devil's horde that robbed you of personality! I know you all want to be a thousand things and not just one, a born being, a simple human, but the truth is, always has been, and always will be, that you're either a person or a lousy sock puppet always on the lookout for somebody's limb!'

Enthusiastic applause. The people look at each other and nod to this artistic soul. Just look at how much effort he has invested into his performance, the sweat is pouring over his eyebrows and white streams of saliva are running down his chin. The Fisher King is circling around him with his chalice, catching every last drop of sweat. The elders catch sight of him again and resume their hunt with an asthmatic cry.

'Why are you applauding?'

Ludovico is amazed. They look affectionately right through him. They don't see him. He's just an echo in their heads and what he told them makes absolutely no difference, since they would in any case just sift everything through the sieve of their consciousness and be left exclusively with what they already knew beforehand. Now he begins to understand.

'Sock puppets!' he roars.

Brian and Rupert look at each other. 'Well this man is…'
'Yes.'

/

'Zoia!' 'Zoia!' 'Zoia?' 'Hey, Zoia.' *My name is Zoja.*

Max has managed to push his way through the crowd. His megaphone swings silently at his hip. He stands by Zoja, who is bent down beside the motionless old man. Running along his back are the hot impulses of the anxiety a person feels when they have worked out that some things have a life of their own. All he wanted was for everyone to have a pleasant evening, but now it's not only beauty that's in the air.

A tall, dark-skinned man with an unbelievably thick beard – Anwar – has rushed over from the other side and knelt down beside Zoja. Behind him stands a very attractive black woman in the embrace of a muscular young man and a few soldiers in uniform.

'What's wrong with him?' asks Max.

Zoja's look oozes concern.

'Diabetes.'

'Do you know where the nearest shop is? We need something sweet,' says the man beside her. Max's shoulders drop.

'There's nothing within five miles, little chance of any shop. The nearest one's across the river but the bridges have been closed for hours.'

Max's sense of anxiety thickens and runs down into his legs, which begin to quake. It's not entirely in good taste to think of oneself at such times, but he would really prefer not to see the old guy drop dead on him right here. Would he be held responsible for it? Was he supposed to, in addition to the lighting and the space and the sanitation and the electricity, also have taken care of…sugar?

'Why don't you read something to him?' Max asks her.

'If he isn't conscious, there's no point.'

'Ok, but what are we going to do?'

Zoja grabs his megaphone. She gets up and turns towards the crowd. Everyone sighs in expectation. Max closely observes what it means to be adored.

'Good evening, people. We have a serious problem on our hands. Does anyone happen to have something sweet to eat?'

Hold on a second, Zoja, you know full well that the taste of real food is now available only to the solemn, and sweet stuff only to the most solemn. Max would bet his private library that not one of those types is among them today. Fame lost the privilege of things; either you're swimming in attention, or you're offering attention, or you enjoy material things in blind obscurity.

Anwar searches through the old guy's pockets. He can't believe that somebody in his condition would not have come prepared. He smiles bitterly on finding a gaping hole in one of the pockets. Marjorie and her lover put their heads together, and the soldiers check their own pockets, though they know there's nothing there. It's the gesture that matters.

'We have a diabetic,' says Zoja to the crowd, which, expecting something completely different, still hasn't managed to respond. 'And we desperately need something sweet to bring him back around. So, please, if somebody has something, anything, I'd be incredibly grateful.'

Eyebrows rise, shoulders shrug, people shake their heads. They're powerless, although they would dearly like to help her. Zoja bites her lips in desperation and stares at them, hoping to create a kinder reality through the power of her gaze.

'Anyone?'

A hush falls over the entire car park. Ludovico pouts in silence and pushes away Semyona's constantly advancing hands. The artists have put a stop to their art, the audience puffs their cheeks in embarrassment. Even the two who have been banging away in the bushes all night decide to give it a brief rest.

'If you tell her to get dressed and come home with me, I might have something for you.'

Enough heads swivel to ensure a week's worth of pleasant weather in Boom-Bay. Standing there is a terribly boring man in ironed pants and a horrible beige shirt, his tie is untied and a nervous breakdown looms under his eyes. Mr Bollinger had just about given up, had just about cursed that worthless slut, who busied herself with those heathens, that darling, butterfly, princess of his, whom he took to the zoo where she could ride camels, oh how she laughed, and whose favourite ice cream was blue sky, and when she slept she looked like a rainbow, his angel, his own tiny personal sun, his little sweetie, ever since her mother died they had always stuck together, inseparable, and for as long as he was able he carried her piggy-back and when she peed on his neck on purpose he wasn't even angry because there was nothing left for him in this beloved world but her, his sweet, darling, little Lucy, and you can't even imagine how torturous it was to see her naked in the centre of a circle of long-haired monkeys who had responded to her bare porky gut with low growls, with shrill worshipping, and how soul-wrenchingly humiliating it was to wave a bar of chocolate in front of her, like he was after a fish instead of the most innocent being in this whole wide world, to bait and lure her back into the refuge of a safe home, away from this fallen horde, but as soon as the first unwashed clodhopper's eyes licked her up, she lifted her chin and wrinkled her nose as if she was too good for her own father, and she wiggled her bare arse, that arse he'd wrapped in diapers for years, that bloody…

'No!' cries Lucy.

/

There is nothing left but to smile now, even though I can feel something shatter deep within me. It's too bad you can't see them now, Mr Ž—, you would understand them completely. They rally around the poor man harbouring the miserable piece of chocolate in his fist, and he cries, bending like a hedgehog, I'm not giving it up, I'm not giving it up, *and they quickly grab his limbs and pull them, they go for his fingers and fiercely unclench them,* you have no right, *he cries.* No right. *But they want it. They'll love you. They don't want to punish you with that. Look at them, how they love. Look at their love. Nobody deserves anything. They will love you for free.*

PANCAKE PALACE

✦ ✦ ✦

the individual crumbles
because he is not alone

'Mnemotion is like a photograph of a landscape that's so beautiful you can barely handle looking at it. The sun is setting over a horizon of dark green sheets of trees, casting a pink light over cliffs of razor stone. There's a waterfall carved into the cliffs. A breath of rainbow on the mist of water drops. A black root rises from the earth. Seated on it is a colourful bird cleaning its wings with its beak. It is a frozen image. Nothing moves. It sucks you in and you're frozen along with it, in pure existence. It's so beautiful. You want it to stay. But only for as long as you're staring at the image. If you were there…I mean, if you were really there, bodily, the mere passing of time would shatter the image. The body demands attention. Your shoes are soaked, a stinging cold is prodding the tips of your toes, and you're all sweaty, your shirt is glued to your armpits and a cold wind is driving the air from your lungs. Your nose is running and your woolly jumper is rubbing at and itching your wrists. Ants are crawling under your trousers, and the itching, pinching of their little legs is driving you insane. Your muscles ache. You feel hot in some places, cold in others, and all the beauty of the scene lasts for only a fleeting moment, before becoming just another piece of neglected evidence of the fact that you were not actually meant to be conscious.'

Koito was sitting motionless in her chair, nursing a plastic bag. Evan had woken up and was talking away memories of the night before. He couldn't deny his swollen jaw, but it was easy enough to forget the humiliation and the flight. Koito got up and placed the bag on the pillow, by the side of his face that ached. He leant into it. Cold and numbing.

He stretched lazily and noticed he was naked.

'Was it you who undressed me?"

She didn't respond. He uncovered himself. The bedspread slid to the floor. He was watching her closely, but it didn't seem like his nakedness was having any effect on her. She was staring straight ahead, motionless. Evan cleared his throat and spat thick mucus into the cup by his bedside.

'Will you cook that thing for me again, what you made yesterday? What's it called again? *Stab*-something?'

When she turned her head towards him he thought he heard the droning of a quiet mechanism, as if he'd put his ear to a watch. She held out her hand and he didn't know what for.

'Give me your hand.'

He carefully placed his hand into hers. It was as cold as the bag of ice. He saw a needle coming out of the finger. When it pricked his finger, he leapt up.

'Ouch.'

'This pain will not last,' she said. A white glaze dropped over her eyes. He looked deep into them and caught a dance of tiny sparks. That's her soul, he thought. Her electric soul. A mathematical consciousness calculation, put on display. The whiteness faded and soon the black semi-circles returned, allowing no light to flee.

'It is not necessary,' she said.

'What's not necessary?'

'You may have coffee.'

He lay down and closed his eyes. Tensed his muscles, held his breath. Hunting Zen. He failed. A sliding off into all the wrong corners. He had sweated overnight. The damp sheet clung to his back. Koito hadn't moved an inch. When he opened his eyes, she was still there, motionless.

'I will.'

She turned and walked to the console. He observed her peculiar body. No joints, anywhere, just smooth lines of black plastic. Perfect symmetry. Her outfit evoked deep-sea diving. The skin on the forearms and neck differed only in hue, otherwise it was equally smooth, without hair, without marks, without pores, without bristles, without crinkles or cuts. The curves of her buttocks and breasts held no charm for mammals. A woman made from a mould. Beautiful even in the morning. She pressed a button. Hormones were back in command of Evan's brain. Blood rushing into the points of desire. He pressed his hand against his chest. Who pumps all this desire if not the heart? Maybe his cock was self-fuelling? That would be more acceptable.

Cup in hand she turned around, took a half-step and stopped.

'Evan, that's indecent.'

He smiled. He gyrated his hips obscenely. He wanted a response.

'Come closer,' he said.

She took a hesitant step. Zzz-zzz. Another step.

'Come.'

Her face revealed nothing, but the choppy motions of her body further stoked Evan's urges.

'Come,' he repeated quietly.

Steam rose from the cup. She offered it to him, but he gently took her by the wrist and very slowly pulled her closer. She leant her knees against the bed. Making sure no coffee would spill.

'Evan, you will have to get dressed.'

'Can I touch you?'

Something seized up in her neck.

'Non-aggressively,' she said.

He placed a hand on her thigh. Cold. With his other hand he took the cup and set it on the shelf. Standing firm. She was motionless. He stroked her.

'Evan, what are you doing?'

'You wouldn't understand.'

He went higher. Like he was glissading along porcelain. Her lips narrowed into a pale line and her eyelids gently shook.

'Evan, what are you doing?'

Her voice collapsed into an electronic echo.

'Can't you feel that?' he asked.

'That is too broad a question.'

He grabbed hold of her inner thigh.

'Non-aggressively,' she said. When she opened her mouth, a complete darkness gaped. No tongue, no saliva, no teeth. He wasn't frightened off by that. It excited him. He was overcome by eternal questions and he had to smirk. Life has spun out of control. It is multiplying and piling up over itself, creating realities that are no longer human. A state of heresy, a new sacrilege.

Even hell will have to keep up with the times. Can a machine sin?

He ran a finger between her legs. She didn't react. Everything was perfectly smooth. No slit. That drove him to the edge. He spread his hand and pressed. Her lips parted and her jaw sank. The blackness below her eyes was now the centre of his attention. Everything was aimed at it, and he was allowed to forget. He lay his hand on the nape of her neck. The muscles in his hand obeyed, and pulled.

/

He ran into the bathroom, vomited, soaked his head under cold water, vomited again, and stared into the mirror. Another man was looking back at him. When he spoke, Evan listened.

'Buddy, you know she made everything up just so you wouldn't go, right? You're aware of that? That pregnancy that came at just the wrong time for you, even though you were always careful, and all of a sudden this "spontaneous miscarriage", right when you turned them down?'

Evan shook his head. The thought had never even remotely crossed his mind. The man smiled.

'And you, with each day, sank deeper into those stupid lies. Mojca is pregnant, Edo can wait. Do you think they believed you? You tried so hard to keep up a cheerful appearance. But you didn't fool them. You're a director, not an actor. Everybody knew. They patted you on the back, congratulated you, with their sweaty palms. When jealousy turns into *Schadenfreude* a little bit of cheer marches right in. Chin up, Evan, their eyes said. Chin up.'

Again he leant over the sink to vomit. He was empty. Hollow. Dry heaves. Chin up, Evan.

'And what are you going to do now? Will you spontaneously miscarry your answer to Edo? Not so easy, eh? That's it. You had a chance to be on top of the world, but you decided the way you did. The decision was always yours. Don't use others as an excuse, even though you know you will. Chin up.'

'Shut up.'

'There's nothing in the world that can silence me, Evan. You know that. Admit defeat, accept the loss, be a man. You won't manage to forget. Chin up.'

'Shut up.'

'Chin up.'

He smashed himself with his fist. Shards of mirror fell into the sink. Blood spurted from his knuckles. As he watched it mix with the water, he saw his face multiplied in the jagged frames through the glaze of false light. He wiped himself off with the towel and clenched his teeth. He marched out. She was right where he'd left her. At the bare kitchen table. Irritated skin around her eyes and lips parted into a staged cramp of emptiness. How could he have been so blind?

'Mojca, tell me, why didn't you ever show up for an audition?'

She didn't respond. This role is made for her. The audience is firmly on her side.

He grabbed her by the chin and pulled her face to him.

'Where is he?'

She swallowed her saliva, rolled her eyes, shook and woke up. A sigh in the first row.

'Where is what?' she asked lazily, her mouth barely moving. They won't hear you up in the balcony, Mojca, louder.

'Where is my child? Where's the blood? What have you done with the blood?'

Her eyes narrowed as she gradually imbued the questions with meaning. Then they opened wide as she drew a sharp breath. Then she shrieked and kept shrieking. Evan lay his hand over her mouth, felt the moist, hot breath, she grabbed him, she sank her nails into his skin, freed her mouth and shrieked. A standing ovation.

Evan ran into the kitchen, opened the door of the cupboard under the sink, hauled out the bin and shook the contents out all over the floor. He kicked the rubbish around. Mojca shrieked. Then he ran into the bathroom again and took out the laundry basket. He dumped it out in front of her, over the table, she screamed, he threw the towels, socks, underwear at her. 'What did you do with it?' She caught her breath and shrieked in an even higher note. He ran out of the flat, down the stairs, the screaming following him through the doors, to the rubbish bin, and he started to tear at the plastic bags, digging for evidence that might restore at least a bit of his dignity. Passers-by avoided him. He gave up and sat down on the pile of rubbish. The shrieking coming through the window stopped. He looked up.

Mojca opened the window and put a foot on the ledge. Now it was his turn to scream. He stood up and ran back into the flat. He jerked her away from the window, threw her to the ground and pressed down on her with all his weight. She sobbed, whimpered quietly, the applause continued, flowers flew onto the stage, ladies fainted. 'What did you do with it?' he whispered in her ear. 'In the pancakes,' she said, and shut her eyes. Her body went limp. Evan got up. He closed the window. He went over to the front door. He closed it. Then to the bathroom. He looked through the toilet seat. He spat. He flushed. He swore. He flushed.

'Get out,' he said, and flushed. 'Get out.' The waters drained away.

The suck of emptiness. He was waiting for the cistern to fill. Get lost. Chin up. The show's over. Bravo. Wonderful. Marvellous. He flushed again and stared into the vortex of water.

That night he lost a tooth.

/

That hurts!

'Koito!' he screamed.

Koito's mouth had clamped shut and was holding him tight. He pressed his thumb into her neck and tried to push her away. A hot pain cut into his groin. He'd never felt anything like it. It tore right up into his ribs. He couldn't make it stop. He waved his arms and hit her on the neck, in vain. The mechanical sound grew louder, little cogs were creaking in her jaw, her mouth was closing tighter and he was trapped inside. The vision of a fox gnawing off its leg put him into a total panic. He started punching her, wildly, but that did nothing to stop the progression of those jaws. He grabbed the coffee cup and smashed it against her. The scalding liquid poured over her head and ran between his legs. He screamed. He tried to force the pain out through his throat. It was in no hurry to depart.

But he had succeeded. Koito crashed. Her hair frizzled, smoke rose from her head and the skin on her face slid downwards. Her eyes turned grey. Her grip eased. He had to wait for it to ease before he could escape and run to the bathroom to let the cold water take him in. Blisters surfaced. Swearing, he banged his head against the side of the cabinet. If he'd known how everything would turn out, he'd have ended it all years ago.

Drops fell from him as he moved to the cabinet and opened it in reluctant anticipation. It was empty. Koito had completely disabled him. The trace of drops then led to the console, where he pressed the button for first aid. There were many icons to choose from. *Knife, stomach, a toilet, mercury, fire.* He pressed *fire.* He'd been burned. He saw the airplane ticket on the counter. *What?* He collected his crumpled jeans from the floor and searched through the pockets. A business card. Lefkas. mAk. He felt a pleasant excitement that almost smothered the burning. The doors opened. He grabbed a green tube and a few pieces of gauze. The ointment smelt of urine and when he spread it over his penis he felt a chill. Koito had slid down from the bed to the floor with the hollow sound of an overturned vase falling onto a carpet without breaking. He allowed himself a lengthy smirk.

/

Taxis in Edo are like black, flattened hearses. You flag them down with a feverish shaking of your body under a wet sky which, in thick drops, lends rhythm to the metal and plays longwinded salon jazz inside people's heads. Evan had a bag of ice in his underwear. He showed the business card to the drivers, they looked him right in the face, *are you joking?*, and when they realized he was serious they angrily slammed the door in his face and drove off. Evan screamed after them that he would pay double, triple, what was the problem? When the fourth one drove off he went to the reception desk and showed the business card to the guy behind the table. The smile on his face looked like the irreparable results of surgery gone wrong. Perhaps he took it off at the end of his shift, hung it up with his tie on a hook and was allowed to go home grumpy. It must be hard to speak through such a smile. Nevertheless you could see how the wrinkles around his eyes sank immediately when he realized what Evan wanted to know.

'Mr Z—, I would not recommend going there, really, I just wouldn't. Firstly, speaking on behalf of the Kéki chain, because we care for our guests. Secondly, speaking personally, there's nothing there for you.'

Evan reflected for a moment. By whatever means. It wasn't his decision to make.

'Well, thank you, both you and your chain, for your concern, but I have to go there, today, right this minute, and in any case I am going to go there' – he waited for the non-verbal response – 'so I am absolving you of all professional and moral responsibility and asking you once more to tell me how I can most easily do what it is I want to do.'

The receptionist could not quite understand, though he could see that Evan wasn't going to give up.

'Do you even know where you're going?'

'I know.'

Evan did not know.

'All right,' said the young man and allowed his zeal to wane, 'you'll have to take the underground. The entrance is across the street. I'll write the directions on the business card. You're going to need personal identification and a gas mask.'

'A gas mask?' exclaimed Evan.

'If you don't have one you can buy one at the entrance to that sector. It costs forty asias. You can also rent one. The deposit is also forty asias. I would recommend wearing more robust clothing.'

Evan wanted to conceal his ignorance, not to let his surprise show. People always follow up lies with a confident look. In any case his shirt was soaked through. 'Robust clothing'? What was that supposed to mean? He waited for the receptionist to write down the underground lines and stations, then snatched the card, thanked him heartily and strode back into the lift.

/

Koito's leg was bent 180 degrees at the knee and her big toe was clacking against the floor. Why the hell did she even need nails? He watched her with slight discomfort as he changed clothes. She reminded him of a stormy morning, a crow's nest. Had the cleaning lady been in yet? He dragged her to the bed and covered her with a sheet. He picked up the newspaper from the floor and mulled over whether to take it with him. He glanced at the first page and threw it against the wall. The windows were darkened. The lights turned off by themselves when he left.

Dressed in a black anorak and hardy corduroy trousers he headed back out into the rain, encouraged by the receptionist's raised thumb. He caught a drop on his tongue and grimaced at the taste of chlorine. Artificial rain. Once he'd had a pool. He loved to swim. One birthday, his present was a dead pigeon. He scooped it out with the net, drained the water and left the pool empty.

He went down the stairs into the underground. The walls of black brick coated with varnish reflected the light of the halogen tubes. There weren't many people. A few businessmen in shoddy shoes, some merchants, weighed down by piles of wet goods, and three widows. No children. The benches were dirty, no one sat on them. Evan leant against the wall and looked at the people's backs. He was painting handprints on their shoulder blades, like in those caves in Argentina, and he felt grateful he wasn't a murderer. Called by the void.

The silent train arrived on its magnetic tracks, spilling green light. It made the faces look contagious. The lights inside were colourless. He sat beside a black-haired girl in a school uniform. She was holding a compact mirror and slowly, thoughtfully, applying make-up. Nobody looked at anyone.

The art of avoiding eye contact. He consulted the map on the business card. Easy as can be. He caught the smell of carbide. It was coming from the girl's hair. His eyes lingered over her, she didn't react. With her skirt hiked high above her knees, she looked like a dead bat. He cleared his throat. She inched away from him.

At the next station the car filled up completely. He had to draw his legs in and push them to the side. He was able to put the back of his hand against her thigh. The mirror followed her chin upwards. The people were sweaty. The odour from their bodies transformed the air into a pink fog. Disinfectant bags were hanging empty from the ceiling. Public claustrophobia. When you squeeze people into a small space, they aren't disgusted by the touching; they rub entire swathes of flesh against one another. If you pressed up against a stranger like that out in the open, everyone would find it strange.

He laid his palm over her knee. She didn't look at him. She closed her compact, stood up and fought her way through the throng to the exit, where she fixed her skirt. She was wearing striped black-and-white stockings. She was not at all attractive. A grey-haired gentleman sat down beside Evan and dug an elbow into his side.

'Is that you?' he asked. His hand lay pressed against his body. He raised it to his face and out popped his index finger. Evan followed the finger. He was looking at an advertising panel just below the ceiling. *FILLING*, in screeching letters. A face with a wide-open mouth. Revolting wrinkle canyons. Hair that looked dirty, thousands of tiny cuts and clogged pores, tired, wincing eyes. When had he become so ugly? He couldn't hold anything against Mundo, he'd tried as best he could with the lighting. But his face was radiating decay. He still liked his irises though. Those don't get old. He nodded.

'What happened to you?'

Evan ruminated. He ran a hand over his face. His cheeks

were swollen, his jaw ached. In the gap between his teeth there was a gluey mixture of gums and anxiety.

'I fell.'

'Where?'

'I just fell.'

His fellow passenger inhaled and nodded. A whispering ran through the car. The faces of teenagers and adults were whizzing between him and the advertisement, hiding behind outstretched palms, giggling. An artist on the underground, what kind of a terrible joke is this? When he bent his head and counted shoes, separating them by income, by activity, by sex, the whisperers gained courage. When he looked up again, the crowd's eyes were penetrating him.

'That's not me,' he said unobtrusively and shook his head. The eyeballs didn't move, so he raised his voice. 'That's not me. You've mistaken me for someone else. Would that guy take the underground?' He'd sown confusion, a pinch of doubt. 'I'd love to be him, believe me. Better than being me, that's for sure.' He had just about convinced them when the guy sitting next to him poked him again.

'Why did you lie to me?' 'I didn't,' he replied. The gentleman took another breath and coolly raised his eyebrows. Somebody grabbed Evan by the shoulder. He shook him off. He did it again. 'Really, you're wrong.' They were not wrong. They approached. A forest of bodies. He raised a lip and almost growled, 'Leave me alone.' They were shocked.

'And where's your sponsor?' someone asked.

'In prison.'

'Oh.'

'And the replacement?'

'She crashed.'

'Oh.'

That cooled them down, made them take a step back. A foreigner without a sponsor could be dangerous. They turned back to their individual burdens. Evan remembered he had a mobile. He searched his pockets. Had he taken it with him? He couldn't remember. But it was there. The body is always on the lookout for contact. The battery was almost dead. No signal underground. Thirty-seven missed calls. Oksana I. B., Oksana I. B., Oksana I. B., Oksana I. B., Oksana I. B., Oksana I. B.,…He turned the phone off, put it back, took it out again, slid his finger over its plastic form, threw it onto the floor and stamped on it with his heel. Durable thing. He raised his foot and hammered it down on the phone. It shattered and the frightened people took a step back. He felt better. The red light flashed for the next stop. He got up. A fellow passenger took him by the elbow and from his sedentary position looked at him with mournful eyes.

'Don't tell me you're getting off here?'

Evan retracted his hand then forcefully nudged a woman who was standing in his way. They cracked their knuckles and gritted their teeth in judgement. He didn't apologize. He didn't answer the man. The doors opened and he rushed out. No one else got off. That was good.

/

The pale lights in the corridor were blinking with epileptic pulses of electricity in a long, rhythmless line, giving the impression of a sequence of quickly moving spaces that would crush anyone who remained in the vacuum of darkness. There was a slight twist in the corridor, the end was not visible. Every few seconds a light in the distance revealed the outline of a sitting figure, its back leaning against the wall. Evan gathered his courage. The ice in his underwear was already melting. He waited for the light and looked between his legs to see whether a dark stain of moistness had started to show. It looked dry. The bag hadn't leaked.

His steps produced no echo. The collective buzzing of gases sounded like television snow. The birth of the universe. Even in man-made shafts the nature of all things resonates.

He was getting close to the figure on the floor. He could more clearly make out his outlines in the pulses of light. Was that a violin he was holding? An old vagabond, mentally pulverized, comes during the day to play an old-continent solo into the fragmented darkness, far away from people. He dug around in his pocket for some change.

'Play me a few cents' worth!' he called out. The figure did not move.

He paused, looked down, ok, took a step. Maybe he's sleeping? Is he dead? Why isn't he playing? Evan wanted some music, so he whistled. The whistling travelled down the corridor like a line of wool. Crackling with static. The shadows followed it.

The broad hat like those worn by gauchos on the southern steppes, over a black coat with mould creeping down the sleeves, and the tips of cracked boots. In his lap, a miserable guitar with a broken string that formed a curl of steel at the neck. Evan stood and listened for the lungs to make a sound. Not even the slightest of movements. The coldness between his legs felt like encroaching fear. With each pulse of light he expected the hat to rise and reveal a face of rusted metal, or for the coat to grab him by the leg with pointed compass-toes. He placed a hand over the chest. Stillness. He had to admit he was enjoying this adrenaline game. But he soon tired. This pile of clothes showed no life, not even an appalling one. He reached into his pants and pulled out the transparent bag now filled with icy water. He tossed it onto the guitar.

The guitar collapsed into dust, the lap sunk, the hat rolled off and spat out a grey skull that bounced along the tiled floor with the sound of high heels clacking. The light went out. Evan shrieked and ran.

/

There was no one at the exit. A narrow staircase led Evan up to a platform where he stopped for a moment to marvel at the emptiness. Light entered the space from cloudy windows way up under the ceiling. Thick patches of dust were converging into tiny civilizations, cobwebs divided the ceiling into fractals, the door of the kiosk lay bent on the floor, granting a glimpse of its innards. All around lay colourful oily puddles that smacked of petrol rainbows. The platform had been abandoned for long stretches of eternity. Evan had no time to wonder. It seemed opportune that desire had led him to such a place.

He trudged into the dust. All the exits were closed tight. Beside them were rickety stands full of long rows of gas masks. He took one and looked at it. The snout of a cow and the eyes of a squid. He had a burning sensation and his jaw creaked with pain when he blew the dust off the mask. He ran his hands along the edges of one of the exits. No gaps. His sense of restlessness abated when he spied the console. He wiped it down and stared into the shimmering red light, the tiny eye of the machine. He put the mask over his head. He pressed hard on the button.

When the air pressure had equalized, the tentacles of incoming wind spun the cob-webbed dust into giant drills. The fog from outside crept onto the floor like a tongue. He stepped out. He didn't know whether the rusty orange tones were caused by daylight or by the glass filter in the mask. The tops of the tower blocks vanished in curtains of smog, and then there were the broken-windowed façades, broken streetlamps, scattered letterboxes, motionless, silent and calm. Evan struggled to read the numbers on the faded signs. The path guided him in among the buildings. He looked back and tried to remember where he had turned so he wouldn't get lost. A loaf of bread would come in handy. There were no birds.

At the entrance to a tower block of fired brick he found what he was looking for. The right number with a sign that more or less matched the one on the card. First he knocked boldly, but the sound did not spread. He took a step back and looked around. Aluminium plates were welded over all of the windows. There was no bell, just a square grille over the speaker by the door. He noticed a sort of rope hanging from the ceiling. He looked at it up close and realised it was sewn together out of cat tails. He pulled the sleeve of his anorak over his hand and tugged it. Nothing.

The speaker coughed.

'Who is it?' asked a computerized voice.

Evan went closer so he could be heard through the mask.

'Evan Z— here, I'm here for Mr Saito,' he looked at the card. 'For Lefkas Saito.'

The speaker went silent. Evan's shoulders tensed up as he waited. It was so close again, suddenly, that evasive feeling, that indescribable feeling. It can't bear angles and edges, it hates language, and images as well… You're either present within it, or

'Password?'

Astonished, he downplayed the alarm he felt and pulled himself together. Password? He closed his eyes and tried to repeat that conversation with Lefkas. mAk? What had he said? That he could, what, roll, drown, bathe in it? He looked at the business card again. Through the fog of glass it was hard to make out what was written there.

'Habeas cor?'

A hoarse laugh. The electric flap kicked free. Evan hurried inside. He found himself in a small room and felt anxious when the doors locked behind him. Utter darkness. The sound of sipping and the entry of light through a slot. It blinded him.

'You can take it off,' a man's voice said.

/

'That buzzer hasn't rung in years,' said Lefkas, as they climbed the stairs. 'At first I didn't even realize what it was. Were you waiting long?' Evan inhaled the dry air and looked over the railing into the depths below. The staircase didn't start at the ground floor, it went deeper. Flies were buzzing all around him.

Lefkas was dressed in a dirty pink bathrobe, his hair was dishevelled and he was wearing slippers. Each step he took rattled the keys in his pocket. 'Not at all,' replied Evan. 'It didn't take long for me to find you.'

'And what came over you? What made you come through the air?' asked Lefkas.

'Through the air?'

'From outside.'

'Is there some other way?'

Lefkas smirked. 'Perhaps.'

Evan didn't get the joke.

'I've come for some mAk.'

Lefkas stopped for a moment, but then moved on again with a quiet 'aha'.

'What is this place?' asked Evan.

'It's my home.'

'Home?'

'Everyone has one.'

Silence. Evan could hear a low roaring coming from the depths below that wrapped everything in a gentle vibration. When he grasped the railing, the vibration entered his bones. Evan exhaled loudly to shoo away a fly from his forehead. Lefkas looked at him and mumbled something indecipherable, something like 'insects, yes'. When they were in front of the door to the flat, he turned to Evan.

'Where's your sponsor?'

'Crashed.'

'The replacement?'

Evan nodded.

'But do you know what happens when you go too long without?' asked Lefkas.

Evan looked up in surprise.

'What do you mean, *what happens*? What's supposed to happen?'

Lefkas shook his head, gave a commiserating smile and turned the handle. They entered, but Evan didn't stop.

'Wait a sec. What did you mean by that, by if I *go too long without*? She crashed this morning…'

Now it was Lefkas's turn to be amazed. 'A woman?'

'A woman, yes. Koito something, a few hours ago, I don't know. What time is it anyway? What happens if you go without?'

The flat had seen better days. It looked uninhabited, except for a corner at the far end of a room where a lamp was shining over a stack of books. Orange foam was poking out of the innumerable holes in an armchair by a table. A carpet, grey and threadbare, showed the way through the hall. The eyes of strangers stared out at Evan from the photos hanging in cheap frames on the walls. None of them looked like Lefkas.

'Shut the door, please. Quick. The flies.'

Evan shut the door.

'Tell me what happens.'

'Nothing,' replied Lefkas, to keep him quiet. 'Forget I even mentioned it. It doesn't concern you.'

'How doesn't it concern me? Didn't you just say—'

Lefkas interrupted him with a raised hand.

'Believe me. You came here for a reason, so I'm not going to talk about time. We're here. That's everything.'

Evan's mouth still hung open but no more sound came out. Lefkas picked up what looked like a board, folded it into a chair and offered him a seat. When Evan sat down, Lefkas, quick as a cobra, jumped up, in one motion removed a slipper from a foot and used it to whack at the wall. A black smudge was all that remained. Evan was impressed. He praised Lefkas.

'Ah, flies. Can't live with them, it's even worse without,' said Lefkas darkly, his eyes on the quickly drying smudge.

'What do you mean?'

Lefkas turned his gaze from the wall and looked a little dumbly at Evan, as if he wanted to apologize in advance for the stupidity of what he was about to tell him.

'I bred them myself, up top, in the attic.' Evan focused on the slipper Lefkas was still holding in his hand. 'It was so quiet, and empty, and hollow.' The smudge was crusty, dried, hard. 'But I said to myself, I said, hey, at least there'll be someone here, at least I'll have somebody, no? Do you follow?' Evan nodded. Thousands of stuck wings, feelers, octagons of eyes… 'Now I get mad every day when they get on my nerves. But I can't take the silence either. I get scared.' Evan blanched.

'Then what, what do you do here?'

Lefkas dropped the slipper and put it on.

'I proclaim the faith,' said Lefkas.

'That's what you call it?'

Lefkas slumped into the armchair and spread his arms.

'It might seem funny to you. For you, mAk is a bit of a diversion, a joke, a thrill. Some little mind game, yes? You don't have to defend yourself, I know how it is,' he said as Evan hastened to object. 'Just so you don't think I'm judging you or anything. It's completely legitimate, this. But do you know how many people out there are dead? Ever think about that? Masses of consciousness that suck the days through straws, or the days suck them. Loners. Good-for-nothings. Fools. Millions of them… With broken mirrors for company. Every minute they trip about in the shoals, every moment they want out, they want in, they want…'

Evan felt his lungs constricting. He bent over to catch his breath.

'Are you all right?' asked Lefkas.

Evan had tears in his eyes. He nodded. He swallowed back a lump.

'How should I know what they want?' continued Lefkas. 'For the world to have mercy on them? For them to have mercy on the world? I've been watching them all my life. I know them well. And mAk is a simple combination. It smears a little electricity over the brain and releases a few hormones: neurotrophins, oxytocin, vasopressin and so on. Like I said, nothing special. If you're in love, the brain does it all by itself. But some people have never been in love. If you asked me, honestly, I'd have to say I'm doing charity work. I'm waking the dead, so to speak. Are you all right?'

Evan's throat was parched. He was desperately fighting back a tickle that would lead to a ceaseless coughing fit.

'I'd like a glass of water,' he croaked.

Lefkas sprang up. 'Where are my manners! Don't be offended,' he said on the way to the kitchen. 'You can see I don't get a lot of guests.' He disappeared through the door. Evan was beginning to sweat. He threw the gas mask on the table and skimmed the spines of the books. They were unfamiliar to him.

'Would you like some tea?' he heard from among clanging pots. 'No, water. Please, just water,' replied Evan. He ran a hand over his stomach. He hadn't eaten yet. 'Do you have something I can munch on?' he asked, and winced at his words.

'To munch on?'

'Do you happen to have some food? Sorry, but I haven't eaten anything today…'

Kitchen sounds. The sigh of the refrigerator opening. Tick-tock, tick-tock. Evan rubbed his fingers over his temples. He relaxed in expectation. He would once again feel. Again

Lefkas tottered in with a glass in one hand and a plate of pancakes in the other.

'I apologize. I hope they're still ok. They're left over from yesterday. Unfortunately I used up all the jam, and I've got nothing else to put in them.'

Evan shrugged. He drained the glass in one go. He rolled a pancake. As he bit into it, he fell into a fountain.

/

What doesn't break. What doesn't erase itself. What doesn't end

You're moving through tough places. Sowing shadows. Counting letters. You're hoping. You drop to your knees. Grass drenches. The bird is cleaning its wings with its beak. The cliff is screaming. You hammer a wedge into your back. You're not blown away. You remain.

you remain

/

Lefkas's face seemed very close. He held Evan in his lap like a helpless man. A tiny ad-hoc pietà. He was pouring black liquid into his mouth and Evan was drinking it. The cramp eased off. His limbs had spread out over the carpet.

'I didn't know, I didn't know,' repeated Lefkas between the pauses.

'What didn't you know?' asked Evan. He sent encouraging signals to the muscles. Let's go, guys, off to work. Chin up. Their male bodies grew aware of the delicacy of the situation and sought the most appropriate way of turning this into something ordinary. Evan picked himself up, shook out his trousers and smiled.

'What didn't you know?' he repeated to Lefkas, who, pale, could finally breathe normally.

'That bloody come-here-Mojca, you almost gave me a heart attack.'

'Sorry?'

Lefkas was kneeling down and catching his breath.

'Nothing. As long as you're ok. I didn't know things were so critical. How long have you been without?'

Evan couldn't remember.

'A day, two. Yesterday I had to drink something else.'

Lefkas stood up, took a bag of powder from his pocket and offered it.

'That will do you for a few days. Just keep it hidden from the sponsor. Let him go on taking care of you, and keep it for yourself.'

Evan nodded.

'Thank you.'

Lefkas found himself in a predicament. He pulled his hair over his shoulder and quickly braided and unbraided it down around his stomach.

'Well, I like to help, as I said, I raise the dead, as it were, but, in any case, you probably won't be upset…' Evan stared at him, while Lefkas was fidgeting. Finally he gathered his courage. 'It's not for free.'

Evan trembled.

'Of course not! Of course not! It's never for free, and it shouldn't be!' he rifled furiously through his pockets, pulled out his wallet, grabbed a wad of banknotes and pressed them into Lefkas's hand.

Lefkas responded with a quiet *that's too much*, but Evan wasn't listening.

Soon he was being carried around the room, looking at photographs and leafing through books, leisurely browsing through piles of paper that were lying on the floor, scrupulously ignoring the pancakes. Lefkas shook off his shame, stuffed the money into his pockets and, relaxed, monitored him, when Evan suddenly cried out, 'Do we have a rehearsal?'

He stroked his chin, shuddered at the pain, scratched between his legs, again staving off the pain, and leapt up.

'I think I have a rehearsal, today. We open next week.'

Lefkas whistled in admiration.

'What time is it?' asked Evan.

'I've given up on time. There's no clock in here. Going by feel, I'd say a little after noon.'

'By feel…' Evan tried out the phrase in his mouth. It felt a little short. He looked at Lefkas again.

'I have to go back.'

Lefkas smiled, 'Of course, of course. I'll show you a shortcut so you won't go wandering off again. And you won't need a mask.'

Evan grabbed the mask and marvelled at it. He'd hung it up and forgotten about it.

'Are we done here?' he asked.

He followed Lefkas and slid over the edges of the steps, down, down, down. Lower than the ground floor. The sound was growing louder. Evan could feel his teeth jumping in his mouth.

'What is that?'

'No one knows,' replied Lefkas.

'How's that, *no one knows*?'

'If you had the time, I'd show you.'

'What? Why don't you just tell me?'

Before going on, Lefkas stopped for a second, as if he were pondering very weighty matters.

'Down there, way down there, is a door of sorts without a handle and without hinges.'

'Then how can it be a door?'

'Well, I said it would be tough to explain.'

Evan apologized and asked him to continue.

'The door won't open, ever. People have tried and tried. It's impossible to open it. I have no idea how the door got there and since when it's been there. Behind it there must be some who-knows-what making that endless racket. Some sort of a machine or a reactor, what do I know. If you put your hand on the door, it rattles every fibre in your body. But I wouldn't exactly say it's a bad feeling, it's just so, you know, strong, you know, something you should experience just once in your life, but beware the second time. I don't know if you're following.'

'I'm following.'

Evan was following.

'That's more or less it, actually. I'm used to it now, just

like I'm used to the flies. I'm not saying I'm not interested in what's up with it, but we can't know everything, right?'

Evan was staring dreamily over the railing. The vibration felt good. He left his body and imagined he was there when Lefkas stopped.

'Is that the door?' Evan asked timidly. It looked perfectly normal.

A doory door.

'No, no,' replied Lefkas, 'this one takes you to the station. Just straight ahead, to the sign. You can't miss it. There's one every half hour.'

'Just straight ahead and every half hour,' repeated Evan.

'Yes.'

Lefkas grabbed the handle and opened the door. Evan saw something horrifying in a circle of light, he yelled, grabbed the handle and slammed the door shut.

'What the hell was that?'

Lefkas smiled.

'Don't be afraid, it's just our birdman.'

'Bird?'

'Oh my, no, no. A man. His mother was employed in Okuma. Close to Fukushima. You know it?'

Evan was horrified.

'Oh Jesus.'

'Yes. He spends entire days down here. Completely harmless, nothing to be afraid of. He says he only wants peace. And if anyone deserves it…'

'What did you say? *Birdman?* Why do you call him that?'

'Oh, sorry,' Lefkas turned red. 'It slipped out. I shouldn't have said that. His name is Toto.'

Evan hugged Lefkas. An astonished gasp. A squeeze. They parted. Looked at each other fondly. Threw a bowline across the rift and went their separate ways.

/

Before his eyes adjusted to the darkness – it was hard to say where the blue light that cast twelve shadows on everything was coming from – he stood utterly still. The steam hissing from the pipes and the constant rhythm of the drops gave the place a stamp of heavy industry. A deserted mine shaft or just an abandoned underground line? Off in the distance, Toto's grotesque form swayed. Evan couldn't shake off his discomfort. He felt naked. Aside from his body he had nothing. He saw a metal rod on the floor between some flakes of steel and a pile of boards and snatched it up. Holding it in his fist, he marvelled at its coolness, at its vague intarsia, and felt much better. The tip was sharpened like a harpoon or a pike. He held it in front of him and let his shifted centre of gravity move him forward.

It seemed that Toto hadn't heard him approaching from behind.

Evan's stomach stirred. Pressure in the ears. He went right up to him.

A round lump of naked flesh on two legs, with stunted growths in place of hands, like chicken wings. That's probably why they called him birdman. He looked like those butchered, plucked and scrubbed chickens wrapped in plastic and sold in supermarkets. Wrinkled, slippery, hairless flesh. Evan couldn't believe such a being could exist. A mino-gallus, a poultry-geist, a cockatoo-asterion! So many forms of this world… In spite of himself, he felt loathing. For that gloomy creature, for its mother, for its father, for the world that allowed such splitting of chromosomes, for the origin of all things. What a gaudy, paltry beast! Who let him in here? How did he get here? Why had he been born? He couldn't fathom answers to the questions this unfortunate image stoked. His blood boiled. Commiserate, if you can. Commiserate? How? Who chooses between things that are and things that shouldn't be? Each moment, penal sentences are carried out, in menstrual cramps and on the gallows, in orgasms and car crashes, in dreams, memories, on the plateaus of oblivion, through the word, through silence, through action, things are sparked into existence and things vanish, they manifest themselves, they glow, they disappear without a trace, and some things shriek in the quiet eternity of nothingness, far beyond our gazes… Who chooses? Who decides about all things? Evan raised the metal rod to finish him off.

Toto turned around slowly and aimed his single eye at him. It wasn't clear whether he had gauged Evan's intentions. Between his legs a slit opened, emitting transparent slime that shone blue in the light.

'What?' he asked in a completely ordinary voice.

The rage departed from Evan. He threw down the stick and put his hands on his hips. 'Nothing,' he wanted to say, but the word didn't want to come out. They stood observing each other. Neither of them would ever know what it was like to be on the other side. They were fated to wonder, to stare, to remain silent. Fellow travellers of the image. Every *what* will be left hanging in the air. Evan put his hand on his chest and felt something quiet there.

'Sorry,' he said. 'I didn't really see you.'

Toto's wings fluttered in helplessness. Evan stepped around him and walked, depressed, to the station. He waited for the train.

/

He missed her. He missed himself. To be missing. That used to seem something very cheap. But then, on the train, in the middle of a half-empty carriage, with no noteworthy features on the people around him, missing rained all over him, and he once again felt a shade better. Nothing evoked it, he couldn't say that he was looking at a particular form, recognizing a particular fragrance, a particular taste that might spin the wheels of memory and conjure up before his eyes a pile of little fragments that would make him regret their no longer being real. No, he simply abandoned himself to the stream, he opened a valve in his brain and bent his head down to the vapours. Warmth took over. He lay down his shield of offence, a nasty prism that coloured memories with their consequences and took them instead as pieces of a puzzle. The puzzle has no intentions of its own, it is broken up merely so that it can at some time become whole again. The red coat, yes, just a quilted fabric, travelling under the fingers of young seamstresses from unfortunate lands, rocking on a boat, or flying above the clouds, in cardboard boxes, in forklift trucks, on shelves, folding under the nimble hands of saleswomen, emitting its charm into the air so that she could take it, so that he could buy it for her, that evening, before they went to see the show that he had put on – he no longer wanted to fool himself, it had always been that way – just for her. They wanted to take it too far.

Their highlands had no peak. Just slopes. Sex can be a strange thing.

Sometimes it has to hurt for you to enjoy it. They didn't notice when their descent began. And all that drama about the child, then… Evan wanted to leave. Already long before, and afterwards completely. Was that really his life?

When he, with a lowered chin, looked around, observing his body from above, he saw that it bore no witness to this fact. It could be anyone's body. Where were those elaborate stories hiding? If he opened up his head and took his brain into his lap, would it look any different from the brains of others? If he pushed his finger into it…would he be able to read it? She didn't deserve that. No. Nobody deserved that. All the warm afternoons, all the mornings of longing… Hundreds of Saturdays on the slopes. Yes, they went skiing. He smiled. Up. Down. Up. Down. A polar bipolar sport. There is so much of this… He was sitting and moving his hips. Leafing through the moments. He remembered each of her smiles. She bit her lips and nails, sometimes. She hiccupped. She filled rooms with the scent of sex. She stole people's teeth. He never brought flowers. He fled instead. It seemed easier. Seemed.

Who says that men never get pregnant? If he didn't bear her, somewhere inside him, how was it that she was here? Where is she? He put his elbows on his knees and rested his face in his palms. He grew indulgent. All that missing had warmed him into a good person. But the past rose up before his eyes each time anew, he knew that and if the next moment he was again going to wrestle with hatred…what then? Nothing endures and nothing remains. The rift widens. A pair of men in white work-overalls boarded the train.

Slowly they walked through the carriage, looking up. Evan watched them go by. He was pricked by the acrid smell of glue. They stopped in front of him. In front of him, up there, in two dimensions, trapped open-mouthed under the Plexiglas and blazed through with light. They took out a red square, placed it over his mouth and rolled a paint roller over. They repeated this three times. Then they stood there and marvelled at their work. At the next station they got off, satisfied. Evan went over to see what that was over his mouth.

CANCELLED

/

The fake clouds were shredding under the dome. A strange sun was scattering its rays over wet patches of concrete. Steam from the floor. People placed palms to their foreheads, saluting in vain, shielding their eyes from the glare. Evan staggered out into the street and stopped, out of breath. He had to take off his anorak. It was too hot. He was blocking the path for the people coming from the underground. Someone shoved him.

He caught sight of Oksana. She was leaning against the wall in front of the entrance to the skyscraper, smoking a cigarette, nervously flicking ash as she jerkily turned her head. She was wearing a red dress. He hid himself behind an advertising panel. Observed her with half a face, with one eye. She took her phone out of her pocket and tapped the screen. She leant it against her ear. Desperate, she opened her mouth – he couldn't hear, she was probably swearing – and threw the phone to the ground. Apparently she regretted this, since she immediately stooped to pick it up and put it back together. She couldn't. She straightened up and kicked it over the edge of the pavement, into the street. She put out her cigarette and lit a fresh one. She was going to stay there.

Evan merged with a group of businessmen, using their bodies as cover. When they turned the corner, he went into the street and raised a hand. He summoned an old, shoddy taxi. He knocked on the window and waited for the driver to let him in. A dark face peered out at him. Its cheeks were stamped with bundles of black dots. A tiny incision ran above its right eye. A white membrane clouded the eye. The face wore a catlike smile.

'Where to?' a crackly voice asked.

Evan had tried to put on a friendly face, but failed. It was hot. Sweat was running down over his eyebrows. When he spoke he had to catch his breath.

'Hello. Can you do me a little favour?'

'That's what I'm here for,' the driver replied. 'Though I don't know if it's still a favour when you're paying for it.'

Evan removed his wallet from his pocket. It was empty. He'd given everything to Lefkas.

'She'll pay,' he said.

The driver leant back.

'I don't see anyone.'

Evan smiled distractedly. He ran his hand over his nose. Took in some air.

'Yes, yes. Here's the thing. You'll turn right over there…' The driver raised his eyebrows. '…and you'll go up to the entrance to Kéki, you know it?' Evan waited for the driver, who was losing patience, to nod. 'Well, in front of the entrance there's a woman standing there in a red dress, her name's…

doesn't matter, the main thing is that you can't miss her, tell her that Evan Z— is waiting in MUD, you know it?' The driver was now eyeing him with suspicion, but nodded. '... And drive her over there. She'll pay you. Remember, Evan Z—, to MUD, it's all good, can you manage it?'

The driver was sizing him up. He stuck his head out of the window and stared at the ground. Evan pondered.

'This better not be some kind of scam,' the driver said.

'No, no,' said Evan, 'she'll pay, don't worry.'

'Don't worry...' the driver repeated, looking him in the eye and grinning.

'Give me your shoes and I'll drive her for free.'

'Shoes? My shoes?'

They both stared down at them.

'I like them,' said the driver. 'Are they leather?'

'American bison,' replied Evan proudly, and bit his tongue.

'Bison? What's that?'

'Some sort of bovine species. You know, like a cow.'

The driver whistled. They stared at each other. Then Evan shook his head and pulled his heels out of his shoes. In his socks he stepped onto the damp concrete, bent down, picked up the shoes and held them out to the driver.

'Uh, where have you been?' the driver asked.

Ribbons of dust hung from the soles. Evan lost it.

'What the hell do you care where I've been? Are you going to take them or not?'

With utter tranquillity the driver grabbed the shoes by the laces and threw them onto the seat next to him. Evan sighed and tried to regain his composure.

'Do you still remember what to say?'

'Yeah, yeah. Evan Z—. MUD. The woman in red.'

'That's right. Good. Thank you.'

'Thank you,' said the driver, winked with his blind eye and drove off.

Evan went to the corner and peeked around. The taxi driver kept his word. He stopped in front of Oksana, who was soon persuaded.

She probably rushed into the taxi as soon as she heard his name. When they disappeared down the street, Evan felt relief.

/

As he walked, the rough concrete jabbed at his soles. He was looking at the pavement and avoiding the litter when a few lines from something he'd once heard, a long time ago, echoed through his head… He stopped. He felt a piercing gaze on the nape of his neck and turned around. A boy was pushing a cart loaded with hazelnuts up a slope. Some old men were bickering around a street lamp. The people looked at the ground. Evan bent his head and wiggled his toes. How did it go again?

Give me…

He muttered something to himself and tried to remember. That was one of her lines. A long time ago, in another life, they had been friends. He looked at himself in the reflection of a shop window. Once he'd had friends. He smiled bitterly. Friends. What an empty word that is when you're all alone. He didn't like to remember his youth. Too much had changed. He fixed his hair. Too much… He'd happily disappeared into love, back then. When the funerals suddenly started to pile up, he was quick to chain Mojca to himself. *Be my support*, he'd said, although he needed something entirely different. *Be my oblivion* doesn't sound so good. When had he lost his friends? Why was he thinking of that now?

Give me shoes…give me shoes of…

He pushed the door and stepped onto the cold marble.

The receptionist who had given him directions was no longer behind the desk. He'd lent his smile to a new one. Evan nodded slightly at him and smiled when the young man looked at his feet.

He raised his shoulders. *What can you do?*

Give me shoes…so I can…

He walked over to the lift and gleefully pressed the button. His pocket was weighed down by the little bag of mAk and he was looking forward to the evening. Everything had been ruined. That didn't bother him. He was just a bit sorry about the show. It wasn't bad at all. If he hadn't been so wrapped up in it, if he ever looked at it with sober eyes, he would probably think highly of it. And if it hadn't been his he'd probably even be envious of the director. But what did it matter? Either way, he knew no eyes were going to see it. So what point was there to the whole thing? To open your mind to strangers, to dance without aim… Now they'll throw him out of Edo and he'll go home with a mask of shame cast over his face. He'll take it off in private and try to pass as peacefully as possible the handful of days that were left to him. Quietly he rose into the air.

…so I can walk…

The flat was still dark. He entered, avoided looking at the bed and walked into the bathroom. He took a leak, washed his face, gargled a few ghosts away and spat them down the plughole. He watched them slink off. He took off his socks and threw them in the hamper. His toes reminded him of Toto's wings. He shook off the image with a cough. He collected the newspaper from the floor, sat at the table and lit the light.

Give me shoes out of despair…

A scandal! They'd arrested a network of sponsors who'd been making money with mAk. He laughed loudly. You scoundrel, you, Gordon – all that time he'd taken him for a fool. Friends. At the console he ordered foie gras. It came in an elegant pot, accompanied by a roll. He cut the roll in half. As he read, he smeared it on thickly. Giggling the whole time. Gordon had himself a serious problem. Sponsors were supposed to provide their protégés with mAk for free. He frowned. What kind of a place was Edo then, if the people in it died drugless? He turned to the window. The panes were darkened. He'd been here a whole year but hadn't lifted the veil a single inch. Blind lives…

FILLING *Performance in Financial Trouble. An Interview with Junichiro Marukama: Mockery and Bluff.* Evan felt a touch of anger, which quickly subsided. He didn't read what was written there. Who cares? All this mess of text to make people feel each other. Words hold no truth. A transparent film over the emptiness. You can beat the drum so it's heard far and wide, but when you take the skin off the sound disappears. He pressed the button and waited for coffee. He placed the bag of mAk on the table and stared at it. What had Lefkas said? Infatuation? And not love? Absently he turned the page. The plane ticket wafted to the floor. He stepped away from the table, picked it up and flattened it against his chin. He looked at the clock. A little before six. The flight was at eight. But where to? And who'd left it here? He didn't want to worry himself with that. He would leave when they told him to leave. He put it down and looked away.

A new serial killer on the prowl. He pulled the cup that had appeared in the wall a little closer. He tore a piece off the newspaper, folded it and shook a bit of dust into it. There was no spoon. They never gave him one. He licked the knife. He sprinkled the dust into the coffee and used the blade to mix it in. As he stirred, his gaze rested on the photo-robot. His hand stopped. That smile. The cut eye. The constellation of black dots on the cheeks. He stood up abruptly, tipping over the cup. The coffee spread over the table, staining the newspaper. He was horrified. Oksana. He ran to the door, knife in hand, and stopped. What to do? He went back to the console and pressed the first-aid button. Who should he call? The icons were all wrong. He pushed the button for back, back, back... He remembered the line. The coffee stain had stretched its tentacles over his ticket.

He looked at it. His eyes were opened wide.

'Give me shoes out of despair, so I can walk upon it.'

The sound of his voice filled the room. He turned a button and made the window transparent. The sun

/

the sun had sharpened the edges of all objects the table the bed the bulbs in the lights the frames the chairs the bristle of the carpet the handles the ropes the cupboards the overturned cups and plates the knife of her skin was sticking out of the dress exploding with every pore into an impossible sharpness he sensed the pupils dilating like the arms of scissors they will flay the rawest of things he staggered to her to her legs to her arms to her chest to her he unhooked her from the embrace of the bed he took her away pressed her against him it wasn't on purpose he wanted to say it wasn't on purpose he wanted to hear it wasn't wasn't it it wasn't on purpose he wanted to hear she wasn't cold like ice like a machine like ice she was a machine wasn't she he wanted to hear only a machine and that it isn't so bad wasn't it and he wanted to say that it wasn't on purpose and on her face on her nose on her chin cold like ice and became mad became rough he didn't want to hear on purpose on her neck on her stomach the tightness of her stomach in the rosy sun pale and cold and screamed and became mad and got rough only a machine not a grave but a landfill he wanted to hear that it wasn't so bad that it wasn't on purpose that she didn't know what she was doing that she didn't want to that it wasn't on purpose that she didn't want to press so hard that she just wanted to enjoy herself that she didn't know he didn't get mad got rough on purpose why did she do that why so cold why a machine presses the heart does not press with the heart does not press does a machine have to without a heart on purpose the heart does not press the heart does not press the heart does not press this much on purpose

He sat on Koito's back, rocking and releasing voices. He was holding the knife in his hands. He slid the edge under a shoulder blade and made a shallow incision. A rusty drop swelled. Blood? He wiped it with his finger and raised it to his tongue. The oily taste of oil. He exhaled the air from his lungs and threw himself on his back. He was relieved. Just a machine. She was just a machine. On purpose. A machine has no choice. Nothing gets lost. He felt mad. He got up and pulled her by her legs. He opened the balcony door. The skin on his back felt brambly. There was a blunt sound when her head slid to the floor. He dragged her out, under the sun. A red parrot was squatting on the railing, cleaning its wings with its beak. When it saw him, it calmly moved away. Evan grabbed Koito under the arms and lifted her to the edge. She was heavy, much heavier than he thought she would be. He gathered all his strength. Barely.

'Did you think it would be so simple?'

He yelled and stretched out his arms. She was consumed by desire.

ABRAHAM!

✦ ✦ ✦

A lattice of smoke. Skin, cracked in a webbed pattern. Crosses and crossroads. Curried leather. A cough.

'What?'

The general stands at the window and stares out across the field. A cigar clenched between his teeth. The honey smell of tobacco reminds Kras of the brick oven of his childhood. The fields are windswept and bare. When he exhales, mists ascend. A bee slams into the window, three times, and, dejected, flies off. It mistook the aide's red beret for a flower.

'Wolf, Wolf, Wolf,' chimes the general.

Kras looks at the aide. His face is expressionless. Kras ponders whether to mark him down as violent or daft. Perhaps he is both. Staring through the walls, to the end of the universe, straight into the back of his head. He came just so he'd be here. The general shakes the ash from his cigar onto the windowsill. He waits for the ash to cool and brushes it off. They're in Kras's study. Surrounded by wood.

Kras waits and sees. He knows the military theatre well. The aura of violence that hangs in the air and soaks through into skin like smoke into fabric. Though he's not afraid, he's nevertheless thankful for his lack of a tail. It might have crept between his legs. You know, just in case. His rage has subsided. He has nothing to be ashamed of. In this society they tolerate pathological outbursts from grown men. Only Grace would follow up on her threats. The rest just looked away. He threw the axe to the ground and calmly invited the guests in.

Nobody let anything unprofitable linger in the air.

'So…' says the general and turns to Kras. Kras raises his eyebrows. 'So, Wolf, to get right down to it, I'm ready to believe you, so long as you don't beat around the bush.'

'I don't know what you're talking about.'

The general smiles grimly and the aide moves his head, while Kras sizes them up.

'I hope that is the truth.' He puffs out his cheeks and coils a hard curl of smoke around his mouth. 'Because I have, on account of our friendship, stretched protocol a little. If I were going by the rules, you'd be the one coming to me, come hell or high water. So consider this a birthday present and pledge honesty. You owe me at least that much.'

'I still don't know what you're talking about.'

The aide coughs into his fist.

'Our ship is leaking, Wolf. It is leaking quite a bit and has been for quite some time. Half the agency is spinning around on its axis and constantly biting itself in the arse, and it was only a matter of time before some analyst pointed a finger at you. They've exhausted all other possibilities. And you could say, of course, you could be thinking that they are going to start making all sorts of accusations now, because they are in it up to their necks and will try to cast suspicion all the way up to Breivik just to save themselves from drowning, but…'

Kras doesn't respond. Every twitch of the body counts. The only freedom lies in staying still. Anything else is slavery of character.

'…once they started entering data the probability level skyrocketed. They're claiming, with eighty percent certainty, that you're the leak, Wolf. Factor in all the dead ends they were considering before and the percentage climbs to over ninety. We both know the algorithms are rarely wrong, which is why I haven't come for your confession. Human curiosity got the best of me, so we're not doing this in front of cameras. I'm not interested in how much. I want to ask you – why?'

Kras snarls from the depths of his lungs. The aide adjusts his stance, the general turns his head.

'Wolf?'

'Someone must have slandered me, Globus… I find it hard to believe you two came here to stuff my head with libel. And the damn computers can go to hell.' He bit his tongue. Literally. 'This has got to be some kind of RDR intrigue, no? What went wrong? And now you'll do me for it? Like that guy, Kennedy, via Khrushchev, first you hit your predecessor, then you yourself resign. Gobec fucked something up so soon? How serious is it?'

The general spits into his palm and puts out his cigar.

'This is not part of some elaborate intrigue, Wolf! You are up shit creek and that's that. Everything fits. All the things that kept the algorithm incomplete were things you carried home for analysis. Our strategy was always sound and yet the Chinese always knew what we were up to.'

'If the HRC had really read my data, then HADE would still be in the desert.'

'Don't belittle us! The only thing that can explain the deviations in the results is a leak. And that leak is you, Wolf. That much we know! Now stop lying, because it's insulting to me.'

Wolf storms over to his desk and bends down to the cupboard door and the safe behind it. The aide's muscles tense up. He's ready to fire at any time, but the general's raised hand stays him. The general moves over to Wolf and peers past his fingers as he turns the dial.

21 – 10 – 20 – 21

The safe opens with a vacuum sigh. It's filled to the top with rainbow-coloured folders.

'Everything's in here,' says Kras.

'Show me,' says the general.

Kras pulls a purple folder from the pile and offers it to the general.

He doesn't take it.

'Open it,' he says.

Kras feels the rough cardboard against his fingers. He snaps the folder open. All three stare into it. The sheets of paper are blank, but for the outline of a head with great big round ears.

'Are you taking me for a fool, Wolf?' asks the general.

Kras licks his fingers and flips through the sheets of paper. They're all the same. He flings them furiously in the air, and they glide around. The aide snatches one out of the air. He looks at it and speaks.

Up until now he's been silent. His croaky magpie voice slices into Kras's eardrum.

'That's... Mickey Mouse.'

It takes Kras all of his strength not to sink his teeth into the aide's abnormally thick neck.

'I know that, you bloody moron,' he hisses through clenched teeth. The aide shrugs his shoulders, and even the general ignores this remark.

'What is this? A break-in? Espionage? Who else knew the combination?' asks the general.

'No one,' Kras says, 'but everything points to it being... my little...my own...' he falls silent and stares out the window. This is a feeling Kras doesn't know. It stretches from the pain of betrayal, to disappointment, through shame at his own mistake, to a sort of pride. He'd never expected that sort of a Mitja. He dared break into his father's most forbidden place? He'd rip him a new arsehole if he ever caught him, and even though Mitja must have known that, it didn't stop him. But what did he do with the papers? How was it that some middling little indigenous villages put up a better defence than the headquarters ever expected? Did he warn them? How? Kras thinks of Bernard's stunned look yesterday, just before he punched him. Where did he get Mitja's tape? How did they communicate? If he's going to blame his son for the leak now, they'll throw him in jail somewhere along the equator. Does he deserve it? Would he survive? Would he find out who put him there?

'My own brother,' says Kras and lets indignation take hold. 'That fucking prick stole from me, right from under my nose, and then sold it on. Business has been really good for him these past few years. He paid to get a new church built, he lent money to half the family for any stupid fancy they may have had. I thought he'd actually got himself some competence, and was even grateful for it. Bernard was always useless. I'm not even surprised, now that I see nothing has changed.'

The general's eyes narrow. He's smelt the gentle whiff of a lie.

'Bernard…that dystrophic critter whose nose you busted open yesterday?'

Kras nods and smiles ominously.

'And,' the general asks, 'where is he now, this Bernard?'

'I sent him to the hills.'

'To the hills?'

'He's driving my mum and the aunts to their homestead. Until…hm, until the smoke blows over.'

'Yes, smoke,' the general nods and motions to his aide. 'Smoke. Good. We're leaving now. I'll issue an immediate arrest warrant for Bernard. We can hold off a little with your interrogation. If he's going to drag you into this, you'd better be ready. I'll see what I can do. No promises. But nothing's impossible.'

Kras thanks him with a nod of the head.

'One more thing before we go,' says the general in a quiet voice as he makes his way to the door. 'The 250th Infantry hasn't seen your son in over a month.' Kras takes a step towards him and grabs him by the shoulder. The aide puffs out his chest.

'What?'

'You asked yesterday. I checked the how and the what of it. He's not at any of the posts. I asked around. No sign of him from our ships. Not from any planes either.'

'Wait a minute, Globus. Just what the hell are you trying to tell me? Is that a threat? Are you threatening me?'

The general turns to Wolf and actually looks sincere.

'Sorry, Wolf, but this sort of thing happens all the time. The boys can't take it. They run off into the jungle. They get taken by some dark woman, if they're lucky, or by some other dark thing if they aren't. If he contacts you, tell him to get back to his damn post straight away. If he's not back in a month he'll be listed as a deserter. And then…'

The general motions to his aide to open and hold the door for him. Kras's head is throbbing. His lips have dried out. He's got no words, no strength, no possibilities. Everything is happening beyond him. His arms are dangling by his side. The general's head disappears down the stairs. A ringing telephone cuts the heavy silence.

/

'Hello?'

A sigh.

'Hello? Kras, is that you?'

Kras grinds his teeth and considers hanging up.

'Wolf, who the fuck is this? Say something. Bernard here. There's been an accident.'

That makes him hesitate. He looks around. Nobody.

'Janez is dead, Wolf. Wolf? Is there anybody there? Give me Kras.'

'I'm here, Berdo.'

'Why the fuck are you so silent?'

'I was thinking about just hanging up. I don't have the energy to deal with you. But what's this about an accident?'

'WOLF! Do not hang up. You have to help us. Janez fell asleep at the wheel. Well, first he took a wrong turn, then we got lost, and when we turned back he fell asleep and went over the cliff.'

'And Mum?' asks Kras.

'Mum's fine, the aunts are fine, I'm fine. We wandered around for a few hours until we came across a house. Some old guy, a loner, a weirdo, if you ask me. He's up to something, no idea what. That's why we need somebody to come get us.'

'Did you call an ambulance?'

'Ambulance? We're fine, we just need somebody to…'

'For Janez?'

'Oh, yeah. Wolf, that was a cliff and a half. He didn't stand a chance. I'll take care of everything, don't worry, just come get us.'

'Me?'

'You, anybody. Fuck! I'm going nuts every day for this family, you dumped Mum on me, then you…' Bernard's voice trails off. 'There's something going on up there,' he says, and Kras clears his throat.

'Bernard, I'm not in the mood to listen to some rambling explanation, but maybe you were lucky, getting lost.'

'What? Hang on a second, I hear Mum…'

'I said maybe you're lucky that you didn't make it over there. Headquarters is going to issue a warrant for your arrest anytime now. I told them where you are.'

'Ah, for fuck's sake, Kras…'

'You don't want to know why?'

'What? No. Yes. Because of the Krpans, right?'

'What Krpans?'

'Fuck, Kras, can't you do anything for me?'

'What Krpans, Berdo?'

He can hear quiet snivelling through the receiver. Each of Bernard's sobs produces a light honk. His nose still hurts.

'I knew they'd come sooner or later… Aw, crap… Mitja gave me a hand. Sorry, Kras. Sorry, please, but…but…'

Bernard looks for a means of stirring the greatest degree of compassion. Because he knows who he's dealing with, his despair sounds almost sincere.

'…fuck, Kras, you saved the arse of that moron who

killed his wife, but you can't save the arse of your own brother?
You won't!'

'Evan didn't kill anybody,' says Kras.

'Neither did I!'

'Mojca committed suicide,' says Kras. He sees his friend
before him. Not the one who came to ask for help, the nervous wreck of a widower, madman and weakling, but the one
from back when they were still young and still had clear eyes
and roars of laughter on their lips and acted like the world had
signed them a contract for eternity... The Cut was their first
cry of the real. It broke them apart. A hollow burial. It was as if
a filter had been cast over the world. Staying friends was hard.
They all had to take care of themselves. Kras managed. Evan,
barely. It has been years since he'd heard anything about Zoja.
Her writing was banned in Europe. A threat to the system,
apparently. Kras had never been able to understand grown-
ups who were afraid of poetry. As if they acknowledged that
the nature of the world is sin. But whose? Does everything
really hang in the balance?

'Veronika too,' yells Bernard. 'Yet you're not getting me
any tickets to go East!'

'Would you like to go East?' asks Kras.

Bernard lets out another moan.

'First of all I'd like someone to come get me and take me
out of this wooded wolf-fuckery. I'll figure out how to hide
later.'

'I can't,' says Kras, 'I have to...'

'Tell somebody, please, tell Alenka or...or...tell Grace!
Yes, tell Grace! Tell her she can finally return the favour for
that bacchanalia I paid for, no? Order her to come. White
Wood, she can ask someone where to go, where the old guy
with the dog lives, a huge house, she can't miss it. Will you?'

'White Wood?'

'Yes.'

Kras smiles bitterly.

'I'll tell her, Berdo. You take care of yourself now.'

The line cuts out. Kras looks at the receiver a bit curiously before quietly setting it down.

/

Kras places himself between the doors, turns his mouth towards the hall so there'll be a loud echo, and hollers like an ape: 'Full stop!' He tilts his head in anticipation of a response. When it comes, he nods, content. 'Full stop,' yells a female voice from the courtyard, joined soon by that of an old man. Another voice emerges from the kitchen, hoarse, a little quieter, also a woman's. The voices ring out in tandem from the top floors. One, deep and sonorous, booms from behind Kras's back. He turns around. Edgar is standing there, smiling at him, but the smile fades when their eyes meet. He hasn't seen that expression on Kras's face for years. Hence, *full stop*.

It was Raven who thought it up, when he got divorced and it looked like the family was falling apart. Back then a thousand tiny grievances suddenly found their way to expression, and life among the Wolfs became increasingly excruciating. A pinch of amateur psychology, a few handbooks on relationships, on mediation and arbitration led him to the very simple idea of shutting all the family members into a space where they would, for a moment, cast off the ballast of the body, allow themselves only ears and mouth, and throw a general amnesty over anything said. If nothing else, they'd blow off a little steam. Sometimes that's all a person needs. This would be the fourth *full stop*, ever. Kras was going to do the thing his way.

He walks into the courtyard and looks up into the tree. The priest Meslier is standing under it.

'Dad, if you don't come down, we'll do it without you,' he shouts.

Raven clings onto a branch and yells, 'So what!' He is terribly bothered that he won't hear what's been going through their heads these past years, but for once in his life he wants to stick to a decision. He's never coming down from the trees again.

Kras nods. 'Very well.' The priest walks towards him, but Kras's gaze stops him. 'What is this "full stop"?' he asks.

'It's only for family,' replies Kras. Meslier nods vaguely.

'I'm just going to stay outside,' he says, as if he had made the decision himself. Kras nods and goes into the house.

He finds them at the table. Edgar is sitting in a chair, scratching his nose and staring absently at the floor. His thick, black hair looks like a pile of tape from an audio-cassette. Kras looks at Mila. She has no idea what an audio-cassette is. She's probably never even seen one. She's avoided all the previous full stops; her face is a mixture of disbelief that something like this is really even happening, pride that her presence seems self-evident to everybody, and fear that she might hear too much. Katarina is completely pale. Kras smiles at her. He has been ignoring her these past few days. She's completely worn out, looking more lost by the minute. No word from Mitja, the birthday stress, then all the chaos that unfolded, which now won't stop spreading... Katarina smiles back at him. Grace avoids eye contact. Kras is, in spite of everything, satisfied with her. A sturdy conscience, an independent soul. In a top-down operation you can't help yourself with this sort of people, but they always rise to the challenge of their destiny. Military instinct and family love converge in an amicable gaze. He goes over to her and takes her by the shoulder.

'Thank you,' he says. Her expression is a tired one. Eyes closed, she bows.

'Are we all here?' asks Kras.

From the staircase, the sound of children laughing. Stoja enters the room. Po, Mira and Mina are chasing each other around the house. Stoja's skirt is *full stop*.

'How's Alan?' asks Kras.

'Ah, he's good, good,' replies Stoja suspiciously. She

doesn't trust Kras. Never did. He butchered her first wedding anniversary. Back then she didn't speak the language well and before they managed to explain what was going on she'd had her nineteenth nervous breakdown. 'A sprained ankle, but otherwise nothing. Olive's with him. She'll bandage his leg. Is Bojan…?'

Kras indicates that he's still outside.

'I'm going out,' says Stoja. Mira is hanging off her skirt and Po squeals before running into Mina. 'Out, brats!' yells Stoja, a smile stretching her cheeks. Kras waits for the door to shut behind them before turning back to the table.

'What did the cops want?' he asks Edgar.

'They came for Olga.'

'Why?'

Edgar imitates the voice of the policewoman: 'On suspicion of causing bodily harm to a minor.'

Kras frowns, Edgar continues.

'If I had to guess, I'd say…Alenka.'

'Do you think she called them?'

'I would have,' says Katarina. It slipped out.

'That's quite a wound she gave Voranc…' says Edgar.

'Ah. You still haven't told me anything. What did they say? How are you?'

Edgar's smile is relaxed. 'All right.'

'What did they say at the hospital?'

Mila takes the floor.

'Alenka dreamt up the idea that Voranc is HIV-positive so we'd stay away from them.'

'That's it, basically, yes,' says Edgar.

Kras runs his hands over his temples and looks down. A curse gets tangled up in his vocal chords.

'What if you went to see her, Edgar? Could you go?'

'Could you try to talk to her?' Kras continues, 'She doesn't need to be convinced. Tell her that she has a family here, if she needs it, and that she doesn't need to lie if she wants to do things all on her own. If she wants to press charges, I don't really care. But she shouldn't think that means she's done with us. She's still a Wolf, tell her that. How does that sound to you?'

They seem satisfied. Edgar crosses his arms over his chest and nods calmly.

'It's a deal.'

'Ok. Good. Grace.'

Grace trembles. Kras notices this and raises a hand.

'Calm down. I'm sorry. I wasn't myself. Something came over me. Sorry. Can you forgive me?'

Grace closes her eyes and nods.

'It would be easier if I had the Singing Herb,' she says with a snarled lip and a tart tone. Kras smiles and turns to look at Mila. Her belly is in knots. She doesn't understand what they're talking about. Maybe they know? She stowed away the goods from the tree house as soon as they got home; she was scared to death that Kras would go that same evening to see what Mitja had left there, but he didn't. They'd all, on edge, gone right to bed.

'Unfortunately, we don't have the herb,' says Kras and again looks over Mila's face turning pale. 'But I still have to ask you something. Well, I won't ask you myself. Bernard would like you to – how should I put it? – let him call in a favour?'

He repeats in brief what Bernard told him. Katarina puts a hand over her mouth and screams when she hears what happened to Janez.

'Does Milena know?' she asks.

Kras shakes his head.

'Who's going to tell her?'

'I don't know.'

Grace wrinkles her brow.

'Of course I'll go,' she says, 'I just hope I can find them. White Wood?'

'Yes.'

'Can I take your jeep?'

'You may.'

'Anything else?' asks Grace.

'Thank you.'

Grace smiles at him, warmly and against her will. This disarms him. He sits at the head of the table and exhales broadly.

'I don't really understand where it all went. All of the sudden, I'm old. Don't go thinking I'm getting soft for putting it like that. Well, I don't know. How should I even know what you're thinking? All these years we've been together. But I don't know.' He sizes them all up, with a sharp look which they all recognize for one that can persist to the point of hurt. He inclines his head. 'Do I even know you, I sometimes, not often, only sometimes, ask myself. Are you really what I think you are, or have I just put something into my head and you, who knows why, just act the way I think you should act for as long as I'm looking at you. Who are you when you're alone?' The communal discomfort could feed the hungry. Nobody will open up. 'Am I even allowed to ask that question? Because how do you know who I am? Who I am when I'm alone. You don't know me. You don't know anything. Am I also, in your heads, just some strange puppet jumping around on strings you think you know? You don't know anything. You don't know anything about me.' Katarina is perfectly still, she doesn't want to make the slightest movement since that would attract attention, but that is precisely what her perfect stillness does. 'My wife knows me better than anybody, but even she knows practically nothing. Because she is not allowed to know some things, because some things I've hidden from her, and because other things, well, some things are just invisible as is. And if my own wife doesn't know me, doesn't really know me after all these years of living together, how the hell can I expect to know all of you? And yet I worry about you. I feel a responsibility towards you that I don't feel towards anybody else. Because that's the way it is. Because we're a family. No? Am I right?' For support he looks at Edgar, who's staring at him the way one stares at a leaky roof. 'I'm right. And if I take on this responsibility, without making demands on your privacy, that must be ok, no? But if I ever require your privacy, it's not because I'm tortured by curiosity but because I need to trust. Because I have that need, for trust. Is that too much? Do I want too much?' Outside, crickets. 'I don't want too much. I would kill for you. I have killed for you.'

'Not for me,' says Grace. They all hold their breath, expecting an eruption, but Kras's voice remains steady.

'Also for you. Also for you. You can't avoid it. You can't go off to some elite university in Berlin, and spend your days easing your conscience with petty grievances, and think that you've absolved yourself of the guilt for the shit that some have to do and that we all have to live with. There are no free zones, dammit, there haven't been for decades. All this freedom you have…' Grace lifts a hand and says quietly, *ok, ok,* 'it didn't come for free. And don't delude yourself. Don't delude yourself into thinking you're safe. A ten-year-old boy wakes up in the middle of a minefield… A cruel God has led him out there to that meadow in the middle of the night, given him one more dream, one more dream, and in the morning, when we all see him, we all wave at him not to move, but he waves back with a smile and takes a step forwards into *bang* and horror. Nobody went to help him. Too dangerous. He's writhing away there, no legs, fifty yards away from us, wailing to everybody who's supposed to love him until he finds the presence of mind to crawl to the next mine and plunge himself into death.'

'Why now…?' Grace asked, horrified. All the faces are grey.

'Because we are that little boy, all of us! Surrounded by mines. And you stretch out an arm, you stretch out a finger, dammit, you stretch out your tongue and *bang*. Is it an achievement of our civilization that people aren't even aware of this now? That all of you think everything's ok? Do you know how many people had to die so we could remain silent? You have no idea. So don't think me a barbarian for wanting to know, for needing to know, what is going on with you. I have to trust you because I can't trust anyone else. Do you understand me? I have to trust you because we depend on one another. We share a fate.'

Grace would prefer to remain silent, but she can't. Eyes closed, she lifts her chin, and her cold voice cuts through the silence.

'Kras, this is precisely what has defeated us as a society. Each family has bound itself into a bundle of kindling and if there's one little spark, the whole thing lights up. We don't care about anything else. That's why things are as they are. Because we have to watch out for our children, our brothers, sisters, parents, instead of dealing with the world. Because the threat seems so close, even though the only threat to us all is always out there.'

'What the hell is it you would like to hear, Grace?' asks Kras.

'Are you aware of that fact?'

'Of course I am aware of it!' Frustration contorts his face. 'But what am I supposed to tell you? They won! They crammed us all into half a square inch and laid landmines all around. Seriously. What am I supposed to tell you? We won.'

Mila turns from her father to her aunt and back again. They look like each other. She'd never noticed how similar they looked. Edgar bites his lip and Katarina bites her lip. Kras stretches out in his seat and spreads his arms, as if he wanted to provoke a reply.

'I'd like to hug you,' says Grace. Katarina's facial muscles relax into a kindly smile before returning to their former position when she realizes that Kras is offended.

'Some other time,' he says, relaxing his hands which had

balled themselves into momentary fists.

'Good. So that's it. Now you know. Would anyone else like to add anything? You know, it's *full stop*. Let's put it all out there. Mila?'

Mila immediately shakes her head and catches Grace's look where she can, for a second, see a trace of disappointment. Easy for her, thinks Mila, because she can run back to where she came from whenever she wants. Mila doesn't take her father at his word – she knows full well how long he can feed off even the slightest of grievances.

'Ok. Good. Katarina, Mila, I'd like to talk to you alone…'

Edgar and Grace understand.

'Can you take me to the station?' Edgar asks. 'Sure,' replies Grace. Katarina tosses her the keys. They leave in a curious haste.

/

'When's the last time you spoke to Mitja?' he asks them. 'And, please, it's very important that you tell the truth.'

'Why?' asks Katarina, terrified and immediately imagining the worst.

Kras repeats the question: 'When?' He tries to encourage Katarina with just a look. She again returns her hand to her mouth.

'Before he left,' says Mila, grimly. 'After that, yesterday was the first time I saw and heard him.'

'Yesterday, on the screen?' asks Kras.

'Yes, where else?'

Kras turns to his wife. 'And you?' She shakes her head, convinced she's been left without a son, that the world is a place of ugliness and pain, and that nowhere will she find any consolation…

'Katarina?'

She snaps out of her reveries of misery and looks into the air, 'I don't know. I don't know when. A month, a month and a half ago? On the phone.'

'Did he call you?'

'Yes. At his allotted time.'

Katarina quickly worked out that on the day the soldiers were allowed to call home, Kras, as if by some magical coincidence, was never anywhere near the house, but she wasn't about to make any accusations.

'What did he say?'

'Nothing much. That he's fine. That he misses us. That he wants to come home.'

'He said he wanted to come home?'

'Ah, Kras, he didn't mean it like that…'

'No, I know, Katarina, but do you think he was serious?'

'Tell me exactly what this is about, please?'

Kras leans on his elbows.

'Globus told me that Mitja's no longer with the other soldiers.'

'What? Well, where is he then?' asks Katarina. Mila frowns.

'I don't know. He disappeared, he's been gone for a month. That's why I want to know if he said anything.'

Katarina bites her upper lip and struggles to remember.

'I don't know…nothing like that…I don't think he did… or maybe he did, no, I don't know…'

'What?' asks Kras.

'Yes, basically he asked me if I know what it means, I don't know, it was all so strange, some acronym, I won't be able to remember it now…'

'RDR? HRC? IA? MENZO? OBI-DAU? UIGOPWTSOALSSV?…'

Katarina chops the air with a finger. 'That's it!'

'UIGOPWTSOALSSV?'

Katarina nods. Kras's skin bristles.

'What did you do with the stuff I had on yesterday?'

'What?'

'My clothes, from yesterday, where are they?'

'I put them in the laundry…' says Katarina, quietly. She knows she's done something wrong even though she had done exactly what was expected of her. That happens to her a lot. '…they were all covered in blood.'

'Did you check the pockets?'

'Did I…?' She's not quite sure. Usually she does.

'Did you or did you not?'

'I don't know, Kras, there was nothing…'

Kras jumps up and races to the room where the washing machine is churning. He presses button after button, but the spinning doesn't stop. He reaches for the cord and yanks it out of the socket. The wretched sound would move some to compassion, but Kras hears nothing. He pulls wildly at the little round transparent door and swears as the soapy waterfall splashes over his feet. He extracts a soaking bit of fabric, like a soul from a child. Poor machine.

/

Stoja had covered Po's ears, who had covered Mira's ears, who had covered Mina's ears. Meslier finds the scene a little comical, but Raven's evident nervous breakdown has made his back itch, right in the middle where your hands don't reach. He beseeches Raven to come down from the tree, to cut it out, this childish stubbornness is unbecoming for an adult, and he should once again assume a little responsibility for his family, but Raven just keeps chuckling away to himself and quoting lines from erotic tales to Stoja, who is blushing and barely containing her laughter at the priest's puffed-up red face.

Po is tired of being in her mum's arms and wriggles free. Raven's words die on his lips. He and Po look at each other. He winks at her. She salutes him. This almost moves him to tears, but he hides his response behind a laugh. Po runs into the house. He feels a heartache in his chest. Stoja steps forwards and covers Mira's ears. Meslier gives a muffled sigh.

'Bend down and spread 'em. I want to see what you've got to hide.'

/

Alan fell off the roof. He got dizzy, everything turned blurry for a second, there was a dark pause, a syncope in consciousness, he remembered Borut's seizure and got even more scared, he let go of the reins over his body for just a second and slid down the tiles to the united cries of the whole family, stopped for a bit, hung over the edge, swinging from the gutter, which bent under his weight, and then lost his grip and fell some three yards into the depths, nastily wrenching his ankle.

Now he's in a bedroom with Olive. She has just wrapped his ankle in fresh gauze. Alan looks everywhere but at her. The poster for a dinosaur film his father once gave him has suddenly become very interesting again. The letters are losing their edges. He'll need glasses. The shelves are sagging under the weight of never-opened books. Alan doesn't like to read. Mila is the family bookworm. He remembers how she always complained that someone had mangled her books and looked accusingly at Mitja. But Mitja also wasn't much of a reader.

Olive is quiet. She doesn't know Slovenian, which is why she's just smiling at this poor little boy and trying to catch his eye, even though (or precisely because) he's so obviously embarrassed. His cheeks flare red every time Olive moves. He's embarrassed, thinks Olive, and that makes him so cute she could just pinch him. Poor child, to be born into such a family. Grace was right – after getting to know the Wolfs she'd start to think her own parents were saints, even though they knew how to employ the most complex of psychological models for expressing their resentment. Brutality trumps even the most sophisticated hatred. She gets lost in thought and strokes his leg as if trying to calm him down. Alan's pupils dilate and his heart starts beating faster. Fear or passion? He can't tell.

There's a knock at the door. Grace's head appears.

'How you doing, kiddo?'

'Ah, ok, nothing major. Olive here is a master…' Alan falls silent. In his stomach there's a feeling of having crossed a line. He got off lightly, fairly lightly. Given the circumstances, Grace is ready to forgive him.

'Good,' says Grace, 'good.'

Alan nods and smiles suavely. Grace turns to Olive.

'I have to go,' she says.

'Where?' asks Olive.

'I'll be back tonight.'

'Where?'

'To get my brother and mother. There's been an accident.'

'Oh my. Are they all right?'

'They say they are.'

'Why do you have to go get them?'

'Long story.'

'Is tomorrow still…?'

'We'll see.'

'Ok. Tonight then.'

'Tschüss.'

'Tschüss.'

Grace leaves, Olive turns back to Alan.

'Oh wow!' she exclaims. Alan's face is now a ruddy scarlet. The sheet covering him has risen shamelessly just below his waist. The short exchange in German was a catalyst for his desire. He's aroused and doesn't know what to do about it. Olive responds with kind laughter and a wink, which helps him not one bit. She's proud that her presence can still conjure up magic, even in a boy as cute, young and innocent as Alan. The palm of her hand is still resting on his leg. At this moment, they both realize it. They look at it. An already slightly wrinkled hand and flawless nails over a boy's nearly hairless leg. They don't look at each other. They stare at the hand. Tension rises. They stare at the hand. They wait for it to move.

Grace had left the door slightly ajar. Po peaks through the crack. She sees Alan's chest rising, sees him throw his head back, sees him fervently grasping the edge of the bed. She stays put.

/

Mila leans by the open window and takes hot, long, protracted drags from an enormous joint into which she's sprinkled all the leftover weed. This might be her last ever. Her father's glare might have meant something, but who knows... She sends acrid clouds skywards. There's never anybody on this side of the house. Each puff leaves her lonelier.

She's already all too familiar with her brain's associative network. First she'll work through all the traumas, the mini-traumas and the awkward memories, the relationship with her father (they will never understand each other), the relationship with her mother (she resents her weakness, her indulgence), her relationship with Mitja (negligent fucking pig, if this brands her for life, she'll run a spear through his back), with the whole jam of family, compote, compost, squeezed and pickled, now they're rotting... But no! You're responsible for yourself, Mila, nobody else can do this to you if you don't let them. That's the most horrific part. The awareness that, in the end, you have no one to blame but yourself, that you're alone before your destiny. When it is so alluring to say, 'you destroyed me'. So tempting to say, 'you sucked out all my blood'. That's what Alenka, after she'd returned from Africa, before she left for good, shouted all through the house. Each tug broadens the abyss. Mila! You have to swear to yourself you'll never let yourself be a victim. Martyred, murdered, massacred, ha-ha-ha... She starts laughing, the smoke goes up her nose. What would they think if they saw you now? Now that you're crazy... But so what! Anyway, nobody's around! She sets the remaining half of the joint on the ashtray and starts jumping around the room. Nobody's watching you! On a rock hurtling through emptiness, in the back pocket of space-cowboy jeans, forgotten, overlooked, we dance in solitude… When you're really alone, when you're really alone, when nobody's watching you, the edge of the universe stretches into infinity on all sides. Just imagine, she thinks, next time, when you're going to close the door behind you, the vastness of the hole you're in. And nobody sees you. She is jumping around and letting it go, satisfied with bodily existence, satisfied with an excess of consciousness…

She lifts the mattress and pulls out a thin, black, dog-eared notebook. She opens it. Written on page one: 'To Kras; to the scale of all our insanities, don't give up on us, you know…' In italics: *Self-Published, LEZK. 17.9.2008.* Three signatures. Only Zoja's is legible.

There's a poem in this collection that speaks to Mila's most remote feelings. What is passion? Not affection, love, lust, desire, want, necessity, need, craving, nothing physical, but not only psychological, and all these words, do they even mean anything on their own, independently of… What is

passion

Clouds have form. The tops of trees are roots – stand on your head. Roofs are bare backs under the acupuncture of chimneys and antennas… Magpies nest in nests. Where is

passion

St Nicholas bakes biscuits, the horizon is red, that's what they say, although it's late summer, the equinox will be late, it's always late, when is

passion

The sound of a zip. My own hand slides between my legs. I'm my own puppet. I make a stranger out of my body and I abuse it. Evil. I use it. And no

fear

A young girl's eye watching through the keyhole. She sees her, sees her belt around her knees, sees her writhing around

on the bed… Mila is thinking about Borut. And a little bit
about Mitja.

/

I don't want to go into too much detail, but what Kras is doing
with Katarina seems normal only when one is naked, focused
on feeling and ripped out of time.

The washing machines tremble. Slapping sounds are
echoing off the walls of the bathroom, the sloped walls of
the bathtub, in the toilet bowl, in the bidet. The soap has
slid down to the plughole. The squished and twisted tube of
toothpaste stands upright among the brushes. A roll of toilet
paper has rolled off the shelf. The floor is wet. The paper soaks
up the water and swells.

Katarina is safe.

The moan takes shelter between the towels, inside the
radiator grill and warms itself up there. The hole in the floor,
covered with a grate, ingests the water and foams at the sides.
The saliva mixes with the mucus. Flushed flecks of flesh on
porcelain. The mirrors hide nothing, they keep silent about
almost everything. Beyond here, there's so little that is true.

Kras wants whatever he wants.

His jaw is unmoving. He's trained it. He pursues pleasure with a technical dedication. Methodically. Long years
of practice. He knows where he has to be, what he has to
do, how. To the limit of trust. To the edge of what's safe. A
tricky tightrope-walk, a dance on a razor blade. The shaving
equipment is not where he left it. Somebody borrowed it. He
doesn't know what to think about that. The epilator in the
plastic bag is what allows his hands to slide over Katarina's
legs. They're smooth.

'Quiet!'

He covers her mouth with his hand. The cries should stay
inside her. They should echo off the inside of her skin. They
mustn't escape. This landscape has its own rules. She bites his

hand lightly. It's not a real bite because right now her teeth aren't a part of her body. The scarlet line stings, mocks. He punishes her by firmly grabbing the flesh hanging from her ribs.

'Quiet!'

The word has lost its addressee. The body frees itself of the slavery of consciousness and becomes a thing, wrapped up in a foreign will. This pain has no roots. This pleasure has no wings. She bites him as he climbs onto her. The teardrop is not really her own. She swallows him. Teeth pressed together. Into the cliff. He slides dangerously. Everything depends on the grip. No ropes. Just faith.

The door handle declines, pointlessly. The door is locked. In the keyhole is a concealing key. Po must make do with eavesdropping. Who knows what she's imagining as they make it to the peak.

/

Kras is lying on Katarina's back. They're sweaty. They smile absently, each in their own direction. They part a little shyly. As they drape themselves in the sounds of splashing, they laugh at each other. Kras shows her the ticket that he extracted from the inside pocket of his jacket. It was soaked but the ink hadn't yet run.

'I got this yesterday, you know, when that postman came.'

Katarina nods.

'What is it?'

'A plane ticket.'

'What? To where? '

'Seam.'

'Seam?'

'That's the military designation for the buffer zones.'

'Yes, I know, but which one?'

'You find out when you get there.'

Kras smiles reluctantly. Mila is growing concerned.

'Do you think it's from Mitja?'

'Probably, yes.'

Silence.

'At least I hope it is.'

'And you're going?'

'Yes.'

'What if…'

Kras interrupts her.

'Please. What if what? Isn't it all the same? If I don't go, I'll never forgive myself. And aren't all of you fed up with me here? If I do go, I'll be mad at him for a few weeks, and then things will cool down.'

Katarina is not used to him talking about his feelings as if they were someone else's.

'The miserable little bastard!' shouts Kras.

He stamps his foot on the floor. Splash.

'I'm sorry. You see? I can't stand not having him around. My body doesn't know how to work this way. And now all this stuff with Berdo… I don't even want to know what they'll do to him.'

'What?' asks Katarina. When Kras explains Bernard's situation, she moves her hand to her mouth and winces at its pungent scent.

'Do you think it will be bad?'

'I think that…if it was really him and not Mitja… Though I don't know how he could do it without Mitja's help, but still… If it was really him, we won't see him again.'

'So you're just going to leave?'

Kras evades her accusatory tone by means of a shrug.

'Yes,' he says. 'I'm just going to leave.'

/

When Edgar presses the doorbell, he feels something like dread in his stomach. He has no idea why. The wind blows a cloud of dust into the air. This place hasn't changed in decades. The same cars, the same homeless people, the same pigeons circling above, creating a sense of constant vertigo for anyone underneath. Edgar has a sunny disposition, but in the midst of all this concrete it darkens sometimes. There's a methadone clinic right nearby. During last year's big clean-up they collected two containers' worth of needles. How can a person keep up a cheerful face? Edgar lacks that urban courage that sucks a person dry of all the mystery, of all the solitude (but not a shred of the loneliness), of all the humility before the night sky, leaving behind just a derisive attitude towards all that is human... Inside these towers they even shit with their backs turned towards each other. The only animal here is man. Everything else is noise, error, a cheap ad for something that can't be squeezed into the schedule. Nobody has time. He stares into the camera. Is Alenka even home?

The door screeches as it unlocks. Edgar enters and climbs the stairs. He doesn't like lifts. The door opens even before he manages to knock. Alenka's not wearing make-up. She looks horrible.

'Hi, Alenka.'

'Did Kras send you?'

The question puts him on the spot. His first instinct is to lie, but that would only have worked if he'd ever bothered to visit her before. He can't remember the last time he was here. Ten years ago? Twenty? Is that possible? The things that have happened since then.

'Yes. I mean, he didn't tell me what to say. He even said there's no need to convince you of anything. Just...how you're doing, yeah? Is that ok? Can I come in?'

Alenka scans the flat. When she looks back at him, she resigns herself to fate. 'Come in.'

He enters and takes his shoes off. The flat is completely soulless, he thinks, after his first glance. Everything is cleansed to the point of sterility, devoid of touch. As if for decades Alenka had been flat-sitting for the real owners, who were held up in Cambodia on a round-the-world trip, thus rendering moot any thought of pouring money into it. Even the picture frames hang empty. Her gait is broken and frail. Edgar follows her through the kitchen to the living room.

Voranc is sitting at a table and staring intensely at the cartoons on the TV. When Edgar pats him on the head, he winces and smiles through a mouthful of chocolate.

'How are you, kiddo?'

Voranc nods and waves a bandaged forearm into the air. Edgar whistles with admiration.

'A battle wound, you're a right old guy.'

'It was Grandma,' Voranc says.

This silences Edgar. He nods grimly.

'You, too,' says Voranc.

'Me, too.'

'Come on, show me.'

Edgar turns his side towards him and lifts his shirt. All Voranc can see is a pile of white gauze, but that's obviously fine by him.

'Wow,' he says.

They nod to each other as if they were the sole survivors of a difficult trial. Voranc's head swivels back to the television. Edgar walks slowly over to Alenka and sits down on the couch right next to her.

'Alenka…'

She interrupts him.

'Edgar, please, you know me better than all of them and you should know how offended this will make me feel.'

'Because…?' asks Edgar.

'Because you brought the family along. Because you carry it like a mask, like a shield, a spear. You didn't come to see me because you're interested in me as a person but because you're following the dictates of some social scheme that is supposed to make our relationships more natural, more meaningful, more human, as if we were all aware that by ourselves we are absolutely incapable, in the long run and without faking it, of loving each other. Every family meeting, every single one, proves this to be true.'

The scars etched on her face by chickenpox have deepened over the years. On her right cheek there's a strange red mark that makes it look as if she'd hit herself or as if someone else had hit her. Her eyes are watery, like they've been done in watercolour. She looks rather thin. What used to be a pretty prominent double chin is now just a fold of goitre. She's never smoked, but her voice is raspy.

Edgar doesn't know what to say. He's not yet ready to speak openly. Alenka smiles.

'Do you want some coffee?'

'Yes, that would be lovely.'

While she's making the coffee, Edgar makes faces at Voranc, bringing out warm and mild laughter.

'I didn't bring the family, Alenka. I don't know how to put it. I'm here because…'

Voranc clangs his spoon against the table.

'Mummy's sick!'

Edgar raises his eyebrows. Alenka's fingers twist Voranc's ears for a moment or two.

'Ill,' she says.

'What is it, Alenka? What do you have?'

Alenka doesn't respond. She is staring at the slowly rising coffee vapour.

She puts the pot to the side, waits, and returns it to the heat.

'Alenka?'

'Nothing, Edgar. We are all mere tenants of these bodies. It's just too bad that…'

'What do you mean, *too bad*?'

'It's too bad that we have to share water, and electricity, and the plumbing.'

'I don't understand.'

'That our landlord is such a bloody prick, and that our landlady's such a lousy whore.'

'Alenka…Voranc!'

'That all the renters are, without exception, complete arseholes. That's too bad. And it's just too bad that we…'

Edgar's face drops. He's not going to achieve anything here. The bonds have been cut for good, probably for years now. We delude ourselves, thinking that other people share the affection, even if we don't maintain contact. Every step can rip us apart. If you are not constantly in view, the picture starts to develop on its own. Alenka is an unknowable girl. How is he going to tell Kras that?

'It's too bad that we share blood.'

Horror has a human face.

/

The light drizzle creates an atmosphere of unease. The clouds have dropped low, their undersides linger at neck height. The hills are flowing into the notches of gorges where they'd hid the bodies. Long rows of dead, cold human bodies in the pits of a mercury mine. Do you think a country can exist without regularly shedding its skin? And which is the real body? The strongest one? Or is it the one who is trusted? The traitor is always on the far side of the answer.

Grace turns among the spruces. These are tricky roads. Fog lights are useless here and she can barely see a yard ahead. She doesn't slow down. Sorry, deer, but she'd like to get out of here right now. She's got a bad feeling. She no longer bears responsibility for these people, she's doing all this simply because she would like to help. But it's precisely help that will entangle her again. It's hard to find the balance between what is right and what is necessary.

At the crossroads she stops and gets out of the car. Her shoes sink into the sand by the road. The signposts are too high up to make out through the fog. 'Dew' or 'White Wood'.

Black letters on a yellow background. A lost bee buzzes by, laden down by drops of rain. To the right, then. She can hear talking in the distance.

'…so we now have this, you'll understand, an ideology, an ideology, right? It's nothing special, but it's ours. Kras's people wrote it, yes. Yeah, it's not exactly Tito's…at least not to the letter…but in terms of meaning they're, either way, all the same in the end, you know – this is mine. And then they start competing over who can put it in a more complicated manner, until they get sick of all the blabbering and shoot each other. What's the need for all the claptrap, then? Take what you can keep, then keep quiet. God understands. You can spin whatever tale you want, he will not give up on you. In the end he will take you.'

Headless figures are staggering along the road. Grace bends down and whistles.

'Mum?'

'Andreja?'

Olga's ear recognizes the children and can tell them apart just by their breathing.

'I came to get you! Are you all right?' yells Grace.

They reduce the distance between them to a few steps. The aunts cling to each other. Mother's face is all sweaty. Wrinkled like bark. Dark grey curls cling to her forehead, and she's out of breath. But her gaze is sharp. That gaze of hers. If Grace appreciates her father as much as she pities him (his heart is as good as it is weak), and if she's always been at least as fearful of Kras as she has been grateful to him, the feeling she has for her own mother is like nothing she feels for any other living being. Olga introduced her to the rituals of religion, as if she were passing along the flame of some ancient wisdom that she had to guard against the vulgar fingers of the uninitiated; she was her priestess, her shaman, and yet also an ordinary mother, a worker, a wife, three times broken by a man's hand, three times avenged, with a fate that, in terms of tragedy, did not differ essentially from the average of all those who found themselves in this world without the consolation of a congenital insemination machine. The break with her mother gave Grace enough experience to live a carefree life. Freedom doesn't owe anything, but neither is it innocent.

'So he managed to call…' says Olga.

'Where is Bernard?' Grace asks.

The sisters look at each other.

'We escaped,' says Svetlana.

'Escaped,' nods Magda.

'Bernard stayed behind at Šink's,' says Olga.

'At Šink's?' asks Grace.

'Šink Lovro has him locked up in the basement. He says he's not letting him out until he gets what he's been waiting for, for twenty-five years.'

Grace is baffled.

'And what might that be?'

'How should I know?' says Olga, upset. 'Maybe he wants me in his bed, maybe he wants to strangle me… I didn't hang around long enough to find out. As soon as I sensed what was in the air, we were off.'

Magda and Svetlana smile. Olga looks at them.

'Well, what to do with you two now? I suppose Grace wants to go fetch Bernard? This is Kras's jeep, right? Good. If it's ok with you, I'll go with her. Will you two come with us? If not, walk. You know where you are, don't you?'

'We're heading home,' 'home, Olga,' 'we've been walking all day,' 'give or take an hour,' 'it's not far,' 'not far.'

'Good.'

They embrace almost without awkwardness. They wink goodbye to Grace.

Olga squeezes herself into the car and Grace follows her.

'Did you walk along the road?'

'Yes?' says Olga, fastening her seatbelt.

'You're lucky I stopped. The way I was driving I could have mowed you down like daisies.'

Olga eyes her coldly.

'I was walking beside it.'

/

'Let me out! Let me out! Let me out!'

Bernard is despairing at the top of the stairs behind a closed, barred door.

It's light brown, freshly lacquered, and when he pounds on it with his fist no splinters burrow into his skin. Can nobody hear him? Where's Mother? He has no courage, never had it, no shame in not having it, and there's no need to have it put to the test… If you ask him, he'll admit it. Without hesitation he'll admit that he's a coward. Doesn't that admission mitigate anything? Or should he just keep quiet, lie, pretend? Would that make him better off?

The basement is totally bare, except for the rickety desk with the telephone. The phone went silent, as if someone had cut the cable. The weak light bulb consumptively sputtering under the ceiling outlines the cinders heaped up in the corners. Who knows what this space was used for. The ghosts are silent. Not because they would be afraid, or because they would be ashamed, but simply because to talk you need a mouth. So much that is human can accumulate in the basements of the world that will remain forever without expression, without influence, entirely without consequences…

'Let me out!'

He's settled into a rhythm. Three bashes with the fist, then a shout. Wait. A dozen beats of the heart. Order takes the edge off the terror. Slaps at least a pinch of sense over the anxiety.

He has no detailed visions up his sleeve. Anytime now, adrenaline will drag him into a state of shock. Claustrophobia. Tense expectations of change. Slim chance of it turning out well. Kras told him he'd most probably lose his freedom, but he didn't expect that to happen so soon, so suddenly. When he heard the creaking of the bolt, he took it to be the synaesthetic experience of Kras's words. But sometimes things get caught up in reality. Knock. Knock. Knock.

'Let me out!'

When he hears the snarling dog on the other side of the door, he jumps back and almost tumbles down the stairs. He struggles to catch his footing. He retreats with slow, tentative steps. The musty smell of sticking soil, openings of white light caught under the ceiling, a stone on the tips of the toes – all sensory perceptions pass unnoticed, everything in Bernard's head is focused on the large steel door handle that will go down any second now, and the iron sigh of the bolt that will allow the door to open... He knows that's his only hope.

He must throw himself out of the hole like a bullet from God, rely on surprise and alarm, on old age and the dog's tameness, but... No starting gun had told him when it was time to run. Life yawns. The dog's head pushes through the steadily widening crack. The old man is holding the dog on a leash and containing its thrusts with fierce yanks, so that the dog's front legs are mostly dangling freely in the air. Bernard retreats. His lips are trembling. Sweat drops from his forehead. He can't speak.

He's blinded by a reflection that finally draws at least some sound from his lungs. The old man is holding a long kitchen knife.

'Sir!'

'Don't you *sir* me, Wolf.'

How did he find out? Did Mum tell him? Was he listening in?

'Can you please tell me...'

His voice breaks into a stretched-out peep.

'I'll slaughter you like a pig, Wolf.'

'What did I...what did I...'

'You were born to the wrong brother, Wolf.'

'I wasn't! I'm not a Wolf!'

This stops the old man for a second, then he smiles bitterly and continues to make his way towards Bernard, who has now arrived at the bottom of the stairs, the floor, the cold floor, and is retreating with his back facing the corner that's farthest away.

'I'll do you for Lovro Jr, for Suzana, for Marjana, and I'll do you for Mihaela and for Evgen…'

'I had nothing to do with it! I had nothing to do with it!'

Bernard is yelling hysterically and pounding his chest. The old man opens his mouth and presses out the names of the dead. The dog is strangling itself on its collar.

'For the Gričars, for the Krajcons, for Milč and Trudi I'll slaughter you two times…'

'Please…'

'For…, for…'

' '

/

'You know the police came looking for you?'

'The police?' Olga's baffled. 'What do the police want with me?'

'Alenka,' says Grace.

'Alenka what?' asks Olga.

They're driving. It's not far now. The fog won't let up. There's no visibility.

'Because of Voranc.'

'It's high time that child learnt what the world is really like. And she's a ditz if she thinks she can hide him away from it.'

'Mum, still…'

'Don't call me Mum!'

Silence. Grace takes her foot off the accelerator. She can't see a thing. Olga looks at her.

'What… Are you crying? Andreja! What have you got to cry about? Don't cry now. Don't cry!'

Grace is trying to hold back her tears, she catches her

breath to calm down, but she fails. The jagged crying issues from her lungs in jerks, and for a moment you can see little saliva bubbles on her lips. Olga raises her nose.

'Andreja, come on…'

'It's not fair!'

Olga folds her hands over her chest.

'It's not fair…' repeats Grace between sobs, 'that in the end I'm the only one who can't call you that…even though all the others were ruthless, not me, even though the rest of them didn't give a shit about what was going on, they just wanted peace, just so that Kras could lock himself in his room, so Bernard could laugh at you both, so Alenka could…whatever Alenka was doing… I'm the only one who cared about you, about the both of you, I'm the only one who cared about what was going on… I'm the only one who tried to…'

Olga has had enough of the accusations. She smacks her hand against the dashboard.

'What did you do! Go on, tell me what you did!'

'…only I knew… Why did I hit myself with the belt then? Who traded away our land for the bottle? Who beat you all of those days? That's why I did it…so you wouldn't be alone. That's why! And it's not fair!'

'Oh, please, Andreja, spare me the *who owes what to whom*. I am finally at peace. I've finally reached a state of equilibrium. I don't owe anybody anything and nobody owes me anything. It took a long time,' her snickering is unusually dry, 'God knows it took a long time, but now I'm finally here and I have to tell you I feel great. At some point you have to say – enough. Enough was enough.'

Grace's crying does not lessen.

'But…then why can't I…?'

'What can't you what, Andreja?'

'My name is Grace!' she yells. In the fog in front of them appears, for a second, a dark silhouette of a figure, just for a split second, not long enough for them to react other than with a momentary dilation of the pupils and an embryo of a sigh on the vocal chords, before the silhouette, with a loud *bang* that they feel through the seats, unites with the front bumper and bounces off. Grace instinctively hits the brakes. She manages to keep the car on the road.

'What was that?'

Olga looks over her shoulder, but immediately waves her arm.

'Probably a deer or stag.'

'I don't think—'

'Who cares what it was,' interrupts Olga. 'Drive on so that bastard doesn't abuse our Bernard. It's not far.'

Grace looks at her in amazement. Olga motions for her to drive on.

'It looked like Berdo's Janez.'

Olga rolls her eyes.

'Give me a break,' she says, 'I've already seen him die once today.'

Grace drives on and before a minute has passed Olga squeezes her shoulder and yells for her to stop. Grace strains to see through the fog but all she can see are the hints of shapes. She doesn't know what Olga can see. They stop.

'Open the trunk, please,' says Olga. 'Left button, at the bottom.'

Grace searches for it, Olga gets out. She presses it. Coolness crawls into the car as Olga is opening the trunk, lifting the cover of the spare-tyre well and extracting a silver revolver. She opens the drum, checks whether it's loaded, spins it, and closes it again. Hearing this, Grace gets out of the car and goes to see what her mother's up to.

She turns speechless when she sees her there with purpose on her face and a gun in her hands.

'What is it, Grace?' asks Olga in a dead tone, 'Did you think it would really be so simple?'

With her foot Grace traces a line in the sand on the

ground. She shrugs. Her gaze does not waver. They each seek courage in the other's eyes.

/

This damned life gives you no peace. It doesn't matter how much you give, how much it takes, for sacrifice, for a joke, for a bit of time… It doesn't stay around long. It always finds something to interrupt it, so that it can get back to its old hurdy-gurdy, now, now, now. The possible worlds are disappearing. The real world is turning into a different one. It can't find equilibrium, and it never will. It's not just things that change form in the stomach, it's also content, and desires morph into the means of struggle. Life is a tank tread. An insatiable beast. It constantly pulls itself by the arse and pummels onwards. But you don't know… You don't know, is it driven by birth or by death? Are the thousands of upset explosions in its digestive tract what's pushing it, or is it being pulled forwards by the gravitation of entropy, the final collapse of all things? Do you always have to persist, create, even destructively, in order to, if nothing else, remain at the outset, or do we have to leave and let others set new points where equilibrium will be balanced? What's my life called? Hey! What's my life called? Abraham? Fuck that. In half? That sounds more…fitting.

Because we killed half of all the politicians, half of all the bankers, half of all the craftsmen, half of all the industrialists, half of all the directors, half of all the managers, half of all the shareholders, half of all the priests, half of all the generals, half of all the soldiers, half of all the secretaries, half of all the workers, half of all the poets, half of all the postmen, half of all the drunks, half of all the writers, half of all the bakers, half of all the pirates, half of all the high-school kids, half of all the students, half of all the hunters, half of all the believers, half of all the artists, half of all the nudists, half of all the waiters, half of all the dressmakers, half of all the tailors, half of all the hungry, half of all the full, half of all the cows, half of all the dogs, half of all the cats, half of all the horses, half of all the pigs, half of all the innocent, half of all the guilty, half of all the good, half of all the pesky, half of all the women, half of all the men, half of all the adults, half of all the children, and expelled all foreigners.

The family idyll had never seemed so close to the touch.

And if the schemer, life, is now again setting them in motion, and they will soon again find themselves on spiral orbits whose paths will never again cross, and will fly off from the solid core of idea into space – does that in any way diminish their meaning? It's true. Everything falls apart. But what about that which was never put together?

Kras had already tied his tie when he looked at himself in the mirror and laughed at his own vanity. He stuck a finger into the knot and unravelled it. He took off the tie and threw it to the floor. He doesn't have much in his suitcase. An extra pair of shoes, a few shirts, underwear, socks, pants. If his path leads him north, or very far south, he'll buy a coat at the airport. There's nothing he really needs. Definitely not a tie.

He has no intention of saying goodbye. In any case he won't be away from home for long and he doesn't want to answer questions. Their presence is still alive in his head, gathered as they were in celebration the day before, a family snapshot in living colour. Now they are once again dispersed into their frames, which is why he won't visit them just to make sure before he leaves… Why does it seem like he's running away? He's never run away from things. Not even when he probably should have. When the world became unhinged and when dangerous oaths were taken and hatred called for its pound of flesh. Nowhere was it written that he would be the one to succeed, that he would be the one to survive, and if back then he'd found himself on the wrong side, there would be nothing but silence from him. So he is not running away. He's just going for his son, wherever he is. Just for his child. Though he's no longer a child. He's as old as Kras was when he still had a choice.

The sound of a suitcase zipper. The shudder of doubt on his face. When he still had a choice. He made a choice for himself. He also made a choice for everyone else. How could he leave a free path for his son, if he was born of a choice that set out and closed off the path for Kras? Fathers are selfish. Kras is well aware of this. There are some things a man must hold on to. Those are not just words. Those are not just memories. And freedom means nothing if you have it only in order to avoid what was chosen – for you.

In the courtyard a taxi honks. Kras heads down the stairs, goes outside, where he glances up to his father, way up there, and snarls at the priest who comes running over to hear confession. He's not interested in what's going on here. He and his father dealt with it a long time ago. Everything else was just a dull variation on a theme. Kras inherited the desert. To make something grow, he had to water it with blood. The truth of history presses down on the sense of justice. It bends it in the strong, it breaks it in the weak. Nobody can see innocence, which is good, since there is none.

He sits in the back seat and doesn't look at the driver. He stares out of the window as they drive. A few drops of rain disturb the cover of dust. The clouds are flaunting their fatness. There's no sun. Evening is a long way off. Everything is captured here. His restless knees jump up and down, the leather heels and the rubber mat squeaking each time they come into contact. Everything is captured here. Kras won't let his eyelids interrupt the view, so his eyes begin to water. The landscape curves over the edges of teardrops.

'Is there something…' he mumbles, and though the driver hears him, he has enough common sense to remain silent. 'Is there something here that's larger than me?' asks Wolf. The fields bend. The forest at the edge merges into the sky. 'All this and something more, at least something, at least a little over it?' The colours of sand and blades of grass blend into a dirty green. 'Or is there always a hole,' he clenches his fist and presses it slowly and deliberately against the glass, 'which sucks and sucks and does not let the world be filled? And no matter how much you throw into it, it still wants more and always takes away the fullness of things…!' He bashes his fist against the glass. The driver shifts in his seat but remains quiet.

'What should I fill it with?'

'Come again, sir?'

'I said, what should I fill the hole with?'

'I don't know, sir.'

Kras nods, crosses his legs, loses sight of the horizon and closes his eyes.

'Mr Wolf. Before we get to the airport, we have to cross the checkpoint. I can tell you right now that you will have to take your shoes off.'

Kras bends down towards his laces.

'Will we be there soon?'

'In a minute, Mister Wolf.'

Just one more minute.

POETRYLITICS

✦ ✦ ✦

A sliver of moon peeks through a crack in the clouds and a person, desperate, becomes convinced for a moment that he came into the world for a purpose he has yet to discover, but the next moment again buries his head in his hands and whispers to himself, *it's hopeless.*

At a height of thirty-five thousand feet, circling like a bald eagle, is death with steel wings, sensitive thermal sensors and the sentence GOD IS NOT DEAD…YET written in red spray paint on the fuselage. This is *Avenger*, a crewless combat plane that has been airborne for twenty-five years. Its wings bear a tonne and a half's worth of K01-7025 Hellfire air-to-ground missiles. Without it, no story comes to an end.

You damned bull! Don't give up now, just before the end! You will make it. I believe in you. Love is not greed. Love is not greed. I promise you. I promise

look…

…at this street and all the people in it. And this branch, floating freely in the air just an inch away from his window. In windy storms it taps lightly on the pane, as if it were seeking refuge from the weather. In rain it dresses in black and makes a silent bow to the procession of drops. The tree itself cannot be seen from here.

Look at the clash of shadows on the streetlight's yellow canvas. Listen to the typewriter keys. The constant clacking of their teeth. That herd of wild horses galloping across an embankment of rocks. The people under the window make all sorts of sounds. They have called out all the names, summoned their children and screamed astonished greetings at people they haven't seen in centuries, they have laughed loudly, with no choice, almost under duress, at the thousands of hostile jokes from the mouths of foreign travellers who have arrived here from the primal forests and deserts, underneath broad hats, with cracked lips, and cracked skin over their thumbs... They have dragged metal barbecue grills right out into the street. Bodies are rotating over the flames. Sweet smoke creeps through the tiny cracks between the window frame and the wall. The smell of meat halts the sound of the keys. The chair screeches when the body in it leans back. *The things you do to escape trap you inside.* He remembers a story about a guy in a prison cell who built a cage out of his bunk bed frame and enclosed himself within it. He was trapped under his own conditions and therefore, so he told anyone who would listen, he had made himself completely free.

It was not in vain.

The pile of typed papers in the corner of the room grows and grows. The people under the window are setting off fireworks. You can hear the whistling rockets and observe the blushing façades. It's a holiday. The windows have been freshly washed. The cleaning lady was going on and on about an anniversary as she scrubbed with a brush, but he couldn't make out what it was an anniversary of. Her accent was too thick and for half of the words she'd switched languages. She also scrubbed the floor and swept away the cobwebs. He didn't have to move, he could keep right on typing as if she wasn't there, only once having to lift his feet, which he did without much enthusiasm and without complaint. Now you can see the reflection of the fireworks in the hardwood floor.

It's been twenty-five years since he left home to settle among the cannibals. They're not choosy. They'll eat anything, from memories to respect. As long he's typing, they leave him alone. But as soon as his typewriter falls silent, they come to inquire. Girls with black hair and translucent lips swarm around his body. He's already too old to succumb to their charms. Once they almost cost him his fingers. Back then it was a matter of courage. What has remained? The men are even more annoying. They want to know everything. Who he is, where he's from, who his parents are, what he does. Just draw his lot from the drum and he'll take it.

The smell of meat won't leave him alone. His machine remains silent. He tilts his head towards the door and listens intensely, to hear whether the hardwood will groan under the steps of an intruder. The house remains silent. All of its ghosts have flocked together in the jambs of the front door, waiting to pounce on the first one to enter. The bell at the reception remains silent. Is there really no one there? With his index finger he pushes his glasses higher up on the bridge of his nose. Sweet smoke. He doesn't want to lead anyone by the nose. In three quick steps he's at the door, which opens to a hallway of tumescent wallpaper with a pattern of pale-pink flower buds (one floor higher, a year ago, fat Shat fell asleep in the tub with the tap running and drowned – the wallpaper separated from the walls in a display of mourning), and timidly peeks over the staircase railing to the floor below. There's no one. He puts the inside of his wrist against his ears to convince himself time hasn't stopped. Om. Sssk. Om. Sssk. (*Try it*)

He grabs the lapels of his jacket and mashes them into a ball against his chest. The fabric tightens over his shoulders and a seam creaks. He rushes to the ground floor, watched over by gazing trophies (cats, cuckoos, buffalos) hanging from the wall . All the chairs are upholstered in red velvet. All the tables are ebony and thickly layered with lacquer. Bitten by forks. The chairs have cigarette burns in them. The fan is on but is facing the wall. There's nobody here. Stubborn, decades-old drops of blood, which have ruined the backs of generations of housewives yet remained present, lead from the common space into the kitchen, a reminder of the Battle of Gunslingers, thoroughly investigated by the police and fully covered by the contemporary press. *Combat at the Union.* The owner's forefathers won. The owner's forefathers always win. With the palm of his hand he smacks the stumpy brass bell and lets the sound eat into the air.

Melquiades was asleep under the counter. His face is just a thin sanctuary that his lips, eyes, nose and thin moustache have made for themselves in-between the spilling circles of fat. He's surprised to see him outside his room.

'Where is Guadalupe?'

Melquiades takes a deep breath as he comes to.

'And how should I know where the nogoonblotter is, I was still draven dreamin'?'

'Can you hear it?' he asks, raising an index finger. Neither can resist looking up for a brief moment.

'No.'

'Silence.'

Melquiades's shoulders droop.

'There's nothing I can do about it,' he says. 'If anyone, she should do something. I don't mind the silence.'

'Good. Good. Could I, please, have a glass of water?'

'Water? That's all you want?'

'Water.'

Melquiades, with difficulty, raises his hand to the row of glasses hanging from their stems over the bar, and takes one out. When he turns on the tap, they hear the melliflu-ous strains of an orchestra. They look at each other, stunned. Melquiades turns off the tap and the orchestra falls silent.

'Do it again.'

When he turns it on again, all they hear is the rushing of water. They are both disappointed. Melquiades places the glass under the stream. After a moment he frowns and raises it to his face.

'Damn. Look at this.'
'What?'
'There's a hole.'
'I'm waiting for…' he says.
'Pardon?' says Melquiades.
'Nothing.'

Melquiades sighs unhappily when he has to raise his hand a second time. He switches glasses and checks to see if this one is ok. He throws the one with the crack into the bin. When he runs the tap, someone whispers.

'Rip me in half, otherwise I can't breathe.'
Melquiades looks up.
'Pardon?'
'Nothing.'
'You said something.'
'That came from the tap.'

'Aha. Yes, it's quite possible, you know, the pipes are copper and very old and sometimes they snatch something out of the air.'

'I doubt that very much.'

'It's true,' says Melquiades, offended. 'Sir, you are not going to call me a liar if I tell you that, just last week, we heard reports from the caliphate, through the tap. Can you imagine? There's half a world between us, yet out it comes, straight from the tap.'

'I changed my mind.'
'You won't have any water?'
'No.'

Melquiades puts the glass on the bar. Guadalupe rushes through the front door with a bang and a tuft of hazel branches pressed into her palm, the street hard on her heels. She doesn't look at them, but immediately starts rushing up the stairs.

'Lupe! He's here.'

The colours, smells and sounds from outside are fading away. Guadalupe swivels the figurine that is her head, purses her lips into a perfect O and cries through them.

'Where have you been?' asks Melquiades, his voice oozing accusation. 'You know that sir has to write.'

'Dolly came home all covered in blood! Manuel and Ricardo have sworn they will take revenge. I know I shouldn't have left you alone, sir, but…the men were weeping with wounded pride.'

Melquiades whistles.

'Serious stuff,' he says.

Guadalupe starts coming down the stairs, with eyes fixed upon him.

The hazel branches are raised in the air, ready for the lazy one to feel the lash.

'Are they still out there? Are they still there?' he asks her.

'They're just leaving. They had to wait for Mum to go into the kitchen to get some St John's wort for the blessing.'

All three nod.

'And Dolly?'

'Dolly stayed outside. She's waiting for dinner.'

'Damned canni—'

'Now hold on a second, sir,' interrupts Melquiades, underlining his sharp tone by thwacking a palm against the bar. 'A little respect never bankrupted anyone.'

He raises in hands in apology. Guadalupe, the girl, drops the branches by her side and finds herself in a dilemma. Her black hair is tied into a ponytail from which a few strands have escaped and fallen over the right side of her face. Her slight paleness reminds one of piano keys. Tone and semitone.

'So?' she asks him with an impatient swing of the knee.

'I would like to see her,' he says.

'Dolly?'

'Dolores,' he replies.

'All right,' nods Guadalupe. 'You can, she's still… Come.'

She grabs him by the arm and pulls him along. Melquiades calls out to them just before they're swallowed by the swing of the door.

'Shall I draw a bath for you tonight, sir?'

He and Guadalupe don't look back.

'Because in that case I would have to go get…'

The street chirps and whistles, smoky, full of smiles and red noses, good-hearted back-slaps, children at play, children on the breast, children in the air. When the fog swallows them, he instantly loses all sense of space. He doesn't know where he comes from. He doesn't know where he is. The colourful fireworks sketch different hues in the air and announce a bang that knots his stomach even when he knows it's coming. He lets himself be pulled along, reassured at having someone in front of him.

They find Dolores inside a circle of grievers who are trying, through their cries, to wrench at least a pinch of melancholy from her. The men have already done their grieving, and now they're hunched down at the far end of the street speaking of weightier matters.

To look at her is to look at sadness. Her stocking-cap is still stuck to her sweaty forehead. Her hair is short and getting thinner and thinner in two marked cuts over her temples. Another year and she'll be bald. Where is her wig? Will no one ease at least some of this shame? Ashen rings surround her eyes. Tears have cut grey trenches into them. Her upper lip is curled into a sob. You could hold a party between her incisors.

'…and he had a knife…and he held me, squished me… it hurt…it hurt a lot…and a whole freezer full of dead cats…'

She thrusts her open palm into their faces, as if she wants to stop their advance, though she merely wants to show them the scabby scratch which has deepened her lifeline, and they're already wailing away. Guadalupe lets go so she can wipe the corners of her eyes. He uses this moment of empathy to slip away. If he's not careful, this obscene, vulgar sadness will hang itself around his neck too. The colourful strata of fog soften the edges of everything in the street. It's all becoming less real. He approaches the circle of men, carefully, as if by mere chance, with his eyes turned to the side and down, trying not to arouse their attention. They absently wipe away tears and try to still the bobbing of their Adam's apples by placing a hand over the neck.

'…they have some sort of holiday…'

'…he went there, for sure, our dentist, Curion, saw him…'

'…but is the zone safe? I didn't think you could even assemble there…'

'…you probably can't, but nobody told them…'

'…so why don't we just wait? Why should we expose ourselves to danger, if…'

Ricardo (or Manuel, you can't quite tell who's who – they're twins) raises his voice.

'…because it's a matter of honour! A matter of honour and pride! Nobody but the Perrada brothers is going to take revenge.'

They stamp their heels on the ground, and they nod, and murmur, yes-yes. There used to be three Perrada brothers before the youngest one – Doloretto – surrendered to the needs of his heart and decided to become their sister, which the other two let him do on the condition that he buy off their honour with his honour, according to a payment plan. The money that Dolores now earns is not really money.

'…and so what are you going to do?'

'…what do you mean, we're going to go over there and count all his bones, from the ankles to the crown of his head…'

'…but he's got a knife…'

'…there's two of us!…two!… He can't get both of us… we can split up!'

This puts them in a better mood. *Some flee from their fates. Fates flee from some others.* It's hard to maintain a balance. It's hard to remain impartial. It is so easy to pay attention to elsewhere. Mum is arriving at the head of a thinning procession. It seems that not everyone is interested in the affair. He

never really got to know their politics. The web of demands
knitted by her sons, her brothers, her fathers, seemed too
complicated for a single person to follow, especially for a
guest, but he could never shake off the feeling that everything
might become quite clear with just a little focus. Attentiveness
is a virtue, like anything else. Sometimes you have to pay for
it, sometimes you can buy something with it. And what pays
off? What really pays off?

hide

Her prayer is short and pithy. She silences the chatter of
children rolling behind her back with a glance, then plucks a
handful of dry leaves from the branch, crumbles them into
powder and sprinkles it over the ground in front of their feet.

'That you may hold on to your head, that you may hold
on to our head, that you may watch over the heads of the
others.' In chorus the men rap their knuckles against their
foreheads.

'It is true,' they say.

Without thinking, he repeats after them this gesture of
community.

'Can we go?'

Mum frames her face with her palms. She's done her job.
Manuel and Ricardo head down the street. The remaining
faces are kept aglow by a feeling that transcends them. He
envies them. They all know how. Slowly they blend back into
the holiday. They know how. Not all at once, and not as if they
really cared. For a moment they stay there, a slight twitch of
the knee announcing they're about to move, then they turn
on their heels and bow their heads as if they were taking leave
of something real, before disappearing into the orange smoke.
Into the purple smoke. For a moment Guadalupe's profile is
traced in it (it's already green). Her task is clear. She must
find him. If he stops writing, they'll eat him. That was the
agreement.

hide

He mustn't do it too quickly, that would attract attention. With cat-like movements he retreats to the wall, turns his face to it, and then, like a crab, slowly slips away sideways. His back makes itself sensitive to their gazes. Nobody is watching him. He holds his breath, silences his heart and silently counts the passing bricks with his lips. When he gets to the end of the street, it's completely dark. All he can hear, off in the distance, is leather crackling in the joints of a brown-shoe quartet.

careful

The hazel branch slices through the dark and transforms the tips of his toes into a burning ball of pain. Guadalupe's voice has grown used to a cold, commanding tone.

'Back.'

/

A conspiracy of skyscrapers rises above the rooftops of human homes. The doors lock in bursts. Graffiti drips from the walls of public buildings and discomfort crawls over the empty streets. Whoever has not locked himself in is either dangerous or crazy. At night, the Third World comes knocking on the windows of dreamers. The high volume of iron bars is not in the least surprising. It's funny, when you think that life here used to be carefree. That women in too-high heels and too-mini skirts used to traipse about, and boys used to try their luck and remain in good spirits even if they crashed and burned. Back then, there was no fear of the possibility of coming in last. Reality blithely doled out chances and kept encouraging even the biggest of losers. On the softened edges of the squares and parks people gave vent to their souls and nobody got angry at them for doing so. Teeth bared in smiles. What went wrong? Who begrudged all those people's children?

Ricardo and Manuel do not heed the traffic signs but power straight on. Ignited by purpose. The dull eyes of vagrants follow them from dark corners where the streetlights don't reach. For a moment their eyes flash with the passion of want, but fear chokes every move. Together the Perrada brothers weigh more than forty-seven stone and stand a shade over thirteen feet tall. They won't put up with any crap. If someone wants something, let him come. There's nobody. They stumble upon a pack of rats feasting on a corpse. The rats scatter. The heatwave did not spare a broken heart. The stench has emptied all the surrounding balconies. They are unfalteringly sure-footed.

The path leads them past stagnant neighbourhoods where ghosts take stock of their former lives and try to determine the moment it all went wrong, past the beach, with its black sand and abandoned amusement parks, playgrounds of defeated wills, past miles of dead asphalt. In the graveyard by the church in which the old priest Mandelbrot continues to publicly battle doubt and asthma every evening, gangs of triads are robbing graves. Ricardo and Manuel are able to remember a different world, but it's not one they miss. Even the previous world didn't mean much to them. People like them have the easiest time surviving. Don't attach yourself to the world. Every subsequent one will seem even worse.

Perhaps it would be easier by train, but to get to some places you have to walk. Sometimes you have to pound the pavement, lick it with your soles, immerse yourself into space and contemplate the world rotating under your feet. Their heads are not exactly empty, but they create no extraordinary thoughts. They're angry, but not enraged, and insulted, though not gravely so. They would never admit to being scared, although the thought of a network of machines staring, through thermally sensitive eyes and with a threat of violence, from high up in the stratosphere at the surface of the world ensuring the dispersion of the human community gives them the creeps. Sometimes a man's spirit has to overcome the limitations of nature. That fool had better not think that he can get away without punishment. Nobody is allowed to cast magic all on his own. Especially not with their sister around.

Among the high concrete fencing, which obscures the private worlds of the solemn people, Manuel places a hand on Ricardo's shoulder to stop him. Something has stirred in the half-darkness ahead of them. They strain their eyes to make out the alien outline and their hearts begin to beat faster. It moves towards them, its shadow growing with each step. The emerald globes reflect the cold light of the display. When they see it, they vanish from the thermal scan. Each atom in their bodies comes to a halt. They can't risk any sudden movements. They quickly forge an agreement in thought. All dimensions of their bodies have become superfluous, so they have to bury their courage. Their calves tighten as they slowly, slowly, drop to their knees. The rough concrete surface makes their kneecaps whimper with pain, but they don't acknowledge it. They look at the ground, straight down. They press their lips together. If it sees their teeth, their bodies will soon be tenantless, like the thousands of run-down, sucked-out buildings they have left behind. They touch the ground with their foreheads. The concrete stings imperceptibly. They spread their arms, placing their open palms on the ground. Their rumps remain in the air, unguarded. They are of this world, they say in the language of nature. They know where their place is. The tiger walks silently between them and lashes their hips with its tail.

They don't know how much time they have spent quietly bowing down before the higher force. With bated breath they listen for whether the beast will change its mind. A window fails to contain the cry of an orgasm. The fluttering wings of pigeons spoil the silence. The rocking of the skyscrapers in the high-altitude wind fills the air with the coarse grinding of foundations against rock. They rise in tandem and fill their lungs with air. It doesn't faze them. They're all the more convinced that they are, in spite of everything, right. In their shred of life they have to follow their own decisions. They will not give in to dispersion. They will not allow someone else to settle behind their eyes.

They break into a run. Adrenaline pours into the space left behind by fear. They compete with each other and remain absolutely parallel. Street to street, park to park, dry hydrant to dry hydrant, everything passes and hardly gets noticed. Their steps echo louder and louder, with an ever more forceful meaning, the chopped sound reverberates off the walls and upends paper bins, they go under overpasses, over bridges, past hollow rows of petrol pumps, past watering holes for horses, the sound throwing the slaves of cardboard castles into despair, the bandits retreat from the pavements, the dealers melt into the scenery, the prostitutes finally fall silent for a moment, the night predators respectfully blink in their wake and the whole city inexorably pushes them forth into the embrace of their destiny.

When they find themselves in front of a full car park, they don't stop. They race over the metal roofs that bend under their weight, interrupting some protracted sexual intercourse in the back seat of a black Oldsmobile. They storm into the crowd with the force of a discharge that has been building up for years. They break the membrane without effort and silent cries of complaint hang in the air, unanswered. Whatever survival instinct doesn't move out of the way, they elbow aside. Bare curiosity cannot withstand the onrush of need. If it is justified, even the sea will part in half, not to mention a bunch of people.

/

Chairs have been gathered from everywhere. Worm-eaten bar stools that tilt perilously under the emaciated arses in faded jeans, plush leather sofas with spiral coils peeking through, plastic garden chairs borrowed from a thousand and one family picnics, rows of pews from abandoned religious buildings, stitched up bags filled with styrofoam… Max didn't discriminate. He's thrown everything he could get his hands on into this space. People are very understanding. If anything, they are mad at themselves for not having queued up earlier. Now all that is left are some strange uncomfortable-looking black cubes nobody wants to be the first to try, so they stand around them in a hesitant circle looking at them, slightly befuddled.

Anwar, Marjorie and her lover, the soldier Mus and his cohorts were invited to sit in the first row. Brian and Rupert are lurking about in the corners and surreptitiously passing around a hastily rolled joint so they won't have to share it with anyone. Ludovico, with Semyona behind him, is standing taut as a string almost directly below the stage. The faces of the others blend into each other and play the role of shop-window mannequins. There are so many of them I won't bother telling you who they are. For the most part, they are lovely and fetching.

Zoja is backstage with Max and the old guy, who is recovering from hypoglycaemic shock. A very shy man with a guitar has walked onto the stage, slowly, as if walking on eggshells, and now he's playing in a way that will ensure nobody will want to do him harm. Quietly and gently.

'So you're a soldier, yes?' Marjorie's lover asks Mus, who is sitting next to him. Marjorie is on his other side, beside Anwar.

'Well…you could say that I am, but right now I'm not here to…'

'A soldier in uniform. I've never understood uniforms. Do they really work?'

'What do you mean?'

'I mean, are people really so stupid that they believe in uniforms?'

'People are very receptive to things.'

'Ha, you can say that again.'

'People are…?'

'Just a figure of speech. That reminds me… My father, once, when I was around ten, got an idea, *yeah that's it, that's it, Selena,* my mum's name, *that's it, Selena, we're going to be rich, rich,* this came over him pretty much twice a year, in the morning he would get out of bed and race to his desk and start scribbling crazily over an endless stack of paper, all the while muttering, *we're gonna be rich, Selena, kids, let's go for ice cream,* and he'd take us to the first ice cream shop, Mum would of course have to pay, she worked as a cleaning lady in a building on the East Side, she'd scowl but she believed him anyway, each time, how bloody naive, and my brother and I always warmed up to his enthusiasm, we'd look at each other covertly and cross our fingers, silently mouthing his mantra, *we're going to be rich, we're going to be rich, no more of those second-, third-, fifth-hand clothes, no more of those crappy pencil cases and those always-empty fountain pens, we're going to be rich,* hey, every six months our family moved up ten floors, for a week, you know, before once again having to move down, down, down, and it was back to Father's sunken cheeks, back to Mum's disappointment, which she was actually great at hiding, but the things that she desperately clutched in her fists then lay around the flat broken and bent, their broken form clearly saying what was going through her head, and I was not attentive enough to get it then, but my brother was starting to cotton on to what it all meant, well, what I was saying, that particular time he got the idea of selling uniforms to people around the world, I can clearly remember his lofty airs, the solemn words he spoke, *there are thousands of us, millions like us that have been let down by the nation states and let down by corporations, and we don't have religions, and we don't have traditions, but we're still alive, every man in his own way…'*

Anwar leans forwards and listens more carefully. Mus raises his eyebrows in an attempt to show compassion. Marjorie runs her hand over her lover's taut chest, which is rising and falling in an excited rhythm.

'*…and all these people, all these people will buy uniforms and stand together and show themselves to the world, hey, here* *we are, don't think we're all alone, each for himself, there is strength in unity*, and then he'd rattle off political slogans so old they were already worn out to transparency after being shouted out loud so many times, but back then I still didn't know that, and it all seemed so interesting and wonderful and in any case I had never before seen Father so, almost, yes, strong, strong or something, I was seeing him like that for the first time, and it impressed itself on me like an immensely important thing, *we're going to be rich, we're going to be rich*, because Father had finally come up with something smart, how easy it is to get a child to believe you, well, and then, once again, he took out a loan and bought acres of material and hired a Chinese seamstress, a neighbour, her family was even worse off than we were, and she slaved over that pile of black uniforms for two months, while he was busy writing philosophical advertisements, building a brand, he told us, *I'm building a brand*, and I knew brands only from cigarettes and it all seemed strange to me, Mum just headed obliviously off to work, and it all stopped having any effect on my brother, and he again started going out and not coming home until morning, although he was – how old? – barely fourteen, well, and, of course, when Father went out into the world to sell his wisdom and his uniforms I waited at home for him, breathless, and when he finally came back, not having sold a single one and not having found a single person who was willing to listen to him, he wasn't even ashamed! It didn't work out, he'd tell us. Mum almost fainted because who was it that would have to get us out of the hole? She, who else? But Father, without an ounce of shame, went back to the desk, scribbled, and half a year later, something new, what do I know, wait, let me remember, some system for more efficient mail delivery, a reform of the toll stations, all asinine of course but soon, again, *we're going to be rich, ice cream*, and so forth and so forth, but now I don't know whether I was so angry at him because he never made it, or whether I was angry at him because he managed to get my hopes up every single time.'

Anwar weighs whether to tell him that he thinks he's just met his father in the car park. Mus presses his lips together and nods indulgently.

'I don't think the idea of uniforms is all that bad,' says Marjorie, which, against all expectation, pleases her lover.

'Ok, yeah, the idea, maybe the idea is doable, but, you know, people! Not to mention all the obstacles that your brain itself sets up, so you have to fight with your own physicality, with dopamine receptors, with pride, with will, not to mention family expectations and the fact that your demands also have to reach others, and let's not even talk about all those system structures grinding away on their own, about the thousands of petty resentments, about the disharmony between space and time, about the conspiracy of the whole bloody universe working against you, how hard it is to even get up in the morning, let alone to organize things your way on this planet of apes, and let's just give it a rest with this lousy illusion of freedom… An idea is not enough. Father had no clue that he had to compete not only with the state and the corporation and religion and tradition, but also with football clubs, strip clubs, alcohol, with a thousand and one feelings of inadequacy, with the collapse of entire layers of hopes and dreams, with gambling, with Tetris, with human evil and to the exact same degree with human kindness, with the daily, constant, all-encompassing lowering of standards, that he ultimately had to compete with poetry… Well, I don't know. Only complete loonies are not paralysed by the world.'

Anwar bellows, 'If that were true, we'd still be living in caves!', and a few people listening to the music whisper a fierce *shhhh*. He lowers his voice and continues.

'Look, I don't know you, I don't know your story, although you keep trying to tell it to us, and I can't cross that abyss between you and me, but I'm old enough and I've experienced enough to tell you this. Your father's defeats are not your defeats. Fuck, even your defeats are not really your defeats. And all this drama about a paralysing world is just a miserable flight from yourself. I can confirm, from first-hand experience, that you will know exactly when the world really makes it impossible, when it ties you up and won't let you breathe, closes off all exits and just takes it all out on your fate… And only then, at that moment, will you clearly hear the voice of God: you have been given knowledge of the real value of freedom. Freedom is not the at-will manipulation of facts. Freedom is a moment of peace.'

Marjorie's lover won't give in.

'Maybe we'll have to go back to the caves. Maybe all this civilization was just a brief respite from the truth. A lie borrowed from the future.'

'But why the hell do you seem so satisfied with that being true?'

Shhhh.

Sincerity is contagious. Mus places a fragile hand on the young lover's beefy thigh.

'I'm sorry, I don't know… But, can I tell you… Well, it's all the same… Still, can I tell you something?'

He doesn't answer. He turns his head towards him and cocks his right eyebrow.

'You said… What did you say? That back then your father seemed strong. I understand what you're talking about. I don't know how to start, basically. Um… Yeah. A strong father.' A nervous laugh. 'I come from a different place. I won't go on and on about it, but, yeah, it's very different. Time flows more slowly. People are…different. I'm not so good with words. What I want to say is… My father is very strong. He always was. My grandfather, for example, isn't and I know that too, but for all his many faults, it was always easier to hang out with him. Maybe it shifts from generation to generation. Maybe my son, if I ever have one, will also be a hard man. I'm not. Maybe that's why you're a hard man. I don't know. I don't know you. But, just now when you were talking about it, it made me think of… Where I'm from, my family is practically an institution. They've been there for, oh, so long. Ever since… God knows when, I'm not so good at history, just the bits I got from older people. But a long time ago. And that shows on people, I can't say it doesn't. They grow sort of, like, in accord with things. They grow into old clothes. I don't know if you're following. But, you know, while we're on the topic… they grow into uniforms. They adapt to them, like they were special to them. And that's all well and good. But, my experience, you know, has taught me that things aren't always the way they seem. Have you ever seen Japanese watermelons?'

'Watermelons?'

'You know what watermelons are?'

'Of course I know.'

'Well, I thought of them because…watermelon transporters in Japan used to be extremely bothered by the fact that watermelons are round, since they took up too much space in shipping, more than they actually deserved.'

A nervous laugh. 'So they found a solution. When watermelons are still really small, they stick them into square boxes, and then when they grow, they reach the edges and can't grow any wider, they fill every inch of every corner, so that in the end they're nice and square and ready for the lorry, even if it's not in their nature. Do you understand?'

'I understand.'

'Now, I don't know if any watermelon exists that simply doesn't give in, breaks the box and, all strong and round, flexes its round muscles in the gardener's face… There probably aren't any like that, but I've always asked myself what happens to those that don't even reach the edge. That chill out in the box, stay small, and nevertheless manage to keep their roundness. I've complicated things a bit…'

'No, no, I'm following.'

'People are just different, that's want I want to say. And we just don't fit into some of those uniforms that float down to us from above. In such cases strong fathers don't help. Of course, that doesn't stop them, because it's not in their nature to leave anything alone. Especially if they have clear expectations and if experience has taught them that reality is at their service. Strong people don't understand freedom like you, you know?' This is for Anwar, who is beginning to bristle. 'And where does all this lead? If the watermelon has reached its limit, there's no force in the world that will push it farther. Any efforts in that direction turn into the usual barbarity. The crazy gardeners can then bother them for years, can badmouth them, abuse them with their hands, they can flatter, try to bribe, they can tattoo their will in big fat letters on the arse, and what will they achieve? Nothing. And when I was listening to you, I had to think… What if our lives are just a long experiment to find out whether or not we manage, in spite of everything, to sew our own uniform? My father went the well-trodden way. Your dad at least tried.'

'Bold words from someone wearing a soldier's uniform.'

'I'm still sewing.'

When Anwar leans back, the back of his chair sags slightly and the sensation of falling fills his stomach. He quickly levels himself and exhales to let out the weight of the world.

'Oh, boys. Anyone who is twenty and doesn't believe in a better world needs a heart. Anyone who is forty and still believes in it, needs a head. But I don't want to lecture you. Sew, sew away. For as long as you can. But watch that you don't find yourselves all sewed up. Every stitch costs something. And unstitching becomes more and more difficult. There are no instructions. No path is the right one. Sometimes hatred leads you into a trap. Sometimes love does. Sometimes good intentions, sometimes bad ones. I finally went down on my knees when the Sherdedovs killed my father and sisters.

Maybe that's the easiest path...but, you know, today I can't say that I regret it. It's hard to renounce courage and hope, and may you never have to. Maybe a few lucky ones really will manage to get through everything, through life, with their sense of control intact. But those who will fail – who will realize that they're desperately clutching sand. Who will then unclasp their fists...'

He covers his mouth and shuts his eyes. Mus stares at the floor. He's embarrassed and he doesn't quite know why. Marjorie's lover runs a hand over her shoulder and pulls her closer. It's hard to shake off the feeling that he's achieved some sort of tiny victory, but it would be in horribly poor taste to celebrate it. He focuses on her warmth. He's satisfied, somehow, with her. Zoja's leg peeks out from an enclosure at the edge of the stage. Excitement charges the air. That's what they came here for. That's why they risked it.

Marjorie allows herself a smile.

'And I never even knew my father.'

A string breaks. Cries of indignation can be heard coming from outside.

'You remind me of my papa,' Semyona whispers in Ludovico's ear, while he is angrily furrowing his brow and gathering courage for the most radical act of his life.

I am your cruelty. Your drive for the ugly. Your constant restlessness.

Zoja walks onto the stage. Applause envelops her. Whistles. Warm, voracious cries.

'You have the same smell. Of freshly skinned pelt, don't ask where I know that smell from, mixed with the sweat of exhausted people, the sweat of tortured people, the sweat of people on their deathbeds. Don't ask...'

Her movements are so common, almost vulgar in their ordinariness. As if she moved that way every day. In the morning that's how she heads into the bathroom and that's how she goes to answer the door.

I'm the one who pushes your head to the ground at night. I'm the one who drags you back into the cave when you would like to raise your fist in a display of never-fought-for victory. 'And you both hold your shoulders the same way. I could play lullabies on your tendons. But you take pains to make sure that it's only obvious to the touch. You're very careful about how things look. You are both hiding something. Right? What are you hiding?'

She clears her throat, which doesn't strike anyone as strange. It becomes a part of her, her cough, a completely human concern. What right does she have to something like that? And then she just smiles.

'Mmm?'

I am despair cast over the service station of your aimless wandering. I roll you up without warning. I splice myself into you, between consciousness and cognition. I am a dark thing. Dark.

'You both have completely shaved heads. What does that mean? Papa, I never dared to ask him. He'd always been like that, ever since I could remember. And he kept his old pictures of himself hidden away from me. I can't even imagine him with hair. But if he had it, it must have been long. And yours? Did you ever have long hair? Before you shaved it off?'

I am everything that you have, but don't want, and all of what you don't have, but would like. I am the heir of the unelected.

She draws in oxygen and lets carbon dioxide escape from her lungs, through her vocal chords, and into the metal microphone, where it is converted into electric signals and whisked through black cables into the quivering diaphragms of the speakers nailed to the walls, and these then shake the air her way. She laughs and her laughter emerges broad, rough, tremendous. Ludovico shows his teeth.

Semyona puts her hand under his tunic and gently prods at his emaciated ribs.

'But Papa was chunky. You are…you're so skinny. Why are you so skinny? Doesn't Mummy give you anything to eat?'

Ludovico pushes away her encroaching hand. I am the prey of shadows. Your isolation, your disintegration. Her words lick the midget ears of those seated around. Ludovico is trying to catch her eye. He doesn't know whether she can even see him, gazing as she is at the bulb of the spotlight. That irritates him utterly.

I am the real thing. You in your worst moments. When you want to kill, I'm with you. When you rejoice at misfortune, I'm in your hidden smile. When you hate a stranger, I'm in your bitter gaze. When you are making sweet love to all your addictions, it's me whispering in your ear *more. More.* When you take off your cloak of kindness, when you seize the whip of your selfishness, when you would like to put your pain into flesh and word, at that time I am by far, far the kindest.

'What is she doing?'

Semyona pulls down the edge of the tunic. On Ludovico's shoulder blade a corner of a tattoo appears.

Zoja has undone her bra and in a carefree movement whipped off her shirt. She went on stage barefoot. She's in denim shorts. Nothing else. What is she doing? Why is she doing that? The people are breathless. They did not expect such disclosure. She covers her breasts with an arm. What is it that her face is trying to tell us? Is it cold? No courage. No fear. Not a single thought-through emotion. Ludovico's muscles tense up. Semyona is hanging on to the tunic, moving slowly, inch by inch. Ludovico's hand slips behind the fabric over his belly and reaches down to the inside of his thigh where he has taped a knife. He feels its steel against his wrist. A little higher, the loose touch of his castrated sex. Her face looks so damned charitable. He wraps his palm around the handle, grips it and pulls.

'What's that on your back?'

Show me your back, if you dare. I'm a monster on a stake-out. Zoja turns around and the shock that the audience had till now found attractive disappears. We have created a world that was not created for us. Her back is an orgy of hacked-up flesh. The scars have accumulated, overtaking each other in long furrows, the torturous pulls of drunken ploughing cattle. If she managed to get through that, think of everything you, you, sheltered people can do. And Zoja doesn't consider it the price of presence. Suffering can't buy anything, suffering only increases the value of beauty. Those who never put a price on the most valuable things will always find buyers. That's why they're here, all these people. They came without being forced. Fine people, constantly on the lookout for the source of beauty. Like moths to a flame.

That offends Ludovico. Nobody has suffered more than he has suffered. He has a monopoly on pain and he can't bear to see it given away so freely. Is nothing sacred any more? Is there anything they won't throw to these gluttons? Did he suffer all those days for nothing? And his life, his shredded life, will he just let them take away everything he spent years clutching to his heart? Were all those cats sacrificed to uncaring deities? He was the only one facing the storms. The only one devouring anxiety. The only one kicked in every last soft wet rag of his body by the passing of time. And that bloody criminal up there now wants to offer these things to everyone for free?

I am the rage of the one who was scammed.

Even Semyona, who has seen the ugliest of things, is shocked at Zoja's back. She leaves Ludovico's alone. What's a simple tattoo compared to this butchered skin?

'That woman must have seriously insulted someone.'

Ludovico's very bones glow.

I am the wrath of the universe. A tempest of gravity. I'm a black hole, a magnet of galaxies. I am a quantum Gatling gun, the tomb of stars. Light doesn't dare approach me, I drink up all light. I am the greed, the gluttony of all things. I am primeval, elemental, the Pre-prophetic!'

Quietly, silently, though he is yelling at the top of his voice, he climbs on stage and, knife in hand, makes for her.

/

'I've got terrible stage fright,' the guitarist says and squeezes the neck of his guitar like he's strangling a duck.

'Why?' asks Zoja.

'I've never seen a crowd like this.'

Standing by the stage exit, he fixes one eye on the audience and then immediately looks away. His whole body shivers. Zoja takes a step towards him and to him this feels like a tacit threat. He'd like to concentrate on the music, on its autonomy, its independence from the instrument, on its effect, and not think of its cause, its human origin, which is why Zoja's body – which from his perspective is growing bigger and bigger – unsettles him.

Max smiles benevolently at the old man who is resting in the only armchair they have backstage, his legs stretched out over the velvet edges, his arms dangling, his palms facing upwards, and giving the air of a man who has cheated death. His face gradually turns the colour of living skin. He's utterly calm. He keeps watch over the situation through slowly rotating eyeballs. His breathing is deep and steady. Now is not the time for rushing.

Zoja is by the guitarist's side. She takes him by the upper arm, then envelops his hand in hers and squeezes his electric response.

'Don't be afraid,' says Zoja. His lips form a frown, he looks down and exhales sharply.

'Don't be afraid,' she repeats. 'There used to be no end to the crowds. These few hundred people are a drop in the ocean compared to the intertwined bodies that used to flock to see far more awful things. Nobody has come to judge. They've come because they're lonely. Because they're afraid nobody understands them. Because they have it hard.'

'That doesn't really help me much,' he says softly, pale in the face. 'My music is just sound. It can't do anything for anyone.'

'There are no demands here. They've just come to convince themselves that somebody, anybody actually still believes.'

'I don't know whether I believe.'

'It's not your job to believe for them.'

'But when you said…'

'You just have to do your magic.'

'Do magic?'

'When you're up there on stage and you're running your fingers over the strings, just forget where you are. Forget about all that wood and all those stones and all that glass and all that nylon and steel and all those hearts and all those eyeballs, forget that time is passing, beat by beat, forget that everything true is true. Step into the void that's floating unseen in space somewhere beyond our galaxy. Don't sing to the people. Sing to that empty space. There's nothing there but your sound. Your sound is the only thing that exists. Your whole life is your sound. For as long as you're in this place, for as long as this place is your sound, you were never born and you'll never die. You have no parents, you have no children, nobody knows you. Nervousness? Nervousness is something you feel on the train when the conductor comes to see whether you've got a ticket. When a stranger asks you for a favour. When you'd like to say *I love you* to someone you don't love. Nervousness is when you're hungry. But you came to create. You came to light up the emptiness. You came to work magic. Leave the nervousness to them.'

'To them?'

'To those people who came for something.'

'What have they come for?'

'For something that nobody can give them.'

'…'

'Get out there, lose yourself, sing.'

A kaleidoscope of emotion washes over his face, his muscles twitch every which way before stiffly resigning themselves to their fate. But you know that face. It's the one that floats in the mirror on all those difficult mornings. Zoja gently nudges him, and his stride as he moves out onto the stage, into the space, is almost calm.

/

'Lupe!'

The hardwood floor squeaks under her steps. His fingers smart. It goes slowly with just one hand. The handle moves silently downward. The door opens. She wedges her head into the slot.

'Lupe, please bring me a glass of water.'

'Water?' Her voice is dry and smooth.

'Water, yes.'

'Would you like something else?'

'Just water.'

With a rapid swing of the forehead she points at the typewriter keys and nods. Then she disappears.

/

I took my shoes off. Now I'm barefoot. I nudge the shoes under the dirty cloth hanging from a little table bestrewn with flyers that are encircling an almost empty plastic bottle of water. We used the water to moisten the diabetic's forehead. Max observes me with bated breath. Mr Ž— has wandered far, far away. I don't know whether the guitarist heard what I told him, but he seems to be enjoying himself on stage. His eyes are closed and he's turned his face skywards. Forget about them. Become sound.

Life sometimes makes you feel like it's taken you in its hand and moved you closer to the sun. And sometimes it seems that the fingers around you have formed a fist and turned off all the light.

In total darkness, it's easy to forget the light. Did they lie to you? Did they take you for a fool? Did they try to sacrifice your soul on the altar of their failures? Did they conspire against you because prisoners of shadows hate people with rays in their eyes? It's so simple to surround yourself with the drowned. But that is only an illusion. It's so simple to convince yourself that you live among a crowd of gluttons. Then you hide yourself and set up walls, you defend yourself against attacks by imagined armadas and you can no longer tell the difference between an offered hand and the thrust of a knife. That's the worst thing that can happen to you in life. Love should never be allowed to lose its transparency. It should never be allowed to wrap itself in a veil of threats. Love me, otherwise…otherwise…otherwise I will unmask my love as a complicated pulley which I use to try to draw my fears from the well to the light. Under the heavens. To the scarlet fields of our steps. Love me, otherwise…otherwise you're not a part of the community of lovers of life. Love me, otherwise you're a horrible, forgotten, cursed thing. Eat me. Devour me. Love me.

Love is not greed. If someone demands it, he doesn't deserve it. If someone bets on it, he'll lose the bet. If someone uses it as a rope to pull himself free from quicksand, it will snap in his hands. Love will never save anyone.

And it's true. We live among hungry people. They devour everything from memories to respect. But nobody knows the taste of love. With stretched-out tongues they chase after it, and just because they devour everything else, they are convinced that it is the same with love. They will eat beauty and they will eat eternity. They will eat poetry and shit politics. That's the reality of people. But it's not all the same. I'm not going anywhere. I'm staying here. I'll crumple the piece of cardboard in my pocket and throw it in the corner. I'll find a way out of my mouth.

/

The guitarist pushes past Zoja, with his guitar in front of him, and enters backstage as triumphantly as if he'd just broken through the Ubanga front. The broken string hangs from the instrument's neck like a loose, bronze spring. He couldn't finish his set. He's out of breath, beaming, flushed and exhausted. His chest is tight and he'd like to smile, but then he senses Zoja's gaze in the back of his neck and again turns humble, so as not to ascribe too much importance to his fifteen minutes of flourishing. Still, he'd like to keep on feeling proud of himself. They listened to him and they didn't all seem turned off. True, some were chatting, but attentive ears could hear past those surely important conversations that were serving as a backdrop for his sound. Music for the masses. Of course they're going to chat. After all, they're only people!

He wipes his face on his arm and walks over to Max, who has moved towards the seated old guy, laid his hands on the backrest, almost touching his hands, and pushed his face forwards, into his. In profile he looks a little like a pear-shaped mole. The reddish hair on his forehead has congealed into a sweaty wire. Now, when Zoja has gone on stage, Max doesn't even look at the guitarist any more, so it's up to him to convince himself of the niceness of his performance. The pop of the string and the awkward flight from the tolerant gazes buoyed by smiles has robbed him of the applause that he perhaps, or perhaps not, deserved. In the moment before he disappeared from the stage, he felt a kind of restlessness in the air, but he's convinced that it wasn't caused by him. He sang to them of loneliness. What else is there to sing about?

'I've never told anyone this, to be totally honest.'

Max's voice lowers. His nose is dangerously approaching the face of the old man, whose eyes have sunk back into their sockets. His jaw is slipping back and his neck is pressing back into the hard chair to escape the progress of the pale, freckled face that suddenly desires contact.

'But my whole life I've been suffering from a very aggressive form of dissociative identity disorder.'

The guitarist, who has placed his guitar on the floor and

taken a last sip of water from the bottle, suddenly feels as if he's inadvertently barged in on something very intimate, so he purses his lips, raises his eyebrows and tightly clenches his fists. He looks around to see whether he might find something interesting in the space with which he could distract himself and stretch some sort of none-of-my-business cling film of privacy over the painful scene. There's nothing. He turns slowly, takes three quick steps, and leans a shoulder against the wall, making sure that the audience won't see him peeping at Zoja's relaxed form.

'One moment I'm fully present in the secondary order of human existence. I have a past and I am part of history. I am also a collection of my consequences and a shaky node of the consequences of all other people. Where I'm going to be placed and where I will place myself depends on my hand and mouth. I cannot deny myself as an artificial being. My family is my family and those edges of its story that touched me became the edges of my story. When I look at my skin, I see it's sewn together from rags. I know where each rag came from. There are no holes, no empty spaces. I'm composed. My inner feeling is a mere drive to make sure I don't stay in one place. I'm not a stone. I'm not a statue. I am a scarecrow of human things, stuck in the field where ravens come to peck at the seeds of beauty. I know that the word *beauty* triggers in me a semantic drift that facilitates my presence and existence. I know that that's the path to the other side. But as long as I'm not there, all the other words wreck me. I know that it is other people who say when you've succeeded. Success. It makes me sick. I know that there's no other way. That there are no other people other than these. That they are dead, or that they haven't been born yet. I know that contact with empti-ness does not outweigh contact with living beings. Emptiness is attractive because it doesn't have a single determinate form. Emptiness is attractive because it's not proud of being itself. I know that *human* is a technical term. I know it's courage when you transcend this. I would like to believe that I will succeed sometime. I hope. I know that without people things would be harder for people. But I am not happy for them. I know that nobody wants to deny what he's been told he is. I know that this is violence. And I know that nobody deserves it. I know that I'm better off, that I'm worse off, that I am. I know that everything I know is real, because knowing is the only thing I know can appear to me as real.'

Zoja undresses.

'And then…wait, is that really my voice? Do I really speak like that? Your eyes are avoiding mine. What does that mean? The muscles in your hands are retracting, to escape the touch of my hands. What are you afraid of? Do I want something from you? Didn't you come here because you wanted something? What did you want? Would you like to see them? Would you like to see her? She reads. She reads aloud. That's all. Look at me!'

Zoja undresses.

'Thank you. Thank you. Then, without motive, without reason, I land in the primary order, at once, all at once, I just am, and all the crap peels away from me, the entire human lineage, and the letters slip from me, they rinse themselves off, straighten themselves into a point without dimensions, and my self-awareness, my self-knowledge and my self-esteem stretch across the membrane of existence, they make nothingness and light disappear and I become a being. Then everything becomes a moment, and it's deadly serious, and it's deadly funny, and the tongue can only scribble, swing stupidly over all the grated bits that want to show us life as something that has to constantly lie to itself. Then I see what violence is in reality. Violence is people who have built an entire world out of words just to briefly escape what cannot be escaped.'

Zoja is naked. Some guy has climbed on to the stage. He's holding something very empty in his hand.

X

He rushed her and she had no idea he was so strong. For so long he had been sitting there completely still – so utterly had he been merged with the clacking of the typewriter keys, with the restless quiet sliding of his feet across the hardwood floor, with the calm, contemplative shifting of his eyes – that she'd have laughed at anyone who tried to warn her of danger. He's an old man, she would had thought, he's already forgotten his desires. A sort of nobody without anybody, just a black hole for the letters flying from his fingers into nothingness. He is our captive. Our dry-haired captive with a dead smile on his lips.

She didn't expect him to be so fast, so relentless, so unlike everything she had learnt to expect from him during the years of his imprisonment. Years of routine vanished in a single moment; long, long periods when he hadn't even moved from his chair, when all of him went onto paper, his every last bodily need, and she had to burn the sheets in the rubbish bin behind the house, where the stench would ward off the homeless coming into the courtyard to warm their hands. They had to find other fires, other company, other paths to warmth.

She no longer expected anything from him and was so shocked at his wild leap, at the vicious face into which this new occurrence had carved wrinkles that she had never even seen before and whose existence she had never even suspected – convinced that this man had only one face, one everlasting face, slightly softened through boredom, with a mischievous hint of despair, and fat, black eyebrows that gave off the sole remaining trace of confidence – that she was left with no other choice than to remain calm and wait for him to tackle her to the floor.

He got to her even before the edge of the table hit the hardwood. The typewriter flew into the air among the fluttering sheets of paper like a lawnmower crashing through a flock of seagulls. His chair raised its front paws high in a mild request and corroborated that request with the muted blow of its tail against the hardwood. Light from the streetlights came through the windows like something sharp and bounced off the floor like something soft. It was midnight in the city that had forgotten why it exists.

And he threw himself onto her. He grabbed her by the hand in which she was holding a glass of water, squeezed the hand tightly and, in spite of his headless rush, managed to keep the water level parallel to the floor even as they were falling, as his weight upset her balance and her toes jutted into the air; as she, with dug-in heels, with shoulder blades thrust into the wall behind her, slid down hard beside it – more screeched than slipped, since a thousand tiny irregularities in the plaster scraped her skin bloody – as her coccyx cracked loudly against the hardwood and the jolt rattled up her spine into her nape, as though somebody had sowed a whole constellation of tiny white dots into her field of vision, and the metal popped when the typewriter jammed its protuberances into the floor, before everything went dark and he sat down on her chest, drawing a silent whistle accompanied by a fine drizzle of saliva from her mouth, and all this time the water level did not approach the edge of the glass until he put it to her mouth, plugged her nose with his fingers, looked deep into her anthracite eyes and calmly ordered her to *Drink*.

The water drained into her mouth and although her first impulse was to breathe, to fill her lungs with air, and her eyes – still more surprised than frightened – were bulging, his weight on her chest prevented her from inhaling, so, with difficulty, she swallowed – it's only water, she thought, all I did was bring him some water, did he think that, after all these years, all of the sudden I wanted to poison him? – and when he saw it flowing into her he eased off a bit, shifting his weight onto a knee on the floor and his face turned back into the only facial form she knew. She could breathe again, so she did.

But not without difficulty. Tears filled her corneas and spilt over the rims, streamed down her temples and got caught in her ears, and she had to cough and he had to shield his eyes from the white clouds that were coming out of her mouth. She drew a convulsive breath and again coughed hoarsely, tried to force out a word in-between the gasping and the coughing, but to no avail, and this again unleashed an attack of slobbering and welling up of the eyes, and when the tears slid down the nasal canal, on top of everything came mucus from the nose, lazily ooz-ing from her nostrils and crossing her philtrum to form a translucent, greasy moustache above her lips. Her face had melted and ran like it was made of wax or honey and had been exposed to the hot beams of the sun. He had to resist the urge to lick it. Ice cream danced in his mind. Ice cream under the concentrated ray of a magnifying glass.

He got off her and sat on the floor. She closed her mouth and swallowed the saliva, exhaled deeply through her nose, and a bubble appeared under one nostril, popping as soon as she got on her elbows and raised her head, inched back a bit, towards the wall, leant her head against it, and with tearful red eyes stared at him, her throat still jumping agitatedly up and down, dryly swallowing, almost like a fish that a wave has thrown up at the shore and that's surprised to discover that it doesn't in fact know the world at all, that it had been deceived, lied to, that nothing is as it seemed, and that there are places in the world that are hateful to everything.

'Why did you do this?' she asked in a voice that had never before been hers.

'Because I wanted us all to be together again. At least

for a brief moment, again. Because I regret. I regret so many things. Because I wanted…'

'When Father finds out what you did, you will be devoured.'

This she said without emotion, as if she were talking about the facts of nature, not the inclination of the gods. He was grateful that her voice betrayed neither emotion nor compassion. Everything he had written had led to this point, to this outcome. It had begun to have an effect on her. She relaxed her shoulders and gazed dreamily somewhere through him.

'After all these years, devoured… When you came here I was just a little girl, a tiny little thing, and at night I couldn't sleep when you prowled the room, howled for whatever it was you wanted us to give you, but reaped only laughter from the ground floor in response. Always laughter. The jeering noise of old men who knew what you wanted and who also knew that you would get nothing. I'm not a little girl any more, I know that, I have learned how things are done around here. And now it's over. Maybe they will give me a leg. I'll bite into an ankle and when your crusty skin crackles and your warm blood runs over my chin, I will remember your every look. I have never felt like this was really my life, with you, that this was really happening to me, that it was me standing behind your back with a rod in my hand and making sure that you were writing, but, you know, when so much time passes, and your body insists and insists and insists, it becomes hard to deny that the things you do really are a part of your existence. That you are a part of my existence. That you're not just a job or some fluke or something that I do in my free time, but that you've become a part of me. Like my memory. A part of my body. Like my leg.'

She raised her upper lip and bared a row of sharp, filed teeth, the heritage of an ancient family ritual. Then she frowned as it dawned on her just what she had stated and how she had stated it. That wasn't like her.

'What have you done to me?' she asked, and for the first time there was a touch of fear in her voice.

'I want you to see what you're turning us into. To see who I was, once, before I let myself get caught. I want you to know that I wasn't always alone. That I had people who loved me, people I loved. I don't want that ever to be forgotten. When you're rolling me around in your mouth and when I'm slipping, gnawed and chewed, down your throat, I want you to know that there are people in this world who, if they were aware of it, if they ever found out what happened to me, would never forgive you. I wasn't always alone. I want you to bear the mark of this.'

Her jaw dropped and her eyes rolled backwards.

'What have you done to me?' she whispered. Her hands automatically slid along her body, glided over the torso, over the chest, to the neck and started to squeeze.

'I want you to meet them.'

'Why didn't you leave them alone?' she croaked through her constricted windpipe.

'Because *you* didn't want to. Because I was selfish. Because I thought I was helping them. Because I miss them, I miss them in my very bones, and I would so much like to see them together again.'

'You won't make it.'

Her eyes returned to their normal position. Her pupils, so dilated that they banished every last trace of her black irises to the edges and left only two empty holes in the middle of her face, quivered slightly as they watched him. The pressure she felt in her hands subsided and the convulsive breathing in her chest became regular and calm.

'No one will make it, my dear Lupe. No one yet has. But that never stopped anyone from trying. If that weren't so, your family would be reigning over a world of grey.'

His face had changed, and that filled her with horror. His jaw jutted and his beard spilt over his cheeks, over his neck, around his mouth, in black tufts. His nose broke off at the root and the tip folded inwards. She closed her eyes and shook her head to ward off the illusion. When she opened them she saw, sitting before her, with his back resting against the overturned desk, a stranger with a broad smile.

'She's gone,' he said in a voice she didn't recognize. He was wearing a red shirt soaked with sweat, and the soles of his socks – these were protruding strangely out of his faded jeans – were dirty. In the bottom row of his teeth, instead of a left bicuspid, there was a hole.

'Who?'

'My sole desire,' said the stranger and placed his finger over her mouth. 'Now we quietly wait.'

She unclenched the hands and removed them from around her neck. She couldn't understand where he'd disappeared to and who this man before her was. She was scared, scared that the prisoner had escaped, although that wasn't supposed to happen, and although no one else had ever broken the order of things – how did he make it? He should not have been allowed to make it – and left her to the mercy of the wrath of Father, to whom she wouldn't be able to explain what had gone wrong. The thoughts in her head twisted strangely and flew into each other in patterns that were foreign to her; patterns that, when she resisted them and forced them back into order, left her at a loss, yet at the same time invited her into such a warm and gentle embrace, invited her to surrender to them and forget that the technology of the moment exists, that there really is such a thing, which a few minutes ago – or was it hours? Years? She no longer knew – when she came up the stairs with a glass of water in her hand, she could call her true, real voice, and they lured her into a new world of scattered concepts and loose postulates where it wasn't really that bad if anyone got away and strayed from her without a clock, fate and judgement, free of her irrevocable demanding, and that this one time she

could make an exception and take upon herself the punishment of Father, end something only in half and quietly crawl
onwards, onwards, onwards...

The hardwood floor started breathing in concert with
her, rising and falling with her thorax, and the yellow of
the street lights, which was creeping in sheaves through the
window, had taken on the most unusual of qualities, was dis-
integrating into strands that wove themselves, in a rollicking
game and right before her eyes, into lovely lace doilies placed
over the edges inside the room, over her legs, over his chest,
and a cold-coloured scent arose from their bodies, a scent of
noble elements of blue, grey and violet, spiralling through the
spinning wheel of light into a chain that fused the various
consciousnesses of spirits hidden in the corners, which things
and their materiality have denied to eyes... From somewhere
far away she heard an echo of some sort of awareness that
something was seriously wrong, that she was getting lost in a
world that wasn't hers and that someday she would pay dearly
for that, but the blanket of warmth was too attractive, she
wrapped herself in it and silenced the voice that was warning
her against this illusion, smiled at the stranger, and when he
returned a gapped-tooth smile she felt safe.

The air carried a rumbling sound to her ears and at first
she thought that Melquiades was outside again, beating a carpet in stout, rhythmic whacks, but when the window panes
began to vibrate and the sound increased in volume, conjur-
ing up before her eyes an image of a giant epileptic cloud, she
knew it had nothing to do with Melquiades, that something
was coming that was too mighty to be hand-wrought, and she
was prepared to genuflect before the force if only she could
get to her feet – her body wasn't obeying her, she discerned
– so she could only calmly watch the stranger's face, its smile
which, impossible as it seemed, broadened even more, before
the stranger raised an index finger and grinned in relief.

'They're coming.'

She wanted to ask *who* when the window panes exploded into crowns of endless little slivers, each of them catching the light and putting on such a stunningly beautiful display that the cry of alarm died out in her throat and she didn't even fear the black-clad bodies of giants that sailed through the windows on black nylon ropes. The door flew off its hinges with a clap of thunder under the weight of a studded boot, sliced through the air and hit the floor with a bang that reminded her of the summer and the beach and the fat kids cannonballing into the choppy surface of the sea.

The infenestrated men in black helmets and black uniforms and, with black rifles in hand, filled the room, full of strength and purpose, firmly determined to get what they had come for. They tossed a black bag over the stranger's head and thrust him out of the window, while another grabbed her by the waist, slung her over his shoulder and marched her down the stairs – it seemed odd to her that there was nobody else around and she could only mutely form their names with her lips, which was of course so futile a gesture that she nearly broke into hysterics – past the empty dining hall, through the salon door and out, where they flung her headfirst through the gaping door of a black limousine, which drove off before its door had even managed to close. Guadalupe had no idea what was going on. Hands she couldn't see planted her on the seat next to the door, beside a man with a black bag over his head, who was sitting between her and somebody on the other side. When her head jerked to the side as they went around a corner, she was able to observe him. He was a handsome man of rough appearance, with thinly sown grey hair high above his forehead, carved features and a sullen look, thin lips crowned with a bushy moustache and a nose that resembled a fox's or wolf's snout.

He seemed to have one of those faces that look best when they're saying no. He was bent over, with his forehead leaning against the driver's seat, and, incredibly slowly, untying his shoes. He was dressed in a dark suit and his every move gave off the sound of treetops rustling in the breeze. Silk, she thought. He was dressed in silk, and it was entirely obvious that he hated it. If it were up to him, he'd be wearing something rougher, but something had happened to him, something that had softened him. After untying his shoes and slipping them off, he straightened up and disappeared from her sight.

Short, feverish bursts of laughter were coming from the bag. Guadalupe fixed her eyes on the driver and screamed somewhere deep inside. No doubt it was him, hidden beneath a grey hat and taller than he seemed to her when he was seated in his chair, with rolled-up sleeves and forearms that – she had never noticed this before – were covered with long, black hair. A thick, gaudy gold bracelet that didn't quite fit hung from his wrist and swung freely every time he turned the wheel. Every now and then she could catch his reflection in the rear-view mirror.

He was laughing. Laughing from the bottom of his heart, youthfully, almost impishly, exploding with the life and happiness that were taking turns lighting up his face. His eyebrows, even darker and even thicker, almost like a pair a chimney sweep's brushes, showed off on his face and were no longer lowered, as they had been all those years when he was with her, but turned upwards, towards the hat, and if he were to raise them they would knock the hat off his head. *Did he make it?* she thought. How could he think he had? What had he done?

And immediately her attention was caught by the roadside lights, which, like in overexposed photographs, dragged long, shyly inconstant coloured lines across her gaze, and the empty spaces of night between the light – spaces that her mind filled with everything that would be possible, not only probable, there – so forcefully bursting with darkness and surrounded by light, as if it were protecting them from the invasion of anything with form, and they absorbed her, took her eyes and put them on, so that she could, from high up in the sky, trace the path of the racing limousine that, completely alone on the four lanes of this orange motorway, was blazing a smoky trail into the asphalt. Her thoughts were tearing themselves apart, the feeling was too strong to keep in touch with, too strong for her head to know how to articulate what was going on, and so she hid from the thoughts, hid herself into the night and the silver edge of the horizon, the jagged sea-level somewhere far, far to the west.

Not until she saw what was going to happen – and she knew what was going to happen, it was inevitable, necessary, even though the two points were still far apart – and although she was convinced that she couldn't prevent it, did she marshall all her strength so that at least a single word might escape her mouth, at least one essential word with which she would, even if she couldn't change anything, at least assume an ounce of responsibility, so that in the end she could tell – whom? She didn't know – that at least she had tried. No one will make it, he had said to her, nobody has ever made it, and those words appeared before her, denuded of all weight, and she recognized that he was right – this world is not grey, not at all, it never was – so she could then unseal her lips and seduce the man sitting on the other side into speech.

'Watch out,' said the man in silk.

An animal had stepped in front of the headlights, the pair of green reflections came to terms with doom, erasing itself from the world with a blunt thud. Guadalupe didn't have time to make out its specific shape in that swarming of forms, she only knew that the animal had stepped of its own volition onto the sacrificial altar, and this awareness shook her so deeply that she couldn't feel the profound silence that lay over the male passengers, she instead sank into herself and followed the flight of her consciousness into the sky.

Up there the clouds were crowding each other out and growing damp. She hung on to the first drop that emerged from the slimy mist and let it pull her into the depths. The world was rapidly approaching her; its chequered visage reminded her of Father's chessboard, but that was always full of figures, always full of dead pawns and rooks and kings, whereas stretching out under her view now was a field without any game, without figures, with just a bit of grass and ears of wheat that whispered their shades to the grey night. Nobody around for miles.

The drop evaporated on the silken shoulder of the man who had got out of the car, taken a few barefoot, hesitant steps and stood before the bloody carcass. A strange shadow lay across his face and she saw a thin tongue of dark smoke slipping out of his ear. Something had left him and the relief in his eyes was such that Guadalupe's body, still safely stowed in the seat of the car, trembled tangibly. The palm of the man with the bag over his head tried to soothe her with gentle caresses of her thigh, and the driver, him, demurely stared ahead, now without a smile on his face, only with the hard look of someone who doesn't want to stand beside a friend in anguish, because that anguish is his own, but would like at the same time to use his body to relate to his friend that he understands that anguish, its entire extent.

The man in silk returned to the car a decade older, and yet more like a living human being than when he went out. It seemed that he only now realized that he wasn't alone in the back of the car. With a curt nod of the head he greeted his fellow passengers – somebody with a bag over his head and a lame woman beside him – and planted a hand on the driver's shoulder.

'You, just drive me home, ok? I'm not flying anywhere today.'

A smile returned to the driver's face, he turned and joyously tore the bag off the head of the man in the middle.

'Did you hear? We're going home!'

The face, lit up by the soft motorway lights which deepened his hollow cheeks in the play of shadows, slowly pondered the meaning of that sentence. With each second his smile narrowed – the hole in the bottom row of his teeth disappeared – until instead of a mouth there was only a thin pale line.

'Home?' he asked.

The driver, him, stared at him in restrained expectation, like a boy waiting for a magician's final trick, and answered the question with an enthusiastic nod. The man who was now holding the bag in his lap and had started to squeeze it clearly did not share his enthusiasm.

'But…but,' he turned his head from side to side, as if expecting support from his fellow passengers, before rushing forwards and grabbing the driver's sleeves.

'But she's still there, trapped, I didn't want… I didn't mean to, but…but, we have to help her. How are we going to help her?'

The driver laughed and Guadalupe started to doubt whether it was really him. His face was changing, but not in the way it had been changing before, when they were sitting in the room and he suddenly became someone else. Now the transformation seemed to be going in the opposite direction, as if he'd settled into the skin of the stranger, taken on his face, his body – and she had to admit it really seemed like a living, fleshy body – and was now struggling from within for mastery over its appearance. If, just a moment before, his face was completely the way she remembered it, now a shadow had dropped over that face and shortened his nose or bleached his eyes, and he had to strain his jaw for his nose to return, for his eyes to turn dark brown again. He hadn't made it yet. Not entirely.

'Don't worry, Evan. Don't you worry about a thing. Everything's taken care of, I've thought of everything.'

'So we're going to help her?'

Guadalupe caught sight of a flame blazing in an eye.

'We already have. She doesn't need your help. Everything is fine.'

'So I can go home? Go home for real?'

'We're going home.'

The man whose head was formerly bagged – his name was Evan, she had learnt – had flopped back into his seat, exhaled loudly and was grinning again. He looked at Guadalupe.

'She's gone, you know? She is not going to be home. But I'll manage, even at home, without her. You know you look a little like her? I loved her so much. Don't you worry.'

He squeezed her thigh encouragingly a little above the knee and turned to the other side. The driver – him? – turned back to the steering wheel with a persistent smile on his face, on that unsteady, shifting, fluid face, and drove off.

'What's up, man? How are you?' Evan asked the man who was sitting next to him.

'Oh, I'm fine, I'm good,' he answered in a sturdy bass which exuded weariness. 'I just wanted to…'

His voice died away and Guadalupe imagined how he would turn to the window and watch the white posts passing by at the side of the road, each one bearing an unexpressed thought, an unfulfilled desire, a stifled cry. Who are these people and what was she doing here with them?

'What did you want?' Evan poked him. The face – she didn't see, she only knew – turned to him again and allowed itself an open, relieved smile before answering.

'Yeah, you know, I wanted…the kid…'

Now a moment of hesitation, almost confusion, flashed over the face. Two vertical incisions in the forehead above the nose remained there even after the gaze cleared.

'Nothing, well, I just wanted to visit the kid.'

'Oh,' said Evan in an inquisitive tone. 'And how old is he now? Where is he? Travelling? Is he already done with his studies?'

The man swept away the flood of questions with a wave of the hand and a meek smile.

'Leave it. How old? Oh, he's old. His own man. He's old

---

enough for me to leave him alone. I think that's best for him. No?'

Evan looked at the street and turned down the corners of his lips.

'Oh, for sure, for sure,' he said with the voice of someone who knows what he's talking about. 'Nothing became of me until they left me alone. But really alone, metaphysically alone. In fact they didn't leave me alone until I left myself completely alone, without them. Do you know what I mean? They had to leave me so alone that I didn't even have a reason to think that they maybe had not left me alone, and I could no longer imagine that, although they were leaving me alone, they in fact did not want to leave me alone, and probably still wanted to do something with me other than leave me alone. Only when you leave yourself alone do they really leave you alone. Do you get what I'm trying to say? And only then can you to their place for lunch, as if nothing happened. Until…'

The driver laughed. He was chasing the passengers' faces in the rear-view mirror. More than once he winked at Guadalupe. She found it very warm and everything seemed very important, but not so important that she needed to pay complete attention, attempt to follow every little bit and bother herself with every little detail, it's just how it was, everything was simply worthy of being there with her, beside her, together, important just because it was there, independent of other things, and she found all of this beautiful. Even the clouds disappeared. The night suddenly turned that shade of coldish blue where the stars seem so close, and your focus is drawn to the edge of the universe, which perhaps isn't even as large as you imagine it to be on cloudy days. If you could just reach out your hand…

'What about him? What do you think he's been doing these past years?' Evan asked. He gently kicked the seat in front of him and sighed. His voice bore a hint of accusation

– as if he felt he had a right to know more and resented knowing so little.

'How should I know? An eternity went by without us hearing from him. Nothing. As if we didn't exist.'

Evan leant forwards again and grabbed the driver by the shoulder.

'Well, spill it. We want to know everything.'

Even Guadalupe became a part of the curiosity that lay thickly about the passengers in the back seat. What had he been doing all those years, with her? Was he even there? Did he somehow manage to slip away somewhere? Had he found a way out from time-stop and no-space? Did Father know what he was doing and is that why he left him with her? Was that her test? Her path to independence? Were these questions which she had been asking herself with unimaginable rapidity and which served her only as a long row of bottomless wells over which she was jumping, without ever sensing a single drop of water – water! Water! What was it with the water – were these questions even her own? She seemed separated from her purpose. And although she now felt light, impossibly light and free and liberated, had she perhaps let the world down? Would people now imagine things the wrong way?

The driver cleared his throat.

'I didn't make it, back then. I thought I would. But I didn't. I lost. I believed in things I shouldn't have believed in and arrived at the end before I could conclude anything. I was powerless there. I wasn't able to change anything, so I could only wait for my name to be uttered one last time. I must say I was sure you would think of me more often.'

'Wait a minute,' said the man in silk, 'you disappeared without a trace. The last time we saw each other, you said you were leaving, but I didn't know that meant we wouldn't hear a single word from you for a quarter of a century. The longing to see you again slowly faded... I don't know why, and I don't know what it was that replaced it. The bitterness that grows from insult, or the forgetting that comes from missing someone for too long. Either way, each of us, all of us, went our own way.'

Evan was slowly nodding beside him, his expression no longer one of untroubled joy, but a deliberate mask placed over decades of regret.

'Each into the strings of slip-ups people short on sense call lives,' he added cautiously.

'I'm sorry, I wasn't trying make any accusations,' continued the driver. 'I'm just saying. With each mention of my name, with each thought that flew towards me, and with each minute that I, albeit with a strange face and uncertain intentions, spent in your dreams, I received the charge of energy that I needed to arrive here, at this point where we are now, so that I could finally take hold of what I wanted to to take hold of, alive. It took longer than I thought it would. But I completely understand. The times weren't so favourable to you. Why waste them on reminiscence?'

'And now?' asked Evan.

'Now I'll see whether I made it. Whether the seam holds. All in all, it's very selfish. Even over there things haven't changed significantly. I still toyed with the destinies of others and led them around my way. Please excuse me. I wouldn't have put you through all of this if I didn't think you were helping me out.'

'Helping you out how?' asked the person by the window.

'I don't know, I don't know, I don't know,' said the driver softly, his head pushed towards the windshield and his face turned upwards, as if he wanted to get something from the sky to give them in place of silence. Guadalupe knew there was nothing up there – but neither did she stop staring.

'I don't understand,' said Evan. The man in the back next to him exhaled loudly through his nose. The driver, gazing at the sky, spoke as if repeating a phrase he'd learnt by heart years ago, his thoughts entirely somewhere else.

'What compels me to live?' he asked. 'That's all I was asking myself back then, when I got on that plane obsessed with the idea, the only one I had left, that I wanted to live alone. A one-way ticket out, to anywhere, to the edge of the world. I worshipped it like a god. In my head there were immensities of conifers growing, cold dew on the meadows grazed by horses, and it shook me, drowning in the phantasms of the creek, how it deafeningly licks ancient rocks that are there for no purpose whatsoever. Self-sufficient. The crackling fire at night and naked solitude on the open skin of another being. Peace. And I know it's a classic romantic idea, and I know that I wasn't the first who wanted to escape all this accumulation of flesh, in favour of things that leave you alone, but back then it seemed truly important to me. A matter of life and death. If I hadn't been able to flee...'

'I don't understand,' Evan repeated.

'What don't you understand?' the driver asked.

'Just what the hell did we do to you that was so bad?' snapped the man in silk. 'Are you going to say that we didn't know how to accept what you are or what you wanted to be? Are you going to accuse us of not knowing how to leave you alone?'

'Let me finish. I'm not the same person. I was not spared insight. Please.' He waited for the silence to thicken into consent, and continued.

'I ran away from mirrors. I ran away from a culture that was constantly repeating a model of *be what you are*, even as it snatched away the exclusive right to how you could play out and perform your identity. *Be what you are, and we will say what that is.* Do you get it? And nobody got away from it. You couldn't get away. You could play the freedom card and they'd take you for a madman. You could hold on to your soul and be seen as a weakling. You could deny culture, deny the judgement of others, deny the power of the gaze, and nowhere, in no one's, not even in one's own heart, did this sound like an act of courage, more like common weakness. That crazy paradox of those times, when the decision for complete personal autonomy in society took away all the levers that would let you make choices of your own.'

'I don't understand why you wanted to be so independent,' said Evan, quietly. 'Wasn't there anyone you loved?'

The man beside him exhaled through his nose. 'That is a matter of ruined responsibility. A being who has created himself in the image of those around him suddenly finds himself in a position where those images no longer correspond to him. Instead of actively setting to work in his surroundings and leading them, to the best of his abilities, in the direction he believes is right, he prefers to run away. I get you. Don't think I don't. But that problem is the luxury of people who can afford it. Ask what slaves in the clutches of traffickers think about absolute personal autonomy, or what little boys in the middle of minefields think about it. Don't hold it against me if I can't empathize with you.'

The driver laughed bitterly.

'I know, I know. I hope someday you'll find time to think about everything you just said, since either way nothing panned out for me. Does anything ever really pan out for anyone? And I don't need your empathy. I don't need anything anymore, now. Nothing can be changed anymore. After everything that happened… I have no other choice. This is what I have to call being left alone.'

The passengers remained silent.

Guadalupe screamed. She bent at the waist and her head dropped between her knees, she twitched violently a few more times, as if someone was beating her on the back, and then regained composure. Evan stared at her, amazed. He turned to the driver and the other passenger to see how they'd reacted to this strange performance, and then, after realizing they hadn't reacted at all, opted for an independent venture. He gently patted her. Guadalupe didn't feel the touch of his hand. She had left for the altar. When Evan held his hand in front of him and stroked the first and middle fingers with the thumb, he felt dampness. He stretched out the arm and looked at it under the light. It was dark in colour.

The drops glided off it. Was that—

'Stop! Stop! This girl here is bleeding!' he cried.

The driver briefly turned to him and the look on his face silenced Evan.

'We're not going to help her?' he asked quietly.

'If you knew, Evan, what you were asking…'

The man in silk winced in his seat and pressed a finger to the glass.

'Look,' he said.

The driver looked up into the sky that was split by a bright light. A smile escaped him, but evaporated.

'I hope it will work,' he whispered, and then asked them. 'Is there something you want to wish for?'

They both shook their heads.

The shooting star gained in strength and bit into the edge of the horizon, producing a subdued *pop* that reached them a few seconds later. A fiery cloud had risen ahead of them.

'That's where we're going,' said the driver.

'There?' asked Evan. 'Didn't you just say we were going home?'

'Tell me, Evan, where is your home?'

'Well…' began Evan, as if he wanted to say something very obvious and then, mouth closed, turned in amazement to his fellow passenger. 'Well, home, right? There, where we are at home. Where we were at home. Where our people are. Right? Tell him, Kras, tell him where our home is.'

Kras's gaze was aimed squarely at the purplish cascading mushroom of dust on the horizon and the surrounding thousands of little, momentary flashes. 'Kras, tell him, won't you?'

'You tell him, dammit. How should I know where your home is?'

Evan's eyes filled with tears and his choice of words betrayed a trace of hysteria.

'No. No. You know, both of you know, where home is for me, why are you making fun of me? Tell me. I don't know. I don't know where home is, but that,' pointing ahead, 'that's certainly not where it is, I've never been there in my life. How could over there be home? Tell me, please, please, tell me.'

They remained silent.

'Please, tell me.'

'You are nowhere at home, my dear Evan,' said a female voice smothered by the fabric of the lap into which her lips were pressed. She straightened up. Evan was startled.

'Look – it speaks! But…'

'Hi, Evan. Hi, Kras.'

'…you're not the same woman!'

'And you're not the same piddly scumbag who chased after each and every skirt, except for mine. So?'

'Zoja?'

Kras turned to her and laughed, something his face wasn't used to. It creaked.

'Zoja? Shit, Zoja, it's really you.'

'How are you, boys?'

Evan stared at her, mouth agape.

'But where…how did you get here? Zoja? Is that really you? Why…?'

'My eldest daughter will be utterly envious when I tell her who I met.'

'Where did the one from before go? I liked her. I think we got on well.'

'Did you know that they banned you back there? That you've been banned for twenty years? A poet, yet banned, can you imagine?'

'No, seriously, can someone tell me what's going on? Why is *nowhere* my home, why did you say that?'

'That poetry collection you once gave me for my birthday, I showed it to her once and she held onto it like a treasure. I'm pretty sure she knows it by heart. Do you remember?'

'Please, if you'd just tell me what's go— Look!'

Evan shouted, and pointed to the right of the motorway, where the field sank into nothingness, leaving behind a sheet of white stars.

'No, you have to tell me what's going on, right now. This is not normal.'

'But aren't you an artist?' asked Zoja, with a smile on her lips. Kras reached over and grabbed her knee between his hands and turned to her like a divorcee towards a friend's still sexy wife.

'Tell me, I heard you had some sort of problem in Paris.'

'What kind of artist? Where is home for me?'

'Yes, as I understand it, they were your people. They weren't exactly gentle.'

'Forgive me. If only I'd known. I found that out later, so much later that there was no longer anybody I could call to account. But are you going to tell me now that back then you really had nothing to do with it?'

'Ha-ha, when did I ever have *nothing to do with it*? Sometimes I think problems get so terribly lonely if they don't have me for company.'

'You haven't changed a bit.'

'Oh come on, everything is falling down…'

The emptiness of dots now beckoned from the other side as well.

'You're a liar, you. I can hardly keep myself together. One real cough and my body will fall apart, why do you have to bring this foolishness up now?'

'But I didn't say a word about how you look, although I see that your relationship to beauty hasn't changed. You still hold it captive, don't you? The Stockholm syndrome is at work, it must be.'

The driver cleared his throat.

'When was the last time you paid somebody a compliment? A little practice wouldn't have killed you.'

'What are you two blabbing about? The laws of physics are going extinct here!'

'So the laws of logic shouldn't get off any more lightly.'

The driver laughed.

'I'm happily married, if you're implying something, and I have four children, so don't imagine too much. I just mentioned it. I haven't seen you in ages! How are you?'

'Look at all those stars. Where did all those stars come from? Would you two prefer to sit together?'

'To be perfectly honest, I don't know whether there is anything left of me that might have any sort of qualitative state, so I guess the question should rather be: Are you?'

'Ah, come on. I look at you and I see you. You're here. How is everything perfectly fine? How?'

'Come on, man, tell them, just tell them to take their heads out of their arses and to look at what's going on. This is not fine. Nothing is fine at all.'

The cloud ahead of them was spreading. They were getting closer and closer.

'Have you gone a little soft, Evan? Were the years hard on you? Where's your spirit?'

'I'll show you *spirit*.'

'This is a little embarrassing. Aren't you going to tell her? Don't you want to talk about it?'

'What was it?'

'I do not know if it is ok for me to say something.'

'La-la-la-la-la.'

Kras looked at her and shook his head. Zoja raised her eyebrows and her shoulders.

'I'll be fine, man. Now we're together. Nothing can hurt us.'

'You always act like – you always did act like – it's nothing.'

'And now here I am, just like you. It seems that our relationship with reality has no impact on our destiny.'

'Wow, Kras, what happened to that cynic who only had armed resistance on his mind? Don't touch me, please, I'm not clean.'

'But isn't your back all bloody? What the hell's going on now?'

'Undress a cynic and you'll find an idealist.'

'If I remember correctly, I was naked just a few moments ago, so the absence of blood is not so surprising. And who undressed you?'

'No. It was the other woman that was bloody. Where did she go?'

'I don't know? I was just on my way to the airport, because God commanded me to do something. Now, to be perfectly honest, I'm a little lost.'

'God, upper-case?'

'The years have obviously soured both of your brains.'

'Kronos? Upper-case, of course.'

'You…believe?'

'No. Come on, just a moment, please, come on, every-one together, let's focus on our situation.'

'We're on a rock hurtling through the universe.'

'We exist.'

'Is there anything stranger than that?'

'You're crazy. You've gone crazy.'

'I have in my possession a mechanical thing that has me in its possession, otherwise I'm a ghost.'

'That sounds like something I'd be inclined to doubt.'

'Matter is energy.'

'We depend on thought.'

'We depend on dead things.'

'No, seriously. You…believe?'

'I have to pee.'

'I love you guys.'

'Who said that?'

'It came from outside.'

'There's nothing outside! Look, look out!'
'I think my father is going to commit suicide.'
'He won't make it.'
'Who said that?'
'From outside?'
'You can't even see the end, there's no more end, it just stretches and stretches, there's just emptiness, everywhere.'
'Is that what you wanted?'
'Absolutely not. Perhaps. I don't know. It's also much easier, in a way.'
'Without edges? A rift? A hole?'
'How do you feel?'
'Terrible, for as long as I don't get rid of the feeling that I'm alone.'
'So you understand?'
'Who said that?'
'I can only be honest with you. Only with you can I be myself. Am I putting too much of a burden on you? I don't want you to feel responsible for me.'
'What's all this fucking responsibility? An empty word. I'm all for activability.'
'For love?'
'Is that it?'
'That's what I want to believe in.'
'You can lean on me if you want.'
'Just let me be me. I'm not here to hurt anyone. Don't feel threatened. Please.'
'Danger always arrives with exactly that on its mouth.'
'Would you like to be safe? What does that mean?'
'Do you know how much effort is needed for me to make at least a somewhat clear picture?'
'One that's a lie?'
'Only if you're lying. Are you lying?'
'I'd like to be honest.'
'That's dangerous.'

'For whom?'

'You, primarily.'

'And for us?'

'Us?'

'Well, then, go ahead and be honest.'

'Who did you say that to?'

'The thermal death of the universe. The Boltzmann constant. I can't believe I can still remember that. Hard to believe I was ever even at school. Is that it? Is that what you wanted to show us?'

'It's just an illusion, right? Calm down.'

'If this is an illusion, then I am delusional, and if I am delusional, how am I supposed to calm down? Maybe I am also de-lingual, and de-emotional, and de-aware. Maybe I'm in a straitjacket somewhere, right now, and the pre-death DMT is pumping into my veins, I am recalling my miserable life in dreamy gusts and quickly departing into the eternal nothing.'

'So we, your long-lost friends, are so important to you that you incarnated us in your last moment? That's a lovely thought, I suppose, although I am a little concerned about the ease with which you're taking on my personality.'

'About this DMT…'

'Didn't he get death high on acid in one of his stories?'

'He? Who are you talking about?'

'The old person with the scythe? The dead man in black? A zombie? That loathsome personification.'

'No, that's just it – death must be something young and juicy. It becomes what it takes from you. It feeds itself on that.'

'I'm dying.'

'Me too!'

'I would have expected a little less enthusiasm.'

'What do you know about enthusiasm?'

'Just a little more…'

'And how did he get it high?'

'That I've forgotten.'

'I'm thirsty.'

'Didn't you just say you had to pee?'

'I'm thirsty and I have to pee. Our bodies are just one big hole.'

'Nobody's hungry?'

'Hungry for sense.'

'How presumptuous. Either way, you end up just flushing the toilet.'

'A choice thought.'

'Exactly this one out of all of them, right?'

'Oh come on, now the stars are going out. Come on, come back, well, at least the stars, at least that, please. I don't care if there are no more fields and signs and blades of grass, I can give that up, but the stars…'

'Is this by any chance the first time you're eye to eye with this?'

'I'd rather pluck them out.'

'Pull them out.'

'Aaaaaaaaaaaa!'

'Anyone else cold?'

'No.'

'Me neither, I'm just asking because since everything is fading out, I think cold would have to follow.'

'Logic.'

'I know.'

'Darkness. Pure green darkness.'

'Are you sure?'

'The universe is green.'

'That's such a human sentence.'

'Well, sorry. That's the only kind I have.'

'Just a little bit more…'

'Do you have any children?'

'Uh, can we change the subject?'

'Out of the blue?

'And you?'

'God forbid.'

'Upper-case?'

'Lowly, lowly, lower case.'

'Come on, something else, please.'

'I have four of them.'

'Can I have one?'

'Be my guest.'

'Just kidding.'

'Me too, probably.'

'What are we even driving on? I can't see anything. Before there was asphalt at least, orange asphalt. It's disappeared. The car's not even shaking any more. Are we even moving?'

'The cloud is bigger. Maybe it's growing or maybe we're getting closer and closer.'

'Perspective, right? We're all dependent on perspective.'

'I hope so.'

'So that cloud is our goal?'

'So it was said.'

'By whom?'

'They're all dead.'

'How do you know?'

'Look at the cloud. That's a cruel cloud. That's a killer, for sure, look at it. All grey and curled and furious. That's what killers look like. Do you think it left something underneath? That it didn't position itself over ground zero, over the naked desert? It got everything.'

'You can't even begin to imagine how happy I am to have met you.'

'Do you think he really won't make it? That he'll jump up and grab the raven by the claws and fall up into the slot in the sky, into some sort of celestial womb? Be born in reverse?'

'In my experience, till now things have all gone straight down. But given the current state, I would not be surprised in the least if something took off in the wrong direction.'

'So you accept it?'

'Not in the least. I'm just saying.'

'We're safe?'

'What do you mean by that?'

'I'm worried it will just end, that I'll open my mouth and let out a simple word that will be cut in half.'

'That seems like a legitimate concern to me.'

'Hold your breath.'

'Tense up every muscle in your body.'

'Any minute now.'

'Be prepared.'

'It's getting tense.'

'I'm drooling.'

'So you are hungry.'

'I've never been so hungry.'

'Starving.'

'I could eat that whole cloud, skin and bones and all.'

'And I'm the crazy one?'

'Have you ever eaten clouds?'

'If you must know, I have.'

'And?'

'Rather empty.'

'Entirely empty.'

'You too?'

'No. By feel.'

'Any second now.'

'I've been holding my breath for five minutes.'

'What's five minutes?'

'In relation to?'

'You know.'

'If there's still time, tell me what you mean by I'm *nowhere at home*.'

'Look.'

'Look.'

'We're here.'

The missile had flown straight into the middle of the

car park. The shock wave scattered cars around the edges and formed a metal wall out of them. The walls on the side of the building facing the car park have disappeared and the building has tipped onto its side. There are flames everywhere. The smoke is white and thick. A few people, naked and hairless, stagger around over the cracked concrete. Their eyes radiate a greed for life. No blood to be seen. Their bodies are intact.

Kras, Evan and Zoja get out of the car and look around. Silence lies over everything. No one dares speak. A crumpled-up black car rolls off a pile of other cars and lands on its roof. A naked couple crawls out of it. Pleasure has narrowed her pupils. Her hands hang freely at her sides. The boy gets up, pounds his fists against his chest and roars. The sound rattles the scene. Like an echo, one hears the roaring of a tiger from the opposite side of the car park. Courage is in the air. Courage.

'He isn't coming?' asks Evan.

'Who?' asks Zoja.

Kras returns to the car and pulls a whirl of smoke to himself. The door opens.

Zoja gets weak in the knees.

A muffled scream resounds over the car park. At the foot of a building a huge rock moves and reveals a dark hole. Out of it, into the white mist, steps the outline of a naked young man with a heavenly body. He turns and looks back to where he came from. There's a hazy tattoo on his back. Swearing nastily, he gives the finger to the darkness. He moves backwards from a pile of crushed gravel and almost keels over. As he catches his balance, he looks towards the limousine.

'Zoia?'

He breaks into an easy jog. His face is obscured, so no one knows whether he poses a threat. Evan takes a step back, Kras steps in front of Zoja.

'Zoia?'

'Hi.'

He stops in front of them and puts his hands on his knees.

'What a load of crap, Zoia. I've had enough. Totally enough. So that's it, no? We're dead. We're all dead. I know, don't you dare try to tell me we aren't. Because if you say we aren't, I have no other choice than to believe you. And if I believe you, then I'll have to, as soon as possible, find a way to kill myself. Because this is too much. If there's anything that's too much, it's this. I just saw them eat my brother. Can you imagine? Can you image that I would ever say that sentence out loud, without lying? That the meaning of that sentence would ever be completely bound to the truth? I saw them eat my brother. And he let them do it. He spoke of Osiris and cats and Bacchus and Christ when he put himself into their mouths. He said they'd stay alive because of him. That, compared to his, your wonders are fairy tales. And they believed him. They rushed him, I just watched. He laughed as they devoured him, Zoia. We're dead. And this hell is unacceptable. This hell is unacceptable. I don't feel any different. Nothing's changed. This is unacceptable, Zoia.'

'Where is Marjorie? Anwar? Did they stay inside?'

'Go inside and take a look at those bloody lunatics. This hell is an unacceptable one, and even if I talk about it this fact doesn't change. What kind of sentences are these? How could anyone expect to get by with these sentences? You read your stuff, you see, everything was still all right, that was still bearable, you read and when you turned your back to us, even that was all right, that I accept, it's your artistic prerogative, to turn any way you want, I have no problem with that, but then everything became completely not all right and very, very wrong. Somebody I only later realized was my own brother – can you imagine? – climbed on stage and made for you, for your back, with a knife in his hands, and he stabbed you as hard as he could and we all cried out and he stabbed you, stabbed you right there, in front of

all of us, my own brother – can you imagine? – never in a
thousand years would I have expected something like that,
it's true, my brother was always a little weird, but that sort of
thing, and you collapsed on the floor, but, and this was the
weirdest thing of all, you see, how should I accept that, how
should I even imagine that nothing I've said till now was the
weirdest, but the weirdest thing was that it wasn't even you
up there but some stranger, some complete stranger, I know,
because I looked her in the face, when you collapsed, when
she collapsed, and the people were screaming, but I just
stayed silent, because it was entirely obvious, suddenly, that
this was no longer real, and that there was no point adding
my bodily sound to that stupidity, so I fell silent and I would
have liked most to close my eyes if I hadn't then slowly come
to understand that the man who stabbed you, who stabbed
her, was in fact someone I know very well and with whom
I spent a considerable part of this foolish existence together
and for whom in the right world my feelings would come
out and I would try somehow to change or I don't know
what, I mean, what are you going to do, you understand me?
This is unacceptable. This you just can't accept. As a matter
of fact I don't even want to hear what you're going to tell me.
I am just saying this out loud in order to convince myself of
how stupid it all sounds. And then from one side of the stage
some idiot with a guitar came running and started hitting
him with it and from the crowd of people that, gradually,
like some sort of retarded earthly slide, moved closer to the
stage, two beasts jumped out, angry, two truly livid, tough
motherfuckers, huge, twenty-three and a half stone each,
rushed him so that the air was crackling with static and all
our hair stood up. How stupid it all is. I can't believe that
happened in my head. Why did that happen in my head,
Zoia? No, don't say anything. Then there was a loud bang
and a flash over everything, utter darkness, utter silence and
I had just enough time to thank the emptiness that finally

cut short that madness before the fire came. Fire, Zoia. Waves and waves of fire, one after another and with each wave the people cheered like they were at a stadium, but in the blinding sunlight that the flames washed over us, in the endless hot flames, we all remained unscathed. Unscathed, Zoia. Our clothes were singed and our hair was singed, look at my eyelashes, can you see them? No. They're gone. I no longer have any hair on my body. But look at me. Touch me. No, you don't have to. Do you see me? Do I seem alive to you? This is unacceptable. The pipes cracked open and the water rushed over us, immediately there was steam all over the place and vapour and sweaty naked human bodies, and Anwar stood up and shouted that we should all drink water, bloody fool, who cares about water at a time like that? But he cupped his hands under the jets and drank long gulps and a few followed him because, what can you do, the people were completely lost, whatever line of sense that might come upon them at that time would find followers, no matter what kind of a line it was, and that's why they probably also listened to Jerry, who found himself alone on stage and immediately exploited that mental void, that chaos, that collapse of everything that was normal, and started to scream that he now had come to earth to save humanity from death, bloody lunatic, oh that bloody lunatic, Zoia…but I'm crying? Am I really crying? You know how long it's been since I cried? This is unacceptable.'

The young man breaks into sobs. Someone with a bloodied mouth escapes from the opening and his rapturous scream triggers an avalanche of naked bodies all coming out into the air with bloody faces and shiny, happy eyes. Among them is also Mitja. When he sees his father, his head drops for a split second and then immediately pivots up again. He moves towards him. All that nudity is arousing. When they're standing a yard apart, eye to eye, they wait for a word.

'Aren't you going to cover up?' asks Kras.

Mitja spreads his arms, palms outwards.

Kras takes a step. Mitja takes a step.

They fall into each other's arms.

Evan, with a sunken face, directs his gaze right into the aperture from which people are still emerging. Every female body takes his breath away and he presses his hands together until they hurt.

'She's not coming, is she?' he asks the driver, who is sitting on the hood of the limousine and staring at him with sad eyes.

'I'm sorry, Evan.'

'It's ok. I didn't really think…'

'I'll get you home.'

'You don't have to.'

'They have water in Edo too. Don't worry. I'll get you home. I promise.'

Marjorie's head peeks out from the entrance. Zoja waves to her and Marjorie waves back. She doesn't dare enter the light. She's ashamed to be looked at. After all this, shame's still around. Zoja looks at the driver. Her expression is slightly hostile.

'Come with me,' she commands, and the driver obeys.

They walk together, slowly, to the opening.

'That wasn't very nice of you.'

He takes his hat from his head and throws it on the ground.

'I never stopped loving you.'

'Does that matter now?'

'Yes.'

'Loving someone is not a state of consciousness but a state of action. Daily, constant, unimaginably small acts. A wink and a held breath and a chin slightly tilted into a kiss. A smile when you meet, an honest smile, again and again and again. It's a matter of how you listen and how you touch. How you look. How you recognize. Loving someone is hard work.

It's a search for contact, a tireless search for contact. Hard work that insincerity can't pull off. That non-love can't pull off. Words and thoughts cannot. Only acts. An endless series of the tiniest of responses. Goosebumps, again and again. A whiff of fragrance, again and again. A touch. And another touch. And so many touches that the body runs out of free spots. And again. And yet again. Years and years and years of touches. Not even an inkling of greed in-between. Not even an illusion of desire. Just hard and constant bodily work. You, unfortunately, aren't capable of that.'

He doesn't say anything.

'When I'm alone, I can love the whole world. Not only can I like it. I can love it, you understand? Actually love it. But only for as long as I'm alone. Until the body comes into play. For as long as I'm satisfied with the illusions in my head, I have enough love for twenty worlds. But the body is reality. You've forgotten that. You shouldn't have forgotten that. Matter is energy, that's true. But energy is only matter. Only matter. Will you come back? Will you ever come back? Because just by expressing you have done nothing. I can't help myself with your text. Bring your body and dare to love. If you think that courage and will are to be found beyond the sphere of the body, you're mistaken. There's nothing beyond us. Emptiness lies within us, not outside. You can fill that emptiness, you can really fill it. But you have to be there, entirely. Do you dare? Do you dare to fill the emptiness?'

He doesn't answer.

'Where were you?' asks Marjorie.

She doesn't answer.

'Anwar told me to drink water and I drank, but now I feel so strange. Like I'm dying. But I'm not dying, even though I am completely sure it's the same feeling, only now I am bursting with energy. Do you know what happened?'

'Your boyfriend told me.'

'Where is he?'

'Outside. Crying.'

'Oh, hell,' she says, collects herself, and is gone.

They step together into the darkness.

'Do you know what I wanted to tell you before?'

'I know.'

'And?'

'After all this, now you want from me precisely that which means nothing. For me to tell you something.'

They walk in silence. On the way they encounter a few lost souls who are slowly working their way towards the light. A strong odour of burnt hair hangs in the air. The hall is almost empty. Anwar, sitting on a chair and with his hands over his knees, is smiling, eyes closed. Brian and Rupert are lying on the floor, staring at the ceiling with eyes as wide open as possible and poking each other in the sides between salvos of hushed laughter. Semyona is sitting on Guadalupe's body, sliding her finger along the blood-covered floor and dipping it into her mouth at short intervals. Max and Mr Ž— are sitting in the corner and trying, with an air that brings to mind a bickering married couple, to determine at least the most fundamental theoretical and historical context for what they have just witnessed. Zoja's gaze locks itself onto the unfortunate countenance of a being that is squatting below the stage and pressing the cup in his hands against the edge of the boards that are dripping streams of blood mixed with water. The being is completely wrinkled, white cataracts cloak his eyes, he has no teeth and on his bones is a barely noteworthy measure of flesh. He senses that he's being observed. He turns his head in their direction, lifts his nose and sniffs the air.

'My little pot cracked,' he says. 'Everything's running all over the floor.'

Silence.

'Is this what you wanted? Is this what you really wanted?'

JASMIN B. FRELIH

' … '
'I'm asking you. What are you doing?'
'Waiting.'
'Hoping?'
'Waiting for it to go in

/

Oneworld, Many Voices

Bringing you exceptional writing
from around the world

The Unit by Ninni Holmqvist (Swedish)
Translated by Marlaine Delargy

Twice Born by Margaret Mazzantini (Italian)
Translated by Ann Gagliardi

Things We Left Unsaid by Zoya Pirzad (Persian)
Translated by Franklin Lewis

The Space Between Us by Zoya Pirzad (Persian)
Translated by Amy Motlagh

The Hen Who Dreamed She Could Fly by Sun-mi Hwang
(Korean) Translated by Chi-Young Kim

The Hilltop by Assaf Gavron (Hebrew)
Translated by Steven Cohen

Morning Sea by Margaret Mazzantini (Italian)
Translated by Ann Gagliardi

A Perfect Crime by A Yi (Chinese)
Translated by Anna Holmwood

The Meursault Investigation by Kamel Daoud (French)
Translated by John Cullen

Minus Me by Ingelin Røssland (YA) (Norwegian)
Translated by Deborah Dawkin

Laurus by Eugene Vodolazkin (Russian)
Translated by Lisa C. Hayden

Masha Regina by Vadim Levental (Russian)
Translated by Lisa C. Hayden

French Concession by Xiao Bai (Chinese)
Translated by Chenxin Jiang

The Sky Over Lima by Juan Gómez Bárcena (Spanish)
Translated by Andrea Rosenberg

A Very Special Year by Thomas Montasser (German)
Translated by Jamie Bulloch

Umami by Laia Jufresa (Spanish)
Translated by Sophie Hughes

The Hermit by Thomas Rydahl (Danish)
Translated by K. E. Semmel

The Peculiar Life of a Lonely Postman by Denis Thériault
(French) Translated by Liedewy Hawke

Three Envelopes by Nir Hezroni (Hebrew)
Translated by Steven Cohen

Fever Dream by Samanta Schweblin (Spanish)
Translated by Megan McDowell

The Postman's Fiancée by Denis Thériault (French)
Translated by John Cullen

The Invisible Life of Euridice Gusmao by Martha Batalha
(Brazilian Portuguese) Translated by Eric M. B. Becker

The Temptation to Be Happy by Lorenzo Marone
(Italian) Translated by Shaun Whiteside

Sweet Bean Paste by Durian Sukegawa (Japanese)
Translated by Alison Watts

They Know Not What They Do by Jussi Valtonen (Finnish)
Translated by Kristian London

The Tiger and the Acrobat by Susanna Tamaro (Italian)
Translated by Nicoleugenia Prezzavento and Vicki Satlow

The Woman at 1,000 Degrees by Hallgrímur Helgason
(Icelandic) Translated by Brian FitzGibbon

Frankenstein in Baghdad by Ahmed Saadawi (Arabic)
Translated by Jonathan Wright

Back Up by Paul Colize (French)
Translated by Louise Rogers Lalaurie

Damnation by Peter Beck (German)
Translated by Jamie Bulloch

Oneiron by Laura Lindstedt (Finnish)
Translated by Owen Witesman

The Boy Who Belonged to the Sea by Denis Thériault
(French) Translated by Liedewy Hawke

The Baghdad Clock by Shahad Al Rawi (Arabic)
Translated by Luke Leafgren

The Aviator by Eugene Vodolazkin (Russian)
Translated by Lisa C. Hayden

Lala by Jacek Dehnel (Polish)
Translated by Antonia Lloyd-Jones

Bogotá 39: New Voices from Latin America
(Spanish and Portuguese) Short story anthology

Last Instructions by Nir Hezroni (Hebrew)
Translated by Steven Cohen

The Day I Found You by Pedro Chagas Freitas (Portuguese)
Translated by Daniel Hahn

Solovyov and Larionov by Eugene Vodolazkin (Russian)
Translated by Lisa C. Hayden

In/Half by Jasmin B. Frelih (Slovenian)
Translated by Jason Blake

ONEWORLD TRANSLATED FICTION PROGRAMME

Co-funded by the
Creative Europe Programme
of the European Union

IN/HALF by Jasmin B. Frelih
Translated from the Slovenian by Jason Blake
Publication date: November 2018 (UK & US)

WHAT HELL IS NOT by Alessandro D'Avenia
Translated from the Italian by Jeremy Parzen
Publication date: January 2019 (UK & US)

GOD IS NOT SHY by Olga Grjasnowa
Translated from the German by Katy Derbyshire
Publication date: March 2019 (UK) / April 2019 (US)

THINGS THAT FALL FROM THE SKY by Selja Ahava
Translated from the Finnish by Emily and Fleur Jeremiah
Publication date: April 2019 (UK) / May 2019 (US)

MRS MOHR GOES MISSING by Maryla Szymiczkowa
Translated from the Polish by Antonia Lloyd-Jones
Publication date: April 2019 (UK) / May 2019 (US)

Oneworld's award-winning translated fiction list is dedicated to publishing the best contemporary writing from around the world, introducing readers to acclaimed international writers and brilliant, diverse stories. With these five titles from across Europe, generously supported by the Creative Europe programme as well as various in-country literary and cultural organizations, we are continuing to break boundaries and to bring new and exciting voices into English for the first time.

We will be organizing various events and publicity in 2019 to celebrate this talented group of authors and translators.
For the latest updates, visit oneworld-publications.com/creative-europe